Thanks for the Memories

Thanks for the Memories

Cecelia Ahern

HARPER

An Imprint of HarperCollins*Publishers*
www.harpercollins.com

HarperCollins books may be purchased for educational, business, or sales promotional use. For information, please write: Special Markets Department, HarperCollins Publishers, 10 East 53rd Street, New York, NY 10022.

Originally published in 2008 in Great Britian, in a slightly different form, by HarperUK.

FIRST U.S. EDITION

Designed by William Ruoto

Library of Congress Cataloging-in-Publication Data

Ahern, Cecelia, 1981–
    Thanks for the memories : a novel / by Cecelia Ahern.—1st ed.
        p.   cm.
    ISBN 978-0-06-170623-3   1. Memory—Fiction.   2. Blood—
Transfusion—Fiction.   3. Psychological fiction.   I. Title.
    PR6101.H47T45   2009
    823'.92—dc22

                                                            2008026028

        09 10 11 12 13   OV/RRD   10 9 8 7 6 5 4 3 2 1

Dedicated, with love, to my grandparents,
Olive and Raphael Kelly and Julia and Con Ahern,
thanks for the memories

Thanks for the Memories

Prologue

◇◇◇◇◇

CLOSE YOUR EYES AND STARE into the dark.
My father's advice when I couldn't sleep as a little girl.
He wouldn't want me to do that now, but I've set my mind to
the task regardless. I'm staring into that immeasurable blackness
that stretches far beyond my closed eyelids. Though I lie still on
the ground, I feel perched at the highest point I could possibly be;
clutching at a star in the night sky with my legs dangling above
cold black nothingness. I take one last look at my fingers wrapped
around the light and let go. Down I go, falling, then floating, and,
falling again, I wait for the land of my life.

I know now, as I knew as that little girl fighting sleep, that
behind the gauzed screen of shut-eye lies color. It taunts me, dares
me to open my eyes and lose sleep. Flashes of red and amber, yellow and white, speckle my darkness. I refuse to open them. I rebel,
and I squeeze my eyelids together tighter to block out the grains of
light, mere distractions that keep us awake, but a sign that there's
life beyond.

But there's no life in me. None that I can feel, from where I
lie at the bottom of the staircase. My heart beats quicker now, the

lone fighter left standing in the ring, a red boxing glove pumping victoriously into the air, refusing to give up. It's the only part of me that cares, the only part that ever cared. It fights to pump the blood around to heal, to replace what I'm losing. But it's all leaving my body as quickly as it's sent; forming a deep black ocean of its own around me where I've fallen.

Rushing, rushing, rushing. We are always rushing. Never have enough time here, always trying to make our way there. Need to have left here five minutes ago, need to be there now. The phone rings again, and I acknowledge the irony. I could have taken my time and answered it now.

Now, not then.

I could have taken all the time in the world on each of those steps. But we're always rushing. All but my heart. That slows now. I don't mind so much. I place my hand on my belly. If my child is gone, and I suspect this is so, I'll join it there. There . . . where? Wherever. It; a heartless word. He or she so young; who it was to become, still a question. But there, I will mother it.

There, not here.

I'll tell it: I'm sorry, sweetheart, I'm sorry I ruined your chances, my chance—our chance of a life together. But close your eyes and stare into the darkness now, like Mummy is doing, and we'll find our way together.

There's a noise in the room, and I feel a presence.

"Oh God, Joyce, oh God. Can you hear me, love? Oh God. Oh God. Oh, please no, good Lord, not my Joyce, don't take my Joyce. Hold on, love, I'm here. Dad is here."

I don't want to hold on, and I feel like telling him so. I hear myself groan, an animal-like whimper, and it shocks me, scares me. I have a plan, I want to tell him. I want to go; only then can I be with my baby.

Then, not now.

He's stopped me from falling, but I haven't landed yet. Instead he helps me balance on nothing, hover while I'm forced to make the decision. I want to keep falling, but he's calling the ambulance and he's gripping my hand with such ferocity it's as though it is he who is hanging on to dear life. As though I'm all he has. He's brushing the hair from my forehead and weeping loudly. I've never heard him weep. Not even when Mum died. He clings to my hand with all of the strength I never knew his old body had, and I remember that I am all he has and that he, once again just like before, is my whole world. The blood continues to rush through me. Rushing, rushing, rushing. We are always rushing. Maybe I'm rushing again. Maybe it's not my time to go.

I feel the rough skin of old hands squeezing mine, and their intensity and their familiarity force me to open my eyes. Light fills them, and I glimpse his face, a look I never want to see again. He clings to his baby. I know I've lost mine; I can't let him lose his. In making my decision, I already begin to grieve. I've landed now, the land of my life. And still, my heart pumps on.

Even when broken, it still works.

PART ONE

One Month Earlier

Chapter 1

◇◇◇◇◇

B LOOD TRANSFUSION," DR. FIELDS ANNOUNCES from the podium of a lecture hall in Trinity College's Arts Building, "is the process of transferring blood or blood-based products from one person into the circulatory system of another. Blood transfusions may treat medical conditions such as massive blood loss due to trauma, surgery, shock, and where the red-cell-producing mechanism fails.

"Here are the facts. Three thousand donations are needed in Ireland every week. Only three percent of the Irish population are donors, providing blood for a population of almost four million. One in four people will need a transfusion at some point. Take a look around the room now."

Five hundred heads turn left, right, and around. Uncomfortable sniggers break the silence.

Dr. Fields elevates her voice over the disruption. "At least one hundred and fifty people in this room will need a blood transfusion at some stage in their lives."

That silences them. A hand is raised.

"Yes?"

"How much blood does a patient need?"

"How long is a piece of string, dumb-ass?" a voice from the back mocks, and a scrunched ball of paper flies at the head of the young male inquirer.

"It's a very good question." She frowns into the darkness, unable to see the students through the light of the projector. "Who asked that?"

"Mr. Dover," someone calls from the other side of the room.

"I'm sure Mr. Dover can answer for himself. What's your first name?"

"Ben," he responds, sounding dejected.

Laughter erupts. Dr. Fields sighs.

"Ben, thank you for your question—and to the rest of you, there is no such thing as a stupid question. This is what Blood for Life Week is all about. It's about asking all the questions you want, learning all you need to know about blood transfusions before you possibly donate today, tomorrow, the remaining days of this week on campus, or maybe regularly in your future."

The main door opens, and light streams into the dark lecture hall. Justin Hitchcock enters, the concentration on his face illuminated by the white light of the projector. Under one arm are multiple piles of folders, each one slipping by the second. A knee shoots up to hoist them back in place. His right hand carries both an overstuffed briefcase and a dangerously balanced Styrofoam cup of coffee. He slowly lowers his hovering foot down to the floor, as though performing a tai chi move, and a relieved smile creeps onto his face as calm is restored. Somebody sniggers, and the balancing act is once again compromised.

Hold it, Justin. Move your eyes away from the cup and assess the situation. Woman on podium, five hundred kids. All staring at you. Say something. Something intelligent.

"I'm confused," he announces to the darkness, behind which he senses some sort of life-form. There are twitters in the room, and he feels all eyes on him as he moves back toward the door to check the number.

Don't spill the coffee. Don't spill the damn coffee.

He opens the door, allowing shafts of light to sneak in again, and the students in its line shade their eyes.

Twitter, twitter, nothing funnier than a lost man.

Laden down with items, he manages to hold the door open with his leg. He looks back to the number on the outside of the door and then back to his sheet, the sheet that, if he doesn't grab it that very second, will float to the ground. He makes a move to grab it. Wrong hand. Styrofoam cup of coffee falls to the ground. Closely followed by sheet of paper.

Damn it! There they go again, twitter, twitter. Nothing funnier than a lost man who has spilled his coffee and dropped his schedule.

"Can I help you?" The lecturer steps down from the podium.

Justin brings his entire body back into the classroom, and darkness resumes.

"Well, it says here . . . well, it said there"—he nods his head toward the sodden sheet on the ground—"that I have a class here now."

"Enrollment for international students is in the exam hall."

He frowns. "No, I—"

"I'm sorry." She comes closer. "I thought I heard an American accent." She picks up the Styrofoam cup and throws it into the bin, over which a sign reads "No Drinks Allowed."

"Ah . . . oh . . . sorry about that."

"Graduate students are next door." She adds in a whisper, "Trust me, you don't want to join this class."

Justin clears his throat and corrects his posture, tucking the folders tighter under his arm. "Actually, I'm lecturing the History of Art and Architecture class."

"You're lecturing?"

"Guest lecturing. Believe it or not." He blows his hair up from his sticky forehead. A haircut, remember to get a haircut. There they go again, twitter, twitter. A lost lecturer who's spilled his coffee, dropped his schedule, is about to lose his folders, and needs a haircut. Definitely nothing funnier.

"Professor Hitchcock?"

"That's me." He feels the folders slipping from under his arm.

"Oh, I'm so sorry," she whispers. "I didn't know . . ." She catches a folder for him. "I'm Dr. Sarah Fields from the IBTS. The faculty told me that I could have a half hour with the students before your lecture, your permission pending, of course."

"Oh, well, nobody informed me of that, but that's no problemo." Problemo? He shakes his head at himself and makes for the door. Starbucks, here I come.

"Professor Hitchcock?"

He stops at the door. "Yes."

"Would you like to join us?"

I most certainly would not. There's a cappuccino and cinnamon muffin with my name on them. No. Just say no.

"Um . . . nn-es." Nes? "I mean yes."

Twitter, twitter, twitter. Lecturer caught out. Forced into doing something he clearly didn't want to do by attractive young woman in white coat claiming to be a doctor of an unfamiliar initialized organization.

"Great. Welcome."

She places the folders back under his arm and returns to the podium to address the students.

"Okay, attention, everybody. Back to the initial question of blood quantities. A car accident victim may require up to thirty units of blood. A bleeding ulcer could require anything between three and thirty units of blood. A coronary artery bypass may use between one and five units of blood. It varies, but with such quantities needed, now you see why we always want donors."

Justin takes a seat in the front row and listens with horror to the discussion he's joined.

"Does anybody have any questions?"

Can you change the subject?

"Do you get paid for giving blood?"

More laughs.

"Not in this country, I'm afraid."

"Does the person who is given blood know who their donor is?"

"Donations are usually anonymous to the recipient, but products in a blood bank are always individually traceable through the cycle of donation—testing, separation into components, storage, and administration to the recipient."

"Can anyone give blood?"

"Good question. I have a list here of donor disqualifications. Please all study it carefully, and take notes if you wish." Dr. Fields places her sheet under the projector, and her white coat lights up with a rather graphic picture of someone in dire need of a donation. She steps away, and it fills the screen on the wall.

People groan and the word "gross" travels around the tiered seating like a wave. Twice by Justin. Dizziness overtakes him, and he averts his eyes from the image.

"Oops, wrong sheet," Dr. Fields says cheekily, slowly replacing it with the promised list.

Justin searches with great hope for needle or blood phobia in an effort to eliminate himself as a possible blood donor. No such luck—not that it matters, as the chances of him donating a drop of blood to anyone are as rare as ideas in the morning.

"Too bad, Dover." Another scrunched ball of paper goes flying from the back of the hall to hit Ben's head again. "Gay people can't donate."

Ben coolly raises a middle finger in the air.

"That's discriminatory," one girl calls out.

"It is also a discussion for another day," Dr. Fields responds, moving on. "Remember, your body will replace the liquid part of the donation within twenty-four hours. With a unit of blood at almost a pint, and everyone having eight to twelve pints of blood in their body, the average person can easily spare giving one."

Pockets of juvenile laughter at the innuendo.

"Everybody, please." Dr. Fields claps her hands, trying desperately to get attention. "Blood for Life Week is all about education as much as donation. It's all well and good that we can have a laugh and a joke, but at this time I think it's important to note the fact that someone's life, be it woman, man, or child, could be depending on you right now."

How quickly silence falls upon the class. Even Justin stops talking to himself.

Chapter 2

◇◇◇◇◇

PROFESSOR HITCHCOCK." DR. FIELDS APPROACHES Justin, who is arranging his notes at the podium while the students take a five-minute break.

"Please call me Justin, Doctor."

"Please call me Sarah." She holds out her hand.

"Nice to meet you, Sarah."

"I just want to make sure we'll see each other later?"

"Later?"

"Yes, later. As in . . . after your lecture." She smiles.

Is she flirting? It's been so long, how am I supposed to tell? Speak, Justin, speak.

"Great. A date would be great."

She purses her lips to hide a grin. "Okay, I'll meet you at the main entrance at six, and I'll bring you across myself."

"Bring me across where?"

"To where we've got the blood drive set up. It's beside the rugby pitch, but I'd prefer to bring you over myself."

"The blood drive . . ." He's immediately flooded with dread. "Ah, I don't think that—"

"And then we'll go for a drink after?"

"You know what? I'm just getting over the flu, so I don't think I'm eligible for donating." He parts his hands and shrugs.

"Are you on antibiotics?"

"No, but that's a good idea, Sarah. Maybe I should be . . ." He rubs his throat.

"Oh, I think you'll be okay." She laughs.

"No, you see, I've been around some pretty infectious diseases lately. Malaria, smallpox, the whole lot. I was in a very tropical area." He remembers the list of contraindications. "And my brother, Al? Yeah, he's a leper." Lame, lame, lame.

"Really." She lifts an eyebrow, and though he fights it with all his will, he cracks a smile. "How long ago did you leave the States?"

Think hard, this could be a trick question. "I moved to London three months ago," he finally answers truthfully.

"Oh, lucky for you. If it was two months, you wouldn't be eligible."

"Now hold on, let me think . . ." He scratches his chin and randomly mumbles months of the year aloud. "Maybe it was two months ago. If I work backward from when I arrived . . ." He trails off while counting his fingers and staring off into the distance with a concentrated frown.

"Are you afraid, Professor Hitchcock?" She smiles.

"Afraid? No!" He throws his head back and guffaws. "But did I mention I have malaria?" He sighs at her failure to take him seriously. "Well, I'm all out of ideas."

"I'll see you at the entrance at six. Oh, and don't forget to eat beforehand."

"Of course, because I'll be ravenous before my date with a giant homicidal needle," he grumbles as he watches her leave.

The students begin filing back into the room, and he tries to hide the smile of pleasure on his face, mixed as it is. Finally the class is his.

Okay, my little twittering friends. It's payback time.

They're not yet all seated when he begins.

"Art," he announces to the lecture hall, and he hears the sounds of pencils and notepads being extracted from bags, loud zips and buckles, tin pencil cases rattling; all new for the first day. Squeaky-clean and untarnished. Shame the same cannot be said for the students. "The products of human creativity." He doesn't stall to allow them time to catch up. In fact, it's time to have a little fun. His speech speeds up.

"The creation of beautiful or significant things." He paces as he speaks, still hearing zipping sounds and rattling.

"Sir, could you say that again ple—"

"No," he interrupts. "Engineering," he moves on, "the practical application of science to commerce or industry." Total silence now.

"Creativity and practicality. The fruit of their merger is architecture."

Faster, Justin, faster!

"Architecture-is-the-transformation-of-ideas-into-a-physical-reality. The-complex-and-carefully-designed-structure-of-something-especially-with-regard-to-a-specific-period. To-understand-architecture-we-must-examine-the-relationship-between-technology-science-and-society."

"Sir, can you—"

"No." But he slows slightly. "We examine how architecture through the centuries has been shaped by society, how it continues to be shaped, but also how it, in turn, shapes society."

He pauses, looking around at the youthful faces staring up at him, their minds empty vessels waiting to be filled. So much to learn, so little time to do it in, so little passion within them to understand it truly. It is his job to give them passion. To share with them his experiences of travel, his knowledge of all the great masterpieces of centuries ago. He will transport them from the stuffy lecture theater of this prestigious Dublin college to the rooms of the Louvre, hear the echoes of their footsteps as he walks them through the cathedral of Saint-Denis, to Saint-Germain-des-Prés and Saint-Pierre-de-Montmartre. They'll know not only dates and statistics but the smell of Picasso's paints, the feel of Baroque marble, the sound of the bells of Notre Dame. They'll experience it all, right here in this classroom. He will bring it to them.

They're staring at you, Justin. Say something.

He clears his throat. "This course will teach you how to analyze works of art and how to understand their historical significance. It will enable you to develop an awareness of the environment while also providing you with a deeper sensitivity to the culture and ideals of other nations. You will cover a broad range: history of painting, sculpture and architecture from Ancient Greece to modern times; early Irish art; the painters of the Italian Renaissance; the great Gothic cathedrals of Europe; the architectural splendors of the Georgian era; and the artistic achievements of the twentieth century."

He allows a silence to fall.

Are they filled with regret on hearing what lies ahead of them for the next four years of their lives? Or do their hearts beat wildly with excitement as his does, just thinking about all that is to come? Even after all these years, he still feels the same enthusiasm for the buildings, paintings, and sculptures of the world. His exhilaration often leaves him breathless during lectures; he has to remember to slow down, not to tell them everything at once. Though he wants them to know everything, right now!

He looks again at their faces and has an epiphany.

You have them! They're hanging on your every word, just waiting to hear more. You've done it, they're in your grasp!

Someone farts, and the room explodes with laughter.

He sighs, his bubble burst, and continues his talk in a bored tone. "My name is Justin Hitchcock, and in my special guest lectures scattered throughout the course, you will study the introduction to European periods and schools such as the Italian Renaissance and French Impressionism. This includes the critical analysis of paintings, the importance of iconography, and the various technical methods used by artists from the Book of Kells to the modern day. There'll also be an introduction to European architecture. Greek temples to the present day, blah blah blah. Two volunteers to help me hand these out, please."

And so it was another year. He wasn't at home in Chicago now; he had chased his ex-wife and daughter to London and was flying back and forth between there and Dublin for his guest lectures. A different country perhaps, but the same class. First week and giddy. Another group displaying an immature lack of understanding of his passions; a deliberate turning of their backs on the possibility—no, not the possibility, the surety—of learning something wonderful and great.

It doesn't matter what you say now, pal; from here on out, the only thing they'll go home remembering is the fart.

Chapter 3

◇◇◇◇◇

"WHAT IS IT ABOUT FART jokes, Bea?"

"Oh, hi, Dad."

"What kind of a greeting is that?"

"Oh, gee whiz, wow, Dad, so great to hear from you. It's been, what, ah shucks, three hours since you last phoned?"

"Fine, you don't have to go all Porky Pig on me. Is your darling mother home yet from a day out at her new life?"

"Yes, she's home."

"And has she brought the delightful Laurence back with her?" He can't hold back his sarcasm, which he hates himself for, but unwilling to withdraw it and incapable of apologizing, he does what he always does, which is to run with it, thereby making it worse. "Laurence," he drawls, "Laurence of A— inguinal hernia."

"Oh, you're such a geek. Will you ever give up talking about his trouser leg?" She sighs with boredom.

Justin kicks off the scratchy blanket of the cheap Dublin hotel he's staying in. "Really, Bea, check it next time he's around. Those trousers are far too tight for what he's got going on down there. There should be a name for that. Something-itis."

Balls-a-titis.

"You know, there are only four TV channels in this dump, one in a language I don't even understand. It sounds like they're clearing their throats after one of your mother's terrible coq au vins. You know, in my wonderful home back in Chicago, I had over two hundred channels." Dick-a-titis. Dickhead-a-titis. Ha!

"Of which you watched none."

"But one had a choice not to watch those deplorable house-fixer-upper channels and music channels of naked women dancing around."

"I appreciate one going through such an upheaval, Dad. It must be very traumatic for you, a sort-of-grown man, while I, at sixteen years old, had to take this huge life adjustment of parents getting divorced and a move from Chicago to London all in stride."

"You got two houses and extra presents, what do you care?" he grumbles. "And it was your idea."

"It was my idea to go to ballet school in London, not for your marriage to end!"

"Oh, ballet school. I thought you said, 'Break up, you fool.' My mistake. Think we should move back to Chicago and get back together?"

"Nah." He hears the smile in her voice and knows it's okay.

"Hey, you think I was going to stay in Chicago while you're all the way over on this side of the world?"

"You're not even in the same country right now." She laughs.

"Ireland is just a work trip. I'll be back in London in a few days. Honestly, Bea, there's nowhere else I'd rather be," he assures her.

Though a Four Seasons would be nice.

"How's Porrúa doing?" He asks after his cactus plant.

"Really, Dad, you have to get a life. Or a dog or a cat or something. You can't have a pet cactus."

"Well, I do, and she's very dear to me. Tell me you've remembered to water her, I don't quite trust you after your attempted assassination of her with a tennis ball."

"It was years ago, the cactus survived, get over it. I'm thinking of moving in with Peter," she says far too casually.

"So what is it about fart jokes?" he asks again, ignoring her, unable to believe his dear cactus and Peter, the jerk who is corrupting his daughter, have been mentioned in the same sentence. "I mean, what is it about the sound of expelling air that can stop people from being interested in some of the most incredible masterpieces ever created?"

"I take it you don't want to talk about my moving in with Peter?"

"You're a child. You and Peter can move into your old dollhouse, which I still have in storage. I'll set it up in the living room. It'll be real nice and cozy."

"I'm eighteen. Not a child anymore. I've lived alone away from home for two years now."

"One year alone. Your mother left me alone the second year to join you, remember."

"You and Mum met at my age."

"And we did not live happily ever after. Stop imitating us and write your own fairy tale."

"I would, if my overprotective father would stop butting in with his version of how the story should go." Bea sighs and steers the conversation back to safer territory. "Why are your students laughing at fart jokes, anyway? I thought your seminar was a one-off for postgrads who'd elected to choose your boring subject. Though why anybody would do that is beyond me. You lecturing me on Peter is boring enough, and I love him."

Love! Ignore it, and she'll forget what she said.

"It wouldn't be beyond you, if you'd listen to me when I talk. Along with my postgraduate classes, I was asked to speak to first-year students throughout the year too, an agreement I may live to regret, but no matter. On to my day job and far more pressing matters . . . I'm planning an exhibition at the gallery on Dutch painting in the seventeenth century. You should come see it."

"No, thanks."

"Well, maybe my postgrads over the next few months will be more appreciative of my expertise."

"You know, your students may have laughed at the fart joke, but I bet at least a quarter of them donated blood."

"They only did because they heard they'd get a free Kit Kat afterward," Justin huffs, rooting through the insufficiently filled minibar. "You're angry at me for not giving blood?"

"I think you're an asshole for standing up that woman."

"Don't use the word 'asshole,' Bea. Anyway, who told you that I stood her up?"

"Uncle Al."

"Uncle Al is an asshole; he should keep my business to himself. And you know what else, honey? You know what the good doctor said today about donating blood?" He struggles with opening the film on a Pringles box.

"What?" Bea yawns.

"That the donation is anonymous to the recipient. Hear that? Anonymous. So what's the point in saving someone's life if they don't even know you're the one who saved it?"

"Dad!"

"What? Come on, Bea. Lie to me and tell me you wouldn't want a bouquet of flowers for saving someone's life?"

Bea protests, but he continues.

"Or a little basket of those, whaddaya call those muffins that you like, coconut—"

"Cinnamon," she laughs, finally giving in.

"A little basket of cinnamon muffins outside your front door with a little note tucked into the basket saying, 'Thanks, Bea, for saving my life. Any time you want anything done, like your dry cleaning picked up, or your newspaper and a coffee delivered to your front door, a chauffeur-driven car for your own personal use, front-row tickets to the opera . . .' Oh, the list could go on and on."

He gives up pulling at the film and instead picks up a corkscrew and stabs the top. "It could be like one of those Chinese things; you know, the way someone saves your life and then you're forever indebted to them. It could be nice having someone tailing you every day, catching pianos flying out of windows and stopping them from landing on your head, that kind of thing."

Bea calms herself. "I hope you're joking."

"Yeah, of course I'm joking." Justin makes a face. "The piano would surely kill them, and that would be unfair."

He finally pulls the film open and throws the corkscrew across the room. It hits a glass on top of the minibar, and the glass smashes.

"What was that?"

"Housecleaning," he lies. "You think I'm selfish, don't you?"

"Dad, you uprooted your life, left a great job and a nice apartment, and flew thousands of miles to another country just to be near me. Of course I don't think you're selfish."

Justin smiles and pops a Pringle into his mouth.

"But if you're not joking about the muffin basket, then you're definitely selfish. And if it was Blood for Life Week at my college, I would have taken part. But you have the opportunity to make it up to that woman."

"I just feel like I'm being bullied into this entire thing. I was going to get my hair cut tomorrow, not have people stab at my veins."

"Don't give blood if you don't want to, I don't care. But remember, if you do it, a tiny little needle isn't gonna kill you. In fact, the opposite may happen. It might save someone's life, and you never know, that person could follow you around for the rest of your life leaving muffin baskets outside your door and catching pianos before they fall on your head. Now, wouldn't that be nice?"

Chapter 4

◇◇◇◇

IN A BLOOD DRIVE BESIDE Trinity College's rugby field, Justin tries to hide his shaking hands from Sarah while he hands over his consent form and health and lifestyle questionnaire, which frankly discloses far more about him than he'd reveal on a date. She smiles encouragingly and talks him through everything as though giving blood is the most normal thing in the world.

"Now I just need to ask you a few questions. Have you read, understood, and completed the health and lifestyle questionnaire?"

Justin nods, words failing him in his clogged throat.

"And is all the information you've provided true and accurate to the best of your knowledge?"

"Why?" he croaks. "Does it not look right to you? Because if it doesn't, I can always leave and come back again another time."

She smiles at him with the same look his mother wore before tucking him into bed and turning off the light.

"Okay, we're all set. I'm just going to do a hemoglobin test," she explains.

"Does that check for diseases?" He looks around nervously at the equipment in the van. Please don't let me have any diseases. That would be too embarrassing. Not likely anyway. Can you even remember the last time you had sex?

"No, this just measures the iron in your blood." She takes a pinprick of blood from the pad of his finger. "Blood is tested later for diseases and STDs."

"Must be handy for checking up on boyfriends," he jokes, feeling sweat tickle his upper lip. He studies his finger.

She quietens as she carries out the test before motioning for Justin to lie supine on the cushioned bench and to extend his left arm. Sarah wraps a pressure cuff around his upper arm, making the veins more prominent, and she disinfects the crook of his arm.

Don't look at the needle, don't look at the needle.

He looks at the needle, and the ground swirls beneath him. His throat tightens.

"Is this going to hurt?" Justin swallows hard as his shirt clings to his saturated back.

"Just a little sting." She smiles, approaching him with a tube in her hand.

He smells her sweet perfume, and it distracts him momentarily. As she leans over, he sees down her V-neck sweater. A black lace bra.

"I want you to take this in your hand and squeeze it repeatedly."

"What?" he laughs nervously.

"The ball." she smiles.

"Oh." He accepts the small soft ball. "What does this do?" His voice shakes.

"It's to help speed up the process."

He pumps at top speed.

Sarah laughs. "Not yet. And not that fast, Justin."

Sweat rolls down his back. His hair clings to his sticky forehead. You should have gone for the haircut, Justin. What kind of a stupid idea was this— "Ouch."

"That wasn't so bad, was it?" she says softly, as though talking to a child.

Justin's heart beats loudly in his ears. He pumps the ball in his hand to the rhythm of his heartbeat. He imagines his heart pumping the blood, the blood flowing through his veins. He sees it reach the needle, go through the tube, and he waits to feel faint. But the dizziness never comes, and so he watches his blood run through the tube and down under the bed into the collection bag she has thoughtfully hidden down there.

"Do I get a Kit Kat after this?"

She laughs. "Of course."

"And then we get to go for drinks, or are you just using me for my body?"

"Drinks are fine, but I must warn you against doing anything strenuous today. Your body needs to recover."

He catches sight of her lace bra again. Yeah, sure.

Fifteen minutes later, Justin looks at his pint of blood with pride. He doesn't want it to go to some stranger; he almost wants to take it to the hospital himself, survey the wards, and present it to someone he really cares about, someone special, for it's the first thing to come straight from his heart in a very long time.

PART TWO

Present Day

Chapter 5

◇◇◇◇◇

I OPEN MY EYES SLOWLY.

White light fills them. Objects gradually come into focus, and the white light fades. Orangey pink now. I move my eyes around. I'm in a hospital. A television high up on the wall. Green fills its screen. I focus more. Horses. Jumping and racing. Dad must be in the room. I lower my eyes, and there he is with his back to me in an armchair. He thumps his fists lightly on the chair's arms. I see his tweed cap appearing and disappearing in front of the chair back as he bounces up and down. The springs beneath him squeak.

The horse racing is silent. So is he. Like a silent movie being carried out before me, I watch him. I wonder if it's my ears that aren't allowing me to hear him. He springs out of his chair now, faster than I've seen him move in a long time, and he raises his fist at the television, quietly urging his horse on.

The television goes black. His two fists open, and he raises his hands in the air, looks up to the ceiling, and beseeches God. He puts his hands in his pockets, feels around, and pulls the material out. They're empty, and the pockets of his brown trousers hang inside out for all to see. He pats down his chest, feeling for money.

Checks the small pocket of his brown cardigan. Grumbles. So it's not my ears.

He turns to feel around in his overcoat beside me, and I shut my eyes quickly.

I'm not ready yet. Nothing has happened to me until they tell me. Last night will remain a nightmare in my mind until they tell me it was true. The longer I close my eyes, the longer everything remains as it was. The bliss of ignorance.

I hear him rooting around in his overcoat, I hear change rattling and then the clunk of coins falling into the television meter. I risk opening my eyes again, and there he is, back in his armchair, cap bouncing up and down, raising his fists in the air.

My curtain is closed to my right, but I can tell I share a room with others. I don't know how many. It's quiet. There's no air in the room; it's stuffy with stale sweat. The giant windows that take up the entire wall to my left are closed. The light is so bright I can't see out. I allow my eyes to adjust and finally see a bus stop across the road. A woman waits by the stop, shopping bags by her feet and a baby on her hip, bare chubby legs bouncing in the Indian-summer sun. I look away immediately and see Dad watching me. He is leaning out over the side of the armchair, twisting his head around, like a child from his cot.

"Hi, love."

"Hi." I feel I haven't spoken for such a long time, and I expect to croak. But I don't. My voice is pure, pours out like honey. Like nothing's happened. But nothing has happened. Not yet. Not until they tell me.

With both hands on the arms of the chair he slowly pulls himself up. Like a seesaw, he makes his way over to the side of the bed. Up and down, down and up. He was born with a leg length discrepancy, his left leg longer than his right. Despite the special shoes he was given in later years, he still sways, the motion instilled in him since he learned to walk.

He hates wearing those shoes and, despite our warnings and his back pains, he goes back to what he knows. I'm so used to the sight of his body going up and down, down and up. I recall as a child holding his hand and going for walks. How my arm would move in perfect rhythm with him. Being pulled up as he stepped down on his right leg, being pushed down as he stepped on his left.

He was always so strong. Always so capable. Always fixing things, lifting things. Always with a screwdriver in his hand, taking things apart and putting them back together—remote controls, radios, alarm clocks, plugs. A handyman for the entire street. His legs may have been uneven, but his hands, always and forever, were steady as a rock.

He takes his cap off as he nears me, clutches it with both hands, moves it around in circles like a steering wheel as he watches me with concern. He steps onto his right leg, and down he goes. Bends his left leg. His position of rest.

"Are you . . . em . . . they told me that . . . eh." He clears his throat. "They told me to . . ." He swallows hard, and his thick messy eyebrows furrow and hide his glassy eyes. "You lost . . . you lost, em . . ."

My lower lip trembles.

His voice breaks when he speaks again. "You lost a lot of blood, Joyce. They . . ." He lets go of his cap with one hand and makes circular motions with his crooked finger, trying to remember. "They did a transfusion of the blood thingy on you, so you're, em . . . you're okay with your bloods now."

My lower lip still trembles, and my hands automatically go to my belly, long enough gone to no longer show swelling under the blankets. I look to him hopefully, only realizing now how much I am still holding on, how much I have convinced myself the awful incident in the labor room was all a terrible nightmare. Perhaps I imagined my baby's silence that filled the room in that final moment. Perhaps there were cries that I just didn't hear. Of course it's possible—by that stage I had little energy and was fading away—maybe I just didn't hear the first little miraculous breath of life that everybody else witnessed.

Dad shakes his head sadly. No, it had been me that had made those screams instead.

My lip trembles more now, bounces up and down, and I can't stop it. My body shakes terribly, and I can't stop that either. The tears; they well, but I keep them from falling. If I start now, I know I will never stop.

I'm making a noise. An unusual noise I've never heard before. Groaning. Grunting. A combination of both. Dad grabs my hand and holds it hard. The feel of his skin brings me back to last night, me lying at the bottom of the stairs. He doesn't say anything. But what can a person say? I don't even know.

I doze in and out. I wake and remember a conversation with a doctor and wonder if it was a dream. Lost your baby, Joyce, we did all we could . . . blood transfusion . . . Who needs to remember something like that? No one. Not me.

When I wake again, the curtain beside me has been pulled open. There are three small children running around, chasing one another around the bed while their father, I assume, calls to them to stop in a language I don't recognize. Their mother lies in the bed next to me. She looks tired. Our eyes meet, and we smile at each other.

I know how you feel, her sad smile says, I know how you feel.

What are we going to do? my smile says back to her.

I don't know, her eyes say. I don't know.

Will we be okay?

She turns her head away from me then, her smile gone.

Dad calls over to them. "Where are you lot from then?"

"Excuse me?" her husband asks.

"I said where are you lot from, then?" Dad repeats. "Not from around here, I see." Dad's voice is cheery and pleasant. No insults intended. No insults ever intended.

"We are from Nigeria," the man responds.

"Nigeria," Dad replies. "Where would that be, then?"

"In Africa." The man's tone is pleasant too. Just an old man starved of conversation, trying to be friendly, he realizes.

"Ah, Africa. Never been there myself. Is it hot there? I'd say it is. Hotter than here. Get a good tan, I'd say, not that you need it." He laughs. "Do you get cold here?"

"Cold?" The African smiles.

"Yes, you know." Dad wraps his arms around his body and pretends to shiver. "Cold?"

"Yes." The man laughs. "Sometimes I do."

"Thought so. I do too, and I'm from here," Dad explains. "The chill gets right into my bones. But I'm not a great one for heat either. Skin goes red, just burns. My daughter, Joyce, goes brown. That's her over there." He points at me, and I close my eyes quickly.

"A lovely daughter," the man says politely.

"Ah, she is." Silence while I assume they watch me. "She was on one of those Spanish islands a few months back and came back black, she did. Well, not as black as you, you know, but she got a fair ol' tan on her. Peeled, though. You probably don't peel."

The man laughs politely. That's Dad. Never means any harm but has never left the country in his entire life, and it shows. A fear of flying holds him back. Or so he says.

"Anyway, I hope your lovely lady feels better soon. It's an awful thing to be sick on your holliers."

With that I open my eyes.

"Ah, welcome back, love. I was just talking to these nice neighbors of ours." He seesaws up to me again, his cap once more in his hands. Rests on his right leg, goes down, bends his left leg. "You know, I think we're the only Irish people in this hospital. The nurse that was here a minute ago, she's from Sing-a-song or someplace like that."

"Singapore, Dad." I smile.

"That's it." He raises his eyebrows. "You met her already, did you? They all speak English, though, the foreigners do. Much better than being on your holidays and having to do all that sign-languagey stuff." He puts his cap down on the bed and wiggles his fingers around.

"Dad"—I smile—"you've never been out of the country in your life."

"Haven't I heard the lads at the Monday Club talking about it? Frank was away in that place last week—oh, what's that place?" He shuts his eyes and thinks hard. "The place where they make the chocolates?"

"Switzerland."

"No."

"Belgium."

"No," he says, frustrated now. "The little round ball-y things all crunchy inside. You can get the white ones now, but I prefer the original dark ones."

"Maltesers?" I laugh, but feel pain and stop.

"That's it. He was in Maltesers."

"Dad, it's Malta."

"That's it. He was in Malta." He is silent. "Do they make Maltesers?"

"I don't know. Maybe. So what happened to Frank in Malta?"

He squeezes his eyes shut again and thinks. "I can't remember what I was about to say now."

Silence. He hates not being able to remember. He used to remember everything.

"Did you make any money on the horses?" I ask, changing the subject.

"A couple bob. Enough for a few rounds at the Monday Club tonight."

"But today is Tuesday."

"It's on a Tuesday on account of the bank holiday," he explains, seesawing around to the other side of the bed to sit down.

I can't laugh. I'm too sore, and it seems some of my sense of humor was lost in the accident.

"You don't mind if I go, do you, Joyce? But I'll stay if you want, I really don't mind, it's not important."

"Of course it's important. You haven't missed a Monday night for twenty years."

"Apart from bank holidays!" He lifts a crooked finger, and his eyes dance.

"Apart from bank holidays." I smile, and grab his finger.

"Well"—he takes my hand—"you're more important than a few pints and a singsong."

My eyes fill again. "What would I do without you?"

"You'd be just fine, love. Besides . . ."—he looks at me warily—"you have Conor."

I let go of his hand and look away. What if I don't want Conor anymore?

"I tried to call him last night on the hand phone, but there was no answer. But maybe I got the numbers wrong," he adds quickly. "There are so many more numbers on the hand phones."

"Cell phones, Dad," I say distractedly.

"Ah, yes. The cell phones. He keeps calling when you're asleep. He's going to come home as soon as he can get a flight. He's very worried."

"That's nice of him. Then we can get down to the business of spending the next ten years of our married life trying to have babies." Back to business. A nice little distraction to give our relationship some sort of meaning.

"Ah now, love . . ."

The first day of the rest of my life, and I'm not sure I want to be here. I know I should be thanking somebody for this, but I really don't feel like it. Instead, I wish they hadn't bothered.

Chapter 6

◇◇◇◇◇

I WATCH THE THREE CHILDREN playing together on the floor of the hospital, little fingers and toes, chubby cheeks and plump lips—the faces of their parents clearly etched on theirs. My heart drops into my stomach, and it twists. My eyes fill again, and I have to look away.

"Mind if I have a grape?" Dad chirps. He's like a little canary swinging in a cage beside me.

"Of course you can. Dad, you should go home now, go get something to eat. You need your energy."

He picks up a banana. "Potassium." He smiles and moves his arms rigorously. "I'll be jogging home tonight."

"How did you get here?" It suddenly occurs to me that he hasn't been into the city for years. It all became too fast for him, buildings suddenly sprouting up out of nowhere, roads with traffic going in different directions from before. With great sadness he sold his car, his failing eyesight too much of a danger for him and others on the roads. Seventy-five years old, his wife dead ten years. Now he has a routine of his own around the local area: church every Sunday and Wednesday, Monday Club every Monday (apart from bank holidays), butcher on Tuesday, his crosswords, puzzles, and TV shows during the days, his garden all the moments in between.

"Fran from next door drove me in." He puts the banana down, still laughing to himself about his jogging joke, and pops another grape into his mouth. "Almost had me killed two or three times. Enough to let me know there is a God if ever there was a time I doubted." He frowns. "I asked for seedless grapes; these aren't seedless." Liver-spotted hands put the bunch back on the side cabinet. He takes seeds out of his mouth and looks around for a bin.

"Do you still believe in your God now, Dad?" It comes out crueler than I mean to, but the anger is almost unbearable.

"I do believe, Joyce." As always, no offense taken. He puts the seeds in his handkerchief and places it back in his pocket. "The Lord acts in mysterious ways, in ways we often can neither explain nor understand, tolerate nor bear. I understand how you can question Him now—we all do at times. When your mother died, I . . ." He trails off and abandons the sentence as always, the furthest he will go toward being disloyal about his God and toward discussing the loss of his wife. "But this time God answered all my prayers. He sat up and heard me calling last night. He said to me"—Dad puts on a broad Cavan accent, the accent he had as a child before moving to Dublin in his teens—" 'No problem, Henry. I hear you loud and clear. It's all in hand, so don't you be worrying. I'll do this for you, no bother at all.' He saved you. He kept my girl alive, and for that I'll be forever grateful to Him, sad as we may be about the passing of another."

I have no response to that, but I soften.

He pulls his chair closer to my bedside, and it screeches along the floor.

"And I believe in an afterlife," he says, a little quieter now. "That I do. I believe in the paradise of heaven, up there in the clouds, and everyone that was once here is up there—including the sinners. God's a forgiver, that I believe."

"Everyone?" I fight the tears. I fight them from falling. "What about my baby, Dad? Is my baby there?"

He looks pained. We hadn't spoken much about my pregnancy. Only days ago we'd had a minor falling-out over my asking him to store our spare bed in his garage. I had started to prepare the nursery, you see . . . Oh dear, the nursery. The spare bed and junk just cleared out. The crib already purchased. Pretty yellow on the walls. "Buttercup Dream" with a little duckie border.

Five months to go. Some people, my father included, would think preparing the nursery at four months is premature, but we'd been waiting six years for a baby, for this baby. Nothing premature about that.

"Ah, love, you know I don't know . . ."

"I was going to call him Sean if it was a boy," I hear myself finally say aloud. I have been saying these things in my head all day, over and over, and here they are now, spilling out of me instead of the tears.

"Ah, that's a nice name. Sean."

"Grace, if it was a girl. After Mum. She would have liked that."

His jaw sets at this, and he looks away. Anyone who doesn't know him would think this has angered him. I know this is not the case. I know it's the emotion gathering in his jaw, like a giant reservoir storing and locking it all away until absolutely necessary, waiting for those rare moments when the drought within him calls for those walls to break and for the emotions to gush.

"But for some reason I thought it was a boy. I don't know why, but I just felt it somehow. I could have been wrong. I was going to call him Sean," I repeat.

Dad nods. "That's right. A fine name."

"I used to talk to him. Sing to him. I wonder if he heard." My voice is far away. I feel like I'm calling out from the hollow of a tree, where I hide.

Silence while I imagine a future that will never be with little imaginary Sean. Of singing to him every night, of marshmallow skin and splashes at bathtime. Of chubby legs and bicycle rides. Of sand-castle architecture and football-related hotheaded tantrums. Anger at a missed life—no, worse, a lost life—overrides my thoughts.

"I wonder if he even knew."

"Knew what, love?"

"What was happening. What he would be missing. I hope he doesn't blame me. I was all he had, and—" I stop. Torture over for now. I feel seconds away from screaming with such terror, I must stop.

"Ah, love." Dad takes my hand and squeezes it again, long and hard. He pats my hair, and with steady fingers takes the strands from my face and tucks them behind my ears. He hasn't done that since I was a little girl.

"If you want my tuppence worth, I think he's in heaven, love. Oh, there's no thinking involved—I know so. He's up there with your mother, yes he is. Sitting on her lap while she plays rummy with Pauline, who's robbing her blind and cackling away. She's up there, all right." He looks up and wags his forefinger at the ceiling. "Now, you take care of baby Sean for us, Gracie, you hear?" He looks back at me. "She'll be tellin' him all about you, she will, about when you were a baby, about the day you took your first steps, about the day you got your first tooth. She'll tell him about your first day of school and your last day of school and every day in between, and he'll know all about you so that when you walk through those gates up there, as an old woman far older than me now, he'll look up from rummy and say, 'Ah, there she is now. The woman herself. My mammy.' Straight away he'll know."

The lump in my throat, so huge I can barely swallow, prevents me from saying the thank-you I want to express, but perhaps he sees it in my eyes. He nods in acknowledgment and then turns his attention back to the TV while I stare out the window at nothing.

"There's a nice chapel here, love." He breaks into my thoughts. "Maybe you should go visit, when you're good and ready. You don't even have to say anything, He won't mind. Just sit there and think. I find it helpful."

I think it's the last place in the world I want to be.

"It's a nice place to be," Dad says, reading my mind. He watches me, and I can almost hear him praying for me to leap out of bed and grab the rosary beads he's placed by the bedside.

"It's a rococo building, you know," I say suddenly, and have no idea what I'm talking about.

"What is?" Dad's eyebrows furrow, and his eyes disappear underneath, like two snails disappearing into their shells. "This hospital?"

I think hard. "What were we talking about?"

Then he thinks hard. "Maltesers. No!"

He's silent for a moment, then starts answering as though in a quick-fire round of a quiz.

"Bananas! No. Heaven! No. The chapel! We were talking about the chapel." He flashes a million-dollar smile, jubilant he succeeded in remembering the conversation of less than one minute ago. He goes further now. "And then you said it's a rickety building. But honestly it felt fine to me. A bit old, sure, but there's nothin' wrong with being old and rickety." He winks at me.

"The chapel is a rococo building, not rickety," I correct him, feeling like a teacher. "It's famous for the elaborate stucco work that adorns the ceiling. It's the work of French *stuccadore* Barthelemy Cramillion."

"Is that so, love? When did he do that, then?" He moves his chair in closer to the bed. Loves nothing more than a lesson.

"In 1762." So precise. So random. So natural. So inexplicable that I know it.

"That long? I didn't know the hospital was here since then."

"It's been here since 1757," I reply, and then frown. How on earth do I know that? But I can't stop myself, almost like my mouth is on autopilot, completely unattached to my brain. "It was designed by the same man who did Leinster House. Richard Cassells was his name. One of the most famous architects of the time."

"I've heard of him, all right," Dad lies. "If you'd said Dick, I'd have known straightaway." He chuckles.

"It was Bartholomew Mosse's brainchild," I explain, and I don't know where the words are coming from, don't know where the knowledge is coming from. Like a feeling of déjà vu. I think maybe I'm making it up, but I know somewhere deep inside that I'm correct. A warm feeling floods my body.

"In 1745 he purchased a small theater called the New Booth, and he converted it into Dublin's first lying-in hospital."

"It stood here, did it? The theater?"

"No, it was on George's Lane. This was all just fields. But eventually that became too small, and he bought the fields that were here. In 1757 the new lying-in hospital, now known as the Rotunda, was opened by the Lord Lieutenant. On the eighth of December, if I recall correctly."

Dad is confused. "I didn't know you had an interest in this kind of thing, Joyce. How do you know all that?"

I frown. I didn't know I knew any of that either. Before I have time to even ponder my response, the door to the room opens and the nurse enters.

"Visitors here to see you, Joyce," she says delicately, as though a raised voice would break me. "I'm sorry, Mr. Conway, but we can only allow two guests at a time. You'll have to wait outside."

Dad is delighted to be ejected from the room, so violent is the look I've thrown him. I had already informed him, quite firmly, that I wasn't in the mood for visitors of any sort. His face is pink, revealing his guilt, if not of arranging this visit, at least of the failure to prevent it. He flies out of the room, up and down, down and up, like a fly that's lost a wing.

As soon as he's out of the room, two faces poke around the edge of the door. Kate and Frankie, my oldest and best friends. They enter the room like two virgins approaching a gigolo; Kate's hands clasped across her front, Frankie's lips pursed, both their eyes wide and concerned. I feel my body tense, rejecting their presence, and they instantly know not to greet me with their usual hugs and kisses. Like the game of musical chairs that we so often played as children, they race for the armchair next to my bed, and their bums fight for space. Frankie wins, as usual, and relaxes in the seat, smug and lazy like a cat. Kate, momentarily caught in a time warp, glares at her childishly, and then finally, remembering the passing of thirty years and where she is, decides to perch on the armrest instead. She wobbles a few times on thin wood, searching for the correct place to place her backside. She can't be comfortable, but she stops squirming to fix her gaze upon me. Her look is similar to the consistency of the food she spends her days making at home; puréed and organic, soft enough to squeeze through the gaps of baby teeth, the sounds from her kitchen not dissimilar to the Dublin roads ripped apart by roadworks, endless drilling and pounding. Her eyes melt down into her cheeks, her cheeks into her mouth, everything downward, sad, sympathetic.

"You didn't have to come," I say. My politeness valve isn't working, and the words gush out mean and cold; they sound more like "I wish you didn't come."

Kate is momentarily taken aback, and then compassion oozes back onto her face, like a slow mush.

"With the kids and everything . . . ," I add lifelessly, an attempt at damage control, but the words are limp and hang in the air and then slither down to the ground in the silence that follows.

"Oh, the kids are outside, on their best behavior." She smiles.

Behind her, I see a solo wheelchair race by with a teddy bear strapped inside. Seconds later, Dad runs after it in a panic. I'm glad I don't see Sam, Kate's baby. I couldn't take that. Only adult life-forms to pass my eyeline from now on.

Frankie remains uncharacteristically quiet from her place in the armchair, looking around the room like a child in a waiting room, bored and uninterested, waiting for Mother to finish her adult duties so that the fun of life can begin again.

My eyes fall to her lap.

"What's that?"

Realizing it's her turn, she looks at me. "Oh—" She bites her lip and looks at Kate, whose expression has quite dramatically altered to one of extreme anger. "Oh, *this*." Her voice goes up a notch. "This is, um, it's a . . ." She angles her head left and right, examining it. "It's a gift," she finally says and lifts it up so that I can see. "For you. From us." She gives me her best, cheekiest, broadest smile.

I look at Kate, whose mushy face has now tightened with anger. Words are bubbling beneath her lips, jumping to get out like heated kernels exploding in her mouth.

"Okay, so I made a bit of a mistake." Frankie tries to hide her smile now.

"I told you to get her *flowers*," Kate finally explodes.

"I wasn't too far off," Frankie defends herself. "It's a plant."

"It's. A. Cactus," Kate spits.

I smile at their usual bickering, surprised they managed to last this long without going at each other. They've been carrying on like an old married couple ever since they were six. While they snap at each other, I gaze at the cactus, a small green prickly ball in the center of a cracked plastic pot. A few balls of dried soil fall into Frankie's lap. The plant is nothing short of ugly, but it seems familiar, and its presence comforts me.

"You got me one of these before." I interrupt their debate on the meaning of "something appropriate."

"We most certainly did not," Kate says with disgust.

"I have one at home?" I ask, studying it further.

"Unless you mean Conor, there's nothing else in your house prick-related—ow!" She rubs her ribs from where Kate had elbowed her.

"Porrúa," I say, holding out my hands and taking it from Frankie.

"Huh?"

"I'm going to call it Porrúa."

Silence. Their confusion, at least, agreed on.

"Named after the Porrúa Bookshop stone that was found embedded in the wall of the Librería Porrúa in Mexican City," I explain, running my fingers along the thin thistles. "It was a giant Aztec barrel cactus carved from basalt rock, a powerful symbol of their tribal roots and quite rare because in Aztec art, they rarely sculpted plants, more often animals, rulers, and gods." I smile at them, my darkness lifting with each sentence.

Kate's eyes widen; Frankie's lips part in a smile.

"Are you on morphine?" Frankie asks, a glint appearing in her eye. "If you are, can I have some? Pass me that tube thing, quick before the nurse comes. What do I do, inhale or stick it in my arm?"

"Frankie—" Kate's elbow meets her ribs again, and her voice softens toward me, as though I weren't a witness to her violence. "I wanted to get you something prettier than that," she apologizes, taking the cactus from my hands and placing it by the bed beside the seeded grapes and mineral water. "Something with flowers, you know. Petals"—her words are more aimed at Frankie now—"soft and delicate. You know? *Appropriate.*"

I study it again, feeling my head heat up. I have seen this cactus before. I see it on a windowsill in some distant memory, but it's not a windowsill I have at home. Where is it? I swallow hard, feeling out of sorts, uncomfortable with the words coming out of my mouth, wondering if a kind of dementia has set in. I've seen it in wildlife programs, mothers who've lost their cubs, going crazy without their child. Perhaps that's what was happening. I realize they're looking at me for an explanation.

"Oh, don't worry, she'll flower all right."

Frankie looks pleased by the news in an I-told-you-so kind of way.

"With some cacti, the flower will open toward the evening and die the following morning," I add, and Frankie's smile quickly fades.

"How do you know so much about cacti, Joyce?" Kate asks, in the same tone with which a cop would talk down someone from a rooftop.

"It's not necessarily cacti that I'm interested in. Cacti can be found repeatedly in pictorial representations and drawings among the remains of the Aztec civilization." I finish that statement with a shrug. I have no idea what I'm saying.

"Are you seeing an Aztec behind Conor's back?" Frankie jokes nervously.

Kate is silent, and our eyes lock momentarily. I'm as concerned as she. Where on earth is this coming from?

"You should rest," Kate says quietly, and I close my eyes, not needing to be told twice.

When I open them again, the two of them are gone, and Dad has replaced them beside me. He pours my mineral water into the cactus.

I sit up, and he smiles at me. "Hello, sunshine."

"Do you have a cactus on a windowsill at home?"

He frowns and shakes his head. "No, love."

"Who has one, then?" I close my eyes and study the image embedded in my memory. A sunny day, a cactus on a windowsill, white voile curtains billowing out an open window. I smell a barbecue, I hear children laugh outside the window and the sound of a ball bouncing. I move closer to the window and see a girl with white-blond hair looking up at me. There's a look of horror on her face, and then I see the ball headed toward me. It flies through the window, knocks the cactus from the sill and to the ground. I jump with fright in the bed.

"What's wrong, love? Should I call a nurse?"

"No, it's just—" I feel beads of sweat breaking out on my forehead. I feel dizzy and confused, madness setting in, a mother without her cub. Suddenly frustration overwhelms me, and I shake my head aggressively. "I want a haircut," I say angrily, blowing my fringe off my forehead. "I want to get out of here."

"Okay, love." Dad's voice is quiet. "A little longer, is all."

Chapter 7

◇◇◇◇◇

GET A HAIRCUT! JUSTIN BLOWS the mop out of his eyes and glares with dissatisfaction at his reflection in the mirror.

Until his image caught his eye, he was packing his bag to go back to London while whistling the happy tune of a recently divorced man who's just been laid by the first woman since his wife. Well, the second time that year, but the first that he could recall with some small degree of pride. Now, standing before the full-length mirror, his whistling stalls, the image of his Fabio self failing miserably against the reality. He corrects his posture, sucks in his cheeks, and flexes his muscles, vowing that now that the divorce cloud has lifted, he will get his body back in order. Forty-three years old, he is handsome and he knows it, but it's not a view that is held with arrogance. His opinions on his looks are merely understood with the same logic he applies to tasting a fine wine. The grape was merely grown in the right place, under the right conditions. Some degree of nurturing and love mixed with later moments of being completely trampled on and walked all over. He possesses enough common sense to recognize he was born with good genes and features that were in proportion, in the right places. He should be neither praised nor blamed for this. It's just how it is.

At almost six feet, he is tall, his shoulders broad, his hair still thick and chestnut brown, though graying at the sides. This he does not mind; he's had gray hairs since his twenties and has always felt they give him a distinguished look. For Justin, moving on and change are what he expects. He is not one for pausing, for becoming stuck in life, though he didn't expect his particular philosophy of aging and graying to apply to his marriage. Jennifer left him two years ago to ponder this, though not just this, but for a great many other reasons too. So many, in fact, he wishes he had taken out a pen and notepad and listed them as she bellowed at him in her tirade of hate. In the dark lonely nights that initially followed, Justin wondered if his solid, tight philosophy could make things all right. Would he wake up in the morning and find Jennifer in their bed; would the light scar on his chin have healed from where the wedding ring had landed; would the list of things about him she hated so much be the very things she loved?

Through strands of the long hair hanging over his eyes, he has a vision of the man he expects to see. Leaner, younger, perhaps with fewer wrinkles around the eyes. Any faults, such as the expanding waistline, are partly due to age and partly of his own doing—he often took to beer and take-out for comfort during his divorce process.

Repeated flashbacks of the previous night draw his eyes back to the bed where he and Sarah got to know each other intimately. All day he definitely felt like the big man on campus, and he was just seconds away from interrupting his talk on Dutch and Flemish painting to give details of his previous night's performance. Only three-quarters of the class, first-year students in the midst of Rag Week, had shown up after the previous night's foam party, and he was sure those who were in attendance wouldn't notice if he launched into a detailed analysis of his lovemaking skills. He didn't test his assumptions, all the same.

Blood for Life Week is over, much to Justin's relief, and Sarah has moved on from the college, back to her base. On his return to Dublin this month he coincidentally bumped into her in a bar, one that he just happened to know she frequented, and they went from there. He isn't sure if he will see her again, though his inside jacket pocket is safely padded with her number.

He has to admit that while the previous night was indeed delightful—a couple too many bottles of Château Olivier (which until last night he's always found disappointing, despite its ideal location in Bordeaux) in a lively bar on the Green, followed by a trip to his hotel room—he feels much was missing from his conquest. He acquired some Dutch courage from his hotel minibar before calling round to see her, and by the time he arrived at the bar, he was already incapable of serious conversation, or more seriously, incapable of conversation— Oh, for Christ's sake, Justin, what man do you know cares about the damn conversation? But he feels that, despite ending up in his bed, Sarah did care about the conversation. Perhaps there were things she wanted to say to him, and perhaps she did say them while he saw those sad blue eyes boring into his and those rosebud lips opening and closing, but his Jameson whiskey wouldn't allow him to hear, instead singing in his head over her words like a petulant child.

With his second seminar in two months complete, Justin throws his clothes into his bag, happy to be leaving this miserable musty room. Friday afternoon, time to fly back to London. Back to his daughter and to his younger brother, Al, and sister-in-law, Doris, visiting from Chicago. He departs the hotel, steps out onto the cobbled side streets of Temple Bar and into his waiting taxi.

"The airport, please."

"Here on holidays?" the driver asks immediately.

"No." Justin looks out the window, hoping this will end the conversation.

"Working?" The driver starts the engine.

"Yes."

"Where do you work?"

"A college."

"Which one?"

Justin sighs. "Trinity."

"You the janitor?" The driver's green eyes twinkle playfully at him in the mirror.

"I'm a lecturer on art and architecture," Justin says defensively, folding his arms and blowing his floppy mane from his eyes.

"Architecture, huh? I used to be a builder."

Justin doesn't respond.

"So where are ye off to? Off on holiday?"

"Nope."

"What is it, then?"

"I live in London." And my U.S. social security number is . . .

"And you work here?"

"Yep."

"Would you not just live here?"

"Nope."

"Why's that, then?"

"Because I'm a guest lecturer here. A colleague of mine invited me to give a seminar once a month."

"Ah." The driver smiles at him in the mirror as though he'd been trying to fool him. "So what do you do in London?"

I'm a serial killer who preys on inquisitive cabdrivers.

"Lots of different things." Justin sighs and caves in as the driver waits for more. "I'm the editor of the *Art and Architectural Review*, the only truly international art and architectural publication," he says proudly. "I started it ten years ago, and we're still unrivaled. Highest-selling magazine of its kind." Only twenty thousand subscribers, you liar.

There's no reaction.

"I'm also a curator."

The driver winces. "You've to touch dead bodies?"

Justin scrunches his face in confusion. "What? No." Then adds unnecessarily, "I'm also a regular panelist on a BBC art and culture show."

Twice in five years doesn't quite constitute regular, Justin. Oh, shut up.

The driver studies Justin now. "You're on TV?" He narrows his eyes. "I don't recognize you."

"Do you watch the show?"

"No."

Well, then.

Justin rolls his eyes. He throws off his suit jacket, opens another of his shirt buttons, and lowers the window. His hair sticks to his forehead. Still. A few weeks have gone by, and he hasn't been to the barber. He blows the strands out of his eyes.

They stop at a red light, and Justin looks to his left. A hair salon.

"Hey, would you mind pulling over for just a few minutes? I won't be long."

"Look, Conor, don't worry about it. Stop apologizing," I say into the cell phone tiredly. He exhausts me. Every little word with him drains me. "Dad is here with me now, and we're going to get a taxi to the house together, even though I'm perfectly capable of sitting in a car by myself."

We're outside the hospital, and Dad has hailed a cab and now holds the door open for me. I'm finally going home, but I don't feel the relief I was hoping for. There's nothing but dread. I dread meeting people I know and having to explain what has happened, over and over again. I dread walking into my house and having to face the half-decorated nursery. I dread having to get rid of the nursery, having to replace it with a spare bed and fill the wardrobes with my own overflow of bags and shoes I'll never wear. I dread having to go to work instead of taking the leave I had planned. I even dread seeing Conor. I dread going back to a loveless marriage with no baby to distract us. I know it would be common sense for me to want my husband to come rushing home to me—in fact, for my husband to *want to* come rushing home to me—but there are many buts in our marriage. And to behave the right way, to do the adult thing, feels wrong right now; I don't want anybody around me. I've been poked and prodded physically and psychologically. I want to be on my own to grieve. I want to feel sorry for myself without sympathetic words and clinical explanations. I want to be illogical, self-pitying, self-examining, bitter and lost, for just a few more days, please, world, and I want to do it alone.

As I said, that is not unusual in our marriage.

Conor's an engineer. He travels abroad to work for months before coming home for one month and then going off again. I used to get so used to my own company and routine that for the first week of him being home I'd be irritable and wish he'd go back. Now that irritability stretches to the entire month of his being home. And it's become glaringly obvious I'm not alone in that feeling.

I always thought our marriage could survive anything as long as we both tried. But then I found myself having to try to try. I dug beneath the new layers of complexities we'd created over the years to get to the beginning of the relationship. What was it, I wondered, that we had then that we could revive now? What was the thing that could make two people want to spend every day of the rest of their lives together? Ah, I found it. It was a thing called love. A small, simple word. If only it didn't mean so much, our marriage would be flawless.

My mind wandered a lot while I was lying in that hospital bed. At times it stalled in its wandering, like when a person enters a room and then forgets what for. It stood alone, dumbstruck.

Sometimes, when staring at the pink walls, I thought of nothing but of the fact that I was staring at pink walls.

On one occasion while my mind was wandering far, I dug deep to find a memory of when I was six years old and had a favorite tea set given to me by my grandmother Betty. She kept it in her house for me to play with when I came over on Saturdays, and during the afternoons, when my grandmother was "taking tea" with her friends, I would wear one of my mother's pretty childhood dresses and have afternoon tea with Aunt Jemima, the cat. The dresses never quite fit, but I wore them all the same, and Aunt Jemima and I never did take to tea, but we were both polite enough to keep up the pretense until my parents came to collect me at the end of the day. I told this story to Conor a few years ago, and he laughed, missing the point.

It was an easy point to miss—I won't hold him accountable for that—but what I was aching for him to understand was that I've increasingly found that people never truly tire of playing games and dressing up, no matter how many years pass. Our lies now are just more sophisticated; our words to deceive, more eloquent. From cowboys and Indians, doctors and nurses, to husband and wife, we've never stopped pretending. But sitting in the taxi beside Dad while listening to Conor on the phone, I realize I've finally stopped pretending.

"Where is Conor?" Dad asks as soon as I've hung up.

He opens the top button of his shirt and loosens his tie. He dresses in a shirt and tie every time he leaves the house, never forgets his cap. He looks for the handle on the car door, to roll the window down.

"It's electronic, Dad. There's the button. He's still in Japan. He'll be home in a few days."

"I thought he was coming back yesterday." He puts the window all the way down, and the wind topples the cap off his head; the few strands of hair left on his scalp stick up. He fixes the cap

back on his head and has a mini battle with the button before finally figuring out how to successfully leave a small gap at the top
for air.

"Ha! Gotcha." He smiles victoriously, thumping his fist at the
window.

I wait until he's finished celebrating to answer. "I told him
not to."

"You told who what, love?"

"Conor. You were asking about Conor, Dad."

"Ah, that's right, I was. Home soon, is he?"

I nod.

The day is hot, and I blow my bangs up from my sticky forehead. I feel my hair sticking to the back of my clammy neck. Suddenly it feels heavy and greasy on my head. I have the overwhelm-
ing urge to shave it all off. I become agitated in my seat, and Dad,
sensing it again, knows not to say anything. I've been doing that all
week: experiencing anger beyond comprehension, so much that
I want to drive my fists through the walls and punch the nurses.
Then I become weepy and feel such loss inside me, it's as if I'll
never be whole again. I prefer the anger. Anger is better. Anger is
hot and filling and gives me something to cling to.

We stop at a set of traffic lights, and I look to my left. A hair
salon.

"Pull over here, please."

"What are you doing, Joyce?"

"I can't take it anymore, Dad, I have to get my hair cut."

Dad looks at the salon and then to the taxi driver, and they
both know not to say anything. Just then, the taxi directly in front
of us moves over to the side of the road too. We pull up behind it.

"Will you be long, love?"

"Ten minutes, fifteen max. Do you want to come in with
me?"

Dad shakes his head vigorously, and his chin wobbles along

with it. Keeping the taxi waiting for me is indulgent, I know, but having Dad outside the salon, distracted, is better.

I watch the cab in front of us. A man gets out, and I freeze with one foot out of the car to watch him. He looks familiar, and I think I know him. He pauses and looks at me. We stare at each other for a while. Search each other's face. He scratches at his left arm; something that holds my attention for far too long. The moment is unusual, and goose bumps rise on my skin. I decide the last thing I want is to see somebody I know, and I look away quickly.

He turns and begins to walk.

"What are you doing?" Dad asks far too loudly, and I finally get out of the car.

I start walking toward the hair salon, and it becomes clear that my destination is the same as that of the man in front of me. My walk becomes mechanical, awkward, self-conscious. Something about him makes me disjointed. Unsettled. Perhaps it's the possibility of having to tell somebody, a stranger, that there will be no baby. Yes, a month of nonstop baby talk, and there will be no baby to show for it. Sorry, guys. I feel guilty for it, as though I've cheated my friends and family. The longest tease of all. A baby that will never be. My heart is twisted at the thought of it.

The man holds open the door to the salon and smiles. Handsome. Fresh-faced. Tall. Broad. Athletic. Perfect. Is he glowing? Do I know him?

"Thank you," I say.

"You're welcome."

We both pause, look at each other, and over to the two identical taxis waiting for us by the curb, and then back to each other. He looks me up and down.

"Nice cactus." He smiles. I notice he has an American accent.

"What?" I ask, confused, then, following his eyeline, notice I'm still carrying the cactus that I brought from the hospital. "Oh!

Oh, my God, I meant to leave it in the car." I feel my face turn pink. "It was a gift," I explain.

"Nice gift. I have one at home."

I think he's joking with me, and I wait for a laugh that never comes. We enter the salon, which is empty save for two staff members who are sitting down, chatting. They are two men; one has a mullet, the other is bleached blond. They see us and spring to attention.

"Which one do you want?" the American says out of the side of his mouth.

"The blond." I smile.

"The mullet it is, then," he says.

My mouth falls open, but I laugh.

"Hello there, loves." The mullet man approaches us. "How can I help you?" He looks back and forth from the American to me. "Who is getting their hair done today?"

"Well, both of us, I assume, right?" The American looks at me, and I nod.

"Oh, pardon me, I thought you were together."

I realize we are so close, our hips are almost touching. We both look down and then take one step away in the opposite direction.

"You two should try synchronized swimming." The hairdresser laughs, but the joke dies when we fail to react. "Ashley, you take the lovely lady. You come with me." The American makes a face at me while being led away, and I laugh again. The two of us get seated at nearby stations.

"I just want two inches off, please," I hear the American say. "The last time I got it done, they took off like, twenty. Just two inches," he stresses. "I've got a taxi waiting outside to take me to the airport, so as quick as possible too, please."

His hairdresser laughs. "Sure, no problem. Are you going back to America?"

The man rolls his eyes. "No, I'm not going to America, I'm not going on holiday, and I'm not going to meet anyone at arrivals. I'm just going to take a flight. Away. Out of here. You Irish ask a lot of questions."

"Do we?"

"Y—" He stalls and narrows his eyes at the hairdresser.

"Gotcha." The hairdresser smiles, pointing his scissors at him.

"Yes, you did." Gritted teeth.

I chuckle aloud, and the American immediately looks at me. He seems slightly confused. Maybe we do know each other. Maybe he works with Conor. Maybe I went to school with him. College. Perhaps he's in the property business, and I've worked with him. But I can't have; he's American. Maybe he's famous, and I shouldn't be staring. I become embarrassed, and I turn quickly away yet again.

My hairdresser wraps a black cape around me, and I steal another glance in the mirror at the man beside me. He looks at me. I look away, then back at him. He looks away. And our tennis match of glances is played out for the duration of our visit.

"How about I just take this from you," my hairdresser says as he reaches for the cactus still in my hands. I hold on to it, not wanting to let go, and a minor tug-of-war is played out. He wins. "I'll just place it here for you." He talks to me as though I'm a patient out on a day trip. "So what will it be for you, madam?"

"All off," I say, trying to avoid my reflection, but I feel cold hands on the sides of my hot cheeks raising my head, and I am forced to stare at myself face-to-face. There is something unnerving about being forced to look at yourself when you are unwilling to come to terms with something. Something raw and real that you can't run away from. I see in the mirror that I am not okay. The truth of it stares me in the face. My cheeks are sunken, small black semicircles hover below my eyes, my red eyes still sting from my night tears. But apart from that, I still look like me. Despite this huge change in my life, I look exactly the same. Tired, but me. Yet the mirror told me this: you can't know everything by looking at me. You can never know just by looking at someone.

I'm five foot five, with medium-length hair that is midway between blond and brown. I'm a medium kind of person. I'm pretty, not stunning, not ugly; not fat, not skinny; I exercise three times a week, jog a little, walk a little, swim a little. Nothing to excess. Not obsessed, not addicted to anything. I'm neither outgoing nor shy but a little of both, depending on my mood, depending on the occasion. I like my job, but don't love it. I'm okay. Nothing spectacular, but sometimes special. I look in the mirror and see this medium average person. A little tired, a little sad, but not falling apart. I peek at the man beside me, and I see the same.

"Excuse me?" The hairdresser breaks into my thoughts. "You want it all off? Are you sure? You've such healthy hair." He runs his fingers through it. "Is this your natural color?"

"Yes, I used to put a little color in it but I stopped because of the—" I stop as my eyes fill, and I look down to my stomach, which is hidden under the gown.

"Stopped because of what?" he asks.

I pretend to be doing something with my foot. An odd shuffle maneuver. I can't think of anything to say, so I pretend not to hear him. "Huh?"

"You were saying you stopped because of something?"

"Oh, em . . ." Don't cry. Don't cry. If you start now, you will never stop. "Oh, I don't know," I mumble, bending over to play with my handbag on the ground. It will pass, it will pass. Someday it will all pass, Joyce. "Chemicals. I stopped because of chemicals."

"Right. Well, this is what it'll look like." He takes my hair and ties it back. "How about we do a Meg Ryan in *French Kiss*?" He pulls clumps out in all directions, and I look like I've just woken up. "It's the sexy messy bed-head look. Or else we can do this." He messes with my hair some more.

"Can we hurry this along? I've got a taxi waiting outside too." I look out the window. Dad is chatting to the taxi driver. They're both laughing and I relax a little.

"O . . . kay. Something like this really shouldn't be rushed. You have a lot of hair."

"It's fine. I'm giving you permission to hurry. Just cut it all off."

"Well, we must leave a few inches on it, darling." He directs my face back toward the mirror. "We don't want Sigourney Weaver in *Aliens*, do we? No GI Janes allowed in this salon. We'll give you a side-swept fringe, very sophisticated, very now. It'll suit you, I think, show off those high cheekbones. What do you think?"

I don't care about my cheekbones. I just want it off.

"Actually, how about we just do this?" I take the scissors from his hand, cut my ponytail, and then hand them both back to him.

He gasps. But it sounds more like a squeak. "Or we could do that. A . . . bob."

American man's mouth hangs open at the sight of my hairdresser with a large pair of scissors and five inches of hair dangling from his hand. He turns to his stylist and grabs the scissors before he makes another cut. "Do not"—he points—"do that to me!"

Mullet man sighs and rolls his eyes. "No, of course not, sir."

The American starts scratching his left arm again. "I must have got a bite." He tries to roll up his shirtsleeve, and I squirm in my seat, trying to get a look at his arm. I can't help myself.

"Could you please sit still?"

"Could you please sit still?"

The hairdressers speak in perfect unison. They look to one another and laugh.

"Something funny in the air today," one of them comments, and the American and I look at each other. Funny, indeed.

My hairdresser places a finger under my chin and tips my face back to the center. He hands me my ponytail.

"Souvenir."

"I don't want it." I refuse to take my hair in my hands. Every inch of that hair was from a moment that has now gone. Thoughts, wishes, hopes, desires, dreams that are no longer. I want a new start. A new head of hair.

He begins to snip it into style now, and as each strand falls, I watch it drift to the ground. My head feels so much lighter.

The hair that grew the day we bought the crib. Snip.

The hair that grew the day we decided on the name. Snip.

The hair that grew the day we announced our news to friends and family. Snip.

The day of the first scan. The day I found out I was pregnant. The day my baby was conceived. Snip. Snip. Snip.

The more recent memories will remain at the root for a little while longer. I will have to wait for them to grow out until I can be rid of them too, and then all traces will be gone, and I will move on for good.

The American man joins me at the register as I'm paying.

"You forgot your cactus." He hands it to me.

Our fingers brush, and my body zings from head to toe. "Thank you."

"That suits you," he comments, studying me.

I go to tuck some hair behind my ear self-consciously, but there's nothing there. I feel lighter, light-headed, delighted with giddiness, giddy with delight.

"So does yours."

"Thank you."

He opens the door for me.

"Thank you." I step outside.

"You're far too polite," he tells me.

"Thank you." I smile. "So are you."

"Thank you." He nods.

We laugh. We both gaze at our waiting taxis and look back at each other curiously. He gives me a smile. I feel like I should stay in this place and not move. I feel like moving away from him is the wrong way, that everything in me is being pulled toward him.

"Do you want to take the first taxi or the second?" he asks. "My driver won't stop talking."

I study both taxis and see Dad in the second, leaning forward and talking to the driver.

"I'll take the first. My dad won't stop talking either."

He studies the second taxi, where Dad has now pushed his face up against the window, staring at me as though I'm an apparition.

"The second taxi it is, then," the American says and walks to his taxi, glancing back twice.

"Hey," I protest and watch him get in his car, entranced.

I go to my own taxi, and we both pull our doors closed at the same time. The taxi driver and Dad look at me like they've seen a ghost.

"What?" My heart beats wildly. "What happened?"

"Your hair," Dad simply says, his face aghast. "You're like a boy."

Chapter 8

◇◇◇◇◇

A S THE TAXI GETS CLOSER to my home in Phisboro, my stomach knots tighter.

"That was funny how the man in front kept his taxi waiting too, Gracie, wasn't it?"

"Joyce. And yes," I reply, my leg bouncing with nerves.

"Is that what people do now when they get their hairs cut?"

"Do what, Dad?"

"Leave taxis waiting outside for them."

"I don't know."

He shuffles his bum to the edge of the seat and pulls himself closer to the taxi driver. "I say, Jack, is that what people do when they go to the barbers now?"

"What's that?"

"Do they leave their taxis outside waiting for them?"

"I've never been asked to do it before," the driver explains politely.

Dad sits back, satisfied. "That's what I thought, Gracie."

"It's Joyce," I snap.

"It's a coincidence. And you know what they say about coincidences?"

"Yep." We turn the corner onto my street, and my stomach flips.

"That there's no such thing as a coincidence," Dad finishes. "Indeedy no," he says to himself. "No such thing. Oh, there's Patrick." He waves. "I hope he doesn't wave back." He watches his friend from the Monday Club walking with two hands on his hips. "And David out with the dog." He waves again, although David is stopping to allow his dog to poop and is looking the other way. I get the feeling Dad feels rather grand in a taxi. It's rare he's in one, the expense being too much and everywhere he needs to go being within walking distance or a short bus ride away.

"Home, sweet home," he announces as we reach my house. "How much do I owe you, Jack?" He leans forward again. He takes two five-euro notes out of his pocket.

"The bad news, I'm afraid . . . twenty euro, please."

"What?" Dad looks up in shock.

"I'll pay, Dad, put your money away." I give the driver twenty-five and tell him to keep the change. Dad looks at me like I've just taken a pint out of his hand and poured it down the drain.

Conor and I have lived in the red-brick terraced house in Phisboro since our wedding ten years ago. The houses have been here since the 1940s, and over the years we've pumped our money into modernizing it. It's finally how we want it, or it was until this week. A black railing encloses a small patch of a front garden where my mother planted rosebushes. Dad lives in an identical house two streets away, the house I grew up in. Though we're never done growing up, and when I return to it, I regress to my youth.

My front door opens just as the taxi drives off. Dad's neighbor Fran smiles at me from my own doorstep. She looks at us awkwardly, failing to make eye contact with me. I'll have to get used to this.

"Oh, your hair!" she says first, then gathers herself. "I'm sorry, love, I meant to be out of here by the time you got home." She opens the door fully and pulls a checked rolling suitcase behind her. She is wearing a single rubber glove on her right hand.

Dad looks nervous and avoids my eye.

"What were you doing, Fran? How on earth did you get into my house?" I try to be as polite as I can, but the sight of someone in my house without my permission both surprises and infuriates me.

She pinks and looks to Dad, who looks at her hand and coughs. She looks down, laughs nervously, and pulls off the glove. "Oh, your dad gave me a key. I thought that . . . well, I put down a nice rug in the hallway for you. I hope you like it."

I stare at her in utter confusion.

"Never mind, I'll be off now." She walks by me, grabs my arm, and squeezes hard but still refuses to look at me. "Take care of yourself, love." She walks on down the road, dragging her suitcase behind her, her brown tights in rolls around her thick ankles.

"Dad"—I look at him angrily—"what the hell is this?" I push into the house, looking at the disgusting dusty rug on my beige carpet. "Why did you give a near stranger my house keys so she could come in and leave a rug? I am not a charity!"

He takes off his cap and scrunches it in his hands. "She's not a stranger, love. She's known you since the day we brought you home from the hospital—"

Wrong story to tell at this moment, and he knows it.

"I don't care!" I splutter. "It's my house, not yours! You can't just do that. I hate this ugly piece-of-shit rug!" I pick it up from one side and drag it outside, then slam the door shut. I'm fuming, and I look at Dad to shout at him again. He is pale and shaken and is looking at the floor sadly. My eyes follow his.

Various shades of faded brown stains, like red wine, splatter the beige carpet. It has been cleaned in some places, but most of the carpet hairs still give away that something once lay there. My blood.

I put my head in my hands.

Dad's voice is quiet, injured. "I thought it would be best for you to come home with that gone."

"Oh, Dad."

"Fran has been here every day now and has tried different things on it. It was me that suggested the rug," he adds in a smaller voice. "You can't blame her for that."

I despise myself.

"I know you like all nice new matching things in your house"— he looks around—"but Fran or I wouldn't have the likes of that."

"I'm sorry, Dad. I don't know what came over me. I'm sorry I shouted at you. You've been nothing but helpful this week. I'll . . . I'll call around to Fran soon and thank her properly."

"Right." He nods. "So I guess I'll leave you at it. I'll bring the rug back to Fran. I don't want any of the neighbors seeing it outside and telling her."

"No, I'll put it back where it was. It's too heavy for you to carry anyway. I'll keep it for the time being and return it to her soon." I open the front door and drag it back into the house with more respect, laying it down so that it once more hides the scene where I lost my baby.

"I'm so sorry, Dad."

"Don't worry." He seesaws up to me and pats my shoulder. "You're having a hard time, that I know. Remember I'm only round the corner if you need me for anything."

With a flick of his wrist, his tweed cap is on his head, and I watch him seesaw down the road. The movement is familiar and comforting, like the motion of the sea. I wait until he disappears, and then I close the door.

Alone. Silence. Just me and the house. Life continues as though nothing has happened.

It seems as though the nursery upstairs vibrates through the walls and floor. *Thump-thump. Thump-thump.* Like a heart, it's trying to push out and send blood flowing down the stairs and through the hallways to reach every little nook and cranny. I walk away from the stairs, the scene of the crime, and wander around the rooms. I place the cactus on the kitchen windowsill. It appears everything is exactly as it was, though on further inspection I see that Fran has tidied around. The cup of tea I was drinking is gone from the coffee table in the living room. The galley kitchen hums with the sound of the dishwasher Fran has set. The taps and draining boards glisten, the surfaces are gleaming.

Upstairs the nursery still throbs.

I notice the red light on the answering machine in the hall is flashing and walk over to it. Four messages. I flick through the list of missed calls and recognize friends' numbers. I turn away from the answering machine, not able to listen to their condolences quite yet. Then I freeze. I go back. I flick through the list again. There it is. Monday evening, 7:10 p.m. Again at 7:12 p.m. My second chance to take the call. The call for which I had foolishly rushed down the stairs and sacrificed my child's life.

They have left a message. With shaking fingers, I press play.

"Hello, this is Xtra-vision, Phisboro, calling about *The Muppet Christmas Carol* DVD. It says in our system that it's one week late. We'd appreciate it if you could return it as soon as possible, please."

I inhale sharply. Tears spring in my eyes. What did I expect? A phone call worthy of losing my baby? Something so urgent that I was right to rush for it? Would that somehow warrant my loss?

My entire body trembles with rage and shock. Breathing in shakily, I make my way into the living room. I look straight ahead to the DVD player. On top is the DVD I rented while babysitting my goddaughter. I reach for the DVD and hold it tightly in my hands, squeezing it as though I can stop the life in it. Then I throw it hard across the room. It knocks our collection of photographs off the top of the piano, cracking the glass on our wedding photo, chipping the silver coating of another.

I open my mouth. And I scream. I scream at the top of my lungs, the loudest I can possibly go. It's deep and low and filled with anguish. I scream again and hold it for as long as I can. One scream after another from the pit of my stomach, from the depths of my heart. I let out deep howls that border on laughter, that are laced with frustration. I scream and I scream until I am out of breath and my throat burns.

Upstairs, the nursery continues to vibrate. *Thump-thump, thump-thump.* It beckons me, the heart of my home beating wildly. I go to the staircase, step over the rug and onto the stairs. I grab the banister, feeling too weak even to lift my legs. I pull myself upstairs. The thumping gets louder and louder with every step until I reach the top and face the nursery door. It stops throbbing. All is still now.

I trace a finger down the closed door, press my cheek to it, willing all that happened not to be so. I reach for the handle and open the door.

A half-painted wall of Buttercup Dream greets me. Soft pastels. Sweet smells. A crib with a mobile of little yellow ducks dangling above. A toy box decorated with giant letters of the alphabet. On a little rail hang two baby onesies. Little booties on a dresser.

A bunny rabbit sits up enthusiastically inside the crib. He smiles stupidly at me. I take my shoes off and step barefoot onto the soft shag-pile carpet, try to root myself in this world. I close the door behind me. There's not a sound. I pick up the rabbit and carry it around the room with me while I run my hands over the shiny new furniture, clothes, and toys. I open a music box and watch as the little mouse inside begins to circle round and round after a piece of cheese to a mesmerizing tinkling sound.

"I'm sorry, my baby," I whisper, and my words catch in my throat. "I'm so, so sorry."

I lower myself to the soft floor, pull my legs close to me, and hug the blissfully unaware bunny. I look again to the little mouse whose very being revolves around eternally chasing a piece of cheese he will never ever reach, let alone eat.

I slam the box shut, and the music stops. I am left in the silence.

Chapter 9

◇◇◇◇◇

I CAN'T FIND ANY FOOD in the apartment; we're going
to have to get take-out," Justin's sister-in-law, Doris, calls
into the living room as she roots through the kitchen cabinets.

"So maybe you know the woman," Justin's younger brother,
Al, says as he sits down on the plastic garden furniture chair in Justin's half-furnished living room.

"No, you see, that's what I'm trying to explain. It's like I know
her, but at the same time, I didn't know her at all."

"You recognized her."

"Yes. Well, no." Kind of.

"And you don't know her name."

"No. I definitely don't know her name."

"Hey, anyone out there or am I talking to myself?" Doris interrupts again. "I said there's no food here, so we're going to have
to get take-out."

"Yeah, sure, honey," Al calls automatically. "Maybe she's a
student of yours, or she went to one of your talks. You usually
remember people you give talks to?"

"There are honestly hundreds of people at a time." Justin shrugs. "And they mostly sit in darkness."

"So that's a no, then." Al rubs his chin.

"Actually, forget the take-out," Doris calls. "You don't have any plates or cutlery—we're going to have to eat out."

"And just let me get this clear, Al. When I say 'recognize,' I don't mean I actually knew her face."

Al frowns.

"I just got a feeling. Like she was familiar." Yeah, that's it, she was familiar.

"Maybe she just looked like someone you know."

Maybe.

"Hey, is anybody listening to me?" Doris interrupts them and stands at the living-room door with her inch-long leopard-print nails on her skintight leather-trouser-clad hips. Thirty-five-year-old fast-talking Italian-American Doris has been married to Al for the past ten years and is regarded by Justin as a lovable but annoying younger sister. There's not an ounce of fat on her bones, and everything she wears looks like it comes out of the closet of *Grease*'s Sandy, post-makeover.

"Yes, sure, honey," Al says again, not taking his eyes off Justin. "Maybe it was that déjà vu thingy."

"Yes!" Justin clicks his fingers. "Or perhaps *vécu* or *senti*. Or *visité*."

"What the heck is that?" Al asks. Doris pulls over a cardboard box filled with books to sit on and joins them.

"*Déjà vu* is French for 'already seen,' and it describes the experience of feeling that one has witnessed or experienced a new situation previously," Justin explains. "The term was coined by a French psychic researcher named Emile Boirac, in an essay that he wrote while at the University of Chicago."

"Go Maroons!" Al raises his beer in the air and then gulps it down.

Doris looks at him with disdain. "Please continue, Justin."

"Well, the experience of déjà vu is usually accompanied by a compelling sense of familiarity, and also a sense of eeriness or strangeness. The experience is most frequently attributed to a dream, although in some cases there is a firm sense that the experience genuinely happened in the past. Déjà vu has been described as remembering the future."

"Wow," Doris says breathily.

"So what's your point, bro?" Al belches.

"Well, I don't think this thing today with me and the woman was déjà vu." Justin frowns and sighs.

"Why not?"

"Because déjà vu relates just to sight, and I felt . . . oh, I don't know." I felt. "*Déjà vécu* is translated as 'already lived,' which explains the experience of not only sight but also of having a weird knowledge of what is going to happen next. *Déjà senti* specifically means 'already felt,' which is exclusively a mental happening, and *déjà visité* involves an uncanny knowledge of a new place, but that's less common. No"—he shakes his head—"I definitely didn't feel like I had been at the salon before."

They all go quiet.

Al breaks the silence. "Well, it's definitely déjà something. Are you sure you didn't just sleep with her at some point?"

"Al." Doris hits her husband's arm. "Why didn't you let *me* cut your hair, Justin, and who are we talking about, anyway?"

"You own a doggie parlor." Justin frowns.

"Dogs have hair." She shrugs.

"Let me try to explain this," Al interrupts. "Justin saw a woman yesterday at a hair salon in Dublin, and he says he recognized her but didn't know her face, and he felt that he knew her but didn't actually know her." He rolls his eyes melodramatically, out of Justin's view.

"Oh, my God," Doris sings, "I know what this is!"

"What?" Justin asks, taking a drink from a toothbrush holder.

"It's obvious." She holds her hands up and looks from one brother to another for dramatic effect. "It's past-life stuff." Her face lights up. "You knew the woman in a paaast liiife." She enunciates the words slowly. "I saw it on *Oprah*." She nods her head, her eyes wide.

"Not more of this crap, Doris." Al looks to Justin. "It's all she talks about now. She sees somethin' about it on TV, and that's all I get on the plane, all the way from Chicago."

"I don't think it's past-life stuff, Doris, but thanks."

Doris tuts. "You two need to have open minds about this kind of thing, because you never know."

"Exactly—you never know," Al fires back.

"Oh, come on, guys. The woman was familiar, that's all. Maybe she just looked like someone I knew from home. No big deal." Forget about it and move on.

"Well, you started it with all your déjà stuff," Doris huffs. "So how do you explain it?"

Justin shrugs. "The optical pathway delay theory."

They both stare at him, dumb-faced.

"The idea is that one eye may record what is seen fractionally faster than the other, creating that strong recollection sensation upon the same scene being viewed milliseconds later by the other eye. Basically it's the product of a delayed optical input from one eye, closely followed by the input from the other eye, which should be simultaneous. This misleads conscious awareness and suggests a sensation of familiarity when there shouldn't be one."

Silence.

Justin clears his throat.

"Believe it or not, honey, I prefer your past-life thing." Al snorts.

"Thanks, sweetie." Doris places her hands on her heart, over-whelmed. "Anyway, as I was saying when I was talking to myself in the kitchen, there's no food, cutlery, or crockery here, so we'll have to eat out tonight. Look at how you're living, Justin. I'm worried about you." Doris looks around the room with disgust. "You've moved all the way over to this country on your own, and you've got nothing but garden furniture, unpacked boxes, and an ugly cactus in a basement that looks like it was built for students. Clearly Jennifer also got all the taste in the settlement too."

Justin's eyes light up, and he clicks his fingers for their attention. "She had a cactus too!"

"Who?"

"The woman at the salon!"

"She carried a cactus into a hair salon?" Doris's upper lip rolls upward. "Oh, my God, the woman is insane, she was made for you." She looks around the room again and shudders. "This place gives me the creeps. Whoever built it is probably still hanging around these walls. I can feel him watching me."

"Don't flatter yourself." Al rolls his eyes.

"This is a Victorian masterpiece, Doris. It was a real find, and it's the only place with a bit of history as well as an affordable price. All the place needs is a bit of TLC, and it'll be fine," Justin says, trying to forget the apartment he loved and recently sold in the affluent and historic Old Town neighborhood of Chicago.

"Which is why I'm here." Doris claps her hands with glee.

"Great." Justin's smile is tight. "Let's go get some dinner now. I'm in the mood for a steak."

"But you're vegetarian, Joyce." Conor looks at me as though I've lost my mind. I probably have. I can't remember the last time I've eaten red meat, but I have a sudden craving for it now that we've sat down at the restaurant.

"I'm not vegetarian, Conor. I just don't like red meat."

"But you've just ordered a medium-rare steak!"

"I know." I shrug. "I'm just one crazy cat."

He smiles as if remembering there once was a wild streak in me. Tonight we are like two friends meeting up after years apart. So much to talk about, but not having the slightest clue where to start.

"Have you chosen the wine yet?" the waiter stops by and asks Conor.

I quickly grab the menu and point. "Actually, I would like to order this one, please."

"Sancerre 1998. That's a very good choice, madam."

"Thank you." I have no idea whatsoever why I've chosen it.

Conor laughs. "Did you just do eeny, meeny, miny moe?"

I smile but get hot under the collar. I don't know why I've ordered that wine. It's too expensive, and I usually drink white, but I act natural because I don't want Conor to worry. He already thought I was crazy when he saw I'd chopped all my hair off. He needs to think I'm back to my normal self in order for me to say what I'm going to say tonight.

The waiter returns with the bottle of wine.

"You can do the tasting," Al says to Justin, "seeing as it was your choice."

Justin picks up the glass of wine, dips his nose into it, and inhales deeply.

I inhale deeply and then swivel the wine in the glass, watching for the alcohol to rise and sweep the sides. I take a sip and hold it on my tongue, suck it in, and allow the alcohol to burn the inside of my mouth. Perfect.

"Lovely, thank you." I place the glass back on the table.

Conor's glass is filled, and mine is topped up, when I begin to tell him the story.

"I found it when Jennifer and I went to France years ago," Justin explains. "She was there performing in the Festival des Cathédrales de Picardie with the orchestra, which was a memorable experience. In Versailles, we stayed in Hôtel du Berry, an elegant 1634 mansion full of period furniture. It's practically a museum of regional history—you probably remember my telling you about it. Anyway, on one of her nights off in Paris, we found this beautiful little fish restaurant tucked away in one of the cobbled alleys of Montmartre. We ordered the sea bass special, but you know how much of a red wine fanatic I am, even with fish, so the waiter suggested we go for the Sancerre.

"You know I always thought of Sancerre as a white wine, as it's famous for using the sauvignon blanc grape, but as it turns out it also uses some pinot noir. And the great thing is that you can drink the red Sancerre cooled exactly like white, at twelve degrees. But when not chilled, it's also good with meat. Enjoy." He toasts his brother and sister-in-law.

Conor is looking at me with a frozen face. "Montmartre? Joyce, you've never once been to Paris. How do you know so much about wine? And who the hell is Jennifer?"

I pause, snap out of my trance, and suddenly hear the words of the story that just came out of my mouth. I do the only thing I can do under the circumstances. I start laughing. "Gotcha."

"Gotcha?" He frowns.

"They're the lines to a movie I watched the other night."

"Oh." Relief floods his face, and he relaxes. "Joyce, you scared me there for a minute. I thought somebody had possessed your body." He smiles. "What film are they from?"

"Oh, I can't remember." I wave my hand dismissively, wondering what on earth is going on with me. I haven't seen a movie in months.

"You don't like anchovies now?" He interrupts my thoughts and looks down at the little collection of anchovies I've gathered in a pile at the side of my plate.

"Give them to me, bro," Al says, lifting his plate closer to Justin's. "I love 'em. How you can have a Caesar salad without anchovies is beyond me." He turns to Doris. "Is it okay that I have anchovies?" he asks sarcastically. "The doc didn't say anchovies are going to kill me, did he?"

"Not unless somebody stuffs them down your throat, which is quite possible," Doris says through gritted teeth.

"Thirty-nine years old, and I'm being treated like a kid," Al says.

"Thirty-five years old, and the only kid I have is my husband," Doris snaps, picking an anchovy from the pile and tasting it. She wrinkles her nose and looks around the room. "They call this an Italian restaurant? My mother and her family would roll in their graves if they saw this place." She blesses herself quickly. "So, Justin, tell me about this lady you're seeing."

Justin frowns. "Doris, it's really no big deal, I told you I just thought I knew her." And she looked like she thought she knew you too.

"No, not her," Al says loudly with a mouthful of anchovies. "She's talking about the woman you were banging the other night."

"Al!" Food wedges in Justin's throat.

"Joyce," Conor says with concern, "are you okay?"

My eyes fill as I try to catch my breath and keep from coughing.

"Here, have some water." He pushes a glass in my face.

People around us are staring, concerned.

I'm coughing so much I can't even take a breath to drink. Conor gets up from his chair and comes around to me. He pats my back, and I shrug him off, still coughing, with tears running down my face. I stand up in a panic, overturning my chair in the process.

"Al, Al, do something. Oh, Madonn-ina Santa!" Doris panics. "He's going purple."

Al untucks his napkin from his collar and coolly places it on the table. He stands up and positions himself behind his brother. He wraps his arms around his waist, and pumps hard on his stomach.

On the second push, the food is dislodged from Justin's throat.

As a third person races to my aid, or rather to join the growing panicked discussion of how to perform the Heimlich maneuver—I suddenly stop coughing. Three faces stare at me in surprise while I rub my throat, confused.

"Are you okay?" Conor asks, patting my back again.

"Yes," I whisper, embarrassed by the attention we are receiving. "I'm fine, thank you. Everyone, thank you so much for your help."

They are slow to back away.

"Please go back to your seats and enjoy your dinner. Honestly, I'm fine. Thank you." I sit down quickly and rub my streaming mascara from my eyes, trying to ignore the stares. "God, that was embarrassing."

"That was odd; you weren't chewing anything. You were just talking, and then, bam! You started coughing."

I shrug and continue to rub my throat. "I don't know, something got caught when I inhaled."

The waiter comes over to take our plates away. "Are you all right, madam?"

"Yes, thank you, I'm fine."

I feel a nudge from behind me, and I see our neighbor from the block lean over to our table. "Hey, for a minute there I thought you were going into labor, ha-ha! Didn't we, Margaret?" He looks at his wife and laughs.

"No," Margaret says, her smile quickly fading and her face turning puce. "No, Pat."

"Huh?" He's confused. "Well, I did anyway. Congrats, Conor." He gives a suddenly pale Conor a wink. "There goes sleep for the next twenty years, believe you me. Enjoy your dinner." He turns back to face his table, after which we hear murmured squabbling.

Conor reaches for my hand across the table. "Are you okay?" he asks yet again.

"That's happened a few times now," I explain, and instinctively place my hand over my flat stomach. "I've barely looked in the mirror since I've come home. I can't stand to look."

Conor makes appropriate sounds of concern, and I hear the words "beautiful" and "pretty," but I silence him. I need for him to listen and not solve anything. I want him to know that I'm not trying to be pretty or beautiful but for just once need to appear as I am. I want to tell him how I feel when I force myself to look closely and study my body, which now feels like a shell.

"Oh, Joyce." His grip on my hand tightens as I speak, squeezing my wedding ring into my skin.

A wedding ring but no marriage.

I wriggle my hand a little to let him know to loosen his grip. Instead he lets go. A sign.

"Conor," is all I say. I give him a look, and I know he knows what I'm about to say. He's seen this look before.

"No, no, no, no, Joyce, not this conversation now." He withdraws his hand from the table completely and holds both of them up in defense. "You—we—have been through enough this week."

"Conor, no more distractions." I lean forward with urgency in my voice. "We have to deal with us now, or before we know it, ten years will have gone by, and we'll be wondering every single day of our miserable lives what might have been."

We've had this conversation in some form or another on an annual basis over the last five years, and I wait for the usual retort from Conor. That no one says marriage is easy, we can't expect it to be so, we promised each other that marriage is for life, and he's determined to work at it. Salvage from the Dumpster what's worth saving, my itinerant husband preaches. I focus on my dessert spoon while I wait for his usual comments. I realize minutes later they still haven't come. I look up and see he is battling tears, and is nodding in what looks like agreement.

I take a breath. This is it.

Justin eyes the dessert menu.

"You can't have any, Al." Doris plucks the menu out of her husband's hands and snaps it shut.

"Why not? Am I not allowed to even read it?"

"Your cholesterol goes up just reading it."

Justin zones out as they squabble. He shouldn't be having any either. Since his divorce he's started to let himself go, eating as a comfort and skipping his usual daily workout. He really shouldn't, but his eyes hover above one item on the menu like a vulture watching its prey.

"Any dessert for you, sir?" the waiter asks.

Go on.

"Yes. I'll have the . . ."

"Banoffee pie, please," I blurt out to the waiter, to my own surprise.

Conor's mouth drops.

Oh, dear. My marriage has just ended, and I'm ordering dessert. I bite my lip and stop a nervous smile from breaking out.

To new beginnings. To the pursuit of . . . somethingness.

Chapter 10

◇◇◇◇◇

A GRAND CHIME WELCOMES ME to my father's humble home. It's a sound far more than deserving of the two up-two down, but then again, so is my father.

The sound teleports me back to my life within these walls and how I used to identify visitors by their call at the door. When I was a child, short, piercing sounds told me that friends, too short to reach, were hopping up to punch the button. Years later, fast and weak snippets alerted me to boyfriends cowering outside, terrified of announcing their very existence, never mind their arrival, to my father. Unsteady rings late in the night sang Dad's homecoming from the pub without his keys. Joyful, playful rhythms were family calls, and short, loud bursts warned us of door-to-door salespeople. I press the bell again, but not just because at ten a.m. nothing has yet stirred inside the quiet house; I want to know what my own call sounds like.

Apologetic, short, and clipped—as if it doesn't want to be heard. It says, Sorry, Dad, sorry to disturb you. Sorry the thirty-three-year-old daughter you thought you were long ago rid of is back home after her marriage has fallen apart.

Finally I hear sounds inside and I see Dad's seesaw movement coming closer, shadowlike and eerie in the distorted glass.

"Sorry, love," he says as he opens the door, "I didn't hear you the first time."

"If you didn't hear me, then how did you know I rang?"

He looks at me blankly and then down at the cactus in my hands and the suitcases at my feet. "What's this?"

"You . . . you told me I could stay for a while."

"I thought you meant till the end of *Dancing with the Stars*."

"Oh . . . well, I was hoping to stay for a bit longer than that."

"Long after I'm gone, by the looks of it." He surveys my baggage on his doorstep. "Come in, come in. Where's Conor? Something happen to the house? You haven't mice again, have you? It's that time of year for them all right, so you should have kept the windows and doors closed. Block up all the openings, that's what I do. I'll show you when we're inside and settled."

"Dad, I've never called around to stay here because of mice."

"There's a first time for everything. Your mother used to do that. Hated the things. Used to stay at your grandmother's while I ran around here like that cartoon cat trying to catch them. Tom or Jerry, was it?" He squeezes his eyes closed to think, then opens them again, none the wiser. "I never knew the difference. But by God they were impossible to catch." He raises a fist, looks feisty for a moment while captured in the thought, then stops suddenly and carries my suitcases into the hall.

"Dad?" I say, frustrated. "I thought you understood me on the phone. Conor and I have separated."

"Separated what?"

"Ourselves."

"From what?"

"From each other!"

"What on earth are you talking about?"

"We're not together anymore. We've split up."

He puts the bags down underneath the wall of photographs, there to provide any visitor who crosses the threshold with a crash course on the Conway family history. Dad as a boy, Mum as a girl; Dad and Mum courting, then married; my christening, communion, debutant ball, and wedding. Capture it, frame it, display it; Mum and Dad's school of thought. It's funny how people mark their lives, choose certain benchmarks to show when one moment is more of a moment than any other. For life is made of countless of them. I like to think the best ones are in my mind, that they run through my blood in their own memory bank for no one else to see.

Dad doesn't pause at the revelations of my failed marriage and instead works his way into the kitchen. "Cuppa?"

I stay in the hall looking for my favorite photo of Mum and breathe in that smell. The smell that's carried around every day on every stitch of Dad's back, like a snail carries its home. I always thought it was the smell of Mum's cooking that drifted around the rooms and seeped into every fiber, including the wallpaper, but it's ten years since Mum has passed away. Perhaps the scent was *her*; perhaps it's still her.

"What are you doin' sniffin' the walls?"

I jump, startled and embarrassed at being caught, and make my way into the kitchen. It hasn't changed since I lived here, and it's as spotless as the day Mum left it; nothing has been moved, not even for convenience's sake. I watch Dad move slowly about, resting on his left foot to access the cupboards below, and then using the extra inches of his right leg as his own personal footstool to reach above. The kettle boils too loudly for us to have a conversation, and I'm glad of that. Dad, clearly upset, grips the handle so tightly his knuckles are white. A teaspoon is cupped in his left hand, which rests on his hip, and it reminds me of how he used to stand with his cigarette shielded in his cupped hand, stained yellow from nicotine. He looks out the window to his immaculate garden and grinds his teeth. He's angry, and I feel like a teenager once again, awaiting my talking-down.

"What are you thinking about, Dad?" I finally ask as soon as the kettle stops hopping about.

"The garden," he replies, his jaw tightening once again.

"The garden?"

"That bloody cat from next door keeps pissing on your mother's roses." He shakes his head angrily. "Fluffy"—he throws his hands up—"that's what she calls him. Well, Fluffy won't be so fluffy when I get my hands on him. I'll be wearin' one of them fine furry hats the Russians wear and dance the Hopak outside Mrs. Henderson's front garden while she wraps a shiverin' Baldy up in a blanket inside."

"Is that what you're really thinking about?" I ask incredulously.

"Well, not really, love," he confesses, calming down. "That and the daffodils. Not far off from planting season for spring. And some crocuses. I'll have to get some bulbs."

Good to know my marriage breakdown isn't my dad's main priority. Nor his second. On the list after crocuses.

"Snowdrops too," he adds.

It's rare I'm around the house so early on in the day. Usually I'd be at work showing property around the city. It's so quiet here now, I wonder what on earth Dad does in this silence.

"What were you doing before I came?"

"Thirty-three years ago or today?"

"Today." I try not to smile because I know he's serious.

"Quiz." He nods at the kitchen table, where he has a page full of puzzles. Half of them are completed. "I'm stuck on number six. Have a look at it." He brings the cups of tea to the table, managing not to spill a drop despite his swaying. Always steady.

I read the clue aloud. "'Who was the influential critic who summed up one of Mozart's operas as having too many notes?'"

"Mozart," Dad shrugs. "Haven't a clue about that lad at all."

"Emperor Joseph the Second," I say.

"What's that now?" Dad's caterpillar eyebrows go up in surprise. "How did you know that, then?"

I frown. I don't know. "I must have just heard it somewh— Do I smell smoke?"

He sits up straight and sniffs the air like a bloodhound. "Toast. I made it earlier. Had the setting on too high and burned it. They were the last two slices, too."

"Hate that." I shake my head. Then I remember to ask, "Where's Mum's photograph from the hall?"

"Which one? There are thirty of her."

"You've counted?" I laugh.

"Nailed them up there, didn't I? Forty-four photos in total, that's forty-four nails I needed. Went down to the hardware store and bought a pack of nails. Forty nails it contained. They made me buy a second packet just for four more nails." He holds up four fingers and shakes his head. "Still have thirty-six of them left over in the toolbox. What is the world comin' to?"

Never mind terrorism or global warming. The proof of the world's downfall, in his eyes, comes down to thirty-six wasted nails in a toolbox.

"You know which one. So where is it?"

"Right where it always is," he says unconvincingly.

We both look at the closed kitchen door, in the direction of the hall. I stand up to go out and check. These are the kinds of things you do when you have time on your hands.

"Ah"—he jerks a floppy hand at me—"sit yourself down." He rises. "I'll check." He goes and closes the kitchen door behind him, blocking me from seeing out. "She's there, all right," he calls to me. "Hello, Gracie, your daughter was worried about you. Thought she couldn't see you, but of course you've been there all along, watchin' her sniffin' the walls, thinkin' the paper's on fire. But sure it's madder she's gettin', leaving her husband and packing in her job."

I haven't mentioned anything to him about taking leave from my job, which means Conor has spoken to him, which means Dad knew my exact intentions for being here from the very first moment he heard the doorbell ring. I have to give it to him, he plays stupid very well. He returns to the kitchen, and I catch a glimpse of the photo on the hall table.

"Ah!" He looks at his watch in alarm. "Ten twenty-five! Let's go inside, quick!" He moves faster than I've seen him move in a long time, grabbing his weekly television guide and his cup of tea.

"What are we watching?" I follow him into the television room, regarding him with amusement.

"*Murder, She Wrote*, you know it?"

"Never seen it."

"Oh, wait'll you see, Gracie. That Jessica Fletcher is a strange one for catching the murderers. Then over on the next channel we'll watch *Diagnosis Murder*, where the dancer solves the cases." He takes a pen and circles the listing on the TV page.

I'm captivated by Dad's excitement. He sings along with the show's theme song, making trumpet noises with his mouth.

"Come in here and lie on the couch, and I'll put this over you." He picks up a tartan blanket draped over the back of the green velvet couch and places it gently over me as I lie down, tucking it around my body so tightly I can't move my arms. It's the same blanket I rolled on as a baby, the same blanket they covered me with when I was home sick from school and was allowed to watch television on the couch. I watch Dad with fondness, remembering the tenderness he always showed me when I was a child, feeling right back there again.

Until he sits at the end of the couch and squashes my feet.

Chapter 11

◇◇◇◇◇

"WHAT DO YOU THINK—WILL BETTY be a millionaire by the end of the show?"

I have sat through an endless number of half-hour morning shows over the last few days, and now we are watching *Antiques Roadshow*.

Betty is seventy years old, from Warwickshire, and is currently waiting with anticipation as the dealer tries to price the old teapot she has brought to the show.

I watch the dealer handling the teapot delicately, and a comfortable, familiar feeling overwhelms me. "Sorry, Betty," I say to the television, "it's a replica. The French used them in the eighteenth century, but yours was made in the early twentieth century. You can see from the way the handle is shaped. Clumsy craftsmanship."

"Is that so?" Dad looks at me with interest.

We watch the screen intently and listen as the dealer repeats my remarks. Poor Betty is devastated but tries to pretend it was too precious a gift from her grandmother for her to have sold anyhow.

"Liar," Dad shouts. "Betty already had her cruise booked and her bikini bought." He turns to me. "How do you know all that about the pots and the French? Read it in one of your books, maybe?"

"Maybe." I have no idea. I'm starting to get a headache thinking about all this newfound knowledge.

Dad catches the look on my face. "Why don't you call a friend or something? Have a chat."

I don't want to but I know I should. "I should probably give Kate a call."

"The big-boned girl? The one who plowed you with poteen when you were sixteen?"

"Yup, that was Kate." I laugh. He has never forgiven her for that.

"She was a messer, that girl. Has she come to anything?"

"You saw her last week at the hospital, Dad," I remind him. "She just sold her shop in the city for two million to become a stay-at-home mother." I try not to laugh at the shock on his face.

"Ah, sure, give her a call. Have a chat. You women like to do that. Good for the soul, your mother always said. Your mother loved talking, was always blatherin' on to someone about somethin' or other."

"Wonder where she got that from," I say under my breath, but just as if by a miracle, my father's ears work for once.

"Her star sign is where she got it from. Taurus. Talked a lot of bull."

"Dad!"

"What? I loved her with all my heart, but the woman talked a lot of bull. Not enough to talk about something, I had to hear about how she felt about it too. Ten times over."

"You don't believe in astrology." I nudge him.

"I do too. I'm a Libra. Weighing scales." He rocks from side to side. "Perfectly balanced."

I laugh and escape to phone Kate. I go upstairs and enter my old bedroom, practically unchanged since the day I left it. Despite the rare guest staying over after I'd moved out, my parents never removed any of my belongings. The Cure stickers remain on the door; wallpaper is still ripped from the tape that had once held my posters. Once as a punishment for ruining the walls, Dad forced me to cut the grass in the back garden, but while doing so I ran the lawn mower over a shrub in the bedding. He refused to speak to me for the rest of that day. Apparently it was the first year the shrub had blossomed since he'd planted it. I couldn't understand his frustration then, but now, after spending years of hard work cultivating a marriage, only for it to wither and die, I can understand his plight. But I bet he didn't feel the relief I feel right now.

My childhood bedroom can only fit a bed and a wardrobe, but for years it was my whole world. My only personal place to think and dream, to cry and laugh and wait until I became old enough to finally do all the things I wanted to do. My only space in the world then, and my only space now, at thirty-three. Who knew I'd find myself back here again without any of the things I'd yearned for, and, even worse, still yearning for them? Not a member of the Cure or married to Robert Smith. No baby and no husband. The wallpaper is floral and wild; completely inappropriate for a place of rest. Millions of tiny brown flowers clustered together with tiny splashes of faded green stalks. No wonder I'd covered them with posters. The carpet is brown with light brown swirls, stained from spilled perfume and makeup. The old and faded brown leather suitcases still lie on top of the wardrobe, gathering dust since Mum died. Dad never goes anywhere—a life without Mum, he decided long ago, is enough of a journey for him.

The duvet cover is the newest addition to the room. New as in over ten years old; Mum purchased it when my room became the guest room. I moved out to live with Kate a year before she died, and I wish every day since that I hadn't, all those precious days of not waking up to hear her long yawns turn into songs, to hear her talking to herself as she listened to Gay Byrne's radio show. She loved Gay Byrne; her sole ambition in life was to meet him. The closest she got was when she and Dad got tickets to sit in the audience of *The Late Late Show*; she spoke about it for years. I think she had a thing for him. Dad hated him. I think he knew about her thing.

He likes to listen to him now, though, whenever he's on. I think Gay Byrne reminds Dad of time spent with Mum, as though when he hears Gay Byrne's voice, he hears Mum's instead. When she died, Dad surrounded himself with all the things she adored. He put Gay on the radio every morning, watched Mum's television shows, bought her favorite biscuits even though he didn't enjoy them. He liked to see them on the shelf when he opened the cupboard, liked to see her magazines beside his newspaper. He liked her slippers staying beside her armchair by the fire. He liked to remind himself that his entire world hadn't fallen apart. Sometimes we need all the glue we can get, just to hold ourselves together.

At sixty-five years old, Dad was too young to lose his wife. At twenty-three, I was too young to lose my mother. At fifty-five she shouldn't have lost her life, but cancer, undetected until far too late, stole it from her and us all. Dad had married late in life for his generation, and he always says he passed more days of his life waiting for Mum than actually being with her, but that every second spent looking for her and, eventually, remembering her, was worth it for all the moments in between.

Mum never met Conor, so I don't know whether she would have liked him, though she would have been too polite to have shown it if she didn't. Mum loved all kinds of people, but particularly those with high spirit and energy, people who lived and exuded that life. Conor is pleasant. Always just pleasant. Never overexcited. Never, in fact, excited at all. Just pleasant, which is simply another word for nice. Marrying a nice man gives you a nice marriage, but never anything more. And nice is okay when it's among other things, but never when it stands alone.

Dad would talk to anyone anywhere and not have a feeling about them one way or another. The only negative thing he ever said about Conor was "What kind of a man likes *tennis?*" A football man, Dad had spat the word out as though it had dirtied his mouth.

Our failure to produce a child didn't do much to sway Dad's opinion. He blamed it on the little white tennis shorts Conor sometimes wore, whenever pregnancy test after pregnancy test failed to show blue. I know he said it to put a smile on my face; sometimes it worked, other times it didn't, but it was a safe joke because we both knew it wasn't the tennis shorts or the man wearing them that was the problem.

I sit down carefully on the duvet cover bought by Mum, not wanting to crease it. A two-pillow and duvet cover set from Dunnes with a matching candle for the windowsill, which has never been lit and which has since lost its scent. Dust gathers on the top, incriminating evidence that Dad is not keeping up with his duties. As if at seventy-five years old the removal of dust from anywhere but his memory shelf should be a priority. I place the cactus on the windowsill beside the candle.

I turn on my cell phone, which has been switched off for days, and it begins to beep as a dozen messages filter through. I have already made my calls to those near, dear, and nosy. Like pulling off a Band-Aid; don't think about it, move quickly, and it's almost painless. Flip open the phone book, and bam, bam, bam: three minutes each. Quick, snappy phone calls made by a strangely upbeat woman who'd momentarily inhabited my body. An incredible woman, in fact, positive and perky, yet emotional and wise at all the right moments, her timing impeccable, her sentiments so poignant I almost wanted to write them down. She even attempted a bit of humor, which some members of the near, dear, and nosy coped well with, while others seemed almost insulted—not that she cared, for it was her party and she was refusing to cry if she wanted to.

Fortunately, I don't have to put on an act for the woman I am calling now.

Kate picks up on the fourth ring.

"Hello," she shouts, and I jump. There are manic noises in the background, as though a mini-war has broken out on the other side.

"Joyce!" she yells, and I realize I'm on speakerphone. "I've been calling you and calling you. Derek, *sit down. Mummy is not happy!* Sorry, I'm just doing the school run. I've to take six kids home, then a quick snack before I take Eric to basketball and Jayda to swimming. Want to meet me there at seven? Jayda is getting her ten-meter badge today."

Jayda howls in the background about hating ten-meter badges.

"How can you hate it when you've never had one?" Kate snaps. Jayda howls even louder and I have to move the phone from my ear. *"Jayda! Give Mummy a break! Derek, put your seat belt on!* If I have to brake suddenly, you will go *flying* through the windscreen and *smash your face in.* Hold on, Joyce."

There is silence while I wait.

"Gracie!" Dad yells up to me. I run to the top of the stairs in a panic, not used to hearing him shout like that since I was a child.

"Yes? Dad! Are you okay?"

"I got seven letters," he shouts.

"You got what?"

"Seven letters!"

"What does that mean?"

"In *Countdown!*"

I stop panicking and sit on the top stair in frustration. Suddenly Kate's voice is back, and it sounds as though calm has been restored.

"Okay, you're off speakerphone. I'll probably be arrested for holding the phone, not to mention cast off the carpool list, like I give a flying fuck about that."

"I'm telling my mammy you said the F word," I hear a little voice say.

"Good. I've been wanting to tell her that for years," Kate murmurs to me, and I laugh.

"Fuck, fuck, fuck, fuck," I hear a crowd of kids chanting.

"Jesus, Joyce, I better go. See you at the leisure center at seven? It's my only break. Or else I have tomorrow. Tennis at three or gymnastics at six? I can see if Frankie is free to meet up too."

Frankie. Christened Francesca but refuses to answer to it. Dad was wrong about Kate. She may have sourced the poteen, but technically it was Frankie who held my mouth open and poured it down my throat. As a result of this version of the story's never being told, he thinks Frankie's a saint, very much to Kate's annoyance.

"I'll take gymnastics tomorrow," I say as the children's chanting gets louder. Kate's gone, and then there's silence.

"*Gracie!*" Dad calls again.

"It's Joyce, Dad."

"I got the conundrum!"

I make my way back to my bed and cover my head with a pillow.

A few minutes later Dad arrives at the door, scaring the life out of me.

"I was the only one that got the conundrum. The contestants hadn't a clue. Simon won anyway, goes through to tomorrow's show. He's been the winner for three days now, and I'm half bored lookin' at him. He has a funny-looking face; you'd have a right laugh if you saw it. Do you want a HobNob? I'm going to make another cuppa."

"No, thanks." I put the pillow back over my head. He uses so many words.

"Well, I'm having one. I have to eat with my pills. Supposed to take it at lunch, but I forgot."

"You took a pill at lunch, remember?"

"That was for my heart. This is for my memory. Short-term memory pills."

I take the pillow off my face to see if he's being serious. "And you forgot to take it?"

He nods.

"Oh, Dad." I start to laugh while he looks on as though I'm having an episode. "You are medicine enough for me. Well, you need to get stronger pills. They're not working clearly."

He turns his back and makes his way down the hall, grumbling, "They'd bloody well work if I remembered to take them."

"Dad," I call to him and he stops at the top of the stairs. "Thanks for not asking any questions about Conor."

"Well, I don't need to. I know you'll be back together in no time."

"No, we won't," I say softly.

He walks back into my room. "Is he stepping out with someone else?"

"No, he's not. And I'm not. We just don't love each other. We haven't for a long time."

"But you married him, Joyce. Didn't I take you down the aisle myself?" He looks confused.

"What's that got to do with anything?"

"You both promised each other in the house of our Lord, I heard you with my own ears. What is it with you young people these days, breaking up and remarrying all the time? What happened to keeping promises?"

I sigh. How can I answer that? He begins to walk away again. "Dad."

He stops but doesn't turn round.

"I don't think you're thinking of the alternative. Would you rather I kept my promise to spend the rest of my life with Conor, but not love him and be unhappy?"

"If you think your mother and I had a perfect marriage, you're wrong, because there's no such thing. No one's happy all the time, love."

"I understand that, but what if you're never happy? Ever."

He thinks about that for what looks like the first time, and I hold my breath until he finally speaks. "I'm going to have a Hob-Nob."

Halfway down the stairs he shouts back rebelliously, "A chocolate one."

Chapter 12

◇◇◇◇◇

I'M ON VACATION, BRO, WHY are you dragging me to a gym?"
Al half walks, half skips alongside Justin in an effort to keep up
with his lean brother's long strides.

"I have a date with Sarah next week," Justin says as he
power-walks from the tube station, "and I need to get back into
shape."

"I didn't realize you were out of shape," Al pants, wiping
trickles of sweat from his brow.

"The divorce cloud was preventing me from working out."

"The divorce cloud?"

"Never heard of it?"

Al, unable to speak, shakes his head.

"The cloud moves to take the shape of your body, wraps itself
nice and tight around you so that you can barely move. Or breathe.
Or exercise. Or even date, let alone sleep with other women."

"Your divorce cloud sounds like my marriage cloud."

"Yeah, well, that cloud has moved on now." Justin looks up at
the gray London sky, closes his eyes, and breathes in deeply. "It's
time for me to get back into action." He opens his eyes and walks

straight into a lamppost. "Jesus, Al!" He doubles over, head in his hands. "Thanks for the warning."

Al's beet-red face wheezes up at him, words not coming easily. Or at all.

"Never mind my having to work out, look at yourself," Justin admonishes his brother. "Your doctor's already told you to drop a few hundred pounds."

"Fifty pounds . . . ," Al gasps, "aren't exactly"—gasp—"a few hundred, and don't start on me too." Gasp. "Doris is bad enough." Wheeze. Cough. "What she knows about dieting is beyond me. The woman doesn't eat. She's afraid to bite a nail in case they've too many calories."

"Doris's nails are real?"

"Them and her hair is about all. I gotta hold on to something." Al looks around, flustered.

"Too much information," Justin says, misunderstanding. "I can't believe Doris's hair is real."

"All but the color. She's a brunette. Italian, of course. Dizzy."

"Yeah, she is a bit dizzy. All that past-life talk about the woman at the hair salon." Justin laughs.

"I meant I'm dizzy." Al glares at him and reaches out to hold on to a nearby railing.

"Oh . . . I knew that, I was kidding. It looks like we're almost here. Think you can make it another hundred yards or so?"

"Depends on the 'or so,'" Al snaps.

"It's about the same as the week 'or so' vacation that you and Doris were planning on taking here. Looks like that's turning into a month."

"Well, we wanted to surprise you, and Doug is able to take care of the shop while I'm gone. The doc advised me to take it easy, Justin. With heart conditions in the family history, I really need to rest up."

"You told the doctor there's a history of heart conditions in the family?" Justin asks.

"Well, yeah, Dad died of a heart attack. Who else would I be talkin' about?"

Justin is silent.

"Besides, you won't be sorry. Doris will have your apartment done up so nice that you'll be glad we stayed. You know she did the doggie parlor all by herself?"

Justin's eyes widen in horror.

"I know." Al beams proudly. "So, how many of these seminars will you be doing in Dublin? Me and Doris might accompany you on one of your trips over there—you know, see the place Dad was from."

"Dad was from Cork."

"Oh. Does he still have family there? We could go and trace our roots. What do you think?"

"Not a bad idea." Justin thinks of his schedule. "I have a few more seminars ahead. You probably won't be here that long, though." He eyes Al sideways, testing him. "And you can't come next week because I'm mixing that trip with a date with Sarah."

"You're really hot on this girl?"

His almost-forty-year-old brother's vocabulary never ceases to amaze Justin. "Am I hot on this girl?" he repeats, amused and confused at the same time. "Good question. Not really, but she's company. Is that an acceptable answer?"

"Did she have you at 'I vant your blood'?" Al chuckles.

"Wow, that was uncanny," Justin says. "Sarah happens to be a vampire from Transylvania." He changes the subject. "Let's do an hour at the gym. I don't think 'resting up' is going to make you any better. That's what got you into this state in the first place."

"One hour?" Al almost explodes. "What are you planning on doing on this date, rock-climbing?"

I WAKE UP TO THE sound of banging pots and pans coming from downstairs, and it takes me a moment to remember where I am. Then I remember everything all over again. My daily morning pill, hard to swallow as usual. One of these days I'll wake up, and I'll just know. But I'm not sure which scenario I prefer; the moments of forgetfulness are such bliss.

I didn't sleep well last night between the thoughts in my head and the sound of Dad flushing the toilet every hour. Then when he was asleep, his snores rattled through the walls of the house.

Despite the interruptions, my dreams during those rare moments of sleep are still vivid in my mind. They almost feel real, like memories, though who's to know what's real, with all the altering our minds do? I remember being in a park, though I don't think I was me. I twirled a young girl with white-blond hair around in my arms while a woman with red hair looked on, smiling, with a camera in her hand. The park was colorful, with lots of flowers, and we had a picnic. . . . I try to remember the song playing in the background, but it fails me. Instead I hear Dad downstairs singing "The Auld Triangle," an old Irish song he has sung at parties all of my life and probably most of his too. He'd stand there, eyes closed, pint in hand, a picture of bliss as he sang his story of how "the auld triangle went jingle jangle."

I swing my legs out of the bed and groan with pain, suddenly feeling an ache in both legs from my hips right down my thighs, all the way down to my calf muscles. I try to move the rest of my body and feel paralyzed with the pain that also runs through my shoulders, biceps, triceps, back muscles, and torso. I massage my muscles in complete confusion and make a note to go see the doctor, just in case it's something to be worried about. I'm sure it's my heart, either looking for more attention or so full of pain it's needed to ooze its ache around the rest of my body, just to relieve itself. Each throbbing muscle is an extension of the pain I feel inside, though a doctor will tell me it's due to the thirty-year-old bed I slept on, manufactured before the time people claimed nightly back support as their God-given right.

I throw a dressing gown around me and slowly, stiff as a board, make my way downstairs, trying my best not to bend my legs.

The smell of smoke greets me as I enter the hall, and I notice once again that Mum's photograph isn't there. Something urges me to slide open the table drawer, and there she is, lying facedown. Tears spring in my eyes; I'm angry that something so precious has been hidden away. This photograph has always been more than just a photograph to the both of us; it represents her presence in the house, so she can greet us whenever we come in the front door or climb down the stairs. I take a deep breath and decide to say nothing for now, assuming that Dad has his reasons, though I can't think of any acceptable ones at this moment. I slide the drawer closed and leave Mum where Dad has placed her, feeling like I'm burying her all over again.

When I limp into the kitchen, chaos greets me. There are pots and pans everywhere—tea towels, eggshells, and what looks like all the contents of the cupboards covering the counters. Dad is wearing an apron with an image of a woman in red lingerie and suspenders over his usual sweater, shirt, and trousers. On his feet are Manchester United slippers, shaped as large footballs.

"Morning, love." He sees me and steps up on his left leg to give me a kiss on the forehead.

I realize it's the first time in years that somebody has made breakfast for me, but it's also the first time in just as many years that Dad has had somebody to cook breakfast for. Suddenly the singing, the mess, the clattering pots and pans, all make sense. He's excited.

"I'm making waffles!" he says with an American accent.

"Ooh, very nice."

"That's what the donkey says, isn't it?"

"What donkey?"

"The one . . ." He stops stirring whatever is in the frying pan and closes his eyes to think. "The story with the green man."

"The Incredible Hulk?"

"No."

"Well, I don't know any other green people."

"You do, you know the one . . ."

"The Wicked Witch of the West?"

"No! There's no donkey in that! Think about stories with donkeys in them."

"Is it a religious one?"

"Were there talking donkeys in the Bible, Gracie? Did Jesus eat waffles, do you think?" he says, exasperated.

"My name is Joyce."

"Maybe I've been reading the wrong Bible all my life," he continues.

I look over his shoulder. "Dad, you're not even making waffles!"

He sighs. "Do I look like a donkey to you? Donkeys make waffles, I make a good fry-up."

I watch him poking sausages around in the pan, trying to get all the sides evenly cooked. "I'll have some of those, too."

"But you're one of those vegetarianists."

"Vegetarian. And I'm not anymore."

"Sure, of course you're not. You've only been one since you were fifteen years old after seeing that show about the seals. Then tomorrow I'll wake up and you'll be tellin' me you're a man. Saw it on the telly once. This woman on the telly, about the same age as you, brought her husband live on the telly in front of an audience to tell him that she decided she wanted to turn her—"

Feeling frustrated with him, I blurt out, "Mum's photo isn't on the hall table."

Dad freezes, a reaction of guilt, and this makes me suddenly angry, as if I didn't realize he was the culprit.

Then he clicks his fingers, and his eyes light up. "*Shrek* is the fella I was trying to think of." He chuckles. "His friend in the movie is the donkey." He gets back to work, keeping himself busy by clattering around with plates and cutlery.

"Don't try to change the subject. Tell me why."

"Why what? Why are you walking like that? is what I want to know." Dad eyes me as I limp across the room to take a seat at the table.

"I don't know," I snap. "Maybe it runs in the family."

"Hoo hoo hoo," Dad hoots and looks up at the ceiling, "we've got a live one here, boss! Now set the table like a good girl."

He brings me right back, and I can't help but smile. And so I set the table and Dad makes the breakfast and we both limp around the kitchen pretending everything is as it was and forever shall be. World without end.

Chapter 13

◇◇◇◇◇

"S o, Dad, what are your plans for the day? Are you busy?"

A forkful of sausage, egg, bacon, pudding, mushroom, and tomato stops on its way into my dad's open mouth. Amused eyes peer out at me from under wild, wiry eyebrows.

"Plans, you say? Well, let's see, Gracie, while I go through the ol' schedule of events for the day. I was thinking after I finish my fry in approximately fifteen minutes, I'd have another cuppa tea. Then while I'm drinking me tea, I might sit down in this chair at this table, or maybe that chair where you are, the exact venue is TBD, as my schedule would say. Then I'll go through answers to yesterday's crossword to see what we got right. Then I'll do the Dusoku, then the word game. I already saw that we've to try and find nautical words today. Seafaring, maritime, yachting, yes, I'll be able to do that, sure. Then I'm going to cut out my coupons, and that should fill my early morning right up. Next I'd say I'll have another cuppa after all of that, before my programs start. If you'd like to make an appointment, talk to Maggie." He finally shovels the fork into his mouth, and egg drips down his chin. He doesn't notice and leaves it there.

I laugh. "Who's Maggie?"

He swallows and smiles, amused with himself. "I don't know why I said it." He thinks hard and finally laughs. "There was a fella I used to know in Cavan—this is goin' back sixty years now—Brendan Brady was his name. Whenever we'd be tryin' to make arrangements, he'd say"—Dad deepens his voice—" 'Talk to Maggie,' like he was someone awful important. She was either his wife or his secretary, I hadn't a clue. 'Talk to Maggie,' " he repeats. "She was probably his mother." He continues eating.

"So basically, according to your schedule, you're doing exactly the same thing as yesterday."

"Oh, no, it's not the same at all." He thumbs through his TV guide and stabs a greasy finger on today's section. He looks at his watch and slides his finger down the page. He picks up his highlighter with his other hand and marks another show. *"Animal Hospital* is on instead of *Antiques Roadshow*. Not exactly the same day as yesterday, now is it? It'll be doggies and bunnies today instead of Betty's fake teapots." He continues to highlight more shows, his tongue licking the corners of his mouth in concentration.

"The Book of Kells," I blurt out of nowhere, though that is nothing odd these days. My random ramblings are becoming something of the norm.

"What are you talking about now?" Dad puts the guide down and resumes eating.

"Let's go into town today. Do a tour of the city, go to Trinity College, and look at the Book of Kells."

Dad stares at me and munches. I'm not sure what he's thinking. He's probably thinking the same of me.

"You want to go to Trinity College. The girl who never wanted to set foot near the place either for studies or for excursions with me and your mother. Suddenly out of the blue she wants to go. Wait, aren't 'suddenly' and 'out of the blue' one and the same?

They shouldn't go together in a sentence, Henry," he corrects himself.

"Yes, I want to go." I suddenly, out of the blue, very much want to go to Trinity College.

"If you don't want to watch *Animal Hospital*, just say so. You don't have to go darting into the city. There's such a thing as changing channels."

"You're right, Dad, and I've been doing some of that recently."

"Is that so? I hadn't noticed, what with your marriage breaking up, your moving in with me, your not being a vegetarianist any more, your not mentioning a word about your job. There's been so much action around here, how's a man to tell if a channel's been changed or if a new show has just begun?"

"I just need to do something new," I explain. "We need a change of schedule, Dad. I've got the big remote control of life in my hands, and I'm ready to start pushing some buttons."

He stares at me for a moment and puts a sausage in his mouth in response.

"We'll get a taxi into town and catch one of those tour buses, what do you think? Maggie!" I shout out at the top of my voice, making Dad jump. "Maggie, Dad is coming into town with me to have a look around. Is that okay?"

I cock my ear and wait for a response. Happy I've received one, I nod and stand up. "Right. Dad, it's been decided. Maggie says it's fine if you go into town. I'll have a shower, and we'll leave in an hour. Ha! That rhymes." With that I limp out of the kitchen, leaving my bewildered father behind with egg on his chin.

"I doubt Maggie said yes to me walkin' at this speed, Gracie," Dad says, trying to keep up with me as we dodge pedestrians on Grafton Street.

"Sorry, Dad." I slow down and link his arm with mine. Despite his corrective footwear, he still sways, and I sway with him. Even if he got an operation to make his legs equal length, I'd imagine he'd still sway, it's so much a part of who he is.

"Dad, are you ever going to call me Joyce?"

"What are you talkin' about? Sure, isn't that your name?"

I look at him with surprise. "Do you not notice you always call me Gracie?"

He seems taken aback but makes no comment and keeps walking. Up and down, down and up.

"I'll give you a fiver every time you call me Joyce today." I smile.

"That's a deal, Joyce, Joyce, Joyce. Oh, how I love you, Joyce." He chuckles. "That's twenty quid already!" He nudges me and says seriously, "I didn't notice I called you that, love. I'll do my best from now on."

"Thank you."

"You remind me so much of her, you know."

"Ah, Dad, really?" I'm touched; I feel my eyes prick with tears. He never says that. "In what way?"

"You both have little piggy noses."

I roll my eyes.

"I don't know why we're walking farther away from Trinity College. Didn't you want to go there?"

"Yes, but the tour buses leave from Stephen's Green. We'll see it as we're passing. I don't really want to go in now anyway."

"Why not?"

"It's lunchtime."

"And the Book of Kells goes off for an hour's break, does it?" Dad jokes. "A ham sambo and a flask of tea, and then it props itself back up on display, right as rain for the afternoon."

"Maybe so." I don't know why, but it feels right to wait. I hug my red coat around me.

◆ ◆ ◆

Justin darts through the front arch of Trinity College and bounds up the road to Grafton Street. Lunchtime with Sarah. He beats away the nagging voice within him telling him to cancel the date. Give her a chance. Give yourself a chance. He needs to try, he needs to find his feet again, he needs to remember that not every meeting with a woman is going to be the same as the first time he laid eyes on Jennifer. The *thump-thump, thump-thump* feeling that made his entire body vibrate, the butterflies that did acrobatics in his stomach, the tingle when his skin brushed hers. He thought about how he'd felt on his first date with Sarah. Nothing. Nothing but flattery that she was attracted to him and excitement that he was back out in the dating world again. He had more of a reaction to the woman in the hair salon a few weeks ago, and that was saying something. Give her a chance. Give yourself a chance.

Grafton Street is crowded at lunchtime, as though the gates to the Dublin Zoo have been opened and all the animals have flooded out, happy to escape confinement for an hour. Justin has finished work for the day, his specialist seminar "Copper as Canvas, 1575–1775" being a success with the third-year students who had elected to hear him speak.

Conscious that he'll be late for Sarah, he attempts to break into a run, but the aches and pains in his overexercised body almost cripple him. Hating that Al's warnings were correct, he limps along, trailing behind what seem to be the two slowest people on Grafton Street. His plan to overtake them on either side is botched as people-traffic prevent him from leaving his lane. With impatience he slows, surrendering to the speed of the two before him, one of whom is singing happily to himself and swaying.

Drunk at this hour, honestly.

◆ ◆ ◆

Dad meanders up Grafton Street as though he has all the time in the world. I suppose he does, compared to everybody else, though a younger person would think differently. Sometimes he stops and points at things, joins circles of spectators to watch a street act, and when we continue on, he steps out of line to really confuse the situation. Like a rock in a stream, he sends people flowing around him; he's a small diversion, yet he's completely oblivious. He sings as we move up and down, down and up.

> *Grafton Street's a wonderland,*
> *There's magic in the air,*
> *There's diamonds in the ladies' eyes and gold-dust in their*
> *   hair.*
> *And if you don't believe me,*
> *Come and see me there,*
> *In Dublin on a sunny summer morning.*

He looks at me and smiles and sings it all over again, forgetting some words and humming them instead.

During my busiest days at work, twenty-four hours just don't seem enough. I almost want to hold my hands out in the air and try to grasp the seconds and minutes as if I could stop them from moving on, like a little girl trying to catch bubbles. You can't hold on to time, but somehow Dad appears to. I always wondered how on earth he filled his moments, as though my opening doors for clients and talking about sunny angles, central heating, and wardrobe space was worth so much more than his pottering. In truth, we're all just pottering, filling the time that we have here, only we like to make ourselves feel bigger by compiling lists of importance.

So this is what you do when it all slows down and the

minutes that tick by feel a little longer than before. You take your time. You breathe slowly. You open your eyes a little wider and look at everything. Take it all in. Rehash stories of old, remember people, times, and occasions gone by. Allow everything you see to remind you of something. Talk about those things. Find out the answers you didn't know to yesterday's crosswords. Slow down. Stop trying to do everything now, now, now. Hold up the people behind you for all you care, feel them kicking at your heels but maintain your pace. Don't let anybody else dictate your speed.

Though if the person behind me kicks my heels one more time . . .

The sun is so bright, it's difficult to look straight ahead. It's as though it's sitting on the top of Grafton Street, a bowling ball ready to knock us all down. Finally we near the top of the street—escape of the human current is in sight. Dad suddenly stops walking, enthralled by the sight of a mime artist nearby. As I'm linking his arm, I'm forced to a sudden stop too, causing the person behind to run straight into me. One grand final kick of my heels. That is it.

"Hey!" I spin around. "Watch it!"

The man grunts at me in frustration and power-walks off. "Hey, yourself," an American accent calls back. Familiar.

I'm about to shout again, but Dad's voice silences me.

"Look at that," Dad marvels, watching the mime trapped in an invisible box. "Should I give him an invisible key to get out of that box?" He laughs again. "Wouldn't that be funny, love?"

"No, Dad." I examine the sandy-duffel-coated back of my road-rage nemesis, trying to recall the voice.

"You know de Valera escaped prison by using a key that was smuggled in to him in a birthday cake. Someone should tell this fella that story." He spins round beside me, looking about. "Now where do we go from here?" He walks off in another direction, straight through a group of parading Hare Krishnas, without taking the slightest bit of notice.

The duffel coat turns round again and throws me one last dirty look before he hurries on in a huff.

Still, I stare. If I was to reverse the frown. That smile. So familiar.

"This is where you get the tickets. I've found it," Dad shouts from afar.

"Hold on, Dad." I watch after the duffel coat. Turn round one more time and show me your face, I plead.

"I'll just go get the tickets, then."

"Okay." I continue to watch the duffel coat moving farther away. I don't—correction, can't—move my eyes away from him. I mentally throw a cowboy's rope around his body and begin to pull him back toward me. His strides become smaller, his speed gradually slows.

He suddenly stops dead in his tracks. Yee-haw.

Please turn. I pull on the rope.

He spins round, searches the crowd. For me?

"Who are you?" I whisper.

"It's me!" Dad is beside me again. "Why are you just standing in the middle of the street?"

"I know what I'm doing," I snap. "Here, go get the tickets." I hold out some money.

I step away from the Hare Krishnas, keeping my eye on the man in the duffel coat, hoping he'll see me. The crisp pale wool of his coat almost glows among the dark and gloomy colors of others around him. I clear my throat and smooth down my shortened hair.

The man's eyes continue to search the street, and then they ever so slowly fall upon mine. I remember him in the second it takes them to register me. "Him" from the hair salon. The most handsome ordinary man my eyes have ever fallen upon. The family of caterpillars that had moved into my stomach the very second I laid eyes on this man outside the hair salon have now decided to molt and transform into butterflies. They flutter about with excitement, hitting the walls of my stomach like a fly against the window, looking for the exit sign. Even during the highest moments of my relationship with Conor, my few good years of truly loving him, I never experienced this feeling.

What now? Perhaps he won't recognize me at all. Perhaps he's just still angry that I shouted at him. I'm not sure what to do. Should I smile? Wave? Neither of us moves.

He holds up a hand. Waves. I look behind me first, to ensure it's me he's waving to. Though I was so sure anyway, I would have bet my father on it. Suddenly Grafton Street is empty. And silent. Just me and this man. I wave back. He mouths something to me.

Hungry? Horny? No.

Sorry. He's sorry. I try to figure out what to mouth back, but I'm smiling. Nothing can be mouthed when smiling, it's as impossible as whistling through a grin.

"I got the tickets!" Dad shouts. "Twenty euro each—it's a crime, that is. Seeing is for free, I don't know how they can charge us to use our eyes. I'm planning to write a strongly worded letter to somebody about that. Next time you ask me why I stay in and watch my programs, I'll remind you that it's free. Two euro for my TV guide, one hundred and fifty for a yearly license fee—a better value than a day out with you," he huffs.

Suddenly I hear the traffic again, see the people crowding around, feel the sun and breeze on my face, feel my heart beating wildly in my chest as my blood rushes around in frenzied excitement. Dad is tugging on my arm.

"The line's moving now. Come on, Gracie, we have to take a bus. It's a bit of a walk up the road, we have to go. Near the Shelbourne Hotel. Are you okay? You look like you've seen a ghost, and don't tell me you have, because I've dealt with enough today already. Forty euro," he mutters to himself.

A steady flow of pedestrians gather at the top of Grafton Street to cross the road, blocking my view of him. I feel Dad pulling me back, and so I begin to move with him down Merrion Row, walking backward, trying to keep the man in sight.

"Damn it!"

"What's wrong, love? It's not far up the road at all. What on earth are you doing, walking backward?"

"I can't see him."

"Who, love?"

"A guy I think I know." I stop walking backward and stand in line with Dad, continuing to look down the street and scouring the crowds.

"Well, unless you know that you know him for sure, I wouldn't be stopping to chat in the city," Dad says protectively. "What kind of a bus is this, anyway? It looks a bit odd. I'm not sure about this. I don't come to the city for a few years, and look what the CIE tours do."

I ignore him and let him lead us onto the bus while I'm busy looking the other way, searching furiously through the—curiously—plastic windows. The crowd finally moves on, but reveals nothing.

"He's gone."

"Is that so? Can't have known him too well then, if he just ran off."

I turn my attention to my father. "Dad, that was the weirdest thing."

"I don't care what you say, there's nothing weirder than this." Dad looks around us in bewilderment.

Finally I too look around the bus and take in my surroundings. Everyone else is wearing Viking helmets, with life jackets on their laps.

"Okay, everybody," the tour guide speaks into the micro-phone, "we finally have everyone on board. Let's show our new ar-rivals what to do. When I say the word I want you all to rooooooar just like the Vikings did! Let me hear it!"

Dad and I jump in our seats, and I feel him cling to me, as the entire bus does just that.

Chapter 14

◇◇◇◇◇

GOOD AFTERNOON, EVERYBODY, I'M OLAF the White, and welcome aboard the Viking Splash bus! Historically known as DUKWs, or Ducks, their affectionate nickname. We are sitting in the amphibious version of the General Motors vehicle built during World War II. Designed to withstand being driven onto beaches in fifteen-foot seas to deliver cargo or troops from ship to shore, they are now more commonly used as rescue and underwater recovery vehicles in the United States, United Kingdom, and other parts of the world."

"Can we get off?" I whisper in Dad's ear.

He swats me away, enthralled.

"This particular vehicle weighs seven tons and is thirty-one feet long and eight feet wide. It has six wheels and can be driven in rear-wheel or all-wheel drive. As you can see, it has been mechanically rebuilt and outfitted with comfortable seats, a roof, and roll-down sides to protect you from the elements, because as you all know, after we see the sights around the city, we have a 'splash-down' into the water with a fantastic trip around the Grand Canal Docklands!"

Everyone cheers, and Dad looks at me, eyes wide like a little boy.

"Sure, no wonder it was twenty euro. A bus that goes into the water. A bus? That goes into the water? I've never seen the likes of it. Wait till I tell the lads at the Monday Club about this. Bigmouth Donal won't be able to beat this story for once." He turns his attention back to the tour operator, who, like everyone else on the bus, is wearing a Viking helmet with horns. Dad collects two, props one on his head, and hands the other, which has blond side plaits attached, to me.

"Olaf, meet Heidi." I pop it on my head and turn to Dad.

He laughs quietly in my face.

"Sights along the way include our famous city cathedrals, St. Patrick's and Christchurch, Trinity College, government buildings, Georgian Dublin . . ."

"Ooh, you'll like this one," Dad elbows me.

". . . and of course Viking Dublin!"

Everyone roars again, including Dad, and I can't help but laugh.

"I don't understand why we're celebrating a bunch of oafs who raped and pillaged their way around our country."

"Oh, would you ever lighten up, at all, and have some fun?"

"And what do we do when we see a rival DUKW on the road?" Olaf asks.

There's a mixture of boos and roars.

"Okay, let's go!" Olaf says enthusiastically.

Justin frantically searches over the shaven heads of a group of Hare Krishnas who have begun to parade by him and obstruct his view of his woman in the red coat. A sea of orange togas, they smile at him merrily through their bell-ringing and drum-beating. He hops up and down on the spot, trying to get a view down Merrion Row.

A mime artist appears suddenly before him, dressed in a black leotard with a painted white face, red lips, and a striped hat. They stand opposite one another, each waiting for the other to do something, Justin praying for the mime to grow bored and leave. He doesn't. Instead, the mime squares his shoulders, looks mean, parts his legs, and lets his fingers quiver around his holster area.

Keeping his voice down, Justin speaks politely, "Hey, I'm really not in the mood for this. Would you mind playing with someone else, please?"

Looking forlorn, the mime begins to play an invisible violin.

Justin hears laughter and realizes they have an audience. Great.

"Yeah, that's funny. Okay, enough now."

Ignoring the antics, Justin distances himself from the growing crowd and continues to search down Merrion Row for the red coat.

The mime appears beside him again, holds his hand to his forehead, and searches the distance as though at sea. His herd of spectators follow, bleating and snap-happy. An elderly Japanese couple take a photograph.

Justin grits his teeth and speaks again quietly, hoping nobody but the mime can hear. "Hey, asshole, do I look like I'm having fun?"

With the lips of a ventriloquist, a voice with a gruff Dublin accent responds, "Hey, asshole, do I look like I give a shit?"

"You wanna play like this? Fine. I'm not sure whether you're trying to be Marcel Marceau or Coco the Clown, but your little pantomime street performance is insulting to both of them. This crowd might find your stolen routines from Marceau's repertoire amusing, but I don't. Unlike me, they're not aware that you've failed to notice the fact that Marceau used these routines to tell a story or to sketch a theme or a character. He did not just randomly stand on a street trying to get out of a box nobody could see. Your lack of creativity and technique gives a bad name to mimes all over the world."

The mime blinks once and proceeds to walk against an invisible strong wind.

"Here I am!" a voice calls beyond the crowd.

There she is! She recognized me!

Justin shuffles from foot to foot, trying to catch sight of her red coat.

The crowd turns and parts to reveal Sarah, looking excited by the scene.

The mime mimicks Justin's obvious disappointment, plastering a look of despair on his face and hunching his back so that his arms hang low to the ground.

"Oooooooo," goes the crowd, and Sarah's face falls.

Justin nervously replaces his look of disappointment with a smile. He makes his way through the crowd, greets Sarah quickly, and leads her away from the scene while the crowd claps and drops coins into the mime's container nearby.

"Don't you think that was a bit rude? Maybe you should have given him some change or something," she says, looking over her shoulder apologetically at the mime, who is covering his face and moving his shoulders up and down violently in a false fit of tears.

"I think *he* was a bit rude." Distracted, Justin continues to look around for the red coat as they make their way to the restaurant where he's made reservations for lunch, which he now definitely wants to cancel.

Tell her you feel sick. No. She's a doctor, she'll ask too many questions. Tell her you made a mistake and that you have a lecture right now. Tell her, tell her!

Instead Justin finds himself continuing to walk with Sarah, his mind as active as Mount Saint Helens, his eyes jumping around like an addict needing a fix. When they reach the basement restaurant, they are led to a quiet table in the corner. Justin eyes the door.

Yell "fire" and run!

Sarah shuffles her coat off her shoulders to reveal much flesh, and pulls her chair closer to his.

Such a coincidence he bumped, quite literally, into the woman from the salon again. Though maybe it wasn't such a big deal; Dublin's a small town. Since being here, he's learned that everyone pretty much knows everyone, or at least someone related to somebody that someone else once knew. But the woman—he definitely has to stop calling her that. He should give her a name. Angelina.

"What are you thinking about?" Sarah leans across the table and gazes at him.

Or Lucille. "Coffee. I'm thinking about coffee. I'll have a black coffee, please," he says to the waitress setting up their table. He looks at her name badge. Jessica. No, his woman wasn't a Jessica.

"You're not eating?" Sarah asks, disappointed and confused.

"No, I can't stay as long as I'd hoped. I have to get back to campus earlier than planned." His leg bounces beneath the table, hitting the surface and rattling the cutlery. The waitress and Sarah eye him peculiarly.

"Oh, okay, well—" She studies the menu. "I'll have a chef's salad and a glass of the house white, please," she says to the waitress, and then to Justin, "I have to eat or I'll collapse. I hope you don't mind."

"No problem." He smiles. Even though you ordered the biggest fucking salad on the menu. How about Susan? Does my woman look like a Susan? *My* woman? What the hell is wrong with me?

"We are now turning onto Dawson Street, so named after Joshua Dawson, who also designed Grafton, Anne, and Henry streets. On your right you will see the Mansion House, which is home to the Lord Mayor of Dublin."

All horned Viking helmets turn to the right. Video cameras, digital cameras, and camera phones are suspended from the open windows.

"You think this is what the Vikings did way back when, Dad? Went clickety-click with their cameras at buildings that weren't even built yet?" I whisper.

"Oh, quiet," he says loudly, and the tour operator stops speaking, shocked.

"Not you." Dad waves a hand at him. "Her." He points, and the entire bus looks at me.

"To your right you will see St. Anne's Church, which was designed by Isaac Wells in 1707." Olaf continues to the thirty-strong crew of Vikings aboard. "The interior dates back to the seventeenth century."

"Actually the Romanesque facade wasn't added until 1868, and that was designed by Thomas Newenham Deane," I whisper to Dad.

"Oh," Dad responds to this, eyes widening. "I didn't know that."

My own eyes widen at this random piece of information. "Me neither."

Dad chuckles.

"We are now on Nassau Street, and we will pass Grafton Street on the left in just a moment."

Dad starts singing, "Grafton Street's a wonderland." Loudly.

An American woman in front of us turns around, her face beaming. "Oh, do you know that song? My father used to sing it. He was from Ireland. Oh, I would love to hear it again; can you sing it for us?"

A chorus of "Oh, yes, please do . . ." surrounds us.

No stranger to public performance, the man who sings weekly at the Monday Club begins belting out the song, and the entire bus joins in, swaying from side to side. Dad's voice reaches out beyond the plastic fold-up windows of the DUKW and into the ears of pedestrians and traffic going by.

I take a mental photograph of Dad sitting beside me, singing with his eyes closed, two horns propped on top of his head.

Justin watches with growing impatience as Sarah slowly picks at her salad. Her fork playfully pokes at a piece of chicken; the chicken hangs on, falls off, grabs on again, and manages to hang on while she waves the fork around, using it as a sledgehammer to knock pieces of lettuce over to see what's beneath. Finally she stabs a piece of tomato, and as she lifts the fork to her mouth, the same piece of chicken falls off again. That was the third time she'd done that.

"Are you sure you're not hungry, Justin? You seem to be really studying this plate." She smiles, waving another forkful of food around, sending red onion and cheddar cheese tumbling back to the plate. It's like one step forward, two steps back every time.

"Yeah, sure, I wouldn't mind having some." He's already ordered and finished a bowl of soup in the time it took her to have five mouthfuls.

"You want me to feed it to you?" she flirts, moving the fork in circular motions toward his mouth.

"Well, I want more than that, for a start."

She spears a few other pieces of food.

"More," he says, keeping an eye on his watch. The more food he can squeeze into his mouth, the quicker this frustrating experience will be over. He knows that his woman, now called Veronica, is probably long gone by now, but sitting here, watching Sarah burn more calories playing with her food than ingesting it, isn't going to confirm that for him.

"Okay, here comes the airplane," she sings.

"More." At least half of it has fallen off again during its "take-off."

"More? How can you possibly fit more on the fork, never mind in your mouth?"

"Here, I'll show you." Justin takes the fork from her and begins stabbing at as much as he can. Chicken, corn, lettuce, beets, onion, tomato, cheese; he manages it all and hands it back to her. "Now, if the lady pilot would like to bring her plane in to land . . ."

She giggles. "This is not going to fit in your mouth."

"I have a pretty big mouth."

She shovels it in, laughing all the while, barely fitting it all into Justin's mouth. When he's finally chewed and swallowed it all, he looks at his watch and then again at her plate.

"Okay, now your turn." You're such a shit, Justin.

"No way." She laughs.

"Come on." He gathers as much food as possible, including the same piece of chicken she's deserted four times, and "flies" it into her open mouth.

She laughs while trying to fit it all in. Barely able to breathe, chew, swallow, or smile, she still tries to look pretty. For almost a full minute she's unable to speak in her attempts to chew in as ladylike a way as possible. Juices and dressing dribble down her chin, and when she finally swallows, her lipstick-smudged mouth smiles at him to reveal a great big piece of lettuce stuck between her teeth.

"That was fun." She smiles.

Helen. Like Helen of Troy, so beautiful she could start a war.

"Are you finished? Can I take the plate?" the waitress comes by to ask.

Sarah begins to answer, "N—" but Justin jumps in.

"Yes, we are, thank you." He avoids Sarah's stare.

"Actually I'm not quite finished, thank you," Sarah says sternly. The plate is replaced.

Justin's leg bounces beneath the table, his impatience growing. Salma. Sexy Salma. An awkward silence now falls between them.

"I'm sorry, Salma, I don't mean to be rude—"

"Sarah."

"What?"

"My name is Sarah."

"I know that. It's just—"

"You called me Salma."

"Oh. What? Who's Salma? God. Sorry. I don't even know a Salma, honestly."

Sarah speeds up her eating, obviously dying to get away from him now.

He says more softly, "It's just that I have to get back to campus—"

"Earlier than planned. You said." She smiles quickly, and her face falls immediately as she looks back down at her plate. She pierces the food with purpose now. Playtime over. Time to eat. Food fills her mouth instead of words.

Justin cringes inside, knowing his behavior is uncharacteristically rude. Now say it like you mean it, you jerk. He stares at her: beautiful face, great body, smart woman. Dressed smartly in a trouser suit, with long legs and big lips to match. Long elegant fingers, neat French-manicured nails, a smart bag to match her shoes by her feet. Professional, confident, intelligent. There is absolutely nothing wrong with this woman at all. Justin's own distraction is the problem, the feeling that a part of him is somewhere else. A part of him, in fact, that feels so nearby, he is almost compelled to run out and catch it. The problem is, he doesn't know what he is trying to catch, or who. In a city of one million people, he can't expect to walk outside this door and find the same woman standing on the pavement. And is it worth leaving this other beautiful woman sitting with him in this restaurant, just to chase an idea?

He stops bouncing his leg up and down and settles back into his chair, no longer at the edge of his seat or ready to dive for the door the second she puts down her knife and fork.

"Sarah . . ." He sighs, and means it this time when he says, "I'm very sorry."

She stops forking food into her mouth and looks up at him, chews quickly, dabs at her lips with a napkin, and swallows. Her face softens. "Okay." She wipes away the crumbs around her plate, shrugging. "I'm not looking for a marriage here, Justin."

"I know, I know."

"Lunch is all this is."

"I know that."

"Or shall we say just coffee, in case mentioning the former sends you running out the door yelling 'fire'?" She acknowledges his empty cup and continues flicking at imaginary crumbs now.

He reaches out to grab her hand and stop her fidgeting. "I'm sorry."

"Okay," she repeats.

The air clears, the tension evaporates, her plate is cleared away.

"I suppose we should get the check," she says.

"Have you always wanted to be a doctor?"

"Whoa." She pauses while opening her wallet. "It's just intense either way with you, isn't it?" But she's smiling again.

"I'm sorry." Justin shakes his head. "Let's have a coffee before we leave. Hopefully I'll have time to stop this from being the worst date you've ever been on."

"It's not." She shakes her head. "But it's a close second. It was almost the worst, but you pulled it right back there with the doctor question."

Justin smiles. "So. Have you?"

She nods. "Ever since James Goldin operated on me when I was in junior infants. What do you call it, kindergarten? Anyway, I was five years old, and he saved my life."

"Wow. That's young for a serious operation. It must have had a huge effect."

"Profound. I was in the yard at lunch break. I fell during a game of hopscotch and hurt my knee. The rest of my friends were discussing amputation, but James Goldin came running over and gave me mouth-to-mouth. Just like that, the pain went away. And that's when I knew."

"That you wanted to be a doctor?"

"That I wanted to marry James Goldin."

Justin smiles. "And did you?"

"Nah. Became a doctor instead."

"You're good at it."

"And you can tell that from a simple needle insertion at a blood donation." She smiles. "Everything okay in that department, by the way?"

"My arm's a little itchy but it's fine."

"Itchy? It shouldn't be itchy, let me see."

He goes to roll up his sleeve and stops. "Could I ask you something?" He squirms again in his chair. "Is there any way that I can find out where my blood went?"

"Where? As in, which hospital?"

"Well, yeah, or even better, do you know who it went to?"

She shakes her head. "The beauty of this is that it's completely anonymous."

"But someone, somewhere, would know, wouldn't they? With hospital records or even your office records?"

"Of course. Products in a blood bank are always individually traceable. It's documented throughout the entire process—donation, testing, separation into components, storage and administration to the recipient—but—"

"There's a word I hate."

"Unfortunately for you, you can't know who received your donation."

"But you just said that it's documented."

"That information can't be released. Though all our records

are kept in a secure computerized database where your donor details are kept. Under the Data Protection Act, you have the right to access your donor records."

"Will those records tell me who received my blood?"

"Justin, the blood you donated was not transfused directly into someone else's body exactly as it came from your vein. It was broken up and separated into red blood cells, white blood cells, platelets—"

"I know, I know."

"Why are you so keen to know?"

He thinks about it for a while, drops a brown sugar cube into his second coffee, and stirs it around. "I'm just interested to know who I helped, if I helped anyone at all, and if I did, how they are. I feel like . . . no, it sounds stupid, you'll think I'm insane. It doesn't matter."

"Hey, don't be silly," she says soothingly. "I already think you're insane."

"I hope that's not your medical opinion."

"Tell me." Her piercing blue eyes watch him over the brim of her coffee cup as she sips.

"This is the first time I've said this aloud, so forgive me for speaking while I think." He sighs. "At first, it was a ridiculous macho ego trip. I wanted to know whose life I saved. Which lucky person I'd sacrificed my blood for."

Sarah smiles.

"But then, over the last few days, I haven't been able to stop thinking about it. I feel different. Genuinely different. Like I've given something away. Something precious."

"It *is* precious, Justin. We need more donors all the time."

"I know, but not—I don't mean that. I just feel like there's someone out there walking around with something inside them that I gave them, and now I'm missing something—"

"Your body replaces the liquid part of your donation within twenty-four hours."

"No, I mean, I feel like I've given something away, a part of me, and that somebody else has been completed because of that part of me and . . . my God, this sounds crazy. I just want to know who that person is."

"You can't get your blood back, you know," Sarah jokes weakly, and they both fall into deep thought; Sarah looking sadly into her coffee, Justin trying to make sense of his jumbled words.

"I suppose I should never try to discuss something so illogical with a doctor," he says.

"You sound like a lot of people I know, Justin. You're just the first person I've heard blame it on a blood donation."

Silence.

"Well," Sarah says as she reaches behind her chair to get her coat, "you're in a rush, so we should really get going now."

They make their way down Grafton Street in a not uncomfortable silence that's occasionally dotted with small talk. They automatically stop walking at the Molly Malone statue, across the road from Trinity College.

"You're late for your class."

"No, I've got a little while before I—" He looks at his watch and then remembers his earlier excuse. He feels his face redden. "Sorry."

"It's okay," she repeats.

"I feel like this whole lunch date has been me saying sorry, and you saying that it's okay."

"It really is okay." She laughs.

"And I really am—"

"Stop!" She holds her hand to hush him. "Enough."

"I really had a lovely time," he says awkwardly. "Should we . . . you know, I'm feeling really uncomfortable right now with her watching us."

They look to their right where Molly stares down at them with her bronze eyes.

Sarah laughs. "You know, maybe we could make arrangements to—"

"Rooooooaaaaaaaaarrrrrrrrr!!"

Justin almost leaps up from where he's standing, startled by the intense screaming coming from the bus stopped at the traffic light beside them. Sarah yelps with fright, and her hand flies to her chest. Beside them more than a dozen men, women, and children, all wearing Viking helmets, are waving their fists in the air and roaring at passersby. Sarah and the dozens of others on the pavement start laughing, some of them even roaring.

Justin, whose breath has caught in his throat, is silent. He can't take his eyes off the woman on the bus laughing uproariously with an old man next to her. Even with a helmet on her head, long blond plaits flowing on each side, he knows it's her.

"We certainly got them, Joyce," the old man says loudly, roaring lightly in her face and waving his fist.

She looks surprised at first, then hands him a five-euro note, much to his delight, and they both continue laughing.

Look at me, Justin wills her. Her eyes stay on the old man as he holds the note up to the light to check its authenticity. Justin looks to the traffic lights, which are still red. He has time yet for her to see him. Turn around! Look at me just once! Then the pedestrian lights flash to amber.

Her head remains turned, completely lost in conversation.

The lights turn green, and the bus slowly moves off up Nassau Street. He starts to walk alongside it, willing her with everything he has to look at him.

"Justin!" Sarah calls. "What are you doing?"

He keeps on walking alongside the bus, quickening his pace and finally breaking out into a jog. He can hear Sarah calling after him but he can't stop.

"Hey!" he calls.

Not loud enough; she doesn't hear him. The bus picks up

speed, and Justin's jog turns into a run, the adrenaline surging through his body. The bus is beating him, speeding up. He's losing her.

"Joyce!" he blurts out. The surprising sound of his own yell is enough to stop him in his tracks. What on earth is he doing? He doubles over to rest his hands on his knees and tries to catch his breath, tries to center himself in the whirlwind he feels caught up in. He looks back at the bus one last time. A Viking helmet appears from the window, blond plaits moving from side to side like a pendulum. He can't make out the face, but with just that head looking back at him, he knows it has to be her.

The whirlwind stops momentarily while he holds up a hand in salute.

A hand appears out the window and the bus rounds the corner onto Kildare Street, leaving Justin to, once again, watch her disappear from sight, his heart beating wildly. He may not have the slightest clue what is going on, but there is one thing he knows now for sure.

Joyce. Her name is Joyce.

He looks down the empty street.

But who are you, Joyce?

"Why are you hanging your head out of the window?" Dad pulls me in, wild with worry. "You might not have much to live for, but for Christ's sake you owe it to yourself to live it."

"Did you hear somebody calling my name?" I whisper to Dad, my mind a whirl.

"Oh, she's hearing voices now," he grumbles. "I said your bloody name, and you gave me a fiver for it, don't you remember?" He snaps it before her face, and turns his attention back to Olaf.

"On your left is Leinster House, the building that now houses the National Parliament of Ireland."

Snappety-snap, clickety-click, flash-flash, record.

"Leinster House was originally known as Kildare House after the Earl of Kildare commissioned it to be built. It was renamed on his becoming the Duke of Leinster. Parts of the building, which was formerly the Royal College of Surgeons—"

"Science," I say loudly, though still largely lost in thought.

"Pardon me?" Olaf stops talking and heads turn once again.

"I was just saying that"—my face flushes—"it was the Royal College of *Science*."

"Yes, that's what I said."

"No, you said 'surgeons,' " the American woman in front of us speaks out.

"Oh," Olaf says, flustered. "Excuse me, I'm mistaken. Parts of the building, which was formerly the Royal College of"—he looks pointedly at me—"Science, have served as the seat of the Irish government since 1922 . . ."

I tune out.

"Remember I told you about the guy who designed the Rotunda Hospital?" I whisper to Dad.

"I do. Dick somebody."

"Richard Cassells. He designed this too. It's been claimed that it formed a model for the design of the White House."

"Is that so?" Dad says.

"Really?" The American woman twists around in her seat to face me. She speaks loudly. Very loudly. Too loudly. "Honey, did you hear that? This lady says the guy who designed this designed the White House."

"No, I didn't actually—"

Suddenly I notice Olaf has stopped talking and is currently glaring at me with as much love as a Viking Dragon for a Sea Cat. All eyes, ears, and horns are on us.

"Well, I said it's been claimed that it formed a model for the design of the White House. There aren't any certainties as such," I say quietly, not wanting to be dragged into this. "It's just that James Hoban, who won the competition for the design of the White House in 1792, was an Irishman."

Everyone stares expectantly at me.

"Well, he studied architecture in Dublin and would have more than likely studied the design of Leinster House," I finish off quickly.

The people around me ooh, aah, and talk among themselves about that tidbit of information.

"We can't hear you!" someone at the front of the bus shouts out.

"Stand up." Dad pushes me up.

"Dad . . ." I slap him away.

"Hey, Olaf, give her the microphone!" a woman shouts. He grudgingly hands it over and folds his arms.

"Eh, hello." I tap it with my finger and blow into the mike.

"You have to say, 'Testing one, two, three,' Gracie."

"Eh, testing one, two—"

"We can hear you," Olaf snaps.

"Okay, well . . ." I repeat my comments, and the people up front nod with interest.

"And these are part of your government's buildings too?" the American woman points to the buildings we're passing on either side.

I look uncertainly at Dad, and he nods at me with encouragement. "Well, actually no. The building to the left is the National Library, and the National Museum is on the right." I go to sit down again, and Dad whooshes my backside back up. Everyone is still looking at me for more. Olaf now looks sheepish.

"Well, a bit of interesting information may be that the National Library and the National Museum were originally home to the Dublin Museum of Science and Art, which opened in 1890. Both were designed by Thomas Newenham Deane and his son Thomas Manly Deane after a competition held in 1885 and were constructed by the Dublin contractors J. and W. Beckett, who demonstrated the best of Irish craftsmanship in their construction. The museum is one of the best surviving examples of Irish decorative stonework, woodcarving, and ceramic tiling. The National Library's most impressive feature is the entrance rotunda. Internally this space leads up an impressive staircase to the magnificent reading room, with its vast vaulted ceiling. As you can see for yourselves, the exterior of the building is characterized by its array of columns and pilasters in the Corinthian order and by the rotunda with its open veranda and corner pavilions framing the composition. In the—"

Loud clapping interrupts my talk—single sharp claps coming from only one person: Dad. The rest of the bus sits in silence. A child breaks it by asking her mother if they can roar again. An imaginary piece of tumbleweed blows down the aisle, landing at the feet of a grinning Olaf the White.

"I, em, I wasn't finished," I say quietly.

Dad claps louder in response, and a man sitting alone in the back row joins in nervously.

"And . . . that's all I know," I say quickly, sitting down.

The American in front of us turns around. "How do you know all that?" she asks.

"She's a real estate agent," Dad says proudly.

The woman makes an "oh" shape with her mouth and turns around again to face an extremely satisfied-looking Olaf, who has grabbed the microphone from me.

"Now everybody, let's roooooooaaaaaar!"

Everybody comes to life again, while each muscle and organ in my body cringes into a fetal position.

Dad leans into me and crushes me against the window. He

moves his head close to whisper in my ear and our helmets knock against each other.

"How *did* you know all that, love?"

As though I'd used up all of my words in that tirade, my mouth opens and closes, but nothing comes out. How on earth did I know all of that?

Chapter 15

⬦⬦⬦⬦⬦

MY EARS IMMEDIATELY SIZZLE AS soon as I enter the school gymnasium that same evening and spy Kate and Frankie huddled together on the bleachers, looking deep in conversation with concern etch-a-sketched across their faces. Kate looks as though Frankie's just told her that her father's passed away, a face I'm familiar with, as I was the one to give her that very news five years ago at the Dublin airport when she'd cut short her holiday to rush to his side. Now Kate is talking, and Frankie looks as though her dog's been hit by a car, a face I'm also familiar with, as I was once again the one to deliver the news, and the blow, that broke three of her sausage dog's legs. Kate glances in my direction and looks as though she's been caught in the act. Frankie freezes too. Looks of surprise, then guilt, and then smiles to make me think they've just been discussing the weather rather than the recent events in my life, which have been as changeable.

I wait for the usual Lady of Trauma to fill my shoes. To give me a little break while she offers the usual insightful comments that keep inquisitors at bay; explaining my recent loss as more of a continuous journey rather than a dead end, giving me the invaluable opportunity to gain strength and learn about myself, thereby turning this terribly tragic affair into something hugely positive. But the Lady does not arrive, knowing this is no easy gig for her. She is well aware the two people who are currently hugging me close can see through her words and right to the heart of me.

My friends' hugs are longer and tighter today; they consist of extra squeezes and pats, which alternate between a circular rubbing motion and a light pitter-pattering on the back, both of which I find surprisingly comforting. The pity in their faces hammers home my great loss, and my stomach suddenly feels queasy, my head fully loaded again. I realize that swaddling myself in a nest with Dad does not hold the superhealing powers I'd hoped for. Every time I leave the house and meet somebody new, I have to go through it over again. Not just the entire rigmarole, but I have to *feel* it all, which is a far more tiring thing than words. Wrapped in Kate and Frankie's arms, I could easily morph into the baby that they in their minds are coddling, but I don't, because if I start now, I know I'll never stop.

We sit on the bleachers away from the other parents, most of whom are sitting alone reading or watching their children doing unimpressive sideways tumbles on the blue rubber mats. I spot Kate's children, six-year-old Eric and my five-year-old goddaughter, Jayda, the *Muppet Christmas Carol* fanatic I have sworn not to hold anything against. They are enthusiastically hopping about and chirping like crickets, pulling their underwear out from in between the cheeks of their behinds and tripping over untied shoelaces. Eleven-month-old Sam sleeps beside us in a stroller, blowing bubbles from his chubby lips. I watch him fondly, then remember again and look away. Ah, remembering. That old chestnut.

"How's work, Frankie?" I ask, wanting to act as normal as possible.

"Busy as usual," she responds, and I detect guilt, perhaps even embarrassment. I envy her normality. I envy that her today was the same as her yesterday.

"Still buying low, selling high?" Kate pipes up.

Frankie rolls her eyes. "Twelve years, Kate."

"I know, I know." Kate bites her lip and tries not to laugh.

"Twelve years I've had this job, and twelve years you've being saying that. It's not even funny anymore. In fact I don't recall it ever being funny, and yet you persist."

Kate giggles. "It's just that I have absolutely no idea what it is that you do. Something in the stock market?"

"Manager, deputy head corporate treasury and investor solutions desk," Frankie tells her.

Kate stares back blankly, then sighs. "So many words to say that you work at a desk."

"Oh, I'm sorry, what do you do all day again? Wipe shitty asses and make organic banana sandwiches?"

"There are many other aspects to being a mother, Frankie," Kate puffs. "It is my responsibility to prepare three human beings so that if, God forbid, something happens to me, or when they are adults, they will be able to live and function and succeed responsibly in the world all by themselves."

"And you mush organic bananas," Frankie adds. "No, no, hold on, is that before or after the preparation of three human beings? Before?" She nods to herself. "Yes, definitely mush bananas and then prepare human beings. Got it."

"All I'm saying is, you have, what, seven words to describe your paper-pushing job?"

"I believe it's eight."

"I have one. One."

"Well, I don't know. Is 'carpooler' one or two words? Joyce, what do you think?"

I stay out of it.

"The point I'm trying to make is that the word 'mum,'" Kate says, irritated, "a teeny, tiny little word that every woman with a child is called, fails to describe the plethora of duties involved. If I was doing what I do every day at your company, I'd be running the fucking place."

Frankie shrugs nonchalantly. "I can't speak for my colleagues, but personally, I like to make my own banana sandwiches and wipe my own behind."

They do this all the time: talk at each other, never to each other, in an odd bonding ritual that seems to pull them closer when it would do the opposite to anybody else. In the silence that follows they both have time to realize what exactly they were talking about in my company. Ten seconds later Kate kicks Frankie. Oh, yes. The mention of children.

When something tragic has happened, you'll find that you, the tragicee, become the person that has to make everything comfortable for everyone else.

"How's Crapper?" I try to sound upbeat as I ask after Frankie's dog.

"He's doing well; his legs are healing nicely. Still howls when he sees your photograph, though. Sorry, I had to move it from the fireplace."

"Doesn't matter. In fact I was going to ask you to move it. Kate, you can get rid of my wedding photo too."

Now on to divorce talk.

"Ah, Joyce." She shakes her head and looks at me sadly. "That's my favorite photo of me. I looked so good at your wedding. Can I not just cut Conor out?"

"Or draw a little mustache on him," Frankie adds. "Or better yet, give him a personality. What color should that be?"

I bite my lip to hide a smile that threatens to crawl from the corner of my lips. I'm not used to this kind of talk about Conor. It's disrespectful, and I'm not sure I'm completely comfortable with it. But it *is* funny. Instead I look away to the children on the floor.

"Okay, everybody." The gymnastics instructor claps his hands for attention, and the crickets' hopping and chirping momentarily subsides. "Spread out on the mat. We're going to do backward rolls. Place your hands flat on the floor, fingers pointing toward your shoulders as you roll back to a stand. Like this."

"Well, looky-look at our little flexible friend," Frankie remarks.

One by one the children roll backward to a perfect stand. Until it gets to Jayda, who rolls over one side of her head in the most awkward way, kicks another child in the shins, and then gets onto her knees before finally jumping to a stand. She strikes a Spice Girl pose in all of her pink sparkling glory, peace fingers and all, thinking nobody has noticed her error.

"Preparing a human being for the world," Frankie repeats smartly. "Yup. You'd be running the fucking place, all right." She turns to me and softens her voice. "So, Joyce, how are you?"

I have debated whether to tell them, whether to tell anyone. Other than carting me off to the madhouse, I have no idea how anybody will react to what's been happening to me, or even how they should react. But after today's experience, I side with the part of my brain that is anxious to reveal.

"This is going to sound really odd, so bear with me on this."

"It's okay." Kate grabs my hand. "You say whatever you want. Just release."

Frankie works valiantly not to roll her eyes.

"Thanks." I slowly slip my hand out of Kate's. "Okay, here goes. I keep seeing this guy on the street."

Kate tries to register this. I can see her trying to link it with the loss of my baby or my looming divorce, but she can't.

"This gorgeous, handsome man." I smile. "I think I know him, but at the same time, I know I don't. I've seen him precisely three times now, the most recent being today, when he chased after my Viking bus. And I think he called out my name. Though I may have imagined that, because how on earth could he know my name? Unless he knows me, but that brings me back to my being sure that he really doesn't." I stop there. "What do you think?"

"Hold on, I'm way back at the Viking bus part," Frankie says doubtfully. "You say you have a Viking bus."

"I don't have one. I was on one. With Dad. It goes into the water too. You wear helmets with horns and go 'Aaaagh' at everyone." I go close to their faces and wave my fists to show them.

They stare back blankly.

I sigh and slide back on the bench. "So anyway, he keeps reappearing."

"Okay," Kate says slowly, looking at Frankie.

There's an awkward silence as they worry about my sanity. I join them on that.

Frankie clears her throat. "So this man, Joyce. Is he young, old, or indeed a Viking upon your magic bus that travels the high waters?"

"Late thirties, early forties. He's American. We got our hair cut at the same time. That's where I saw him first, at a salon. He said he liked my cactus."

"You brought that cactus to a hair salon?" Kate says, horrified.

I nod, not caring now how crazy this all sounds. "He has one too." I frown. "And somebody else does too, but I can't think of who." I search my memory again.

"Your hair is lovely, by the way," Kate says to change the subject, gently fingering a few front strands.

"Dad thinks I look like Peter Pan."

"So maybe this man remembers you from the hair salon," Frankie reasons.

"No, it felt weird from the first time at the salon. There was a . . . recognition or something."

Frankie smiles. "Welcome to the world of singledom." She turns to Kate, whose face is scrunched up in disagreement. "When's the last time Joyce allowed herself a little flirt with someone? She's been married for so long."

"Please," Kate says patronizingly to Frankie. "If you think that's what happens when you're married, then you're sorely mistaken. No offense, Joyce. No wonder you're afraid to commit."

"I'm not afraid, I just don't agree with it. You know, just today I was watching a makeup show—"

"Oh, here we go."

"Shut up and listen. The makeup expert said that because the skin is so sensitive around the eye, you must apply cream with your ring finger because it is the finger with the least power."

"Wow," Kate says drily. "You sure have revealed us married folk to be the fools that we are."

I rub my eyes wearily and interrupt their bickering. "I know I sound insane. I'm tired and probably imagining things where there is nothing to be imagined. The man I'm supposed to have on the brain is Conor, but he's not. He's really not at all. I don't know if it's a delayed reaction and next month I'm going to fall apart, start drinking and wear black every day—"

"Like Frankie," Kate butts in.

"But right now, I feel nothing but relieved," I continue. "Is that terrible?"

"Is it okay for me to feel relieved too?" Kate asks.

"You didn't like him?" I ask sadly.

"No, he was fine. He was nice. I just hated you not being happy."

"I hated him," Frankie chirps up.

"We spoke briefly yesterday," I tell them. "It was odd. He wanted to know if he could take the espresso machine."

"The bastard," Frankie spits.

"I really don't care about the espresso machine. He can have it."

"It's mind games, Joyce. Be careful," Frankie warns me. "First it's the espresso machine, and then it's the house, and then it's your soul. And then it's that emerald ring that belonged to his grandmother that he claims you stole but that you recall more than clearly that when you first went to his house for lunch he said, 'Help yourself,' and there it was." She scowls.

I look to Kate for help.

"Her breakup with Lee."

"Ah. Well, it's not going to get like that."

"Christian went for a pint with Conor last night," Kate says. "Hope you don't mind."

"Of course I don't; they're friends. Is Conor okay?"

"Yeah, Christian said he seemed fine. He's upset about the, you know . . ."

"Baby. You can say the word. I'm not going to fall apart."

"He's upset about the baby and disappointed the marriage didn't work, but he thinks it's the right thing to do. He's going back to Japan in a few days. He also said you're both putting the house on the market."

"Well, we bought it together, and I don't like being there anymore."

"But are you sure? Where will you live?"

As a tragicee and future divorcee, you'll also find that people will question you on the biggest decisions you've ever made in your life as though you hadn't thought about them at all before—as though, through their twenty questions and dubious faces, they're going to shine light on something that you missed the hundredth time around during your darkest hours.

"Is your dad not driving you insane?" Kate asks.

"Funnily enough, no." I smile as I think about him. "He's actually having the opposite effect. Though he's only managed to call me Joyce once out of every hundred times. I'm going to stay with him until the house is sold and I find somewhere else to live."

"You know at the hospital he told the nurse to check my bag for poteen in case I gave you any," Kate says grumpily. "He still hates me."

"And he still loves me," Frankie says happily.

"I'm going to tell him the truth about what happened, the next time I see him," Kate says, and then turns her attention back to me. "That story about the strange man . . . apart from him, how are you really? We haven't seen you since the hospital, and we've been so worried."

"I know. I'm sorry about that. I really appreciated you coming, though."

"No, you didn't."

"Okay, I didn't then, but I do now."

I think about how to summarize how strange things have been since the hospital.

"I eat meat now. And I drink red wine. I hate anchovies, and I listen to classical music. I particularly love *The JK Ensemble* on Lyric FM with John Kelly, who doesn't play Kylie, and I don't mind. Last night I listened to Handel's 'Mi restano le lagrime' from act three, scene one, of *Alcina* before going to sleep, and I actually knew the words but have no idea how. I know a lot about Irish architecture, but not as much as I know about French and Italian. I've read *Ulysses* and can quote from it ad nauseam, when I couldn't even finish the audio book before. Only today I wrote a letter to the council telling them how their cramming yet another new ugly modern block into a traditional area means that not only is the nation's heritage seriously under threat, but the sanity of its citizens too. I thought my father was the only person who wrote strongly worded letters. That's not such a big deal in itself, but the fact is that just two weeks ago I was excited about the prospect of showing these new properties. Today I'm particularly vexed about talk of bulldozing a hundred-year-old building in Old Town, Chicago, and so I plan to write another letter. I bet you're wondering how I knew about that. Well, I read it in the recent edition of the *Art and Architectural Review*, the only truly international art and architectural publication. I'm a subscriber now." I take a breath. "Ask me anything, because I'll probably know the answer, and I've no idea how."

Kate and Frankie are too stunned to even exchange looks.

"Maybe with the stress of constantly worrying about you and Conor over with, you're able to concentrate on other things more," Frankie suggests.

I consider that before continuing. "I dream almost every night about a little girl with white-blond hair who gets bigger every time. And I hear music—a song I don't know. When I'm not dreaming about her, I have vivid dreams of places I've never been, foods I've never tasted, and strange people that I seem to know well. A picnic in a park with a woman with red hair. A man with green feet. And sprinklers." I think hard. "Something about sprinklers.

"When I wake up, I have to remember all over again that my dreams are not real and that my reality is not a dream. I find that next to impossible, but not completely so, because Dad is there with a smile on his face and sausages in the frying pan, chasing a cat called Fluffy around the garden, and for some unknown reason hiding Mum's photograph in the hall drawer. So after the first few moments of my waking day, when everything is crap, I try to focus on all those other things. And a man I can't get out of my head, who I don't even know."

The girls' eyes are filled, their faces a mixture of sympathy, worry, and confusion.

I don't expect them to say anything, and so I look out to the kids again on the gymnasium floor and watch as Eric takes to the balance beam. The instructor calls out to him to do airplane arms. Eric's face is a picture of nervous concentration. He stops walking as he slowly lifts his arms. The instructor offers words of encouragement, and a small proud smile starts to form around the boy's mouth. He raises his eyes briefly to see if his mother is watching, and in that one moment, he loses balance and falls straight down, the beam quite unfortunately landing between his legs. His face is now one of horror.

Frankie snorts again. Eric howls. Sam starts to cry lightly in his stroller. Kate looks from one son to the other.

"Joyce, can you take care of Sam for me?" she says in a panic, rushing to the child, who's rolled in a ball on the floor, surrounded by the teacher and the entire gym class.

I look into the stroller at Sam, at his bright red lips wobbling with fright, tears starting to form in his worried eyes.

"He better not start screaming." Frankie puts her hands over her ears in preparation.

I move toward Sam and begin fidgeting with the clasp on his safety straps. My heart is banging in my rib cage, and my hands are trembling so much, the buckle won't open. Sam becomes more impatient and squirms about like a worm, his cries getting louder and attracting the attention of the other mums, mums not like me, who know exactly what to do, who watch on judgmentally.

"Oh, please stop him," Frankie moans. "Does he want a breast or something?"

I finally manage to unlatch the straps, and Sam looks at me, tears spilling from his blue eyes, his arms up in the air, looking to be pulled out. But I can't do it. I just can't.

I leave.

Chapter 16

◇◇◇◇◇

D RIVING BACK TO DAD'S, I try not to glance at my former
house as I pass. My eyes lose the battle with my mind, and
I see Conor's car parked outside it. Since our final meal together a
couple weeks ago we have talked a few times, each conversation
varying in degrees of affection for each other. The first call came
late at night the day after our dinner, Conor asking just one last
time if we were doing the right thing. His slurred words and soft
voice drifted in my ear as I lay on my bed in my childhood bedroom and stared at the ceiling, just as I had years ago during those
all-night phone calls when we first met. Living with my father at
thirty-three years of age after a failed marriage, with a vulnerable
husband on the other end of the phone . . . it was so easy right then
to remember only the good times together and to doubt our decision. But more often than not, the easy decisions are the wrong
decisions, and sometimes we feel like we're going backward when
we're actually moving forward.

The next call was a little more stern—an embarrassed apology, and a mention of something legal. The next, a frustrated in-
quiry into why my lawyer hadn't replied to his lawyer yet. The

next, his telling me his newly pregnant sister was going to take the crib, something that made me fly into a jealous rage as soon as I hung up and throw the phone across the room. The last was to tell me he'd boxed everything up; he was leaving for Japan in a few days. And could he have the espresso machine?

Each time I hung up the phone, I felt that my weak good-bye wasn't a good-bye. It was more of a "see you around." I knew that there was always a chance to back out, that he'd be around for a little while longer, that our words weren't really final.

I pull the car over and stare up at the house we've lived in for almost ten years. Doesn't it deserve more than a few weak good-byes?

I ring the doorbell, and there's no answer. Through the front window I can see everything in boxes, the walls naked, the surfaces bare, the stage set for the next family to move in and tread the boards. I turn my key in the door and step inside, making a noise so as not to surprise Conor if he's here. I'm about to call his name when I hear the soft tinkle of music drifting from upstairs. I make my way up to the half-decorated nursery and find Conor sitting on the soft carpet, tears streaming down his face as he watches the musical mouse chase the cheese. I cross the room and reach for him. On the floor, I hold him close and rock him gently. I close my eyes and drift away for a moment.

He stops crying and looks up at me. "What?"

"Hmm?" I snap out of my trance.

"You said something. In Latin."

"No, I didn't."

"Yes, you did. Just there." He dries his eyes. "Since when do you speak Latin?"

"I don't."

"Right," he says sharply. "Well, what does the one phrase that you do know mean?"

"I don't know."

"You must know, you just said it."

"Conor, I don't recall saying anything." He glares at me then, a look of something pretty close to hate, and I swallow hard.

"Okay." He gets to his feet and moves toward the door. No more questions, no more trying to understand me. He no longer cares. "Patrick will be acting as my lawyer now."

Fantastic, his shithead brother.

"Okay," I whisper.

He stops at the door and turns round, grinding his jaw as his eyes take in the room. A last look at everything, including me, and he's gone.

The final good-bye.

I have another restless night at Dad's as more images flash through my mind like lightning, so fast and sharp they light up my head with an urgent bolt before they're gone again. Back to black.

A church. Bells ringing. Sprinklers. A tidal wave of red wine. Old buildings with shop fronts. Stained glass.

A view through banisters of a man with green feet, closing a door behind him. A baby in my arms. A girl with white-blond hair. A familiar song.

A casket. Tears. Family dressed in black.

Park swings. Higher and higher. My hands pushing a child. Me swinging as a child. A seesaw. A chubby young boy raising me higher in the air as he lowers himself to the ground. Sprinklers again. Laughter. Me and the same boy in swimming togs. Suburbs. Music. Bells. A woman in a white dress. Cobbled streets. Cathedrals. Confetti. Hands, fingers, rings. Shouting. Slamming.

The man with green feet closing the door.

Sprinklers again. A chubby young boy chasing me and laughing. A drink in my hand. My head down a toilet. Lecture halls. Sun and green grass. Music.

The man with green feet outside in the garden, holding a hose in his hand. Laughter. The girl with the white-blond hair playing in the sand. The girl laughing on a swing. Bells again.

The view from the banisters of the man with green feet closing a door. A bottle in his hand.

A pizza parlor. Ice-cream sundaes.

Pills in his hand now. The man's eyes seeing mine before the door closes. My hand on a doorknob. The door opening. Empty bottle on the ground. Bare feet with green soles. A casket.

Sprinklers. Rocking back and forth. Humming that song. Long blond hair covering my face. Whispers of a phrase . . .

I open my eyes with a gasp, heart drumming in my chest. The sheets are wet beneath me; my body is soaked in sweat. I fumble in the darkness for the bedside lamp. With tears in my eyes that I refuse to allow to fall, I reach for my cell phone and dial with trembling fingers.

"Conor?" My voice is shaking.

He mumbles incoherently for a little while until he awakens. "Joyce, it's three a.m.," he croaks.

"I know, I'm sorry."

"What's wrong? Are you okay?"

"Yes, yes, I'm fine, it's just that, well, I—I had a dream. Or a nightmare, or maybe it was neither. There were flashes of, well . . . lots of places and people and things and—" I stop myself and try to focus. "Perfer et obdura; dolor hic tibi proderit olim?"

"What?" he says groggily.

"The Latin that I said earlier, is that what I said?"

"Yeah, it sounds like it. Jesus, Joyce—"

"Be patient and tough; someday this pain will be useful to you," I blurt out. "That's what it means."

He is quiet and then he sighs. "Okay, thanks."

"Somebody told me that once. Tonight, they told me."

"You don't have to explain."

Silence.

"I'm going back to sleep now."

"Okay."

"Are you okay, Joyce?"

"I'm fine. Perfect." My voice catches in my throat. "Good night."

Then he's gone.

A single tear rolls down my cheek, and I wipe it away before it reaches my chin. Don't start, Joyce. Don't you dare start now.

Chapter 17

◇◇◇◇◇

A S I MAKE MY WAY downstairs the following morning, I spy Dad placing Mum's photograph back on the hall table. He hears me approaching, whips out his handkerchief from his pocket, and pretends he's dusting it.

"Ah, there she is. Muggins has risen from the dead."

"Yes, well, the toilet flushing every fifteen minutes kept me awake for most of the night." I kiss the top of his almost hairless head and go into the kitchen. I sniff the smoky atmosphere again.

"I'm very sorry that my prostate is bothering your sleep." He studies my face. "What's wrong with your eyes?"

"My marriage is over, and so I decided to spend the night crying," I explain matter-of-factly, hands on hips.

He softens a bit but sticks the knife in regardless. "I thought that's what you wanted."

"Yes, Dad, you're absolutely right, the past few weeks have been every girl's dream."

He moves up and down, down and up, to the kitchen table, takes his usual seat in the path of the sun's beam, props his glasses on the base of his nose, and continues his Sudoku. I watch him for a while, mesmerized by his simplicity, and then continue my sniffing mission.

"Did you burn the toast again?" He doesn't hear me and keeps scribbling away. I check the toaster. "It's on the right setting, I don't understand how it's still burning." I look inside. No crumbs. I check the bin—no toast thrown out. I sniff the air again, grow suspicious, and watch Dad from the corner of my eye. He fidgets.

"You're like that Fletcher woman or that Monk man from TV, snooping around. You'll find no corpses here," he says without looking up from his puzzle.

"Yes, but I'll find something, won't I?"

His head jerks up, quickly. Nervously. Aha. I narrow my eyes.

"What's up with you?"

I ignore him and race around the kitchen, opening drawers, searching inside each one of them.

He looks worried. "Have you lost your mind? What are you doing?"

"Did you take your pills?" I ask, coming across the medicine cabinet.

"What pills?"

With a response like that, there's definitely something up.

"Your heart pills, memory pills, vitamin pills."

"No, no, and . . ." He thinks for a second. ". . . no."

I bring them over to him, line them up on the table. He relaxes a little. Then I continue searching the cupboards, and I feel him tense again. I pull on the knob to the cereal cupboard—

"Water!" he shouts, and I jump and bang the door closed.

"Are you okay?" I ask.

"Yes," he says calmly. "I just need a glass of water for my pills. Glasses are in that cupboard over there." He points to the other end of the kitchen.

Suspiciously, I go and fill a glass with water and deliver it to him. I return to the cereal cupboard.

"Tea!" he shouts. "Let's have a cup of tea. I'll even make it for you. You've been through such a tough time, and you've been great about it all. So brave. Trophy brave, as they say. Now sit down there, and I'll fetch you a cuppa. A nice bit of cake as well. Battenburg—you liked that as a wee one. Always tried to take the marzipan off when no one was lookin', the greedy goat that you were." He tries to steer me back to the table.

"Dad—," I warn. He stops dithering and sighs in surrender.

I open the cupboard door and look inside. Nothing odd or out of place, just the porridge I eat every morning and the Sugar Puffs that I never touch. Dad looks satisfied, lets out a hearty harrumphing sound, and makes his way back to the table. Hold on a minute. I open the door again and reach for the Sugar Puffs that I never eat and never see Dad eat. As soon as I lift it, I know that it's empty of cereal. I look inside.

"Dad!"

"Ah, what, love?"

"Dad, you promised me!" I take out the packet of cigarettes and hold it in front of his face.

"I only had one, love."

"You have not had only one. That smell of smoke every morning is not burned toast. You lied to me!"

"One a day is hardly going to kill me."

"That's exactly what it's going to do. You've had bypass surgery, you're not supposed to smoke at all! I turn a blind eye to your morning fry-ups, but this, this is unacceptable," I tell him.

Dad rolls his eyes and holds his hand up like a puppet's mouth, mimicking me as he snaps it open and closed.

"That's it, I'm calling your doctor."

His mouth drops, and he jumps out of his chair. "No, love, don't do that."

I march out to the hall, and he chases after me. Up, down, down, up, up, down. Goes down on his right, bends his left.

"Ah, you wouldn't do that to me. If the cigarettes don't kill me, the doctor will. She's a battle-ax, that woman."

I pick up the phone that's beside Mum's photograph and dial the emergency number I've memorized. The first number that comes to my mind when I need to help the most important person in my life.

"If Mum knew what you were doing, she would go berserk— Oh." I pause as it hits me. "That's why you hide the photograph?"

Dad looks down at his hands and nods sadly. "She made me promise I'd stop. If not for me, for her. I didn't want her to see," he adds in a whisper, as though she can hear us.

"Hello?" There's a response on the other end of the phone. "Hello? Is that you, Dad?" says a young girl with an American accent.

"Oh—" I'm puzzled, but snap out of it. Dad looks pleadingly at me. "Pardon me," I speak into the phone. "Hello?"

"Oh, I'm sorry, I saw an Irish number and thought you were my dad," the voice on the other end explains.

"That's okay," I say, confused.

Dad is standing before me with his hands together in prayer.

"I was looking for . . ." Dad shakes his head wildly, and I stall.

"Tickets to the show?" the girl asks.

I frown. "To what show?"

"The Royal Opera House."

"Sorry," I say, and rub my eyes tiredly. "Your voice is so familiar, but I can't place it."

Dad rolls his eyes and sits on the bottom stair.

"I'm Bea. And *you* called *me*, by the way."

I try to think of how I can know an American girl named Bea, and as soon as I close my eyes, I hear a singsong voice penetrate my thoughts. A woman singing "Buzzy Bee" over and over. A little girl with white-blond hair wearing a tutu, the same little girl from my dreams, looks at me and giggles from behind an open door.

She places a tiny finger over her lips and hops up and down with excitement. The woman's voice gets closer, and she enters the room; it's the familiar woman with the red hair, and she looks at me. She smiles lovingly, adoringly at me, then tiptoes around the room, calling "Buzzy Bee, Buzzy Bee." The scene then ends in my mind, and I'm afraid to open my eyes. Afraid of what's happening to me again, but as soon as that memory fades, another appears. The blond girl again, older this time, a teenager, looking at me with anger, a face of thunder. We're in the same room as before, hardwood floors and bright white walls filled with cornicing, panels, a wall of shelves bursting with books. "My name isn't Buzzy Bee," she's shouting at me, "it's Bea! And I can do what I want!" A short skirt and long legs stride angrily away from me, and the door that only seconds ago she had hidden behind as a child bangs closed, knocking a book from the shelf and to the floor. Another face comes into focus, angry—the woman with the red hair. She says nothing but throws me a look. A look of love in the last memory, hatred in this one. I open my eyes, unable to take anymore, and I'm back in Dad's hall with the phone to my ear, my heart pounding in my chest. Dad has moved from the stairs and now stands before me, thrusting a glass of water toward me, looking at me nervously.

"Hello?" a voice calls from the other end of the phone. "Is anybody there? Hello?"

"Hello?" I force myself to speak, and my voice is shaky.

"Well, who is this?" Her tone is harder.

"Joyce." My voice is not much louder than a whisper. "I'm sorry, Bea, I think I've dialed the wrong number. Have I called America?"

Happy there isn't a stalker on the other end, her tone is friendly again. "You've called London," she explains. "I saw the Irish number and thought you were my dad. He's not Irish—he's American—but he's flying back from Dublin tonight to make it to my show tomorrow, and I was worried because I'm still a student and it's such a huge deal and I thought he was . . . sorry, I have absolutely no idea why I'm explaining this to you, but I'm so nervous." She laughs and takes a deep breath. "Technically, this is his emergency number."

"I dialed my emergency number too," I say faintly.

"Oh, freaky," she says. "Maybe our wires got crossed, that happens, doesn't it? People can just tune in to each other sometimes, can't they? A friend of mine can often pick up his neighbor's phone conversations when he listens to his radio. Weird, huh?"

I feel weak at the knees at the mention of her American father. Too many coincidences, far too many. But surely I'm just piecing together something that I wish to be the truth. "This may sound like a stupid question, but are you blond?"

Dad sits back down on the staircase and sips the water himself, watching me worriedly.

"Yeah! Why, do I sound blond? Maybe that's not such a good thing," she says.

I have a lump in my throat and must stop speaking. "Just a silly guess," I force out.

"Good guess," she says curiously. "Well, I hope everything's okay. You said you dialed your emergency number?"

"Yes, thanks, everything's fine."

She laughs. "Well, this was weird. I better go. Nice talking to you, Joyce."

"Nice talking to you too, Bea. Best of luck with your ballet show."

"Oh, sweet, thank you."

We say our good-byes, and with a shaking hand I replace the handset.

"You silly dope, did you just dial the Americas?" Dad says, putting his glasses on and pressing a button on the phone. "Joseph down the road showed me how to do this when I was getting the cranky calls. You can see who's called you and who you've called too. Turns out it was Fran bumping off her hand phone. The grandchildren got it for her last Christmas, and she's done nothing with it but wake me up at all hours. Anyway, there it is. First few numbers are 0044. Where's that?"

"That's the UK."

"Why on earth did you do that? Were you trying to trick me? Christ, that alone was enough to give me a heart attack."

"Sorry, Dad." I lower myself to the bottom stair, feeling shaky. "I don't know where I got that number from."

"Well, that sure taught me a lesson," he says insincerely. "I'll never smoke again. No sirree, Bob. Give me those cigarettes, and I'll throw them out."

I hold my hand out, feeling dazed.

He snaps the packet up and shoves it deep into his trouser pocket. "I hope you'll be paying for that phone call, because my pension certainly won't be." He narrows his eyes. "What's up with you?"

"I'm going to London," I blurt out.

"What?" His eyes pop open wildly. "Christ Almighty, Gracie, it's just one thing after another with you."

"I have to find some answers to . . . something. I have to go to London. Come with me," I urge, standing up and stepping toward him. If I go to a doctor, they may lock me away, put me on medication for whatever is wrong with me. If I go to London, I can find out for myself, find out if Bea is the Bea in my dreams and if her father is the man I can't get out of my head. It's a long shot, I know, but . . . well, it's all I have, and I'm clinging to it before I lose that too.

Dad begins to walk backward with his hand held protectively over his pocket containing the cigarettes.

"I can't go to London," he says nervously.

"Why not?"

"I've never been away from here in my life!"

"All the more reason to go away now," I say intensely. "If you're going to smoke, you might as well see outside of Ireland before you kill yourself."

"There are numbers I can call about being spoken to like that. Don't think I haven't heard about all that abuse that children do to their elderly parents!"

"Don't play the victim—you know I'm looking out for you. Come to London with me, Dad. Please."

"But, but," he says as he keeps moving backward, his eyes wide, "I can't miss the Monday Club."

"We'll go tomorrow morning, be back before Monday, I promise."

"But I don't have a passport."

"You just need photo ID."

We're approaching the kitchen now.

"But we've nowhere to stay." He passes through the door.

"We'll book a hotel."

"It's too expensive."

"We'll share a room."

"But I won't know where anything is in London."

"I know my way; I've been plenty of times."

"But . . ." He bumps into the kitchen table and cannot move back any farther. His face is a picture of terror. "I've never been on a plane before."

"There's nothing to it. You'll probably have a great time up there. And I'll be right beside you, talking to you the whole time."

He looks unsure.

"What is it?" I ask gently.

"What will I pack? What will I need for over there? Your mother usually packed all my going-away bags."

"I'll help you pack." I smile, getting excited. "This is going to be so much fun—you and me on our first overseas holiday!"

Dad looks excited for a moment; then the excitement fades. "No, I'm not going. I can't swim. If the plane goes down, I can't swim. I'll fly with you somewhere, but not over the seas."

"Dad, we live on an island; everywhere we go outside of this country has to be over the sea. And there are life jackets on the plane."

"Is that so?"

"Yeah, you'll be fine," I assure him. "They show you what to do in case of emergencies, but believe me, there won't be one. I've flown dozens of times without so much as a hiccup. You'll have a great time. And imagine all the things you'll have to tell the gang at the Monday Club! They'll hardly believe their ears, they'll want to hear your stories all day."

A smile slowly creeps onto Dad's lips, and he concedes. "Big-mouth Donal will have to listen to someone else tell a more inter-esting story for a change. I think secretary Maggie might be able to clear a spot for me in the schedule, all right." His smile then changes to a look of curiosity. "What are we going for?"

I search my mind for an answer. "For me, Dad." I feel my eyes well, and I battle the tears. If I start now, I'll never stop. "I need to get away from here."

"Right." He nods firmly. "And I'll be beside you all the way, love."

Chapter 18

◇◇◇◇◇

"FRAN'S OUTSIDE, DAD. WE HAVE to go!"

"Hold on, love, I'm just making sure everything's okay."

"Everything's fine," I assure him. "You've checked five times already."

"You can never be too sure. You hear these stories of televisions malfunctioning and toasters exploding and people coming back from their holidays to a pile of smouldering ash instead of their house." He checks the socket switches in the kitchen for the umpteenth time.

Fran beeps the horn again.

"I swear one of these days I'm going to throttle that woman. Beep beep beep yourself," he calls back.

"Dad," I take his hand, "we really have to go now. The house will be fine. All your neighbors will keep an eye on it. Any little noise outside, and their noses are pressed up against their windows. You know that."

He nods but still looks about, his eyes watering.

"We'll have great fun, really we will. What are you worried about?"

"That damn Fluffy cat, comin' into my garden and pissin' on my plants. I'm worried that the stranglers will suffocate my poor petunias and snapdragons, and that there'll be no one to keep an eye on my chrysanthemums. What if there's wind and rain when we're away? I haven't staked the plants yet, and the flowers get heavy and might break. Do you know how long the magnolia took to settle? Planted it when you were a wee one, while your mother was lying out catchin' the sun and laughin' at Mr. Henderson from next door, God rest his soul, who was peekin' out the curtains at her legs. And what about your cactus? Who'll water that for you?"

Beep, beeeeeeep. Fran presses down on the horn.

"It's only a few days, Dad. The garden will be fine. You can get to work on it as soon as we get back."

"Okay, fine." He takes one last look around and makes his way to the door.

I watch his figure swaying, dressed in his Sunday finest: a three-piece suit, shirt and tie, extra-shined shoes, and his tweed cap, of course, which he'd never be seen without outside the house. He looks as though he's jumped straight from the photographs on the wall beside him. He stalls at the hall table and reaches for the photograph of Mum.

"You know your mother was always at me to go to London with her." He pretends to wipe a smudge on the glass, but really he runs his finger over Mum's face.

"Bring her with you, Dad."

"Ah, no, that'd be silly," he says confidently, but looks at me unsurely. "Wouldn't it?"

"I think it'd be a great idea. The three of us will go and have a great time."

His eyes tear up again, and with a simple nod of the head, he slides the photo frame into his overcoat pocket and exits the house to more of Fran's beeping.

"Ah, there you are, Fran," he calls to her as he sways down the garden path. "You're late, we've been waiting for you for ages."

"I was beeping, Henry—did you not hear me?"

"Were you now?" He gets into the car. "You should press it a little harder the next time; we couldn't hear a thing in there."

As I slide the key into the lock, the phone sitting just inside the hall begins ringing. I look at my watch. Seven a.m. Who on earth would be calling so early?

Fran's car beeps again, and I turn round angrily and see Dad leaning over Fran's shoulder, pushing his hand down on the steering wheel.

"There you go now, Fran. We'll hear you the next time. Come on, love, we've a plane to catch!" He laughs uproariously.

I ignore the ringing phone and hurry to the car with the bags.

"There's no answer." Justin paces the living room in a panic. He tries the number again. "Why didn't you tell me about this yesterday, Bea?"

Bea rolls her eyes. "Because I didn't think it'd be such a big deal. People get wrong numbers all the time."

"But it wasn't a wrong number." He stops walking and taps his foot impatiently to the sound of the rings.

"That's exactly what it was."

Answering machine. Damn it! Do I leave a message?

He hangs up and frantically dials again.

Bored with his antics, Bea sits on the garden furniture in the living room and looks around the sheet-covered room and at the walls filled with dozens of color samples. "When is Doris going to have this place finished?"

"After she starts," Justin snaps, dialing again.

"My ears are burning," Doris sings, appearing at the door in a pair of leopard-print overalls, her face heavily made up as usual. "Found these yesterday, aren't they adorable?" She laughs. "Buzzy-Bea, sweetie, so lovely to see you!" She rushes to her niece, and they embrace. "We are so excited about your performance tonight, you have no idea. Little Buzzy-Bea all grown up and performing in the Royal Opera House." Her voice rises to a screech. "Oh, we are so proud, aren't we, Al?"

Al enters the room with a chicken leg in his hand. "Mmm-hmm."

Doris looks him up and down with disgust, and then back to her niece. "A bed for the spare room arrived yesterday morning, so you'll actually have something to sleep on when you stay, won't that be a treat?" She glares at Justin. "I also got some paint and fabric samples so we can start planning your room design, but I'm only designing according to feng shui rules. I won't hear of anything else."

Bea freezes. "Oh, gee, great."

"I know we'll have such fun!"

Justin eyes his daughter. "That's what you get for withholding information."

"What information? What's going on?" Doris ties her hair up in a cerise pink scarf and makes a bow at the top of her head.

"Dad is having a conniption fit," Bea explains.

"I told him to go to the dentist already. He has an abscess, I'm sure of it," Doris says matter-of-factly.

"I told him too," Bea agrees.

"No, not that. The woman," Justin says intensely. "Remember the woman I was telling you about?"

"Sarah?" Al asks.

"No!" Justin responds impatiently.

"Who can keep up with you?" Al shrugs him off. "Certainly not Sarah, when you're running at top speed after Viking buses and leaving her behind."

Justin cringes. "I apologized."

"To her voice mail," Al chuckles. "She is never going to answer your calls again."

I wouldn't blame her.

"Are you talking about the déjà vu woman, Justin?" Doris gasps, realizing.

"Yes." Justin gets excited. "Her name is Joyce, and she called Bea yesterday."

"She may not have." Bea's protests falls on deaf ears. "A woman named Joyce rang yesterday. But I do believe there's more than one Joyce in the world."

Ignoring her, Doris gasps again. "How can this be? How do you know her name, Justin?"

"I heard somebody call her that on the Viking bus. And yesterday Bea got a phone call on her emergency number, a number that no one has but me, from a woman in Ireland." Justin pauses for dramatic effect. "Named Joyce."

There's silence. Justin nods his head knowingly. "Yep, I know. Spooky, huh?"

Frozen in place, Doris widens her eyes. "Spooky, all right." She turns to Bea. "You're eighteen years old, and you've given your father an emergency number?"

Justin groans in frustration and starts dialing again.

Bea's cheeks are pink. "Before he moved over, Mum wouldn't let him call at certain hours because of the time difference. So I got another number. It's not technically an emergency number, but he's the only one who has it, and every time he calls he seems to have done something wrong."

"Not true," Justin objects.

"Sure," Bea responds breezily, picking up and flicking through a magazine. "And I'm not moving in with Peter."

"You're right, you're not. Peter"—he spits out the name— "picks strawberries for a living."

"I love strawberries." Al offers his support. "If it wasn't for Petey, I wouldn't get to eat 'em."

"Peter is an IT consultant." Bea shrugs her shoulders in confusion.

Choosing this moment to butt in, Doris turns to Justin. "Sweetie, you know I'm rooting for you and the déjà vu lady—"

"Joyce, her name is Joyce."

"Whatever, but you got nothing but a coincidence. And I'm all for coincidences, but this is . . . well, it's a pretty dumb one."

"I have not got nothing, Doris, and that sentence is atrociously wrong on so many grammatical levels, you wouldn't believe. I have got a name, and now I have a number." He walks over to Doris and squeezes her face in his hands, pushing her cheeks together so that her lips puff out. "And that, Doris Hitchcock, means that I got something!"

"It also makes you a stalker," Bea says under her breath.

You are now leaving Dublin. We hope you enjoyed your stay.

Dad's rubber ears go back on his head, his bushy eyebrows lift upward, as we reach the airport.

"You'll tell all the family that I said good-bye, won't you, Fran?" Dad says a little nervously.

"Of course I will, Henry. You'll have a great time." Fran's eyes smile at me knowingly in the rearview mirror.

"I'll see them all when I come back," Dad adds, closely watching a plane as it disappears to the skies. "It's off behind the clouds now," he says, looking at me unsurely.

"The best part." I smile.

He relaxes a little.

Fran pulls over at the drop-off section, busy with people conscious that they can't stay for more than a minute and quickly unloading bags, hugging, paying taxi drivers. Dad stands still and takes it all in, like the rock thrown into the stream again, as I lift the bags from the trunk. Eventually he snaps out of it and turns his attention to Fran, suddenly filled with warm affection for a woman he usually can't stop bickering with. Then he surprises us all by offering her a hug, awkward as it is.

Once inside, in the hustle and bustle of one of Europe's busiest airports, Dad holds on to my arm tightly with one hand and with the other pulls along the weekend bag I've lent him. It took me the entire day and night to convince him it wasn't anything like the tartan rolling suitcases Fran and all the other older ladies use for their shopping. He looks around now, and I see him registering men with similar bags. He looks happy, if still a little confused. We go to the computers to check in.

"What are you doing? Getting the sterling pounds out?"

"It's not an ATM, this is check-in, Dad."

"Do we not speak to a person?"

"No, this machine does it for us."

"I wouldn't trust this yoke." He looks over the shoulder of the man beside us. "Excuse me, is your yokey-mabob working for you?"

"Scusi?"

Dad laughs. "Scoozy-woozy to you too." He looks back at me with a grin on his face. "Scoozy. That's a good one."

"Mi dispiace tanto, signore, la prego di ignorarlo, è un vecchio sciocco e non sa cosa dice," I apologize to the Italian man, who seemed more than taken aback by Dad's comments. I have no idea what I've said, but he returns my smile and continues checking in.

"You speak Italian?" Dad looks surprised, but I haven't time to consider my new skill while an announcement is being made. "Shhh, Gracie, it might be for us. We better hurry."

"We have two hours until our flight."

"Why did we come so early?"

"We have to." I'm already getting tired now, and the tireder I get, the shorter my answers get.

"Who says?"

"Security."

"Security who?"

"Airport security. Through there." I nod in the direction of the metal detectors.

"Where do we go now?" he asks once I retrieve our boarding passes from the machine.

"To check our bags in."

"Can we not carry them on?"

"No." I walk us toward the counter

"Hello," a woman immediately greets us, then takes my passport and Dad's ID.

"Hello," Dad says chirpily, a saccharine smile forcing itself through the wrinkles of his permanently grumpy face.

I roll my eyes. Always a sucker for the ladies.

"How many bags are you checking in?"

"Two."

"Did you pack your own bags?"

"Yes."

"No." Dad nudges me and frowns. "You packed my bag for me, Gracie."

I sigh. "Yes, but you were with me, Dad. We packed it together."

"Not what she asked." He turns back to the lady. "Is that okay?"

"Yes." She continues, "Did anybody ask you to carry anything for them on the plane?"

"N—"

"Yes," Dad interrupts me again. "Gracie put a pair of her shoes in my bag because they wouldn't fit in hers. We're only going for a couple of days, you know, and she brought three pairs. Three."

"Do you have anything sharp or dangerous in your hand luggage—scissors, tweezers, lighters, or anything like that?"

"No," I say.

Dad squirms and doesn't respond.

"Dad"—I elbow him—"tell her no."

"No," he finally says.

"Well done," I snap.

"Have a pleasant trip." She hands us back our IDs.

"Thank you. You have very nice lipstick," Dad adds before I pull him away.

I take deep breaths as we approach the security gates, and I try to remind myself that this is Dad's first time in an airport, and that if you've never heard the questions before, particularly if you're a seventy-five-year-old, they might indeed seem quite strange.

"Are you excited?" I ask, trying to make the moment enjoyable.

"Delirious, love," he says sarcastically.

I give up and keep to myself.

I collect a clear plastic bag and fill it with my makeup and his pills, and we make our way through the maze that is the security queue.

"Just do what they say," I tell him when we get to the security gates. "You won't cause any trouble, will you?"

"Trouble? Why would I cause trouble? What are you doing? Why are you taking your clothes off?"

I groan quietly. "Dad, you don't understand. I really have to get to London. I can't explain it to you now because you won't understand, I barely do, but I *have* to be there, so please, please just comply. This is what we're supposed to do, okay?" I give him a forced smile as I take off my belt and my coat.

"Sir, could you please remove your shoes, belt, overcoat, and cap?"

"What?" Dad laughs at him.

"Remove your shoes, belt, overcoat, and cap."

"I will do no such thing. You want me walking around in my socks?"

"Dad, just do it," I tell him.

"If I take my belt off, my trousers will fall down," he says angrily.

"You can hold them up with your hands," I snap.

"Christ Almighty," he says loudly.

The young security officer looks round to his colleagues.

"Dad, just do it," I say more firmly now. An extremely long queue of irritated seasoned travelers who already have their shoes, belts, and coats off is forming behind us.

"Empty your pockets, please." An older and angrier-looking security man steps in.

Dad looks uncertain.

"Oh, my God, Dad, this is not a joke. Just do it."

"Can I empty them away from her?" Dad nods at me.

"No, you'll do it right here."

"I'm not looking." I turn away, baffled.

I hear clinking noises as Dad empties his pockets.

"Sir, you were told you could not bring these things through with you."

I spin round to see the security man holding a lighter and toenail clippers in his hands, as well as the packet of cigarettes in the tray with the photograph of Mum. And a banana.

"Dad!" I say.

"Stay out of this, ma'am."

"Don't speak to my daughter like that. I didn't know I couldn't bring them. She said scissors and tweezers and water and—"

"Okay, we understand, sir, but we're going to have to take these from you."

"But that's my good lighter! And what'll I do without my clippers?"

"We'll buy new ones," I say through gritted teeth. "Now just do what they say."

"Okay, okay"—he waves his hands rudely at them—"keep the damn things."

"Sir, please remove your cap, jacket, shoes, and belt."

"He's an old man," I say to the security guard in a low voice so that the gathering crowd behind us doesn't hear. "He needs a chair to sit on to take off his shoes. And he shouldn't have to take them off as they're corrective footwear. Can you not just let him through?"

"The nature of his right shoe means that we must check it," the man begins to explain, but Dad overhears and explodes.

"Do you think I have a *bomb in my shoe?* What kind of eejit would do that? Do you think I have a *bomb* sittin' behind my belt? Is my banana really a *gun,* do you think?" He waves the banana around at the staff, making shooting sounds. "Have you all gone loony in here?"

Dad reaches for his cap. "Or maybe I've a *grenade* under my—"

He doesn't have the opportunity to finish his sentence as everything suddenly goes crazy. He is whisked away right in front of my eyes before I can do anything.

Then I am taken to a small cell-like room and ordered to wait.

Chapter 19

◇◇◇◇◇

A FTER FIFTEEN MINUTES OF SITTING alone in the sparse interrogation room with nothing but a table and chair, I hear the door in the next room open, then close. I hear the squeak of chair legs, and then Dad's voice, as always, louder than everyone else's. I move closer to the wall and press my ear up against it.

"Who are you traveling with?"

"Gracie."

"Are you sure about that, Mr. Conway?"

"Of course! She's my daughter, ask her yourself!"

"Her passport tells us her name is Joyce. Is she lying to us, Mr. Conway? Or are you the one lying?"

"I'm not lying. Oh, I meant Joyce, I meant to say Joyce."

"Are you changing your story now?"

"What story? I got the name wrong, is all. My wife is Gracie, I get confused."

"Where is your wife?"

"She's not with us anymore. She's in my pocket. I mean, the photograph of her is in my pocket. At least, it was in my pocket until the lads out there took her and put her in the tray.

Will I get my toenail clippers back, do you think? They cost me a bit."

"Mr. Conway, you were told sharp items and lighter fluid are not permitted on the flights."

"I know that, but my daughter, Gracie—I mean, Joyce—got mad at me yesterday when she found my pack of smokes hidden in the Sugar Puffs, and I didn't want to take the lighter out of my pocket or she'd lose her head again. I apologize for that, though. I wasn't intending to blow up the plane or anything."

"Mr. Conway, please refrain from using such language. Why did you refuse to take off your shoes?"

"I have holes in me socks!"

Silence.

"I'm seventy-five years old, young man. Why on earth do I have to take my shoes off? Did you think I was going to blow the plane up with a rubber shoe? Or maybe it's the insoles you're worried about. Maybe you're right to arrest me, you can never tell the damage a man can do with a good insole—"

"Mr. Conway, please don't use such language, and refrain from smart-aleck behavior, or you will not be allowed on the plane. You haven't been arrested. We just need to ask you some questions. Behavior such as yours is prohibited at this airport, so we need to ascertain if you are a threat to the safety of our passengers."

"What do you mean, a threat?"

A man clears his throat. "Well, it means finding out if you are a member of any gangs or terrorist organizations before we reconsider allowing you through."

I hear Dad roar with laughter.

"You must understand that planes are very confined spaces, and we can't allow anybody through that we aren't sure of. We have the right to choose who we allow on board."

"The only threat I'd be in a confined space is when I've had a good curry from my local. And terrorist organizations? I'm a member of one, all right. The Monday Club. We meet every Monday except on bank holidays, when we meet on a Tuesday. A bunch of lads and lasses like me gettin' together for a few pints and a sing-song is all it is. Though if you're lookin' for juice, Donal's family was pretty heavily involved in the IRA—"

I hear the man clear his throat again.

"Donal?"

"Donal McCarthy. Ah, leave him alone, he's ninety-seven, and I'm talkin' about way back when his dad fought. The only rebellious thing he's able to do now is whack the chessboard with his cane, and that's only because he's frustrated he can't play. Arthritis in both his hands. Could do with g'ttin' it in his mouth, if you ask me. Talkin' is all he does. Annoys Peter to no end, but they've never gotten along since he courted Peter's daughter and broke her heart. She's seventy-two. Have you ever heard anything more ridiculous? Had a wandering eye, she claimed, but sure, Donal's as cockeyed as they come. His eye wanders without him even knowing it. I wouldn't blame the man for that, though he does like to dominate the conversations every week. I can't wait for him to listen to me for a change." Dad laughs and sighs in the long pause that follows. "Do you think I could get a cuppa?"

"We won't be much longer, Mr. Conway. What is the nature of your visit to London?"

"I'm going because my daughter dragged me here, last minute. She gets off the phone yesterday morning and looks at me with a face as white as a sheet. I'm off to London, she says, like it's somethin' you just do last minute. Ah, maybe it is what you young people do, but not me. Not what I'm used to at all, at all. Never been on a plane before, you see. So she says, Wouldn't it be fun if we both go away? And usually I'd say no, I've loads to be doin' in my garden. Have to put down the lilies, tulips, daffodils, and hyacinths in time for the spring, you see, but she says live a little, and I felt like peltin' her because it's more livin' I've been doing than her.

But because of recent—well, troubles, shall we say—I decided to come with her. And that's no crime, is it?"

"What recent troubles, Mr. Conway?"

"Ah, my Gracie—"

"Joyce."

"Yes, thank you. My Joyce, she's been goin' through a rough patch. Lost her little baby a few weeks back. Had been trying to have one for years with a fella that plays tennis in little white shorts and things finally looked great but she had an accident. Fell, you see, and she lost the little one. Lost a little of herself too, if I'm to be honest with you. Also lost the husband just last week, but don't you be feelin' sorry for her about that—she somehow got a little somethin' in the process she never had before. Can't put my finger on exactly what, but whatever it is, I don't think it's such a bad thing. Generally things aren't goin' right for her, and sure, what kind of a father would I be to let her go off on her own in this state? She's got no job, no baby, no husband, no mother, and soon no house, and if she wants to go to London for a break, even if it is last minute, then she sure as hell is entitled to go without any more people stopping her from what she wants.

"Here, take my bloody cap. My Joyce is a good girl, never did a thing wrong in her life. She has nothing right now but me and this trip, as far as I can see. So here, take it. If I have to go without my cap and my shoes and my belt and my coat, well, that's fine by me, but my Joyce isn't going to London without her father."

Well, if that isn't enough to break a girl.

"Mr. Conway, you do know that you get your clothing back once you go through the metal detector?"

"What?" he shouts. "Why the hell didn't she tell me that? All this feckin' nonsense for nothing. Honestly, you'd think she almost wants the trouble sometimes. Okay, lads, you can take my things. Will we still make the flight, do you think?"

Any tears that had welled have instantly dried.

Finally the door to my cell opens, and with a single nod, I'm a free woman.

"Doris, you cannot move the stove in the kitchen. Al, tell her."

"Why can't I?"

"Honey, first of all it's heavy, and second of all, it's gas. You are not qualified to move around kitchen appliances," Al explains, and prepares to bite into a doughnut.

Doris whisks it away from him, leaving him to lick dribbles of jam from his fingers. "You two don't seem to understand that it's bad feng shui to have a stove facing a door. The person at the stove may instinctively want to glance back at the door, which creates a feeling of unease, which can lead to accidents."

"Perhaps removing the stove altogether will be a safer option for Dad," Bea pipes in.

"You have to give me a break," Justin sighs, sitting down at the new kitchen table. "All the place needs is furniture and a lick of paint, not for you to restructure the entire place according to Yoda."

"It is not according to Yoda," Doris huffs. "Donald Trump follows feng shui, you know."

"Oh, well then," Al and Justin say in unison.

"Yes, well then. Maybe if you did what he did, you'd be able to walk up the stairs without having to take a lunch break halfway up," she snaps at Al. "Just because you sell tires, sweetie, doesn't mean you have to wear them too."

Bea's mouth drops, and Justin tries not to laugh. "Come on, Bea, let's get out of here before it turns to violence."

"Where are you two going? Can I come?" Al asks.

"I'm going to the dentist, and Bea has rehearsals for tonight."

"Good luck, blondie." Al ruffles her hair. "We'll be cheering for you."

"Thanks." She grinds her teeth and fixes her hair. "Oh, that reminds me. One more thing about the woman on the phone, Joyce?"

What, what, what? "What about her?"

"She knows that I'm blond."

"How did she know?" Doris asks with surprise.

"She said she just guessed. But that's not it. Before she hung up she said, 'Best of luck with your ballet show.' "

"So she's a thoughtful lucky-guesser." Al shrugs.

"Well, I was thinking about it afterward, and I don't remember telling her anything about my show being specifically ballet."

Justin immediately looks to Al, a little more concerned now that it involves his daughter, but adrenaline still surges. "What do you think?"

"I think watch your back, bro. She could be a fruitcake." He stands up and heads to the kitchen, rubbing his stomach. "Actually, that's not a bad idea. Fruitcake."

Deflated, Justin looks to his daughter. "Did she sound like a fruitcake?"

"I dunno." Bea shrugs. "What does a fruitcake sound like?"

Justin, Al, and Bea all turn to stare at Doris.

"What?" she squeals.

"No." Bea shakes her head wildly at her father. "Nothing like that at all."

"What's this for, Gracie?"

"It's a sick bag."

"What does this do?"

"It's for hanging your coat up."

"Why is that there?"

"It's a table."

"How do you get it down?"

"By unlatching it, at the top."

"Sir, please leave your tabletop up until after takeoff."

Silence, but only for a moment.

"What are they doing outside?"

"Loading the bags."

"What's that button?"

"An ejector seat for people who ask three million questions."

"What's it, really?"

"For reclining your chair."

"Sir, could you stay upright until after takeoff, please?"

Silence again.

Then, "What does that do?"

"Fan."

"What about that?"

"Light."

"And that one?"

"Yes, sir, can I help you?"

"You pressed the button for assistance."

"Oh, is that what that little woman on the button is for? I didn't know. Actually, can I have a drink of water?"

"We can't serve drinks until after takeoff, sir."

"Oh, okay. That was a fine display you did earlier. You were the image of my friend Edna when you had that oxygen mask on. She used to smoke sixty a day, you see."

The flight attendant makes an O shape with her mouth.

"I feel very safe now, but what if we go down over land?" He raises his voice, and the passengers around us look our way. "Surely the life jackets are hopeless, unless we blow our whistles while we're flying through the air and hope someone below hears and catches us. Do we not have parachutes?"

"There's no need to worry, sir, we won't go down over land."

"Okay. That's very reassuring, indeed. But if we do, tell the pilot to aim for a haystack or something."

I take deep breaths and pretend that I don't know him. I continue reading my book, *The Golden Age of Dutch Painting: Vermeer, Metsu and Terborch*, and try to convince myself this is not the bad idea it's turning out to be.

"Where are the toilets?"

"To the front and on the left, but you can't go until after takeoff," the attendant responds.

Dad's eyes widen. "And when will that be?"

"In just a few minutes."

"In just a few minutes, *that*"—he takes the sick bag out from the seat pocket—"won't be used for what it's supposed to be used for."

"We will be in the air in just a few minutes more, I assure you." The attendant leaves quickly before he can ask another question.

I sigh.

"Don't you be sighing until after takeoff," Dad says, and the man next to me laughs and pretends to turn it into a cough.

Dad looks out the window. "Oh oh oh," he sings, "we're moving now, Gracie."

As soon as we're off the ground, the wheels moan as they're brought back up, and then we are light in the air. Dad is suddenly quiet. He is turned sideways in his chair, head filling the window, watching as we reach the beginning of the clouds, mere wisps at first. The plane bumps around as it pushes through. Dad is agog as we're surrounded by white on all sides of the plane; his head darts around looking at every window possible, and then suddenly it is blue and calm above the fluffy world of clouds. Dad blesses himself. He pushes his nose up against the window, his face lit by the nearby sun, and I take a mental photograph for my own hall of memories.

The Fasten Seatbelt sign goes off with a *bing*, and the cabin crew announces that we may now use electronic devices and the facilities, and that food and refreshments will be served shortly. Dad takes down the tabletop, reaches into his pocket, and takes out his photograph of Mum. He places her on the table, facing out the window. He reclines his chair, and they both watch the endless sea of white clouds disappear below us and don't say a word for the remainder of the flight.

Chapter 20

◇◇◇◇◇

"WELL, I MUST SAY, THAT was absolutely marvelous. Marvelous indeed." Dad pumps the pilot's hand up and down enthusiastically.

We are standing by the just-opened door of the plane, with a queue of hundreds of irritated passengers huffing and puffing down our necks. They are like greyhounds whose trap has opened, with the bunny having been fired off ahead of them, and all that blocks their path is, well, Dad. The usual rock in the stream.

"And the food," Dad continues to the cabin crew, "it was excellent, just excellent."

All this over a ham roll and a cup of tea.

"I can't believe I was eating in the sky." He laughs. "Well done again, just marvelous. Nothing short of miraculous, I'd say. My Lord." He pumps the pilot's hand again, as though he's meeting JFK.

"Okay, Dad, we should move on now. We're holding everybody up."

"Oh, is that so? Thanks again, folks. 'Bye now. Might see you on the way back," he shouts over his shoulder as I pull him away.

We make our way through the tunnel adjoining the plane to the terminal, and Dad says hello and tips his hat to everyone we pass on the way to the baggage claim.

"You really don't have to say hello to everybody, you know."

"It's nice to be important, Gracie, but it's more important to be nice. Particularly when in another country," says the man who hasn't left the province of Leinster for ten years.

"Will you stop shouting?"

"I can't help it. My ears feel funny."

"Either yawn or hold your nose and blow. It will help your ears to pop."

He stands by the conveyor belt, purple-faced, with his cheeks puffed out and his fingers pinched over his nose. He takes a deep breath and pushes. He lets out a fart.

The conveyor belt jerks into motion, and like flies around a carcass, people suddenly swoop in front of us to block our view, as though their life depends on grabbing their bags this very second.

"There's your bag, Dad." I spot it and step forward.

"I'll get it, love."

"No, I will. You'll hurt your back."

"Step back, love, I can do it." He passes over the yellow line and grabs his bag, only to realize that the strength he once had is gone, and he finds himself walking alongside it while tugging away. Ordinarily I would rush to help him, but I'm doubled over laughing. All I can hear is Dad saying, "Excuse me, excuse me," to people who are standing over the yellow line as he tries to keep up with his moving luggage. He does a full lap of the conveyor belt, and by the time he gets back to where I stand (though I'm still doubled over), somebody has the common sense to help the out-of-breath grumbling old man.

He pulls his bag over to me, his face scarlet, his breathing heavy.

"I'll let you get your own bag," he says, pulling his cap farther down over his eyes in embarrassment.

I wait for my bag while Dad wanders around the baggage claim "acquainting himself with London." After the incident at the Dublin airport, the satellite navigational voice in my head has continuously nagged me to head back home, but somewhere inside, another part of me is under strict orders to soldier on, feeling convinced that this trip is the right thing to do. As I collect my bag from the belt, though, I am aware that there is no clear purpose for this trip. A wild goose chase is all it is right now. Instinct alone, caused by a confusing conversation with a girl named Bea, has caused me to fly to another country with my seventy-five-year-old father, someone who has never left Ireland in his entire life. Suddenly what seemed like the "only thing to do" at the time now appears to be completely irrational behavior.

What does it mean to dream about somebody you've never met, almost every night, and then have a chance encounter with them over the phone? I had called my dad's emergency number; she had answered her dad's emergency phone number. Surely there is a message in that. But what am I supposed to learn? Is it just a mere coincidence that an ordinary right-thinking person would ignore, or am I right to think and feel that something more lies beneath this? My hope is that this trip will have some answers for me. Panic begins to build as I watch Dad peering at a poster on the far side of the room. I have no idea what to do with him.

Suddenly Dad's hand flies to his head and then to his chest, and he darts toward me with a manic look in his eyes. I make a grab for his pills.

"Gracie," he gasps.

"Here, quickly, take these." My hand trembles as I hold out the pills and a bottle of water.

"What on earth are you doing?"

"Well, you looked . . ."

"I looked what?"

"Like you were going to have a heart attack!"

"That's because I bloody well will, if we don't get out of here quick." He grabs my arm and starts to pull me along.

"What's wrong? Where are we going?"

"We're going to Westminster."

"What? Why? No! Dad, we have to go to the hotel to leave our bags."

He stops walking and whips around to push his face close to mine, almost aggressively. His voice shakes with adrenaline. "The *Antiques Roadshow* is having a valuation day today from nine thirty to four thirty in a place called Banqueting House. If we leave now we can start lining up. I'm not going to miss seeing it on the telly and then come all the way to London just to miss seeing it in the flesh. We might even get to see Michael Aspel. Michael Aspel, Gracie. Christ Almighty, let's get out of here."

His pupils are dilated, he's all fired up. He shoots off through the sliding doors, with nothing to declare but temporary insanity, and takes a confident left.

I wait there in the arrivals hall while men in suits approach me with placards from all sides. I sigh and wait. Dad reappears from the direction he went in, seesawing and pulling his bag behind him at top speed.

"You could have told me that was the wrong way," he says, passing me and heading in the opposite direction.

Dad rushes through Trafalgar Square, pulling his suitcase behind him and scattering a flock of pigeons into the sky. He's not interested in acquainting himself with London anymore; he has only Michael Aspel and the treasures of the blue-rinse brigade in sight. We've taken a few wrong turns since surfacing from the tube station, but Banqueting House finally comes into view, a seventeenth-century former royal palace, and though I am sure I have never visited it before, it stands before me, a familiar sight.

We join the deep queue already forming outside, and I study the single drawer that is in the hands of the old man in front of us. Behind us, a woman is rolling out a teacup from a pile of newspapers. All around me there is excited and rather innocent and polite chatter, and the sun is shining as we wait to enter the Banqueting House reception area. There are TV vans, camera and sound people going in and out of the building, and cameras filming the long queue while a woman with a microphone picks people out of the crowd to interview. Many people in the queue have brought deck chairs, picnic baskets of scones and finger sandwiches, and canteens of tea and coffee, and as Dad looks around with a grumbling stomach, I feel guilty, like a bad mother who hasn't properly equipped her child. I'm also concerned for Dad that we won't make it past the front door.

"Dad, I don't want to worry you, but I really think that we're supposed to have something with us."

"What do you mean?"

"Like an object. Everybody else has things with them to be valued."

Dad looks around and seems to realize this for the first time. His face falls.

"Maybe they'll make an exception for us," I add quickly, but I doubt it.

"What about these cases?" He looks down at our bags.

I try not to laugh. "I got them at TJ Maxx; I don't think they'll be interested in valuing them."

Dad chuckles. "Maybe I'll give them my undies. You know there's a fine bit of history in them."

I make a face, and he waves his hand dismissively.

We shuffle along slowly in the queue, and Dad has a great time chatting with everybody about his life and his exciting trip with his daughter. After queuing for an hour and a half, we have been invited to two houses for afternoon tea, and the gentleman behind us has instructed Dad how to stop the mint in his garden from taking over the rosemary. Up ahead, just beyond the doors, I see an elderly couple being turned away. Dad sees this too and looks at me, his eyes worried. We will be up next pretty soon.

"Eh . . ." I look around quickly for something.

Both entrance doors have been held open for the flowing crowd. Just inside the main entrance, behind the opened doors, is a wooden wastebasket posing as an umbrella stand. When we reach the doors, and while no one is looking I turn it upside down, emptying it of a few scrunched balls of paper and forgotten umbrellas. I kick them behind the door just in time to hear, "Next."

I carry it up to the reception desk, and Dad's eyes pop out of his head at the sight of me.

"Welcome to Banqueting House," a young woman greets us.

"Thank you." I smile innocently.

"How many objects have you brought today?" she asks.

"Oh, just the one." I raise the bin onto the table.

"Oh, wow, fantastic." She runs her fingers along it, and Dad gives me a look that, if for any second I had forgotten which of us was the parent, would quickly remind me. "Have you been to a valuation day before?"

"No." Dad shakes his head wildly. "But I see it on the telly all the time. Big fan, I am. Even when Hugh Scully was host."

"Wonderful." She smiles. "Once you enter the hall you'll see there are many queues. Please join the queue for the appropriate discipline."

"What queue should we join for this thing?" Dad looks at the item as though there's a bad smell.

"Well, what is it?" she asks.

Dad looks at me, baffled.

"We were hoping you could tell us that," I say politely.

"I'd suggest miscellaneous, and though that is the busiest table, we try to move it along as quickly as possible by having four experts. Once you reach the expert's table, simply show your item, and he or she will tell you all about it."

"Which table do we go to for Michael Aspel?" Dad asks eagerly.

"Unfortunately Michael Aspel isn't actually an expert, he is the host, so he doesn't have a table of his own. But we do have twenty other experts that will be available to answer your questions."

Dad looks devastated.

"There is the chance that your item may be chosen for television," she adds quickly, sensing Dad's disappointment. "The expert shows the object to the television team, and a decision is made whether to record it, depending on rarity, quality, what the expert can say about the object, and, of course, value. If your object is chosen, you'll be taken to our waiting room and made up before talking to the expert about your object in front of the camera for about five minutes. You would meet Michael Aspel under those circumstances. And the exciting news is that for the first time, we are broadcasting the show live in . . . ooh, let's see"—she examines her watch—"in one hour."

Dad's eyes widen.

"Do bear in mind that we have to choose from two thousand people's items before the show," she says to me with a knowing look.

"We understand. We're just here to enjoy the day, isn't that right, Dad?"

He doesn't hear me; he's busy looking around for Michael Aspel.

"Enjoy your day," the woman says finally, calling the next person in line forward.

As soon as we enter the busy hall, I immediately look up at the ceiling of the double-cubed room, already knowing what to expect: nine huge canvases commissioned by Charles I to fill the paneled ceiling.

"Here you go, Dad." I hand him the wastebasket. "I'm going to take a look around this beautiful building while you look at the junk people are putting inside it."

"It's not junk, Gracie. I once saw a show where a man's collection of walking sticks went for sixty thousand pounds sterling."

"Wow, in that case you should show them your shoe."

He seems to consider it for a moment.

"Off you go to have a look around, and I'll meet you back here." He starts to wander away before he even finishes the sentence. Dying to get rid of me.

"Have fun." I wink.

He smiles broadly and looks around the hall with such happiness, my mind takes another photograph.

As I wander the rooms of the only part of the former Whitehall Palace to survive a fire, the feeling that I've been here before comes over me in a giant wave. I find a quiet corner and secretly produce my cell phone.

"Manager, deputy head corporate treasury and investor solutions desk, Frankie speaking."

"My God, you weren't lying. That's a ridiculous amount of words."

"Joyce! Hi!" Her voice is hushed but still audible over the manic sounds of the stock-trading in the Irish Financial Services Centre offices, behind her.

"Can you talk?"

"For a little bit, yeah. How are you?"

"I'm fine. I'm in London. With Dad."

"What? With your dad? Joyce, I've told you before it's not polite to bind and gag your father. What are you doing there?"

"I just decided to come over last minute." For what, I have no idea. "We're currently at the *Antiques Roadshow*. Don't ask."

I leave the quiet rooms behind me and enter the gallery of the main hall. Below me I can see Dad wandering around the crowds with the bin in his hands. I smile as I watch him.

"Frankie, have we ever been to Banqueting House together?"

"Refresh my memory: where is it, what is it, and what does it look like?"

"It's at the Trafalgar Square end of Whitehall. It's a former royal palace designed by Inigo Jones in 1619. Charles I was executed on a scaffold in front of the building. I'm in a room now with nine canvases covering the paneled ceiling." What does it look like? I close my eyes. "The roofline is balustrade. The street facade has two orders of engaged columns, Corinthian over Ionic, above a rusticated basement, which lock together in a harmonious whole."

"Joyce?"

"Yes?" I snap out of it.

"Are you reading from a tourist guide?"

"No."

"Our last trip to London consisted of Madame Tussaud's, a night at G-A-Y, and a party at a flat owned by a man named Gloria. It's happening again, isn't it? That thing you were talking about?"

"Yes." I slump into a chair in the corner, feel a rope beneath me, and jump back up. I quickly move away from the antique chair, looking around for security cameras.

"Has your being in London got anything to do with the American man?"

"Yes," I whisper.

"Oh, Joyce—"

"No, Frankie, listen. Listen, and you'll understand. I hope. Yesterday I panicked about something and called Dad's doctor, a number that is practically engraved in my head, as it should be. I couldn't possibly get it wrong, right?"

"Right."

"Wrong. I ended up dialing a UK number, and a girl named Bea answered the phone. So from our short conversation I figured out that her dad is American but was in Dublin and was traveling to London last night to see her in a show today. And she has blond hair. I think Bea is the little girl I keep dreaming about at different ages."

Frankie is quiet.

"I know I sound insane, Frankie, but this is what's happening. I have no explanation for it."

"I know, I know," she says quickly. "I've known you practically all my life, so I know this is not something you'd be inclined to make up. But even as I take you seriously, please keep in consideration the fact that you've had a traumatic time, and what you're currently experiencing could be due to high levels of stress."

"I've already considered that." I groan and hold my head in my hands. "I need help."

"We'll only consider insanity as a last resort. Let me think for a second." She sounds as though she's writing it all down. "So basically, you have seen this girl, Bea—"

"Maybe Bea."

"Okay, okay, let's just say it's Bea. You've seen her grow up?"

"Yes."

"To what age?"

"From birth to, I don't know . . ."

"Teenager, twenties, thirties?"

"Teenager."

"Okay, so who else is in the scenes with Bea?"

"Another woman. With a camera."

"But never your American man?"

"No. So he probably has nothing to do with this at all."

"Let's not rule anything out. So when you view Bea and the

lady with the camera, are you part of the scene or viewing them as an outsider?"

I close my eyes and think hard, see my hands pushing the swing, taking a photograph of the girl and her mother in the park, feeling the water from the sprinklers spray and tickle my skin . . . "No, I'm part of it. They can see me."

"Okay." She is silent.

"What, Frankie, what?"

"I'm figuring it out. Hold on. Okay. So you see a child, a mother, and they both see you?"

"Yes."

"Would you say that in your dreams you're viewing this girl grow up through the eyes of a father?"

Goose bumps form on my skin.

"Oh, my God," I whisper. The American man?

"I take it that's a yes," Frankie says. "Okay, we're onto something here. I don't know what, but it's something very weird, and I can't believe I'm even entertaining these thoughts. But what the hell, I only have a million other things to do. What else do you dream about?"

"It's all very fast, images just flashing by."

"Try and remember."

"Sprinklers in a garden. A chubby young boy. A woman with long red hair. I hear bells. See old buildings with shop fronts. A church. A beach. I'm at a funeral. Then at college. Then with the woman and the young girl. Sometimes the woman's smiling and holding my hand, sometimes she's shouting and slamming doors."

"Hmm . . . she must be your wife."

I bury my head in my hands again. "Frankie, this sounds so ridiculous."

"Who cares? When has life ever made sense? Let's keep going."

"I don't know, the images are all so abstract. I can't make any sense of it."

"What you should do this: every time you get a flash of something or suddenly know something you never knew, write it down and tell me. I'll help you figure this out."

"Thank you."

"So apart from the place you're in now, what kinds of things do you suddenly just know about?"

"Em . . . mostly buildings." I look around and then up at the ceiling. "And art. I spoke Italian to a man at the airport. And Latin, I spoke Latin to Conor the other day."

"Oh, God."

"I know. I think he wants to have me sent away."

"Well, we won't let him do that. Yet. Okay, so, buildings, art, languages. Wow, Joyce, it's like you've gotten a crash course in an entire college education you never had. Where is the culturally ignorant girl I once knew and loved?"

I smile. "She's still here."

"One more thing. My boss has called me for a meeting this afternoon. What is it about?"

"Frankie, I don't have psychic powers!"

The door to the gallery opens, and a flustered-looking young girl wearing a headset rushes in. She approaches almost every woman on her way in, and I can hear her asking for me.

"Joyce Conway?" she asks when she finally reaches me, out of breath.

"Yes." My heat beats a mile a minute. Please let Dad be okay. Please, God.

"Is your father Henry?"

"Yes."

"He wants you to join him in the green room."

"He what? In the what?"

"He's in the green room. He's going live with Michael Aspel in just a few minutes with his item, and he wants you to join him because he says you know more about it. We really have to move now, there's very little time, and we need to get you made up."

"Live with Michael Aspel . . ." I trail off. I realize I'm still holding the phone. "Frankie," I say, dazed, "put on BBC, quick. You're about to witness me getting into very big trouble."

Chapter 21

◇◇◇◇◇

I HALF WALK, HALF RUN behind the girl with the headset and reach the green room, panting and nervous, to see Dad sitting on a makeup chair facing a mirror lit up by bulbs, tissue tucked into his collar, a cup and saucer in his hand, his bulbous nose being powdered for his close-up.

"Ah, there you are, love," Dad says grandly. "Everybody, this is my daughter, and she'll be the one to tell us all about my lovely piece here that caught the eye of Michael Aspel." This is followed by a chuckle and a sip of tea. "There's Jaffa Cakes over there if you want them, Gracie."

Evil little man.

I look around the room at all the interested nodding heads and force a smile onto my face.

Justin squirms uncomfortably in his chair at the dentist's waiting room, his swollen cheek throbbing, sandwiched between two old dears carrying on about someone they know called Rebecca, who should leave a man named Timothy.

Shut up, shut up, shut up!

The 1970s television in the corner, which is covered by a lace cloth and fake flowers, announces that the *Antiques Roadshow* is about to begin.

Justin groans. "Does anybody mind if I change the channel?"

"I'm watching it," says a young boy no older than seven years old.

Justin smiles at him with loathing, then looks to his mother for backup.

Instead she shrugs. "He's watching it."

"Charming," Justin grunts in frustration.

"Excuse me." Justin finally interrupts the women to his right and left. "Would one of you ladies like to swap places with me, so that you can continue this conversation more privately?"

"No, don't worry, love, there's nothing private about this conversation, believe you me. Eavesdrop all you like."

The smell of her breath silently tiptoes under his nostrils again, tickles them with a feather duster, and runs off with an evil giggle.

"I wasn't eavesdropping. Your lips were quite literally in my ear, and I'm not sure if Charlie or Graham or Rebecca would appreciate that." He turns his nose away.

"Oh, Ethel"—the other laughs—"he thinks we're talking about real people."

With that, Justin turns his attention back to the television in the corner, which the other six people in the room are now glued to.

". . . And welcome to our first live *Antiques Roadshow* special . . ."

Justin sighs loudly again.

The little boy narrows his eyes at him and raises the volume with the remote control that is firmly in his grasp.

". . . coming to you from Banqueting House, London."

Oh, I've been there. A nice example of Corinthian and Ionic locked together in a harmonious whole.

"We have had over two thousand people spilling through our doors since nine thirty this morning, and only moments ago those doors have closed, leaving us to display the best pieces for you to view at home. Our first guests come from—"

Ethel leans across Justin and rests her elbow on his thigh. "So anyway, Margaret—"

He zones in on the television so as not to grab both their heads and smash them together.

"So what do we have here?" the host asks his two guests. "Looks like a designer wastebasket to me." The camera takes a close-up of the piece propped on the table.

Justin's heart begins to palpitate.

"Bo-ring. Do you want me to change it now, mister?" The boy flicks through the channels at top speed.

"No!" he shouts, breaking through Margaret and Ethel's conversation and reaching out rather dramatically. He falls to the carpet on his knees, in front of the television. Margaret and Ethel both jump and go silent. "Go back, go back, go back!" he shouts at the boy.

The boy's lower lip begins to tremble as he looks to his mother.

"There's no need to shout at him." She pulls his head to her chest protectively.

Justin grabs the remote control from the boy and flicks back through the channels. He stops when he comes upon a close-up of Joyce, whose eyes are looking uncertainly to the left and right, as though she has just landed in the cage of a Bengal tiger at feeding time.

At the Irish Financial Services Centre, Frankie is racing through the offices searching for a television. She finally finds one surrounded by dozens of suits studying the figures that are racing by on the screen.

"Excuse me! Coming through!" she shouts, pushing her way through. She rushes to the TV and starts fiddling with the buttons to cries of abuse from the men and women around her.

"I'll be quick, the market won't crash in all of the two minutes this will take." She flicks around and finds Joyce and her dad live on BBC.

She gasps and holds her hands up to her mouth. And then she laughs and throws her fist at the screen. "You go, Joyce!"

The team quickly shuffles off to find another screen, apart from one man, who seems pleased by the change in programming and decides to stay and watch.

"Oh, that's a nice piece," he comments, leaning back against the desk and folding his arms.

"Em . . ." Joyce is saying, "well, we found it . . . I mean we put it, put this beautiful . . . extraordinary . . . eh, wooden . . . bucket outside of our house. Well, not outside—" She quickly withdraws upon seeing the appraiser's reaction. "Inside. We put it inside our front porch so that it's protected from the weather, you see. For umbrellas."

"Yes, and it may have been originally used for that too," the appraiser says. "Where did you get it from?"

Joyce's mouth opens and closes for a few seconds, and Henry jumps in. He is standing upright with his hands clasped over his belly. His chin is raised, there is a glint in his eye, and he ignores the expert and takes on a posh accent to direct his answer at Michael Aspel, whom he addresses as though he's the pope.

"Well, Michael, I was given this by my great-great-grandfather Joseph Conway, who was a farmer in Tipperary. He gave it to my grandfather Shay, who was also a farmer. My grandfather gave it to my father, Paddy-Joe, who was also a farmer in Cavan, and then when he died, I took it."

"I see, and do you have any idea where your great-great-grandfather may have got this?"

"He probably stole it from the Brits," Henry jokes, and is the only one to laugh. Joyce elbows him, Frankie snorts, and on the floor before the television in a dentist's waiting room in London, Justin throws his head back and laughs loudly.

"Well, the reason I ask is because this is a fabulous item you have here. It's a rare nineteenth-century English Victorian era upright jardinière planter—"

"I love gardening, Michael," Henry interrupts the expert, "do you?"

Michael smiles at him politely, and the expert continues, "It has wonderful hand-carved Black Forest–style plaques set in the Victorian ebonized wood framing on all four sides."

"Country English or French decor, what do you think?" Frankie's work colleague asks her.

She ignores him, concentrating on Joyce.

"Inside it has what looks like an original tole painted tin liner. Superb condition, ornate patterns carved into the solid wood panels. We can see here that two of the sides have a floral motif, and the other two sides are figural, one with the center lion's head and the other with griffin figures. Very striking indeed, and an absolutely wonderful piece to have by your front door."

"Worth a few quid, is it?" Henry asks, dropping the posh accent.

"We'll get to that part," the expert says. "While it is in good condition, it appears there would have been feet, quite likely wooden. There are no splits or warping in the sides, and the finger ring handles on the sides are intact. So bearing all that in mind, how much do you think it's worth?"

"Frankie!" Frankie hears her boss calling her from across the room. "What's this I hear about you messing with the monitors?"

Frankie stands up, turns around, and blocking the television with her body, attempts to turn the channel back.

"Ah—" Her colleague tuts. "They were just about to announce the value. That's the best bit."

"Step aside." Her boss frowns.

Frankie moves to display the stock market figures racing across the screen. She smiles brightly, showing all her teeth, and then sprints back to her desk.

Back at the waiting room, Justin is glued to the television, glued to Joyce's face.

"Is she a friend, love?" Ethel asks him.

Justin studies Joyce's face and smiles. "Yes, she is. Her name is Joyce."

Margaret and Ethel ooh and aah.

On-screen, Joyce's father, or at least that's who Justin assumes him to be, turns to Joyce and shrugs.

"What would you say, love? How much lolly for Dolly?"

Joyce smiles tightly. "I really wouldn't have the slightest idea how much it's worth."

"How does between one thousand five hundred and one thousand seven hundred pounds sound to you?" the expert asks.

"Sterling pounds?" the old man asks, flabbergasted.

Justin laughs.

The camera zooms in on Joyce and her father's face. They are both astonished, so gobsmacked, in fact, that neither of them can say anything.

"Now, there's an impressive reaction." Michael laughs. "Good news from this table. Let's go over to our porcelain table to see if any of our other collectors here in London have been as lucky."

"Justin Hitchcock," the receptionist announces.

The room is quiet as everyone looks around at one another.

"Justin," she repeats, raising her voice.

"That must be him on the floor," Ethel says. "Yoo-hoo!" she sings and gives him a kick with her comfortable shoe. "Are you Justin?"

"Somebody's in love, ooohey-ooohey," Margaret sings while Ethel makes kissing noises.

"Louise," Ethel says to the receptionist, "why don't I go in now while this young man runs down to Banqueting House to see his lady? I'm tired of waiting." She stretches her left leg out and makes pained expressions.

Justin stands and wipes carpet lint from his trousers. "I don't know why you're both waiting here anyway, at your age. You should just leave your teeth here and come back later when the dentist's finished with them."

He exits the room as a year-old copy of *Homes and Gardens* flies at his head.

Chapter 22

◇◇◇◇◇

ACTUALLY, THAT'S NOT A BAD idea." Justin stops following the receptionist down the hallway as adrenaline once again surges through his body. "That's exactly what I'll do."

"You're going to leave your teeth here?" she says drily, in a strong Liverpool accent.

"No, I'm going to Banqueting House," he says, hopping about with excitement.

"Great, Dick. Can Anne come too? Let's be sure to ask Aunt Fanny first." She glares at him, killing his excitement. "I don't care what's going on with you, you're not escaping this time. Come now. Dr. Montgomery won't be happy if you don't show for your appointment again."

"Okay, okay, but hold on. My tooth is fine now." He holds out his hands and shrugs like it's all no big deal. "All gone. No pain at all. In fact, chomp, chomp, chomp," he says as he snaps his teeth together. "Look, completely gone. What am I even doing here? Can't feel a thing."

"Your eyes are watering."

"I'm emotional."

"You're delusional. Come on." She continues to lead him down the corridor.

Dr. Montgomery greets him with a drill in his hand, "Hello, Clarisse," he says and bursts out laughing. "Just joking. Trying to run off on me again, Justin?"

"No. Well, yes. Well, no, not run off exactly, but I realized that there's somewhere else I should be and . . ."

All throughout his explanation, the firm-handed Dr. Montgomery and his equally strong assistant manage to usher him into the chair, and by the time he's finished his excuse he realizes he's wearing a protective gown and reclining.

" 'Blah blah blah' was all I heard, I'm afraid, Justin," Dr. Montgomery says cheerily.

He sighs.

"So you're not going to fight me today?" Dr. Montgomery snaps two surgical gloves onto his hands.

"As long as you don't ask me to cough."

Dr. Montgomery laughs as Justin reluctantly opens his mouth.

The red light on the camera goes off, and I grab Dad's arm.

"Dad, we have to go now," I say with urgency.

"Not now," Dad responds in a David Attenborough–style loud whisper. "Michael Aspel is right over there. I can see him standing behind the porcelain table. He's looking around for someone to talk to."

"Michael Aspel is very busy in his natural habitat, presenting a live television show." I dig my fingernails into Dad's arm. "I don't think talking to you is very high on his priority list right now."

Dad looks slightly wounded, and not from my fingernails. He lifts his chin high in the air, which I know from experience has an invisible string attached to his pride. He prepares to approach Michael Aspel, who is standing alone with his finger in his ear.

"Must get waxy buildup, like me," Dad whispers. "He should use that stuff you got for me. Pop! Comes right out."

"It's an earpiece, Dad. He's listening to the people in the control room."

"No, I think it's a hearing aid. Let's go over to him, and remember to speak up and mouth your words clearly. I have experience with this."

I block his path and leer over him in the most intimidating way possible. Dad steps onto his left leg and immediately rises near enough to my eye level.

"Dad, if we do not leave this place right now, we will find ourselves locked in a cell. Again."

Dad laughs. "Ah, don't exaggerate, Gracie."

"I'm bloody Joyce," I hiss.

"All right, bloody Joyce, no need to get your bloody knickers in a twist."

"I don't think you understand the seriousness of our situation. We have just stolen a seventeen-hundred-pound Victorian wastebasket from a once-upon-a-time royal palace and talked about it live on air."

Dad looks at me quickly, his bushy eyebrows raised halfway up his forehead. For the first time in a long time I can clearly see his eyes. They look alarmed. And rather watery and yellow at the corners—I make a note to ask him about that later, when we are not running from the BBC. Or the law.

The production girl with the headset gives me wide eyes from across the room. My heart beats in panic, and I look around quickly. Heads are turning to stare at us. They know.

"Okay, we have to go now. I think they know."

"It's no big deal. We'll put it back." He tries to sound casual. "We haven't even taken it off the premises—that's no crime."

"Okay, it's now or never. Grab it quick so we can put it back and get out of here."

I scan the crowd to make sure nobody big and burly is coming toward us, cracking their knuckles and swinging a baseball bat. Just the young girl with the headset so far, and I'm sure I can take her on. If not, Dad can hit her on the head with his clunky corrective shoe.

Dad grabs the wastebasket from the table and tries to hide it inside his coat. The coat barely makes it a third of the way around, and I look at him bizarrely. We make our way through the crowd, ignoring congrats and well-wishes from those who seem to think we've won the lottery. I see the young girl with the headset pushing her way through the crowd too.

"Quick, Dad, quick."

"I'm going as fast as I can."

We make it to the door of the hall, leaving the crowd behind, and start toward the main entrance. I look back and catch the girl with the headset talking urgently into her mike. She starts to run toward us but gets caught behind two men in brown overalls carrying a wardrobe across the floor. I grab the wooden bin from Dad's hands, and immediately we speed up. Down the stairs, we grab our bags from the cloakroom and then up and down, down and up, all the way along the marble-floored hallway.

As Dad reaches for the gold oversize handle on the main door we hear, "Stop! Wait!"

We stop abruptly and slowly turn to look at each other in fear. I mouth "Run" at Dad. He sighs dramatically, rolls his eyes, and steps down on his right leg, bending his left as a way of reminding me of his struggles with walking, let alone running.

"Where are you two going in such a hurry?" asks a man, making his way toward us.

We slowly turn around, and I prepare to defend our honor.

"It was her," Dad says straightaway, thumb pointed at me.

My mouth falls open.

"It was both of you, I'm afraid." He smiles. "You left your microphone packs on. Worth a bit, these are." He fiddles around the back of Dad's trousers and unclips his battery pack. "Could have gotten into a bit of trouble if you'd escaped with this." He laughs.

Dad looks relieved until I ask nervously, "Were these turned on the entire time?"

"Eh." He studies the pack and flicks the switch to the off position. "They were."

"Who would have heard us?"

"Don't worry, they wouldn't have broadcast your sound while they went to the next item."

I breathe a sigh of relief.

"But internally, whoever was wearing headphones on the floor would have heard you," he explains, removing Dad's mike. "Oh, and the control room too," he add, turning to me next.

After he shuffles back with our packs inside, we hurry to place the umbrella stand back by the entrance door, fill it with broken umbrellas, and exit the scene of the crime.

"So, what's new?" Dr. Montgomery asks.

Justin, who is reclined in the chair with two surgically gloved hands and apparatus shoved in his mouth, is unsure of how to answer, and decides to blink once, having seen that on television. Then unsure of what exactly that signal means, he blinks twice to confuse matters.

Dr. Montgomery misses his code and chuckles. "Cat got your tongue?"

Justin rolls his eyes.

"I might start getting offended one of these days, if people continue to ignore my questions." He chuckles again and leans in over Justin, giving him a good view up his nostrils.

"Arrrgggh." Justin flinches as the cool prong hits his sore point.

"Hate to say I told you so," Dr. Montgomery continues, "but that would be a lie. The cavity that you wouldn't let me look at during your last visit has become infected, and now the tissue is inflamed."

He taps around some more.

"Aaaahh." Justin makes some gurgling sounds from the back of his throat.

"I should write a book on dentistry language. Everybody makes all sorts of sounds that only I can understand. What do you think, Rita?"

Rita, the assistant with the glossy lips, doesn't care much.

Justin gurgles some expletives.

"Now, now." Dr. Montgomery's smile fades for a moment. "Don't be rude."

Startled, Justin concentrates on the television suspended from the ceiling in the corner of the room. Sky News's red banner at the bottom of the screen screams its breaking news, and though it's muted and too far away for him to read, it provides a welcome distraction from Dr. Montgomery's dismal jokes and calms his urge to jump out of the chair and grab the first taxi he can find, straight to Banqueting House.

The broadcaster is currently standing outside Westminster, but as Justin can't hear a thing, he has no idea what it's related to. He studies the man's face and tries to lip-read while Dr. Montgomery comes at him with what looks like a needle. His eyes widen as he catches sight of something on the television. His pupils melt into his eyes, blackening them.

Dr. Montgomery smiles as he holds the tool before Justin's face. "Don't worry, Justin. I know how much you hate needles, but it's necessary for a numbing effect. You need a filling in another tooth before that gets an abscess as well. It won't hurt—it will just feel slightly odd."

Justin's eyes grow wider at the television and he tries to sit up. For once, Justin doesn't care about the needle. He must try to communicate this as best as possible. Unable to move or close his mouth, he begins to make deep noises from the back of his throat.

"Okay, don't panic. Just one more minute. I'm nearly there."

He leans over Justin again, blocking his view of the television, and Justin squirms in his seat, trying to see the screen.

"My goodness, Justin, please stop it. The needle won't kill you, but I might if you don't stop wriggling." Chuckle, chuckle.

"Ted, I think maybe we should stop," his assistant says, and Justin looks at her with grateful eyes.

"Is he having a fit of some sort?" Dr. Montgomery asks her and then raises his voice at Justin, as though his patient has suddenly become hearing-impaired. "I say, are you having a fit of some sort?"

Justin rolls his eyes and makes more noises from the back of his throat.

"TV? What do you mean?" Dr. Montgomery looks up at Sky News and finally removes his fingers from Justin's mouth.

All three focus on the television screen, the other two concentrating on the news while Justin watches the background, where Joyce and her father have wandered into the path of the camera's angle, with them in the foreground, Big Ben in the background. Seemingly unaware, they carry out what looks like a seriously heated conversation, their hands gesturing wildly.

"Look at those two idiots." Dr. Montgomery laughs.

Suddenly Joyce's father pushes his suitcase over to Joyce and then storms off in the other direction, leaving Joyce, alone with two bags, to throw up her hands with frustration.

"Yeah, thanks, that's very mature," I shout after Dad, who has just stormed off, leaving his suitcase behind with me. He is going in the wrong direction. Again. Has been since we left the Banqueting House but refuses to admit it, and also refuses to get a taxi to the hotel, as he is on a penny-saving mission.

He is still within my sights, and so I sit on my case and wait for him to realize the error of his ways and come back. It's evening now and I just want to get to the hotel and have a bath. My phone rings.

"Hi, Kate."

She is laughing hysterically.

"What's up with you?" I smile. "Well, it's nice to hear somebody is in a good mood."

"Oh, Joyce—" She catches her breath, and I imagine she's wiping her teared-up eyes. "You are the best dose of medicine, you really are."

"What do you mean?" I can hear children's laughter behind her.

"Do me a favor and raise your right hand."

"Why?"

"Just do it. It's a game the kids taught me." She giggles.

"Okay." I sigh, and raise my right hand.

I hear the kids howl with laughter.

"Tell her to wiggle her right foot," Jayda shouts in the background.

"Okay," I laugh. This is putting me in a much better mood. I wiggle my right foot, and they laugh again. I can even hear Kate's husband howling, which suddenly makes me uncomfortable again. "Kate, what exactly is this?"

Kate can't answer, she's laughing too much.

"Tell her to hop up and down!" Eric shouts.

"No." I'm irritated now.

"She did it for Jayda," he begins to whine, and I sense tears.

I quickly stand and hop up and down.

They howl again.

"By any chance," Kate wheezes through her laugher, "is there anyone around you who has the time?"

"What are you talking about?" I frown, looking around, still not sure of the joke. I see Big Ben behind me, and as I turn back, only then do I see the camera crew in the distance. I stop hopping.

"What on earth is that woman doing?" Dr. Montgomery steps closer to the television. "Is she dancing?"

"Oo han ee ha?" Justin says, feeling the effects of his numbed mouth.

"Of course I can see her," he responds. "I think she's doing the hokey-pokey. See? You put your left leg in," he begins to sing. "Left leg out. In. Out. In. Out. Shake it all about." He dances around. Rita rolls her eyes.

Justin, relieved that his sightings of Joyce aren't all in his mind, begins to bounce up and down in his seat impatiently. Hurry! I need to get to her.

Dr. Montgomery glances at him curiously, pushes him back in the chair, and places the instruments in his mouth again. Justin continues to gurgle and make noises.

"It's no good explaining it to me, Justin, you're not going anywhere until I have filled this cavity. You'll have to take antibiotics for the abscess, then when you come back I'll either extract it or use endodontic treatment. Whatever I'm in the mood for," he says darkly. "And whoever this Joyce lady is, you can thank her for curing your fear of needles. You didn't even notice I'd injected you."

"Aah haa ooo aaa aa ee a."

"Oh, well, good for you, old boy. I donated blood before too, you know. Satisfying, isn't it?"

"Aa. Ooo aaa iii uuuu."

Dr. Montgomery throws his head back. "Oh, don't be silly,

they'll never tell you who the blood has gone to. Besides, it's been separated into different parts, platelets, red blood cells, and what have you."

Justin gurgles again.

The dentist laughs again. "What kind of muffins would you want?"

"Aa."

"Banana." He considers this. "Prefer chocolate, myself. Air, please, Rita."

A bewildered Rita puts the tube into Justin's mouth.

Chapter 23

◇◇◇◇◇

I SUCCEED IN HAILING A black cab, and I send the driver in the direction of the dapper old man, who is easily spotted on the pavement, swaying in horizontal motions like a drunken sailor amid the crowd's vertical stream. Like a salmon he swims upstream, pushing against the throngs of people going in the opposite direction. Not doing it just for the sake of it or to be deliberately different, and not even noticing he's the odd one out.

Seeing him now reminds me of a tale he once told me when I was so small he seemed as gigantic as our neighbor's oak tree that loomed over our garden wall, raining acorns onto our grass. During the months when playtime was interrupted by the gray world outside, the howling wind would blow the giant tree's branches from side to side, leaves going *swish swash*, left to right, just like my dad, a pin wavering at the end of a bowling lane. But neither of them fell under the wind's force. Not like the acorns, which leaped from their branches like panicked parachutists pushed out unawares.

Back when my dad was as sturdy as an oak tree and when I was bullied at school for sucking my thumb, he recalled the Irish myth of how an ordinary salmon had eaten hazelnuts that had fallen into the Fountain of Wisdom. In doing so, the salmon gained all the knowledge in the world, and the first to eat the salmon's flesh would, in turn, gain this knowledge. The poet Finneces spent seven long years fishing for this salmon, and when he'd finally caught it, he instructed his young apprentice, Fionn, to prepare it for him. When spattered with hot fat from the cooking salmon, Fionn immediately sucked on his burned thumb to ease his pain. Thus he gained incredible knowledge and wisdom. For the rest of his life, when he didn't know what to do, all he needed was to suck on his thumb, and the knowledge would come.

He told me that story way back when I sucked my thumb, and when he was as big as an oak tree. When Mum's yawns sounded like songs. When we were all together. When I had no idea there would ever come a time when we wouldn't be. When we used to have chats in the garden, under the weeping willow. Where I always used to hide, and where he always found me. When nothing was impossible, and when the three of us, together forever, was a given.

I smile now as I watch my great big salmon of knowledge moving upstream, weaving in and out of the pedestrians pounding the pavement toward him.

Dad looks up, sees me, gives me two fingers, and keeps walking.

Ah.

"Dad," I call out the open window, "come on, get in the car."

He ignores me and holds a cigarette to his mouth, inhaling long and hard, so much so that his cheeks go concave.

"Dad, don't be like this. Just get in the car, and we'll go to the hotel."

He continues walking, looking straight ahead, as stubborn as anything. I've seen this face so many times before, arguing with Mum over staying too late and too often at the pub, debating with the Monday Club gang about the political state of the country, holding his ground at a restaurant when his beef is handed to him not resembling a piece of charcoal as he wishes—the "I'm right, you're wrong" look that has set his chin in that defiant stance, jutting outward like Cork and Kerry's rugged coastline from the rest of the land. A stubborn chin, a troubled head.

"Look, we don't even have to talk. You can ignore me in the car too. And at the hotel. Don't talk to me all night, if it'll make you feel better."

"You'd like that, wouldn't you?" he huffs.

"Honestly?"

He looks at me.

"Yes."

He tries not to smile. Scratches the corner of his mouth with his yellow-stained cigarette fingers to hide how he softens. The smoke rises into his eyes, and I think of his yellow eyes, think of how piercingly blue they used to be when, as a little girl, legs swinging, chin on my hands, I'd watch him at the kitchen table dismantling a radio or a clock or some other device. Piercing blue eyes, alert, busy, like a CAT scan sourcing a tumor. His cigarette squashed between his lips, to the side of his mouth like Popeye, the smoke drifting into his squinted eyes, staining them the yellow that he sees through now. The color of age, like old newspapers dipped in time.

I'd watch him, transfixed, afraid to speak, afraid to breathe, afraid to break the spell he'd cast on the contraption he was fixing. Like the surgeon who'd operated on his heart during his bypass surgery ten years ago, there he was with youth on his side, connecting wires and clearing blockages, his shirtsleeves rolled to just below his elbows, the muscles in his arms tanned from gardening, flexing and unflexing as his fingers tackled the problem. His fingernails, always with a trace of dirt under the surface. His right forefinger and middle finger, yellow from the nicotine. Yellow but steady.

Finally he stops walking. He throws his cigarette on the ground and stomps it out with his chunky shoe. I ask the driver to stop. I throw the lifesaving ring around his body, and we pull him out of his stream of defiance and into the boat. Always a chancer, always lucky, he'd fall into a river and come out dry, with fish in his pockets. He gets in the car and sits without a word to me, his clothes, breath, and fingers smelling of smoke. I bite my lip to stop from saying anything.

He is silent for a record amount of time. Ten, minutes, maybe fifteen. Finally words start spilling out of his mouth, as though they'd been queuing up impatiently. Fired from his heart as usual, not from his head, and catapulted to his mouth, only to bounce against the walls of his closed lips. But now the gates open, and the words fly out in all directions like projectile vomit.

"You may have got a sherbet, but I hope you know that I haven't a sausage." He raises his chin, which pulls on the invisible string attached to his pride. He appears pleased with the collection of words that have strung themselves together for him on this particular occasion.

"What?"

"You heard me."

"Yes, but . . ."

"Sherbet dab, cab. Sausage and mash, cash," he explains. "It's the ol' Chitty Chitty."

I try to work that out in my head.

"Bang Bang, rhyming slang," he finishes. "He knows exactly what I'm talking about." He nods at the driver.

"He can't hear you."

"Why? Is he Mutt and Jeff?"

"What?"

"Deaf."

"No." I shake my head, feeling dazed and tired. "When the red light is off, they can't hear you."

"Like Joe's hearing aid," Dad responds. He leans forward and flicks the switch on the back of the seat in front of us. "Can you hear me?" he shouts.

"Yeah, mate." The driver looks at him in the rearview mirror. "Loud and clear."

Dad smiles and flicks the switch again. "Can you hear me now?"

There is no response, and the driver quickly glances at him in the mirror, concern wrinkling his forehead while he keeps an eye on the road.

Dad chuckles.

I bury my face in my hands.

"This is what we do to Joe," he says mischievously. "Sometimes he can go a whole day without realizing we turned his hearing aid off. He just thinks that no one's saying anything. Every half hour he shouts, '*Jaysus, it's very quiet in here!*'" Dad laughs and flicks the switch again. "'Allo, guv," Dad says pleasantly.

"All right, Paddy," the driver responds.

I wait for Dad's gnarled fist to go through the slit in the window. It doesn't. His laughter filters through instead.

"I feel like being on my tod tonight. I say, could you tell me where there's a good jack near my hotel, so I can go for a pig without my teapot?"

The young driver studies Dad's innocent face in the mirror, but he doesn't respond and continues driving.

I look away so Dad isn't embarrassed, but I feel rather superior and hate myself for it. Moments later, at a set of traffic lights, the hatch opens and the driver passes a piece of paper through.

"Here's a list of a few, mate. I'd suggest the first one, that's my favorite. Does good loop and tucker right about now, if you know what I mean." He smiles and winks.

"Thank you." Dad's face lights up. He studies the paper closely as though it's the most precious thing he's ever been given, then folds it carefully and slides it into his top pocket proudly. "It's just that this one here is being a merry ol' soul, if you know what I mean. Make sure she gives you a good bit of rifle."

The driver laughs and pulls over at our hotel. I examine it from the cab and am pleasantly surprised. The three-star hotel is right in the heart of the city, only ten minutes' walk from the main theaters, Oxford Street, Piccadilly, and Soho. Enough to keep us out of trouble. Or put us right in it.

Dad gets out of the car and pulls his case up to the revolving doors at the hotel entrance. I watch him while waiting for my change. The doors are going around so fast, I can see him trying to time his entrance. Like a dog afraid to jump into the cold sea, he inches forward, then stops, jerks forward again and stops. Finally he makes a run for it, and his suitcase gets stuck outside, jamming the revolving doors and trapping him inside.

I take my time getting out of the cab. I lean in the passenger's side window to the sound of Dad rapping on the glass of the revolving doors.

"Help! Someone!" I hear Dad call.

"By the way, what did he call me?" I ask the driver, calmly ignoring the calls behind me.

"A merry old soul?" he asks with a grin. "You don't want to know."

"Tell me," I prompt.

"It means arsehole." He laughs and then pulls away, leaving me at the side of the street with my mouth gaping.

I notice the knocking has quieted and turn to see that Dad has been freed at last. I hurry inside.

"I can't give you a credit card, but I can give you my word," Dad is saying slowly and loudly to the woman behind the reception desk. "And my word is as good as my honor."

"It's okay, here you go." I join them and slide my credit card across the counter to the young lady.

"Why can't people just pay with paper money these days?" Dad says, leaning farther over the counter. "It's more trouble that the youth of today are getting themselves into, debt after debt because they want this, they want that, but they don't want to work for it, so they use those plastic thingies. Well, that's not free money, I can tell you that." He nods his head with finality. "You'll only ever lose with one of those."

The receptionist smiles at him politely and taps away at her computer. "You're sharing a room?" she asks.

"Yes," I respond with dread.

"Two Uncle Teds, I hope?" Dad says.

She frowns.

"Beds," I say quietly. "He means beds."

"Yes, they're twin beds."

"Is it an en suite?" He leans in again, trying to see her name badge. "Breda, is it?" he asks.

"Aakaanksha. And, yes, sir, all our rooms are en suite," she says politely.

"Oh." He looks impressed. "Well, I hope your lifts are working, because I can't take the apples, my Cadbury's playin' up."

I squeeze my eyes together tightly.

"Apples and pears, stairs. Cadbury snack, back," he says.

"I see. Very good, Mr. Conway."

I take the key and head toward the elevator, hearing him muttering phrases over and over as he follows me through the foyer. I hit the button for the third floor, and the doors close.

The room is standard, and it's clean, and that's good enough for me. Our beds are far enough apart for my liking, and there's a television and a minibar, which hold Dad's attention while I run a bath.

"I wouldn't mind a drop of fine," he says, his head disappearing into the minibar.

"You mean wine."

"Fine and dandy, brandy."

When I finally slide down into the hot soothing bathwater, the suds rise like the foam atop an ice-cream float. They tickle my nose and cover my body, overflow and float to the ground, where they slowly fade with a crackling sound. I lie back and close my eyes, feeling tiny bubbles all over my body pop as soon as they touch my skin. I'm relaxing for the first time in ages . . . Then there's a knock at the door.

I ignore it.

Then it goes again, a little more loudly this time.

Still I don't answer.

Bang! Bang!

"What?" I shout.

"Oh, sorry, thought you'd fallen asleep or something, love."

"I'm in the bath."

"I know that. You have to be careful in those things. Could nod off and slip under the water and drown. Happened to one of Amelia's cousins. You know Amelia. Visits Joseph sometimes, down the road. But she doesn't drop by as much as before on account of the bath accident."

"Dad, I appreciate your concern, but I'm fine."

"Okay."

Silence.

"Actually, it's not that, Gracie. I'm just wonderin' how long you'll be in there for?"

I grab the yellow rubber duck sitting at the side of the bath, and I strangle it.

"Love?" he asks in a little voice.

I hold the duck under the water, trying to drown it. Then I let go, and it bobs to the top again, the same silly eyes staring back at me. I take a deep breath, breathe out slowly.

"About twenty minutes, Dad, is that okay?"

Silence. I close my eyes again.

"Eh, love. It's just that you've been in there twenty minutes already, and you know how my prostate is—"

I don't hear any more, because I'm climbing out of the bath with all the gracefulness of a piranha at feeding time. My feet squeak on the bathroom floor, splashing water in all directions.

"Everything okay in there, Shamu?" Dad laughs uproariously at his own joke.

I throw a towel around me and open the door.

"Ah, Willy's been freed." He smiles.

I bow and hold my arm out to the toilet. "Your chariot awaits you, sir."

Embarrassed, he shuffles inside and closes the door behind him. It locks.

Wet and shivering, I browse through the half bottles of red wine in the minibar. I pick one up and study the label. Immediately an image flashes through my mind, so vivid, I feel like my body has been transported.

A picnic basket with a bottle inside, with this identical label, a red-and-white-checked cloth laid out on the grass, a little girl with blond hair twirling, twirling in a pink tutu. The wine swirling, swirling in a glass. The sound of laughter. Birds twittering. Children's laughter far off, a dog barking. I am lying on the checked cloth, barefoot, trousers rolled above my ankles. Hairy ankles. I feel heat beating down on my skin. The little girl dances and twirls before the sun, sometimes blocking the harshness of light, other times spinning in the other direction to send the glare into my eyes. A hand appears before me, a glass of red wine in it. I look to her face. Red hair, lightly freckled, smiling adoringly. At me.

"Justin," she's singing. "Earth to Justin!"

The little girl is laughing and twirling, the wine is swirling, the long red hair is blowing in the light breeze . . .

Then it's gone. I'm back in the hotel room, standing before the minibar, my hair dripping bathwater onto the carpet. Dad is now out and watching me curiously, hand suspended in the air as though he's not sure whether to touch me or not.

"Earth to Joyce," he's singing.

I clear my throat. "You're done?"

Dad nods, and his eyes follow me to the bathroom. On the way there, I stop and turn. "By the way, I've booked a ballet show for tonight if you'd like to come. We need to leave in an hour."

"Okay, love." He nods softly, and watches after me with a familiar look of worry in his eyes. I've seen that look as a child, and I've seen it as an adult—and a million times in between. It's as though I've taken the training wheels off my bicycle for the very first time, and he's running along beside me, holding on tight, afraid to let me go.

Chapter 24

◇◇◇◇◇

D AD BREATHES HEAVILY BESIDE ME and links my arm
tightly as we make our way to Covent Garden. Using my
other hand I pat down my pockets, feeling for his heart pills.

"Dad, we're definitely getting a taxi back to the hotel. And I'm
not taking no for an answer."

Dad stops and stares ahead.

"Are you okay? Is it your heart? Should we sit down? Stop and
take a rest? Go back to the hotel?"

"Shut up and turn round, Gracie. It's not just my heart that
takes my breath away, you know."

I spin round, and there it is, the Royal Opera House, its columns illuminated for the evening performance, a red carpet lining
the pavement outside and crowds filing through the doors.

"You have to take your moments, love," Dad says, soaking in
the sight before him. "Don't just go headfirst into everything like
a bull seeing red."

Having booked our tickets so late, we are seated almost at
the top of the tremendous theater. The position is unlucky, yet
we are fortunate to have gotten tickets at all. And while the view

of the stage is restricted, the view of the boxes opposite is perfect. Squinting through the binoculars situated beside my seat, I spy on the people filling the boxes. No sign of my American man. Earth to Justin? I hear the woman's voice in my head and wonder again if Frankie's theory about seeing the world from his eyes is correct.

Dad is enthralled by our view. "We've got the best seats in the house, love, look." He leans over the balcony, and his tweed cap almost falls off his head. I grab his arm and pull him back. He takes the photograph of Mum from his pocket and places her on the velvet balcony ledge. "Best seat in the house, indeed," he says, his eyes filling.

The voice over the intercom system signals that the ballet is about to begin, prompting the cacophony of the tuning orchestra to die down. The lights dim, and there is silence before the magic begins. The conductor taps, and the orchestra plays the opening bars of Tchaikovsky's ballet. Apart from Dad snorting when the male principal dancer appears onstage wearing tights, it runs smoothly, and we are both entranced by the story of *Swan Lake*. I look away from the prince's coming-of-age party and again study those sitting in the boxes. Their faces are lit, their eyes dancing along with the dancers they follow. It's as though a music box has been opened, spilling music and light, and all those watching have been enchanted, captured by its magic. I continue to spy through my opera glasses, moving from left to right, seeing a row of strange faces until . . . My eyes widen as I reach the familiar face, the man from the hair salon I now know from Bea's biography in the program to be Mr. Hitchcock. Justin Hitchcock? He watches the stage, entranced, leaning so far over the ledge it looks as though he'll topple over. I can't stop watching him; I study his face, his eyes, his lips. He's so close in my view that I feel like I can reach out to touch him. The excitement rushes through me at just seeing him, the feeling of a childhood crush suddenly alive inside me.

Dad elbows me. "Would you stop looking around you, and

keep your eye on the stage? He's about to kill her." He knocks the binoculars away from my hand, and the man is once again far from my reach.

I turn to face the stage and try to hold my eyes on the prince leaping about with his crossbow, but I can't. A magnetic pull turns my face back down to the box, anxious to see who Mr. Hitchcock is sitting with. My heart is drumming loudly, and I secretly raise the binoculars to my eyes again. Beside him is the woman with long red hair, the one who holds the camera in my dreams. Beside her is a sweet-looking man, and squashed together behind them are a young man pulling uncomfortably at his tie, a woman with big curly red hair, and a large round man. I flick through my memory files like I'm going through Polaroids. The chubby boy from the sprinkler scene and seesaw? Perhaps. But the other two, I don't know. I move my eyes back to Justin Hitchcock and smile, finding his face more entertaining than the action onstage.

Suddenly the music changes, the light reflecting on his face flickers, and his expression shifts. I know instantly that Bea is onstage, and I turn to watch. Somehow I'm able to pick her out among the flock of swans moving about so gracefully in perfect unison, dressed in a white fitted corset dress with a raggedy long white tutu, similar to feathers. Her long blond hair is tied up in a bun, covered by a neat headdress. I recall the image of her in the park as a little girl, twirling and twirling in her tutu, and I'm filled with pride. How far she has come. How grown-up she is now. My eyes fill.

"Oh, look, Justin," Jennifer says breathily beside him.

He is looking. He can't take his eyes off his daughter, a vision in white, dancing in perfect unison with the flock of swans, not a movement out of place. She looks so grown-up. How did that happen? It seems like only yesterday she was twirling for him and

Jennifer in the park across from their house, a little girl with a tutu and dreams and now . . . His eyes fill, and he looks beside him to Jennifer, to share a look, to share the moment, but at the same time she reaches for Laurence's hand. He looks away quickly, back to his daughter. A tear falls, and he reaches into his front pocket for his handkerchief.

A handkerchief is raised to my face, catches my tear before it drips from my chin.

"What are you crying for?" Dad says loudly, dabbing at my chin roughly as the curtain lowers for the intermission.

"I'm just so proud of Bea."

"Who?"

"Oh, nothing . . . I just think it's a beautiful story. What do you think?"

"I think those lads have definitely got socks down their tights."

I laugh and wipe my eyes. "Do you think Mum's enjoying it?"

He smiles and stares at the photo. "She must be, she hasn't turned round once since it started. Unlike you, who's got ants in her pants. If I'd known you were so keen on binoculars, I'd have taken you out bird-watching long ago." He sighs and looks around. "The lads at the Monday Club won't believe this at all. Donal McCarthy, you better watch out."

"Do you miss her?"

"It's been ten years, love."

It stings that he can be so dismissive. I fold my arms and look away, silently fuming.

Dad leans closer and nudges me. "And every day I miss her more than I did the day before."

Oh. I immediately feel guilty for wishing that on him.

"It's like my garden, love. Everything grows. Including love. And with that growing every day, how can you expect the missing part to ever fade away? Everything builds, including our ability to cope with it. That's how we keep going."

I shake my head, in awe of some of the things he comes out with, philosophical and otherwise. And this from a man who's been calling me his teapot (lid, kid) ever since we landed.

"And I just thought you liked pottering." I smile.

"Ah, there's a lot to be said for pottering. You know Thomas Berry said that gardening is an active participation in the deepest mysteries of the universe? There are lessons in pottering."

"Like what?"

"Well, even a garden grows stranglers, love. It grows them naturally, all by itself. They creep up and choke the plants that are growing from the very same soil as they are. We each have our demons, our self-destruct button. Even in gardens. Pretty as they may be. If you don't potter, you don't notice them."

He eyes me, and I look away, choosing to clear my already-clear throat. Sometimes I wish he'd just stick to laughing at men in tights.

"Justin, we're going to the bar, are you coming?" Doris asks.

"No," he says, in a huff like a child.

"Why not?" Al squeezes farther into the box to sit beside him.

"I just don't want to." He picks up his opera glasses and starts fiddling with them.

"But you'll be here on your own."

"So?"

"Mr. Hitchcock, would you like me to get you a drink?" Bea's boyfriend, Peter, asks.

"Mr. Hitchcock was my father, you can call me Al. Like the

song." He punches him playfully on the shoulder, but it knocks him back a few steps.

"Okay, Al, but I actually meant Justin."

"You can call me Mr. Hitchcock." Justin looks at him like there's a bad smell in the room.

"We don't have to sit with Laurence and Jennifer, you know," Al says.

Laurence. Laurence of Ahernia, who has elephantitis of the—

"Yes, we do, Al, don't be ridiculous," Doris interrupts.

Al sighs. "Well, give Petey an answer. Do you want us to bring you back a drink?"

Yes. But Justin can't bring himself to say it and instead shakes his head sulkily.

"Okay, we'll be back in fifteen."

Al gives him a comforting brotherly pat on his shoulder before they all leave him alone in the box to stew over Laurence and Jennifer and Bea and Chicago and London and Dublin and now Peter. Over how exactly his life has ended up.

Two minutes later and already tired of feeling sorry for himself, he looks through the opera glasses and begins spying on the trickles of people below him who'd stayed seated for the intermission. He spots a couple fighting, snapping at each other. Another couple kissing, reaching for their coats, and then disappearing quickly to the exits. He spies a mother giving it to her son. A group of women laughing together. He moves to the boxes on the opposite side. They are empty, everyone choosing to have their preordered drinks in the nearby bar. He cranes his neck up higher. How on earth can anyone see anything from up there?

He doesn't see anything unusual, just a small number of people, like everyone else, sitting and chatting. He moves along from right to left. Then stops. Rubs his eyes. Surely he is imagining it. He squints back through the opera glasses again, and sure enough, there she is. With the old man. Every scene in his life is beginning to seem like a page from *Where's Waldo?*

She is looking through her opera glasses too, scanning the crowd below them both. Then she raises her opera glasses, moves slowly to the right, and . . . they both freeze, staring at each other through their respective lenses. He slowly lifts his arm. Waves.

She slowly does the same. The old man beside her puts his glasses on and squints in his direction, mouth opening and closing the entire time.

Justin holds his hand up, intends to make a "wait" sign. Hold on, I'm coming up to you. He holds his forefinger up, as though he's just thought of an idea. One minute. Hold on, I'll be one minute, he tries to signal.

She gives him the thumbs-up, and he breaks into a smile.

He drops the opera glasses and stands up immediately, taking note of where exactly she is sitting. Just then the door to the box opens, and in walks Laurence.

"Justin, I thought maybe we could have a word," he says politely, drumming his fingers on the back of the chair that separates them.

"No, Laurence, not now, sorry." He tries to move past him.

"I promise not to take up too much of your time. Just a few minutes while we're alone. To clear the air, you know?" He opens the button of his blazer, smooths down his tie, and closes his button again.

"Yeah, I appreciate that, buddy, I really do, but I'm in a really big hurry right now." He tries to inch by him, but Laurence moves to block him.

"A hurry?" he says, raising his eyebrows. "But intermission is just about over and . . . ah." He stops, realizing. "I see. Well, I just thought I'd give it a try. If you're not ready to have the discussion yet, that's understandable."

"No, it's not that." Justin looks through his opera glasses and up at Joyce, feeling panicked. She's still there. "It's just that I really am in a hurry to get to somebody. I have to go, Laurence."

Jennifer walks in just as he says that. Her face is stony.

"Honestly, Justin. Laurence just wanted to be a gentleman and talk to you like an adult. Something, it seems, you have forgotten how to be. Though I don't know why I'm surprised about that."

"No, no, look, Jennifer." I used to call you Jen. So formal now, a lifetime away from that memorable day in the park when we were all so happy, so in love. "I really don't have time for this right now. You don't understand, I have to go."

"You can't go. The ballet is about to begin in a few minutes, and your daughter will be onstage. Don't tell me you're walking out on her, too, because of some ridiculous male pride."

Doris and Al enter the box, Al's size alone completely crowding the small space and blocking the path to the door. Al holds a pint of cola in his hand and an oversize bag of chips.

"Tell him, Justin." Doris folds her arms and taps her long fake pink nails against her thin arms.

Justin groans. "Tell him what?"

"Remind him of the heart disease in your family so that he might think twice before eating and drinking that crap."

"What heart disease?" Justin holds his hands to his head while on the other side of him, Jennifer drones on and on in what sounds like Charlie Brown's teacher's voice. *Wah, wah, wah,* is all he hears.

"Your father, dying of a heart attack," Doris says impatiently.

Justin freezes.

"The doc didn't say that it would necessarily happen to me," Al moans to his wife.

"He said there was a good chance. If there's a history in the family."

Justin's voice sounds to him as though it's coming from somewhere else. "No, no, I really don't think you have to worry about that, Al."

"See?" He looks at Doris.

"That's not what the doctor said, sweetheart. We have to be more careful if it runs in the family."

"No, it doesn't run in the—" Justin stalls. "Look, I really have to go now." He tries to move in the crowded box.

"No, you will not," Jennifer blocks him. "You are not going anywhere until you apologize to Laurence."

"It's really all right, Jen," Laurence says awkwardly.

I call her Jen, not you!

"No, it's not, sweetheart."

I'm her sweetheart, not you!

Voices come at him from all sides, *wah wah wah*, until he is unable to make out any words. He feels hot and sweaty; dizziness grips him.

Suddenly the lights dim and the music begins and he has no choice but to take his seat again, beside a fuming Jennifer, an insulted Laurence, a silent Peter, a worried Doris, and a hungry Al, who decides to munch his chips loudly in his left ear.

He sighs and looks up at Joyce.

Help.

It seems the squabble in Justin Hitchcock's box has ended, but as the lights are going down, they are all still standing. When the lights lift again, they are seated with stony faces, apart from the large man in the back, who is eating a large bag of chips. I have ignored Dad all throughout the last few moments, choosing instead to invest my time in a crash course in lipreading. If I have been successful, their conversation involved Carrot Top and barbecued bananas.

Deep inside, my heart drums like a *djembe*, its deep bass and slap reaching down into my chest. I feel it in the base of my throat, throbbing, and all because he saw me, he wanted to come to me. I feel relieved that following my instincts, however flighty, paid off. It takes me a few minutes to be able to focus on anything other than Justin, and when I calm my nerves, I turn my attention back to the stage, where Bea takes my breath away and causes me to sniffle through her performance like a proud aunt. It occurs to me so strongly right now that the only people privy to those wonderful memories in the park are Bea, her mother, her father . . . and me.

"Dad, can I ask you something?" I lean close to him and whisper.

"He's just after telling that girl that he loves her, but she's the wrong girl." He rolls his eyes. "Eejit. The swan girl was in white, and that one is in black. They don't look alike at all."

"She could have changed for the ball. No one wears the same thing every day."

He looks me up and down. "You only took your bathrobe off one day last week. Anyway, what's up with you?"

"Well, it's that, I, em, something has happened and, well . . ."

"Spit it out, for Christ's sake, before I miss anything else."

I give up whispering in his ear and turn to face him. "I've been given something, or actually, something very special has been shared with me. It's completely inexplicable, and it doesn't make any sense at all, in an Our Lady of Knock kind of way, you know?" I laugh nervously and quickly stop, upon seeing his reaction.

No, he doesn't know. Dad looks angry I've used Mary's apparition in County Mayo during the 1870s as an example of nonsense.

"Okay, perhaps that was a bad example. What I mean is, it breaks every rule I've ever known. I just don't understand why."

"Gracie"—Dad lifts his chin—"Knock, like the rest of Ireland, suffered great distress over the centuries from invasion, evictions, and famines, and Our Lord sent His Mother, the Blessed Virgin, to visit with His oppressed children."

"No—" I hold my hands over my face. "I don't mean why did

Mary appear, I mean why has this . . . this thing happened to me? This thing I've been given."

"Oh. Well, is it hurting anyone? Because if it's not, and if you've been given it, I'd as soon stop callin' it a 'thing' and start referring to it as a 'gift.' Look at them dancing. He thinks she's the swan girl. Surely he can see her face. Or is it like Superman when he takes the glasses off and suddenly he's completely different, even though it's as clear as day he's the same person?"

A gift. I'd never thought of it like that. I look over at Bea's parents, beaming with pride, and I think of Bea before the intermission, floating around with her flock of swans. I shake my head. No. No one is being hurt.

"Well, then." Dad shrugs.

"But I don't understand why and how and—"

"What is it with people these days?" he hisses, and the man beside me turns round. I whisper my apologies.

"In my day, something just was. None of this analysis a hundred times over. None of these college courses with people graduating with degrees in Whys and Hows and Becauses. Sometimes, love, you just need to forget all of those words and enroll in a little lesson called 'Thank You.' Look at this story here." He points at the stage. "Do you hear anybody complaining about the fact that she, a woman, has been turned into a swan? Have you heard anything more ludicrous in your life?"

I shake my head, smiling.

"Have you met anyone lately who happens to have been turned into a swan?"

I laugh and whisper, "No."

"Yet look at it. This bloody thing has been famous the world over for centuries. We have nonbelievers, atheists, intellects, cynicists, even him"—he nods at the man who shushed us—"all kinds of what-have-yous in here tonight, but all of them want to see that fella in the tights end up with that swan girl, so she'll be able to get out of that lake. Only with the love of one who has never loved before can the spell be broken. Why? Who the hell cares why? Do you think your woman with the feathers is going to ask why? No. She's just going to say thank you because then she can move on and wear nice dresses and go for walks, instead of having to peck at soggy bread in a stinky lake every day for the rest of her life."

I have been stunned to silence.

"Now, shhh, we're missing the performance. She wants to kill herself now, look. Talk about being dramatic." He places his elbows on the balcony and leans in closer to the stage, his left ear tilted more than his eyes, quite literally eavesdropping.

Chapter 25

◇◇◇◇◇

DURING THE STANDING OVATION, JUSTIN spies Joyce's father helping her into a red coat, the same one from their Grafton Street collision. Together they begin to move to their nearby exit.

"Justin—" Jennifer scowls at her ex-husband, who is more busy spying through his opera glasses up at the ceiling than at his daughter bowing onstage.

He puts the glasses down and claps loudly, cheering, then has an idea.

"Hey, guys, I'm going to go to the bar and save some good seats for us." He starts moving toward the door.

"It's already reserved," Jennifer shouts after him, over the applause.

He holds his hand up to his ear and shakes his head. "Can't hear you."

He escapes and runs down the corridors, trying to find his way upstairs. The curtain must have fallen for the final time as people begin to exit their boxes, suddenly crowding the corridors and making it impossible for Justin to push past.

He has a change of plan: he'll rush to the exit and wait for her there. That way he can't miss her.

⚜

L ET'S GET A DRINK, LOVE," Dad says as we slowly amble behind the crowd exiting the theater. "I saw a bar on this floor somewhere."

We stop to read some directions.

"There's the amphitheater bar, this way," I say, looking out constantly for Justin Hitchcock. Today is the day, I can feel it. We are finally going to meet face-to-face, and I'll explain all these coincidences and memories I've been having. I'm excited, as if it's our first date. Now I just have to find him.

When we reach the bar, an usher announces that it's open only to cast, crew, and family members. Perfect.

"That's great, so we'll have some peace and quiet," Dad says to her, tipping his cap as he walks in. "Oh, you should have seen my granddaughter up there. Proudest day of my life," he says, putting his hand on his heart.

The woman smiles and allows us entry.

"Come on, Dad." After we've bought our drinks, I drag him deep into the room to sit at a table in the far corner, away from the growing crowd.

"If they try to throw us out, Gracie, I'm not leaving my pint. I just sat down."

I wring my hands nervously and perch on the edge of my seat, looking around for him. Justin. His name doesn't stop rolling around in my head.

People filter in and out of the bar, presumably all family, crew, and cast members. Nobody approaches us again to usher us out, perhaps one of the perks of being with an old man. At last I see Bea's mother enter with the two unknown people from the box and the chubby man I recognize. But no Justin. My eyes dart around the room.

"There she is," I whisper.

"Who?"

"One of the dancers. She was one of the swans."

"How do you know? They all looked the same. Even the nancy boy thought they were the same. Didn't he profess his love to the wrong woman? The bloody eejit."

There's still no sign of Justin, and I begin to worry that this is another wasted opportunity. Perhaps he has left early and isn't coming to the bar at all.

"Dad," I say urgently, "I'm just going to take a look around for somebody. Please do not move from this chair. I'll be back soon."

"The only moving I'll be doing is this." He picks up his pint and brings it to his lips. He takes a gulp of Guinness, closes his eyes, and savors the taste, leaving a white mustache around his lips.

I hurry out of the bar and wander around the huge theater, not sure where to start looking. I stand outside the nearby men's restroom for a few minutes, but he doesn't appear. I look in at the balcony he was seated in, but it's empty.

Justin gives up standing by the exit door as the last few people trickle by him. He must have missed her—stupid to think there was only one exit. He sighs with frustration. He wishes he could transport himself back in time to the day in the salon and relive the moment properly this time. His pocket vibrates, snapping him out of his daydream.

"Bro, where the heck are you?"

"Hi, Al. I saw the woman again."

"The Sky News woman?"

"Yeah!"

"The Viking woman?"

"Yeah, yeah, her."

"The *Antiques Roadshow* wo—"

"*Yes!* For Christ's sake, do we have to go through everything?"

"Hey, did you ever think that maybe she's a stalker?"

"If she's a stalker, then why am I always chasing her?"

"Oh, yeah. Well, maybe you're the stalker and you don't know it."

"Al . . ." Justin grits his teeth.

"Whatever, hurry back up here before Jennifer has a conniption fit. Another one."

Justin sighs. "I'm coming."

He snaps his phone shut and takes one last look down the street. Among the crowd something catches his eye, a red coat. Adrenaline surges. He races outside and pushes past the slowly filtering crowd, his eyes not budging from the coat.

"Joyce!" he calls. "Joyce, wait!" he shouts louder.

She keeps walking, unable to hear him.

He bumps and pushes, getting cursed at and prodded by the crowd, until finally she's just inches from him.

"Joyce," he says breathlessly, reaching out and grabbing her arm. She spins around, a face twisted in surprise and fright. The face of a stranger.

She hits him over the head with her leather bag.

"Ow! Hey! Jesus!"

Apologizing, he slowly makes his way back to the theater, trying to catch his breath, rubbing his sore head, cursing and grumbling to himself in frustration. He reaches for the main door. It doesn't open. He tries it again gently, then rattles it slightly a few times. Within seconds, he pulls and pushes the door with full force, finally kicking at it.

"Hey, hey, hey! We're closed! Theater's closed!" a member of staff informs him from behind the glass.

When I return to the bar, I thankfully find Dad sitting in the corner where I'd left him. Only this time he's not alone. Perched on the chair beside him, her head close to his as though in deep conversation, is Bea. I panic and rush over to them.

"Hi." I say, terrified by what verbal diarrhea may have slipped out of his mouth already.

"Ah, there you are, love. Thought you'd abandoned me. This nice girl came to see if I was okay, seeing as someone tried to throw me out."

"I'm Bea." She smiles, and I can't help but notice how grown-up she has become. How self-assured and confident she seems. I almost feel like telling her that the last time I'd seen her she was "yay high," but I stop myself from gushing.

"Hello, Bea."

"Do I know you?" Frown lines appear on her porcelain forehead.

"Um . . ."

"This is my daughter, Gracie," Dad butts in, and for once I don't correct him.

"Oh, Gracie." Bea shakes her head. "No. I was thinking of someone else. Nice to meet you."

We shake hands, and I hold on for a little too long perhaps, entranced by the feel of her real skin, not just a memory. I quickly let go.

"You were wonderful tonight. I was so proud," I say breathily.

"Proud? Oh, yes, your father told me you designed the costumes." She smiles. "They were beautiful. I'm surprised I hadn't met you until now. I guess we had been dealing with Linda for all the fittings."

My mouth drops. Dad shrugs nervously and sips on what looks to be a new pint. A fresh lie for a fresh pint. The price of his soul.

"Oh, I didn't design them, I just . . ." You just what, Joyce? "I just supervised," I say dumbly. "What else has he been telling you?" I nervously sit down and look around for her father, hoping this isn't the moment he chooses to enter and meet me.

"Well, just as you arrived, he was recalling how he'd once saved a swan's life," she says.

"Single-handedly," they both add in unison and laugh.

"Ha-ha," I force out, sounding fake. "Is that true?" I ask him doubtfully.

"Oh, ye of little faith." Dad takes another gulp of Guinness. Seventy-five years old, and he's already had a brandy and a pint: he'll be on his ear in no time. God knows what he'll be saying then. We'll have to leave soon.

"Well, you know what, girls, it's great to save a life, it really, really is," Dad says from his high horse. "Unless you've done it, you have no idea."

"My father, the hero." I smile.

Bea laughs at Dad. "You sound exactly like my father."

My ears perk up. "Is he here?"

She looks around. "No, not yet. I don't know where he is. Probably hiding from my mom and her new boyfriend, not to mention my boyfriend." She giggles. "But that's another story. Anyway, he considers himself Superman—"

"Why?" I interrupt and try to rein myself in.

"About a month ago, he donated blood," she says and holds her hands up. "Ta-da! That's it!" She laughs. "But he thinks he's some kind of hero that's saved somebody's life. I mean, I don't know, maybe he has. It's all he talks about. He donated it at a mobile unit at the college where he was giving a seminar—you guys probably know it, it's in Dublin. Trinity College? Anyway, he only did it because the doctor was cute and for that Chinese thing, what do you call it? The thing where you save someone's life and they're forever indebted to you or something like that?"

Dad shrugs. "I don't speak Chinese. Or know any. She eats the food all the time, though." He nods his head at me. "Rice with eggs, or something." He wrinkles his nose.

Bea smiles. "Anyway, he figured if he was going to save someone's life, he deserved to be thanked every day by the person he saved."

"How would they do that, then?" Dad leans in.

"By delivering a muffin basket, picking up his dry cleaning, having a newspaper and coffee delivered to his door every morning, a chauffeur-driven car, front-row tickets to the opera . . ." She rolls her eyes and then frowns. "I can't remember what else, but they were all ridiculous things. Anyway, I told him he may as well have a slave if he wants that kind of treatment, not save someone's life." She laughs, and Dad joins her.

I make an O shape with my mouth, but nothing comes out. It's like my body is in shock over Bea's words.

"Don't get me wrong, he's a really thoughtful guy," she adds quickly, misunderstanding my silence. "And I was proud of him for donating blood, as he's absolutely terrified by needles. He has a huge phobia," she explains to Dad, who nods along in agreement. "That's him there." She opens the locket around her neck, and if I have regained my power of speech, it is quickly lost again.

On one side of the locket is a photograph of Bea and her mother, and on the other side, one of her and her father when she was a little girl, in the park on that summer day that is clearly embedded in my memory. I remember how she jumped up and down with excitement and how it had taken so long to get her to sit still. I remember the smell of her hair as she sat on my lap and pushed her head up against mine and shouted "Cheeeeese!" so loudly my ears rang. She hadn't done that to me at all, of course, but I remember it with equal fondness as a childhood day spent fishing with my father, feel all the sensations as clearly as the drink I now taste in my mouth. The cold of the ice, the sweetness of the mineral. It's as real to me as the moments spent with Bea in the park.

"I'll have to put my glasses on to see this," Dad says, moving closer and taking the gold locket in his old fingers. "Where was this?"

"The park near where we used to live. In Chicago. I'm five years old there, with my dad. I love this photograph. It was such a special day." She looks at it fondly. "One of the best."

I smile too, remembering it.

"Photograph!" somebody in the bar calls out.

"Dad, let's get out of here," I whisper while Bea is distracted by the commotion.

"Okay, love, just after this pint—"

"No! Now!" I hiss.

"Group photo! Come on!" Bea says, grabbing Dad's arm.

"Oh!" Dad looks pleased.

"No, no no no no no." I try to smile to hide my panic. "We really must go now."

"Just one photo, Gracie." She smiles. "We have to get the lady who's responsible for all these beautiful costumes."

"No, I'm not—"

"Costume supervisor," Bea corrects herself apologetically.

A woman on the other side of the group throws me a look of horror, upon hearing this. I'm stiff beside Bea, who throws one arm around me and the other arm around her mother.

"Everyone say Tchaikovsky!" Dad shouts.

"Tchaikovsky!" They all cheer and laugh.

The camera flashes.

Justin enters the room.

The crowd breaks up.

I grab Dad and run.

Chapter 26

◇◇◇◇◇

B ACK IN OUR HOTEL ROOM it's lights-out for Dad, who climbs into bed in his brown paisley pajamas, and for me, who is wearing more clothes in bed than I've worn for a long time.

The room is black, thick with shadows, and still, apart from the flashing red digits in the time-display panel at the bottom of the television. Lying flat and still on my back, I attempt to process the day's events. My body once again becomes the subject of much Zulu drumming as my heartbeat intensifies. I feel its pounding rebound against the springs in the mattress beneath me. Then the pulse in my neck vibrates so wildly, it causes my eardrums to join in. Beneath my rib cage, it feels like two fists hammering to get out, and I watch the bedroom door and anticipate the arrival of an African tribe, ready to participate in a synchronized dance at the end of my bed.

The reason for these internal war drums? My mind runs through the zinger Bea dropped only hours ago once again. The words fell from her mouth just like a cymbal falling from its drum set. Since then it has rolled around on the floor and only now lands facedown with a crash, ending my African orchestra. The revelation that Bea's dad, Justin, donated blood a month ago in Dublin, the same month I fell down the stairs and changed my life forever, plays over and over in my mind. Coincidence? A resounding yes. Something more? A shaky possibility. A hopeful possibility.

When is a coincidence just a coincidence, though? And when, if at all, should it be seen as something more? At a time like this? When I am lost and desperate, grieving for a child that was never born and tending to my wounds after a defeated marriage? When what was once clear has instead become cloudy, and what was once considered bizarre has now become a possibility?

It is during troubled times like these that people often see straight, though others watch with concern and try to convince them that they can't possibly be doing so. Weighted minds are just so because of all of their new thoughts. When those who have passed through their troubles and come out the other side suddenly embrace their new beliefs wholeheartedly, it is viewed with cynicism. Why? Because when you're in trouble, you look harder for answers than those who aren't, and it's those answers that are usually the ones to help you through.

This blood transfusion—is it the answer or merely an answer I'm looking for? I've learned over time that answers usually present themselves. They are not hidden under rocks or camouflaged among trees. Answers are right there, in front of our eyes. But if you haven't cause to look, then you will probably never find them.

So, the explanation for the sudden arrival of alien memories, the reason for such a deep connection to Justin—I feel it running through my very veins. Is this the answer that my heart is currently raging within me to realize? It hops up and down now, trying to get my attention, trying to alert me to a problem. I breathe in slowly through my nose and exhale, close my eyes gently and place my hands over my chest, feeling the *thump-thump, thump-thump* that is raging within me. Time to slow everything down now, time to get answers.

Taking the bizarre as a given for just one moment, as people in trouble can do: if I did indeed receive Justin's blood during my transfusion, then my heart is now sending his blood around my body. Some of the blood that once flowed through his veins, keeping him alive, now rushes through mine, helping to keep me alive. Something that came from his heart, that beat within him, that made him who he is, is now a part of me.

At first I shiver at the thought, goose bumps rising on my skin, but on further thought, I snuggle down into the bed and hug my body. I suddenly don't feel so lonely, and I actually feel glad of the company within me. But can this really be the reason for the connection I feel with him? That in flowing from his channels to mine, the blood enabled me to tune in to his frequency and experience his personal memories and passions?

I sigh wearily, knowing nothing in my life makes sense anymore, and not just since the day I fell down the stairs. I had been falling for quite some time before that. That particular day . . . that was the day I'd landed. The first day of the rest of my life—and, quite possibly, thanks to Justin Hitchcock.

It has been a long day. The business at the airport, the *Antiques Roadshow*, then the finale at the Royal Opera House. A tsunami of emotions has come crashing down upon me all in twenty-four hours, pulled me under, and overwhelmed me. I smile now, remembering the events, the precious moments with Dad—from tea at his kitchen table to a mini-adventure in London. I offer a toothy grin to the ceiling above me and a heartfelt thanks beyond the ceiling.

From the darkness I hear wheezing, short rasps drifting into the atmosphere.

"Dad?" I whisper. "Are you okay?"

The wheezing gets louder, and my body freezes.

"Dad?"

Then it's followed by a snort. And a loud guffaw.

"Michael Aspel," he splutters through his laughter. "Christ Almighty, Gracie."

I sigh with relief as his laughter intensifies, becomes so much bigger than him that he almost can't bear it. I giggle at the joyous sound. He laughs harder upon hearing me, and I at him. Our sounds fuel each other. The springs of the mattress beneath me squeak as my body shakes, causing us to roar even more. Thoughts of the umbrella stand, going live with Michael Aspel, the group cheering "Tchaikovsky!" at the camera, the hilarity grows with each flickering scene.

"Oh, my stomach," he howls.

I roll onto my side, hands on my belly.

Dad continues to wheeze and bangs his hand repeatedly on the side cabinet that separates us. I can't stop, and Dad's high-pitched wheezing sets me off even more. I don't think I've ever heard him laugh so much and so heartily. From the pale light seeping through the window beside Dad, I see his legs rise in the air and kick around with glee.

"Oh. My. I. Can't. Stop."

We wheeze and roar and laugh, sit up, lie down, roll around, and try to catch our breaths. We stop momentarily and try to compose ourselves, but it takes over our bodies again, laughing, laughing, laughing in the darkness, at nothing and at everything.

Then we calm down, and there is silence. Dad farts, and we are off again.

Hot tears roll from the sides of my eyes and down my plumped cheeks, which ache from smiling, and I squeeze them with my hands to stop. It occurs to me how happiness and sadness are so closely knitted together. Such a thin line, a threadlike divide. In the midst of emotions, it trembles, blurring the territory of exact opposites. The movement is minute, like the thin string of a spider's web that quivers under a raindrop. Here in my moment of unstoppable cheek- and stomach-aching laughter, as my body rolls around—stomach clenched, muscles taut—it's racked by emotion and steps ever so slightly over the mark, and into sadness. Tears of sadness suddenly gush down my cheeks as my stomach continues to shake and ache with happiness.

I think of Conor and me; how quickly a moment of love was snapped away to a moment of hate. One comment to steal it all away. How love and war stand upon the very same foundations. How my darkest moments, my most fearful times, when faced, became my bravest. At your weakest, you end up showing more strength; at your lowest you are suddenly lifted higher than you've ever been. They all border one another, these opposites, and show how quickly we can be altered. Despair can be altered by one simple smile offered by a stranger; confidence can turn to fear by the arrival of one uneasy presence. Just as Kate's son had wavered on the balance beam, and in an instant his excitement had turned to pain. Everything is on the verge, always brimming the surface, with only a slight shake or a tremble to send things toppling.

Dad stops his laughter so abruptly it concerns me, and I reach for the light.

Pitch-black so quickly becomes light.

He looks at me as though he's done something wrong, but is afraid to admit it. He throws the covers off his body and shuffles into the bathroom, grabbing his travel bag and knocking down everything in his path, refusing to meet my eyes. I look away. How quickly such comfort with someone can shift to awkwardness. When you are convinced you know exactly where you're going, you reach a dead end.

Dad makes his way back to bed, wearing a different pair of pajama bottoms and with a towel tucked under his arm. I turn off the light, both of us quiet now. Light so quickly becomes darkness. I continue to stare at the ceiling, feeling lost again, when only moments ago I'd been found. My recent answers transformed back into questions.

"I can't sleep, Dad." My voice sounds childlike.

"Close your eyes and stare into the dark, love," Dad responds sleepily, sounding thirty years younger too.

Moments later his light snores are audible. Awake . . . and then gone.

A veil hangs between the two opposites, a mere slip of a thing that is too transparent to warn us or comfort us. You hate now, but look through this veil and see the possibility of love; you're sad, but look through to the other side and see happiness. Absolute composure shifting to a complete mess—it happens so quickly, all in the blink of an eye.

Chapter 27

◇◇◇◇◇

"O KAY, I'VE GATHERED US ALL here today because—"

"Somebody died."

"No, Kate." I sigh.

"Well, it sounds like— Ow," she yelps as Frankie, I assume, physically harms her for her tactlessness.

"So are you all red-bused out?" Frankie asks.

I'm seated at the desk in the hotel room, on the phone with the girls, who are huddled at Kate's house on speaker. I'd spent the morning looking around London with Dad, taking photographs of him standing awkwardly in front of anything resembling anything English: red buses, postboxes, police horses, pubs, Buckingham Palace, and a completely unaware transvestite, as Dad was so excited to see "a real one," who was nothing like the local priest who'd lost his mind and wandered the streets wearing a dress in his hometown of Cavan when he was young.

While I chat, Dad is lying on his bed watching *Dancing with the Stars*, drinking a brandy and licking the sour cream and onion off Pringles before depositing the soggy chips back in the can.

I've called a conference call to share the latest news, or more to plead for help and sanity. I may have gone one wish too far, but a girl can always dream.

"One of your kids just puked on me," Frankie says. "Your kid just puked on me."

"Oh, that is not puke, that's just a little dribble."

"No, *this* is dribble . . ."

There's silence.

"Frankie, you are disgusting."

"Okay, girls, girls, please, can you two stop, just this once?"

"Sorry, Joyce, but I can't continue this conversation until *it* is out of here. It's crawling around biting things, climbing on things, drooling on things. It's very distracting. Can't Christian mind it?"

I try not to laugh.

"Do not call my child 'it.' And no, Christian is busy."

"He's watching football."

"He doesn't like to be disturbed, particularly by you."

"Well, you're busy too. How do I get it to come with me?"

Another silence.

"Come here, little boy," Frankie says uneasily.

"His name is Sam. You're his godmother, in case you've forgotten that too."

"No, I haven't forgotten. Just his name." Her voice strains, as though she's lifting weights. "Wow, what do you feed it?"

Sam squeals like a pig. Frankie snorts back.

"Frankie, give him to me. I'll take him to Christian."

"Okay, Joyce," Frankie begins in Kate's absence, "I've done some research on the information you gave me yesterday, and I've brought the paperwork with me. Hold on." I hear papers being ruffled.

"What's all this about?" Kate asks, returning.

"This is about Joyce jumping into the mind of the American man, thereby possessing his memories, skills, and intelligence," Frankie responds.

"What?" Kate shrieks.

"I found out that his name is Justin Hitchcock," I say excitedly.

"How?" Kate asks.

"His surname was in his daughter's biography in last night's ballet program, and his first name, well, I heard that in a dream."

No response. I roll my eyes as I imagine them giving each other that look.

"What the hell is going on here?" Kate asks, confused.

"Google him, Kate," Frankie orders. "Let's see if he exists."

"He exists, believe me," I confirm.

"No, sweetie. You see, the way this works is, we're supposed to think you're crazy for a while before eventually believing you. So let us check up on him, and then we'll go from there."

I lean my chin on my hand and wait.

"While Kate's doing that, I looked into the idea of sharing memories—" Frankie starts.

"What?" Kate shrieks again. "Sharing memories? Are you both out of your mind?"

"No, just me," I say tiredly, now resting my head on the desk.

"Actually, surprisingly enough, it turns out that you're not clinically insane," Frankie continues. "On that count, anyway. I went online and did some research. It turns out you're not alone in feeling that."

I sit up, suddenly alert.

"I read interviews with people who have admitted to experiencing somebody else's memories and even acquiring skills or tastes."

"Oh, you two are pulling my leg. I knew this was a setup. I knew it was out of character for you to drop by, Frankie."

"This isn't a setup," I assure Kate.

"So you're trying to tell me honestly that you've magically acquired somebody else's skills."

"She speaks Latin, French, and Italian," Frankie explains. "But we didn't say it was magically. That would be ridiculous."

"And what about tastes?" Kate is not convinced.

"She eats meat now," Frankie says matter-of-factly.

"But why do you think these are somebody else's skills? Why can't she just have learned Latin, French, and Italian by herself and decided that she suddenly likes meat, like a normal person? Lately I like olives and have an aversion to cheese. Does that mean my body has been possessed by an olive tree?"

"I don't think you're quite getting this. What makes you think olive trees don't like cheese?"

Silence.

"Look, Kate, I agree with you about the change of diet being a natural thing, but in all fairness, Joyce did learn three languages overnight without actually learning them."

"Oh."

"And I have dreams of Justin Hitchcock's private childhood moments," I add.

"Where the hell was I when all of this was happening?"

"Making me do the hokey-pokey live on Sky News," I huff.

I place the phone on speaker and pace the room and watch the time on the bottom of the television as both Frankie and Kate laugh heartily on the other end.

Dad's tongue freezes mid-Pringle lick as his eyes follow me.

"What's that noise?" he finally asks.

"Kate and Frankie laughing," I respond.

He rolls his eyes and continues licking his Pringles, his attention back to a middle-aged news anchor doing the rumba.

After two minutes, the laughter finally stops, and I take them off speaker.

"So as I was saying," Frankie says, catching her breath as though nothing had happened, "what you're experiencing is quite normal—well, not normal, but there are other, eh . . ."

"Freaks?" Kate suggests.

". . . *cases* where people have spoken of similar things. The only thing is, these are all people who have had heart transplants, which is nothing to do with what you've been through, so that blows that theory."

Thump-thump, thump-thump. In my throat again.

"Hold on," Kate butts in, "one person says here that it's because she was abducted by aliens."

"Stop reading my notes, Kate," Frankie hisses. "I wasn't going to mention that part to her."

"Listen"—I interrupt their squabbling—"he donated blood. The same month that I went into hospital."

"So?" Kate says.

"I received a blood transfusion."

"That's not even remotely the same thing."

"Concentrate, Kate. She *received* a blood transfusion," Frankie explains. "Not all that different to the heart transplant theory I just mentioned."

We all go quiet.

Kate breaks the silence. "Okay, so, I still don't get it. Somebody explain."

"Well, it's practically the same thing, isn't it?" I say. "Blood comes from the heart."

Kate gasps. "It came straight from his heart," she says dreamily.

"Oh, so now blood transfusions are romantic to you," Frankie comments. "Let me tell you what I got online: 'Due to reports from several heart transplant recipients claiming experiences of unexpected side effects, Channel Four made a documentary about whether it's possible that in receiving a transplanted organ, a patient could inherit some of their donor's memories, tastes, desires, and habits as well. The documentary follows these people making contact with the donor families in an effort to understand the new life within them. It questions science's understanding of how the memory works, featuring scientists who are pioneering research into the intelligence of the heart and the biochemical basis for memory in our cells.' "

"So if they think that the heart holds more intelligence than we think, then the blood that is pumped from someone's heart could carry that intelligence. So in transfusing his blood, he transfused his memories too?" Kate asks. "And his love of meat and languages," she adds a little tartly.

Nobody wants to say yes to that question. Everybody wants to say no. Apart from me, who's had a night to warm to the idea already.

"Did *Star Trek* have an episode of this one time?" Frankie asks. "Because if they didn't, they should have."

"This can easily be solved," Kate says excitedly. "You can just find out who your blood donor was."

"She can't." Frankie, as usual, dampens the mood. "That kind of information is confidential. Besides, it's not as though she received all of his blood. He could only have donated less than a pint in one go. Then it's separated into white blood cells, red blood cells, plasma, and platelets. What Joyce would have got, if Joyce received it at all, is only a part of his blood. It could even have been mixed with somebody else's."

"His blood is still running through my body," I add. "It doesn't matter how much of it there is. And I remember feeling distinctly odd as soon as I opened my eyes in the hospital."

A silence answers my ridiculous statement, as we all consider the fact that my feeling "distinctly odd" had nothing to do with my transfusion and all to do with the unspeakable tragedy of losing my baby.

"We've got a Google hit for Mr. Justin Hitchcock," Kate fills the silence.

My heart beats rapidly. Please tell me I'm not making it all up, that he exists, that he's not a figment of my delusional mind. That the plans I've already put in place are not going to scare him away.

"Okay, this Justin Hitchcock is a hatmaker in Massachusetts. Hmm. Well, at least he's American. You have any sudden knowledge of hats, Joyce?"

I think hard. "Berets, bucket hats, fedoras, fisherman hats, ball caps, porkpie hats, tweed caps."

Dad stops licking his Pringle again and looks at me. "Panama hat."

"Panama hat," I repeat to the girls.

"Newsboy caps, skullcaps," Kate adds.

"Top hat," Dad says, and I repeat this into the phone.

"Cowboy hat," Frankie says, sounding deep in thought. She snaps out of it. "Wait a minute, what are we doing? Anybody can name hats."

"You're right, it doesn't feel right. Keep reading," I urge.

"Justin Hitchcock moved to Deerfield in 1774, where he served as a soldier and fifer in the Revolution . . . I should probably stop reading this. Over two hundred years old is probably too much of a sugar daddy for you."

"Hold on," Frankie takes over, not wanting me to lose hope. "There's another Justin Hitchcock below that. New York Sanitation Department—"

"No," I say with frustration. "I already know he exists. This is ridiculous. Add Trinity College to the search; he did a seminar there."

Tap-tap-tap.

"No. Nothing for Trinity College."

"Are you sure you spoke to his daughter?" Kate asks.

"Yes," I say through gritted teeth.

"And did anybody see you talking to this girl?" she says sweetly.

I ignore her.

"I'm trying the words *art, architecture, French, Latin, Italian* . . ." Frankie says over the *tap-tap-tap* sound.

"Aha! Gotcha, Justin Hitchcock! Guest lecturer at Trinity College, Dublin. The Faculty of Arts and Humanities. Department of Art and Architecture. Bachelor's degree, Chicago; master's degree, Chicago; Ph.D., Sorbonne University. Special interests are history of Italian Renaissance and Baroque sculpture, painting in Europe in 1600–1900. External responsibilities include founder and editor of the *Art and Architectural Review*. Coauthor of *The Golden Age of Dutch Painting: Vermeer, Metsu and Terborch*, author of *Copper as Canvas: Paintings on Copper, 1575–1775*. He's written over fifty articles in books, journals, dictionaries, and conference proceedings."

"So he exists," Kate says, excited now.

Feeling more confident now, I say, "Try his name with the London National Gallery."

"Why?"

"I have a hunch."

"You and your hunches." Kate continues reading, "He is a curator of European art at the National Gallery, London. Oh, my God, Joyce, he works in London. You should go see him."

"Hold your horses, Kate. She might freak him out and end up in a padded cell. He might not even be the donor," Frankie objects. "And even if he is, it doesn't explain anything."

"It's him," I say confidently. "And if he was my donor, then it means something to me."

"We'll have to figure out a way to find out," Kate offers.

"It's him," I repeat.

"So what are you going to do about it?" Kate asks.

I smile lightly and glance at the clock again. "What makes you think I haven't done something already?"

J USTIN HOLDS THE PHONE TO his ear and paces the small office in the National Gallery as much as he can, stretching the phone cord as far as it will go on each pace, which is not far. Three and a half steps up, five steps down.

"No, no, Simon, I said 'Dutch portraits,' though you're correct, as there certainly will be 'much portraits.' " He laughs. "The age of Rembrandt and Frans Hals," he continues. "I've written a book about that subject, so it's something I'm more than familiar with." A half-written book you stopped working on two years ago, liar.

"The exhibition will include sixty works, all painted between 1600 and 1680."

There is a knock on the door.

"Just a minute," he calls out.

The door opens anyway, and his colleague Roberta enters. Though she's only in her thirties, her back is hunched and her chin pressed to her chest as though she is decades older. Her eyes, mostly cast downward, occasionally flicker up to meet his before falling again. She is apologetic for everything, as always, constantly saying sorry to the world, as though her very presence offends. She tries to maneuver her way through the obstacle course that is Justin's cluttered office to reach his desk. This she does the same way she lives her life, as quietly and as invisibly as possible, which Justin would find admirable if it weren't quite so sad.

"Sorry, Justin," she whispers, carrying a small basket in her hand. "I didn't know you were on the phone, sorry. This was at reception for you. I'll just put it here. Sorry." She backs away, barely making a sound as she tiptoes out of the room and closes the door silently behind her.

He simply nods at her and then tries to concentrate on the conversation again, picking up where he left off.

"It will range from small individual portraits meant for the private home to large-scale group portraits of members of charitable institutions and civic guards."

He stops pacing and eyes the basket suspiciously, feeling as though something inside is about to jump out at him.

"Yes, Simon, in the Sainsbury Wing. If there's anything else you need to know, please do contact me here at the office."

He hurries his colleague off the phone and hangs up. His hand pauses on the receiver, half tempted to call for security. The small basket seems alien and sweet in his musty office, like a newborn baby in a cradle left on the dirty steps of an orphanage. Underneath the wicker handle, the contents are covered by a checked cloth. He stands back and lifts it slowly, preparing to jump away at any moment.

A dozen or so muffins stare back at him.

His heart thumps, and he quickly looks around his box-sized office; he knows nobody is with him, but his discomfort at receiving this surprise gift adds an eerie presence. He searches the basket for a card. Taped to the other side is a small white envelope. With what he realizes now are shaking hands, he rips it rather clumsily from the basket and slides the card out. In the center of the card, in neat handwritten script, it simply says:

Thank you . . .

Chapter 28

◇◇◇◇◇

J USTIN POWER-WALKS THROUGH THE HALLS of the National Gallery, part of him obeying and the other part disobeying the no-running-in-the-halls rule as he jogs three steps then walks three steps, jogs three steps and slows to a walk again. Goody Two-shoes and the daredevil within him battling it out.

He spots Roberta tiptoeing through the hallway, making her way like a shadow to the private library where she has worked for the past five years.

"Roberta!" His daredevil is unleashed, disobeying the no-shouting-in-the-halls rule, and his voice echoes and rebounds off the walls and the high ceilings.

It's enough for Roberta to freeze and turn slowly, her eyes wide and terrified like a deer caught in the headlights. She blushes as the half-dozen others in the hall turn to stare at her. Her gulp is visible from where he stands, and Justin's immediately sorry for breaking her code, for pointing her out when she wants to be invisible. He stops his power-walking and tries to walk quietly along the floors, to glide as she does, in an attempt to retract the noise he has made. She stands, stiff as a board and as close to the wall as possible.

Justin wonders if her behavior is a consequence of her career, or if being a librarian in the National Gallery seemed attractive to her because of her natural way. He thinks the latter.

"Yes," she whispers, wide-eyed and frightened.

"Sorry for shouting your name," he says as quietly as he can.

Her face softens, and her shoulders relax a little.

"Where did you get this basket?" He holds it out to her.

"At reception. I was returning from my break when Charlie asked me to give it to you. Is there something wrong?"

"Charlie." He thinks hard. "He's at the Sir Paul Getty entrance?"

She nods.

"Okay, thank you, Roberta. I apologize again for shouting." He dashes off to the East Wing, his daredevil and good side clashing again in a remarkably confused half-run, half-walk combination, while the basket swings from his hand.

"Finished for the day, Little Red Riding Hood?" He hears a croaky chuckle as he nears his destination.

Justin, noticing he has been skipping along with the basket, stops abruptly and spins around to face Charlie, the gallery's six-foot-tall security guard.

"My, Grandmother, what an ugly head you have."

"What do you want?"

"I was wondering who gave you this basket?"

"A delivery guy from . . ." Charlie moves over to behind his small desk and riffles through some papers. He retrieves a clipboard. "Harrods. Zhang Wei," he reads. "Why? Something wrong with the muffins?" He runs his tongue over his teeth and clears his throat.

Justin's eyes narrow. "How did you know they were muffins?"

Charlie refuses to meet his stare. "Had to check, didn't I? This is the National Gallery. You can't expect me to accept a package without knowing what's in it."

Justin studies Charlie, whose face has pinked. He spies crumbs stuck to the corners of his mouth; there are slight traces down his uniform. He removes the checked cloth from his hamper and counts. Eleven muffins.

"Don't you think it's odd to send a person eleven muffins?"

"Odd?" Eyes wander, shoulders fidget. "Dunno, mate. Never sent muffins to anyone in my life."

"Wouldn't it seem more obvious to send a dozen muffins?"

Shoulders shrug. Fingers fidget. Charlie's eyes now turn to study everybody that enters the gallery, far more intently than usual. His body language tells Justin that he's finished with the conversation.

Justin whips out his cell phone as he exits to Trafalgar Square.

"Hello?"

"Bea, it's Dad."

"I'm not talking to you."

"Why not?"

"Peter told me what you said to him at the ballet last night," she snaps.

"What did I do?"

"You interrogated him about his intentions all night."

"I'm your father, that's my job."

"No, what you did is the job of the Gestapo," she fumes. "I swear, I'm not speaking to you until you apologize to him."

"Apologize?" He laughs. "What for? I merely made a few inquiries into his past, in order to ascertain his agenda."

"Agenda? He doesn't have an agenda!"

"So I asked him a few questions, so what? Bea, he's not good enough for you."

"No, he's not good enough for *you*. Anyway, I don't care what you think of him, it's me that's supposed to be happy."

"He picks strawberries for a living."

"He is an IT consultant!"

"Then who picks strawberries?" Somebody picks strawberries. "Well, honey, you know how I feel about consultants. If they are so amazing at something, why don't they do it themselves, instead of just making money telling people how to do it?"

"You're a lecturer, curator, reviewer, whatever. If you know so much, why don't you just build a building or paint a damn picture yourself?" she shouts. "Instead of just bragging to everybody about how much you know about them!"

Hmm.

"Sweetheart, let's not get out of control now."

"No, you are the one out of control. You will apologize to Peter, and if you don't, I will not answer your phone calls, and you can deal with your little dramas all by yourself."

"Wait, wait, wait. Just one question."

"Dad, I—"

"Did-you-send-me-a-hamper-of-a-dozen-cinnamon-muffins?" he rushes out.

"What? No!"

"No?"

"No muffins! No conversations, no nothing—"

"Now, now, sweetheart, there's no need for double negatives."

"I'll have no more contact with you until you apologize," she finishes.

"Okay." He sighs. "Sorry."

"Not to me. To Peter."

"Okay, but does that mean you won't be collecting my dry cleaning on your way over tomorrow? You know where it is, it's the one beside the tube station—"

The phone clicks. He stares at it in confusion. My own daughter hung up on me? I knew this Peter was trouble.

He thinks again about the muffins and dials another number. He clears his throat.

"Hello."

"Jennifer, it's Justin."

"Hello, Justin." Her voice is cold.

Used to be warm. Like honey. No, like hot caramel. It used to bounce from octave to octave when she said his name, just like the piano music he'd wake early on Sunday mornings to hear her play from the conservatory. But now?

He listens to the silence on the other end. Ice.

"I'm just calling to see whether you'd sent me a basket of muffins." As soon as he's said it, he realizes how ridiculous this call is. Of course she didn't send him anything. Why would she?

"I beg your pardon?"

"I received a basket of muffins at my office today along with a thank-you note, but the note failed to reveal the sender's identity. I was wondering if it was you."

Her voice is amused now. No, not amused, mocking. "What would I have to thank you for, Justin?"

It's a simple question, but because he knows her as he does, it has implications far beyond the words, and of course Justin jumps up and snaps at the bait. The hook cuts through his lip, and bitter Justin is back, the voice he grew so accustomed to during the demise of their . . . well, during their demise. She has reeled him right in.

"Oh, I don't know, twenty years of marriage, perhaps. A daughter. A good living. A roof over your head." He knows it's a stupid statement. That before him, after him, and even without him, she had and always would have a roof, of all things, over her head. But it's spurting out of him now, and he can't stop and won't stop, for he is right and she is wrong and anger is spurring on every word, like a jockey whipping his horse as they near the finish line. "Travel all over the world." Whip-crack-away! "Clothes, clothes, and more clothes." Whip-crack-away! "A new kitchen when we didn't need one, a conservatory, for Christ's sake . . ." And he goes on, like a man from the nineteenth century who'd been keeping his wife accustomed to a good life she would otherwise have been without, ignoring the fact that she had made a good living herself playing in an orchestra that traveled the world.

At the beginning of their married life they had no choice but to live with Justin's mother. They were young and had a baby to rear, the reason for their hasty marriage, and as Justin was still attending college by day, bartending at night, and working at an art museum on the weekends, Jennifer had made money playing the piano at an upmarket restaurant in Chicago. She would return home in the early hours of the morning, her back sore and tendonitis in her middle finger, but the memory of this flies out of his mind at this moment. Finally running out of things to list from the last twenty years, and out of steam, he stops.

Jennifer is silent, refusing to spar with him this time.

"Jennifer?"

"Yes, Justin." Icy again.

Justin sighs with exhaustion. "So, was it you?"

"It must have been one of your other women, because it most certainly wasn't me."

Click, and she's gone.

Rage bubbles inside him. Other women. Other women! One affair when he was twenty years old, a fumble in the dark with Mary-Beth Dursoa at college, before he and Jennifer were even married, and she carries on as though he were Don Juan. In their bedroom, he'd even put a print of *A Satyr Mourning over a Nymph* by Piero di Cosimo, which Jennifer had always loathed but which he had always hoped would send her subliminal messages. In the painting there is a young girl, semiclothed, who on first glance seems asleep, but on further viewing has blood seeping from her throat. A satyr is mourning her. Justin's interpretation of the painting is that the woman, mistrusting her husband's fidelity, followed him into the woods. He was hunting, not going astray as she thought, and shot her by accident. Sometimes during his and Jennifer's toughest arguments, their eyes stinging with tears, their hearts breaking from the pain, their heads pounding from the analysis, Justin would study the painting and envy the satyr.

Fuming, he charges down the North Terrace steps, sits down by one of the fountains, places the basket by his feet, and bites into a muffin, wolfing it down so quickly he barely has time to taste it. Crumbs fall at his feet, attracting a flock of pigeons with intent in their beady black eyes. He goes to reach for another muffin, but he is swarmed by even more overenthusiastic pigeons pecking at the contents of his basket. Peck, peck, peck—he watches dozens more flock toward him, coming in to land like fighter jets. Afraid of falling missiles from those that circle his head, he picks up his basket and shoos them away with all the butchness of an eleven-year-old.

A few minutes later he breezes in the front door of his home, not even taking the time to close it, and is immediately greeted by Doris, with a paint palette in her hand.

"Okay, so I've narrowed it down," she begins, thrusting dozens of colors in his face.

Her long leopard-print nails are each decorated with a diamanté jewel. She wears an all-in-one snakeskin jumpsuit, and her feet wobble dangerously in patent lace-up ankle stilettos. Her hair is its usual shock of red; her eyes are catlike, with inky eyeliner sweeping up from the corners of her eyes; and with her painted lips matching her hair, she reminds him of Ronald McDonald.

Not sensing his mood, she begins, "Gooseberry Fool, Celtic Forest, English Mist, and Woodland Pearl, all calm tones, would look so good in this room, or even Wild Mushroom, Nomadic Glow, and Sultana Spice. Cappuccino Candy is one of my faves, but I don't think it'll work next to that curtain, do you?"

She waves a fabric in front of his face, and it tickles his nose, which tingles with such intensity it senses the fight that is about to brew. He doesn't respond, but takes deep breaths and counts to ten in his mind. And when that doesn't stop her from listing more paint colors, he keeps on going to twenty.

"Hello? Justin?" She snaps her fingers in his face. "Hel-lo?"

"Maybe you should give Justin a break, Doris. He looks tired." Al looks nervously at his brother.

"But—"

"Get your sultana spice behind over here," he teases, and she whoops.

"Okay, but just one more thing. Bea will love her room done in Ivory Lace. And Petey too. Imagine how romantic this will be for—"

"*Enough!*" Justin screams at the top of his lungs, not wanting his daughter's name and the word *romantic* to share the same sentence.

Doris jumps and immediately stops talking. Her hand flies to her chest. Al stops mid-gulp, his bottle freezing just below his lips, his heavy breathing above the rim making strange pipe music. Other than that, there's absolute silence.

"Doris"—Justin takes a deep breath and tries to speak as calmly as possible—"enough of this, please. Enough of this Cappuccino Nights—"

"Candy," she interrupts, and quickly falls silent again.

"Whatever. This is a Victorian house, from the nineteenth century, not some painted lady from an episode of *Changing Rooms*." He tries to restrain his emotions, his feelings on behalf of the building. "If you had mentioned Cappuccino Chocolate—"

"Candy," she whispers.

"Whatever! To anyone during that time, you would have been instantly burned at the stake."

She squeaks, insulted.

"It needs sophistication, it needs to be researched, it needs furniture of the period, colors of the period. It can't have a room that sounds like Al's dinner menu."

"Hey!" Al speaks up.

"I think it needs—" Justin takes another deep breath and says gently, "somebody else for the job. Maybe it's just bigger than you thought it was going to be, but I appreciate your help, really I do. Please tell me you understand."

She nods slowly, and he breathes a sigh of relief.

Suddenly the paint palettes go flying across the room as Doris lets rip, "You pretentious little bastaaaaard!"

"Doris!" Al leaps up out of his armchair, or at least makes a great attempt to.

Justin immediately takes three steps back as she walks aggressively toward him, pointing a sparkly animal-print nail at him like a weapon.

"Listen here, you silly little man. I have spent the last two weeks researching this dump of a basement in the kinds of libraries and places you wouldn't even think exist. I've been to dark, dingy dungeons where people smell of old . . . things." Her nostrils flare, and her voice deepens threateningly. "I purchased every historic period paint brochure that I could get my hands on and applied the colors in accordance with the color rules at the end of the nineteenth century. I've shaken hands with people and seen parts of London you don't even wanna know about. I've looked through books so old, the dust mites were big enough to hand them to me from the shelves. I've been to secondhand, thirdhand, even antique stores and have sat in chairs so rickety I could smell the black death that killed the last person who died sitting on them. I have sanded down so much pine, I have splinters in places you don't wanna see. So." She prods him in the chest with her dagger nail as she emphasizes each word, finally backing him up against the wall. "Don't. Tell. Me. That this is too big for me."

She clears her throat and stands up straight. The anger in her voice is replaced with a vulnerable "poor me" tremble. "But despite what you said, I will finish this project. I will go on undeterred. I will do it in spite of you, and I will do it for your brother, who might be dead next month, not that you even care."

"Dead?" Justin's eyes widen.

With that, she turns on her heel and storms off into her bedroom.

She sticks her head back in the doorway. "By the way, just so you know, I would have banged the door behind me *very loudly* to show just how angry I am, but it's currently out in the backyard ready for sanding and priming before I paint it"—and this she spits out rebelliously—"Ivory Lace."

Then she disappears again, without a bang.

I shift from foot to foot nervously outside Justin's front door, which is oddly wide open. Should I ring the bell? Simply call his name? Will he call the police and have me arrested for trespassing? Oh, this was such a bad idea. Frankie and Kate have persuaded me to come here to present myself to him. They pumped me up to such a point I hopped in the first taxi that came my way and took it to Trafalgar Square, to try to catch him at the National Gallery before he left. I ended up trailing him on the street while he was on the phone, hearing him question someone about the basket. I'd felt oddly comfortable just watching him, without his knowing, reveling in the secret thrill of being able to actually see him for who he is instead of just viewing his memories.

His anger at whoever was on the phone—most likely his ex-wife, the woman with the red hair and freckles—convinced me it was the wrong time to approach him, and so I just continued to follow him, figuring I'd build up the courage to talk to him eventually. Would I mention the transfusion? Would he think I was crazy, or would he be open to listening—or even better, open to believing?

But once we were on the tube, the timing again wasn't right. It was overcrowded, people were pushing and shoving, and eye contact, never mind first-time introductions or conversations about the possible intelligence of blood, was impossible. And so after pacing up and down his street, feeling like a schoolgirl with a crush and a stalker at the same time, I now find myself standing on his doorstep with a plan. I am drawn to this man that I have barely met, in ways I've never been drawn to anybody, not even my husband. But my plan is once again being compromised as Justin and his brother Al begin to talk about something I know I shouldn't be hearing, about a family secret I am more than familiar with already.

I move my finger away from the doorbell, keep hidden from all the windows, and bide my time.

Chapter 29

◇◇◇◇◇

JUSTIN LOOKS TO HIS BROTHER in panic and searches quickly
for something to sit on. He drags over a giant paint tub and sits
down, not noticing the wet white ring of paint around the top.

"Al, what was she talking about? About you being dead next
month."

"No, no, no." Al laughs. "She said *might* be dead. That's distinctly different. Hey, you got away lightly there, bro. Good for
you. I think that Valium is really helping her. Cheers." He holds up
his bottle and downs the last of his beer.

"Hold on, hold on. Al, what are you talking about? Is there
something you haven't told me? What did the doctor say?"

"He told me exactly what I've been telling you for the last two
weeks. If any members of a person's immediate family developed
coronary heart disease at a young age, i.e., a male under fifty-five
years old, well then, we have an increased risk of coronary heart
disease."

"Do you have high blood pressure?"

"A little."

"Do you have high cholesterol?"

"A lot."

"So, all you do is make lifestyle changes, Al. It doesn't mean you're going to be struck down like . . . like . . ."

"Dad?"

"No." Justin frowns and shakes his head.

"Coronary heart disease is the number-one killer of American males and females. Every thirty-three seconds an American will suffer some type of coronary event, and almost every minute someone will die from it." He looks at their mother's grandfather clock, half covered by a dust sheet. The minute hand moves. Al grabs his heart and starts groaning. His noises soon turn to laughter.

Justin rolls his eyes. "Who told you that nonsense?"

"The pamphlets at the doc's office said so."

"Al, you're not going to have a heart attack."

"It's my fortieth birthday next week."

"Yeah, I know." Justin hits him playfully on the knee. "That's the spirit, we'll have a big party."

"That's the age Dad was when he died." Al lowers his eyes and peels the label from his beer bottle.

"That's what this is about?" Justin's voice softens. "Dammit, Al, is that what this is all about? Why didn't you say something earlier?"

"I just thought that I'd spend some time with you before, you know, just in case . . ." His eyes tear up, and he looks away.

Tell him the truth.

"Al, listen, there's something you should know." Justin's voice trembles, and he clears his throat, trying to control it. You've never told anyone. "Dad was under a huge amount of pressure at work. He had a lot of difficulties, financial and otherwise, that he didn't tell anyone. Not even Mom."

"I know, Justin. I know."

"You know?"

"Yeah, I get it. He didn't just drop dead for no reason. He was stressed out of his mind. And I'm not, I know that. But ever since I was a kid, I've had this feeling hanging over me that it's gonna happen to me, too. It's been playing on my mind for as long as I can remember, and now that my birthday's next week and I'm not in the greatest of shape . . . Things have been real busy at work, and I haven't been looking after myself. Never could do it like you could, you know?"

"Hey, you don't have to explain it to me."

"Remember that day we spent with him on the front lawn? With the sprinklers? Just hours before Mom found him . . . Well, remember playing around, the whole family?"

"Those were good times." Justin smiles, fighting back tears.

"You remember?" Al says.

"Like it was yesterday," Justin says.

"Dad was holding the hose and spraying us both. He was in such a good mood." Al frowns in confusion and thinks for a while, then the smile returns. "He'd brought Mom a huge bunch of flowers—remember she put that big one in her hair?"

"The sunflower." Justin nods along.

"And it was real hot. Do you remember it being real hot?"

"Yeah."

"And Dad had his pants rolled up to his knees and his shoes and socks off. And the grass was getting wet and his feet were all covered in grass and he just kept chasing us around and around . . ." He smiles into the distance. "That was the last time I saw him."

It wasn't for me.

Justin's memory flashes to the image of his father closing the living-room door. Justin had run into the house from the front yard to go to the bathroom; all that playing around with water was almost making him burst. As far as he knew, everyone else was still outside playing. He could hear his mom chasing and taunting Al, and Al, who was only five years old, screeching with laughter. But as Justin came back downstairs, he spotted his dad coming out of the kitchen and walking down the hall. Justin, wanting to jump out and surprise him, crouched down and watched him from behind the banister.

That was then he saw what was in his father's hand. The bottle of liquid that was always locked away in the kitchen cabinet and only taken out on special occasions when his dad's family came over from Ireland to visit. When they all drank from that bottle, they would change; they would sing songs that Justin had never heard but that his dad knew every word of, and they would laugh and tell stories and sometimes cry. He wasn't sure why that bottle was in his dad's hands now. Did he want to sing and laugh and tell stories today? Did he want to cry?

Then Justin saw the bottle of pills. He knew they were pills, because they were in the same container as the medicine Mom and Dad took when they were sick. He hoped his dad wasn't feeling sick now, and watched as he closed the door behind him with the pills and bottle in his hands. He should have known then what his dad was about to do, but he didn't. Whenever he recalls this moment, years later, he always tries to call out and stop him. But the nine-year-old Justin never hears him. He stays crouched on the stair, waiting for his dad to come out so he can jump out and surprise him. As time went by, he began to feel that something wasn't right, but he didn't quite know why he felt that way and didn't want to ruin the big surprise by checking on his dad.

After minutes that felt like hours, hearing nothing but silence from behind the door, Justin gulped and stood up. He could hear Al still screaming with laughter outside, even as he went inside and saw the green feet on the floor. He remembers the sight of those feet so vividly. He remembers following those feet and finding his dad on the floor, lying there like a big green giant, staring lifelessly at the ceiling.

He didn't say anything then. Didn't scream, didn't touch him, didn't kiss him, didn't try to help him because though he didn't understand much at that time, he knew that it was too late for help. He just slowly backed out of the room, closed the door behind him, and ran out to the front lawn to his mom and younger brother.

They had five minutes. Five more minutes of everything being exactly the same. He was nine years old on a sunny day with a mom and a dad and a brother, and he was happy. All the food they ate for dinner was made by his mom, and when he was bad at school the teachers shouted at him, like they should. Five more minutes of everything being the same, until his mom went into the house and then everything changed. Five minutes later, he wasn't nine years old with a mom, a dad, and a brother. He wasn't happy, neither was Mom, and the neighbors smiled at him with such sadness he wished they wouldn't bother smiling at all. Everything they ate came from containers carried over by women who lived on their street, and when he acted up at school, the teachers just looked at him with that same look of pity. Everyone now had the same face.

Mom told them that Dad had suffered a heart attack. It's what she told the entire family, and anybody who came by with a home-cooked meal or pie.

Justin could never bring himself to tell anyone he knew the truth, partly because he wanted to believe the lie and partly because he thought his mother had started to believe it too. So he kept it to himself. He hadn't even told Jennifer during their marriage, because saying it out loud made it true, and he did not want to validate his father's dying that way. And now, with their mother gone, he was the only person who knew the truth about his dad. The story of their father's death fabricated to help them had ended up hanging like a black cloud over Al and becoming a burden for Justin.

He wanted to tell Al the truth right now, he really did. But how could it help him? Surely knowing the real story would be far worse, and Justin would have to explain how and why he'd kept it from his brother all these years. . . . But then he would no longer have to shoulder all the burden. Perhaps he could finally find some release, helping Al's fear of heart failure in the process.

"Al, there's something I have to tell you," Justin begins.

The doorbell rings suddenly, a sharp sting of a ring that startles them both from their thoughts, smashing the silence like a sledgehammer through glass.

"Is someone gonna get that?" Doris yells.

Justin walks to the door with a white ring of paint around his behind. The door is already ajar, and he pulls it open farther. Before him, on the railings, hangs his dry-cleaning, his suits, shirts, and sweaters all covered in plastic. But nobody is there. He steps outside and runs up the steps to see who has left them there, but apart from the huge trash bin that Doris has set up, the front lawn is empty.

"Who is it?" Doris calls.

"Nobody," Justin responds, confused. He unhooks the hangers from the railing and carries them inside.

"You're telling me that cheap suit just pressed the doorbell itself?" she comes out and asks, still angry at him from before.

"I don't know. It's peculiar. Bea was going to collect all these tomorrow. I hadn't arranged a delivery with the dry cleaners."

"Maybe it's a special delivery for being such a good customer, because by the looks of it, they dry-cleaned your entire wardrobe." She eyes his choice of clothes with distaste.

"Yeah, and I'll bet the special delivery comes with a big bill," he grumbles. "I had a little falling-out with Bea earlier; maybe she organized this as an apology."

"Oh, you are a stubborn man." Doris rolls her eyes. "Do you ever think for a second that it's you who should be making the apologies?"

Justin narrows his eyes at her. "Why did you talk to Bea?"

"Hey, look, there's an envelope here," Al points out, interrupting the beginnings of another fight.

"There's your bill." Doris laughs.

Justin's heart immediately leaps to his mouth as he catches sight of the familiar stationery. He throws the pile of clothes down on the floor and rips off the envelope.

"Be careful! These have just been pressed." Doris takes them and hangs them from the door frame.

He opens the envelope and gulps hard, reading the note.

"What does it say?" Al asks.

"It must be a death threat, by the look on his face," Doris says excitedly. "Or a ransom note. What's wrong, and how much do they want?" She giggles.

Justin takes out the card he received earlier with the muffin basket, and he holds the two cards together so that they make a complete sentence. Reading the words causes a chill to run through his body.

Thank you . . . for saving my life.

Chapter 30

◇◇◇◇◇

I LIE IN THE TRASH bin, breathless, my heart beating at the speed of a hummingbird's wings. I'm like a child playing hide-and-seek, intense nervous excitement rolling around in my tummy. Please don't find me, Justin, don't find me like this, lying at the bottom of the trash bin in your garden, covered in plaster and dust. I finally hear his footsteps move away, then back down the steps to his basement apartment.

What on earth have I become? A coward. I chickened out and rang the doorbell to stop Justin from telling Al the story about their father, and then, afraid of playing God to two strangers, I ran, eventually leaping and landing in the bottom of the bin. How metaphorical. I'm not sure I'll ever be able to speak to him now. I don't know how I'll ever find the words to explain how I'm feeling. The world is not a patient place: Stories such as these are mostly for the pages of the *Enquirer* or for double-page spreads in certain women's magazines. Beside my story would be a photograph of me in my dad's kitchen, looking forlornly at the camera. With no makeup. No, Justin would never believe this story if I told him—so I'm counting on actions speaking louder than words.

Lying on my back, I stare up at the sky. The clouds stare right back down at me. They pass over the woman in the trash with curiosity, calling the stragglers behind them to come see. More clouds gather, eager to witness what the others are grumbling about. Then they too pass over, leaving me staring at empty blue and the occasional white wisp. I almost hear my mother up there laughing aloud, imagine her nudging her friends to come have a look at her silly daughter. I picture her peeping over a cloud, hanging over too far like Dad with the balcony at the Royal Opera House. I smile, enjoying this now.

Now, as I brush dust, paint, and wood chips from my clothes and clamber out of the bin, I try to remember what other things Bea mentioned her father wanted to have done by the person he saved.

"Justin, calm down, for creep's sake. You're making me nervous." Doris sits on a stepladder and watches Justin pace up and down the room.

"I can't calm down. Do you not understand what this means?" He hands her the two cards.

Her eyes widen. "You saved someone's life?"

"Yeah." He shrugs and stops pacing. "It's really no big deal. Sometimes you just gotta do what you gotta do—"

"He donated blood," Al interrupts his brother's failed attempt at modesty.

"You donated blood?"

"It's how he met Vampira, remember?" Al refreshes his wife's memory. "In Ireland, when they say, 'Fancy a pint?' beware."

"Her name is Sarah."

"So you donated blood to get a date." Doris folds her arms. "Is there anything you do for the greater good of humanity, or is it all just for yourself?"

"Hey, I have a heart."

"Though a pint lighter than it was," Al adds.

"I have donated plenty of my time to helping organizations—colleges, universities, galleries—in need of my expertise. Something I don't have to do, but which I have agreed to do for them."

"Yeah, and I bet you charge them per word. That's why he says 'oops-a-daisy' instead of 'shit' when he stubs his toe," Al says.

Al and Doris dissolve into laughter, thumping and hitting each other in their fit.

Justin takes a deep breath. "Let's get back to the matter at hand. Who is sending me these notes and running these errands?" He begins pacing again and biting his nails. "Maybe this is Bea's idea of a joke. She's the only person I talked to about deserving thanks in return for saving a life."

Please, don't be Bea.

"Man, you are selfish," Al says.

"No." Doris shakes her head. Her long earrings whip against her cheeks with each movement, but her back-brushed hair-sprayed hair remains still as ever. "Bea wants nothing to do with you until you apologize. No words can describe how much she hates you right now."

"Well, thank God for that." Justin continues pacing. "But she must have told somebody, or else this wouldn't be happening. Doris, find out from Bea who she spoke to about this."

"Huh." Doris lifts her chin and looks away. "You said some pretty nasty things to me before. I don't know if I can help you."

Justin falls to his knees and shuffles over to her.

"Please, Doris, I'm begging you. I am so, so sorry for what I said. I had no idea how much time and effort you were putting into this place. I underestimated you. Without you, I'd still be drinking from a toothbrush holder and eating from a cat bowl."

"Yeah, I meant to ask you about that," Al interrupts his brother's groveling. "You don't even have a cat."

"So I'm a good interior designer?" Doris lifts her chin.

"A great designer."

"How great?"

"Greater than . . ." He stalls. "Andrea Palladio."

Her eyes look to the left, then look to the right. "Is she better than Ty Pennington?"

"*He* was an Italian architect in the sixteenth century, widely considered the most influential person in the history of Western architecture."

"Oh. Okay. Then you're forgiven." She holds out her hand. "Give me your phone, and I'll call Bea right now."

Moments later they are all seated around the new kitchen table, listening to Doris's half of the phone conversation.

"Okay, Bea told Petey, and the costume supervisor for *Swan Lake*. And her father."

"The costume supervisor? Do you guys still have the program from the performance?"

Doris disappears to her bedroom and returns with her program. She flicks through it and finds the bio pages.

"No." Justin shakes his head upon reading her biography. "I met this woman that night, and it can't be her. But her father was there? I didn't see her father."

Al shrugs.

"Well, this costume supervisor isn't involved in this, I certainly didn't save her life or her father's. The person must be Irish, or at least received medical attention in an Irish hospital."

"Maybe her dad's Irish, or was in Ireland."

"Give me that program, I'm calling the theater."

"Justin, you can't just call her up." Doris dives for the program in his hand, but he dodges her. "What are you going to say?"

"All I need to know is if her father is Irish or was in Ireland during the past month. I'll make the rest up as I go along."

Al and Doris look at each other worriedly while Justin leaves the kitchen to make the call.

"Did you do this?" Doris asks Al quietly.

"No way." Al shakes his head, his chins wobbling.

Five minutes later Justin returns.

"She remembered me from last night, and no, it's not her or her father. So either Bea told somebody else or . . . it must be Peter fooling around. I'm gonna get that little kid and—"

"Grow up, Justin. It's not him," Doris says sternly. "Start looking elsewhere. Call the dry cleaners, call the guy who delivered the muffins."

"I have already. They were charged to a credit card, and they can't release the owner's details."

"Your life is just one big mystery. Between the Joyce woman and these mysterious deliveries, you should hire a private investigator," Doris responds. "Oh! I just remembered." She reaches into her pocket and hands him a piece of paper. "Speaking of investigators . . . I got this for you. I've had it for a few days but didn't say anything because I didn't want you going on a wild goose chase and making a fool of yourself. But seeing as you're choosing to do that anyway, here."

She hands him a piece of paper with Joyce's details.

"I called international directory inquiries and gave them the number of the Joyce person that showed up on Bea's phone last week. They gave me the address that goes with it. I think it'd be a better idea to find this woman, Justin. Forget this good-deeds person. It seems like very odd behavior to me. Who knows who's sending you these notes? Concentrate on the woman; a nice healthy relationship is what you need."

He barely reads the paper before putting it in his jacket pocket, totally uninterested, his mind elsewhere. Ever since the near-miss at the ballet, he's made an effort not to think about Joyce. He doesn't have time for wild goose chases.

"You just jump from one woman to another, don't you?" Doris studies him.

"Hey, it could be the Joyce woman that's sending the messages," Al pipes up.

Doris and Justin both look at him and roll their eyes.

"Don't be ridiculous, Al," Justin dismisses him. "I met her in a hair salon. Anyway, who says it's a woman that's doing this?"

"Well, it's obvious," Al replies. "Because you were given a muffin basket." He scrunches up his nose. "Only a woman would think of sending baked goods. Or a gay man. And whoever it is, he or she—maybe it's a heshe—knows how to do calligraphy, which further backs up my theory. Woman, gay guy, or tranny," he sums up.

"I was the one who thought of the muffin basket idea!" Justin puffs. "And I do calligraphy."

"Yeah, like I said. Woman, gay guy, or tranny." He grins.

Justin throws his hands up in exasperation and falls back in his chair. "You two are no help."

"Hey, I know who could help you." Al sits up.

"Who?" Justin rests his chin on his fist, bored.

"Vampira," Al says spookily.

"I've already asked her for help. All she could tell me were my blood details in the database. Nothing about who received my donation. She won't tell me where my blood went, and in any case, she won't speak to me."

"On account of you leaving her to run after a Viking bus?"

"That had something to do with it."

"Gee, Justin, you really have a beautiful way with women."

"Well, at least somebody thinks I'm doing something right." He stares at the two cards he's placed in the center of the table.

But are you?

"You don't have to ask Sarah straight out. Maybe you could snoop around in her office." Al gets excited.

"No, that would be wrong," Justin says unconvincingly. "I could get into trouble. I could get her into trouble, and besides, I've treated her so badly."

"So a really lovely thing to do," Doris says slyly, "would be to drop by her office and tell her you're sorry. As a friend."

A smile slowly creeps onto each of their faces.

"But can you take a day off work next week to go to Dublin?" Doris asks, breaking their evil moment.

"I've already accepted an invitation from the National Gallery in Dublin to give a talk on Terborch's *Woman Writing a Letter*," Justin says excitedly.

"What's the painting of?" Al asks.

"A woman writing a letter, Sherlock," Doris snorts.

"What a boring story." Al scrunches up his nose, then watches as Justin reads the notes over and over, hoping to decipher a hidden code.

"*Man Reading a Note*," Al says rather grandly. "Discuss."

He and Doris crack up again as Justin takes that moment to exit the room.

"Hey, where are you going?"

"Man booking a flight." He winks.

Chapter 31

◇◇◇◇◇

A T SEVEN FIFTEEN THE NEXT morning, just before Justin leaves for work, he stands poised at the front door, hand on the door handle.

"Justin, where's Al? He wasn't in bed when I woke up." Doris shuffles out in her slippers and robe. "What on earth are you doing now, you funny little man?"

Justin holds a finger to his lips, hushing her, and jerks his head in the direction of the closed door.

"Is the blood person out there?" she whispers excitedly, kicking off her slippers and tiptoeing like a cartoon character to join him at the door.

He nods excitedly.

They press their ears up against the door, and Doris's eyes widen. "I can hear!" she mouths.

"Okay, on three," he whispers, and they mouth together, One, two— He pulls the door open with full force. "Ha! Gotcha!" he shouts, striking an attacker's pose and pointing his finger with more aggression than intended.

"Aaaah!" the postman screams with fright, dropping envelopes by Justin's feet. He fires a package at Justin and holds another parcel by his head in defense.

"Aaaah!" Doris shouts.

Justin doubles over as the package hits between his legs. He falls to his knees, his face turning red as he gasps for air.

They all hold their chests, panting.

The postman remains cowered, his knees bent, his head covered by the package.

"Justin"—Doris picks up an envelope and hits Justin across the arm—"you idiot! It's the postman."

"Yes," Justin rasps, making choking sounds. "I can see that now." He takes a moment to compose himself. "It's okay, sir, you can lower your package now. I'm sorry to have frightened you."

The postman slowly lowers the parcel, fear and confusion in his eyes. "What was that about?"

"I thought you were someone else. I'm sorry, I was expecting . . . something else." He looks to the envelopes on the floor. All bills. "Is there nothing else for me?"

His left arm starts to niggle at him. Tingling as though a mosquito has bitten him. He starts to scratch. Lightly at first, and then he pats his inner elbow, smacking the itch away. The tingling becomes more intense, and he digs his nail into his skin, scratching over and over. Beads of sweat break out on his forehead.

The postman shakes his head and starts to back away.

"Did nobody give you anything to deliver to me?" Justin climbs back to his feet and moves closer, unintentionally appearing threatening.

"No, I said no." The postman rushes up the steps to get away.

Justin watches him flee, confused.

"Leave the man alone. You almost gave him a heart attack." Doris continues picking up the envelopes. "If you have that reaction to the real person, you'll scare them off too. If you ever do meet this person, I advise you to rethink the 'Ha! Gotcha!' routine."

Justin pulls up the sleeve of his shirt and examines his arm, expecting to find red lumps or a rash, but there are no marks on his skin apart from the scratch marks he has made himself.

"Are you on something?" Doris narrows her eyes.

"No!"

She shuffles back into the kitchen with a harrumphing sound. "Al?" her voice echoes around the kitchen. "Where are you?"

"Help! Help me! Someone!"

In the distance they hear Al's voice, muffled as though his mouth is stuffed with socks.

Doris gasps, "Baby?" Justin hears the fridge door opening. "Al?" A few seconds later she returns to the living room, shaking her head, alerting Justin to the fact that her husband was not in the fridge after all.

Justin rolls his eyes. "He's outside, Doris."

"Then for goodness' sake, stop just standing there looking at me and help him!"

He opens the front door again, and Al sits slumped on the ground at the base of the steps. Wrapped around his sweaty head, Rambo style, is one of Doris's tangerine headbands. His T-shirt is soaked with sweat, beads of perspiration run down his face, and his legs are spandex-clad and crumpled underneath him, still in the same position as when he'd fallen.

Doris pushes by Justin aggressively and charges toward Al. She falls to her knees. "Baby? Are you okay? Did you fall down the stairs?"

"No," he says weakly, his chins resting on his chest.

"No, you're not okay, or no, you didn't fall down the stairs?" she asks.

"The first one," he says with exhaustion. "No, the second. Hold on, what was the first?"

She shouts at him now as though he is deaf. "The first was, Are you okay? And the second was, Did you fall down the stairs?"

"No," he responds, rolling his head back to rest it against the wall.

"To which one? Shall I call an ambulance? Do you need a doctor?"

"No."

"No what, baby? Come on, don't go to sleep on me, don't you dare go anywhere." She slaps his face. "You have to stay conscious."

Justin leans against the door frame and folds his arms, watching the two of them. He knows his brother is fine, lack of fitness being his only problem. He goes to the kitchen for some water for him.

"My heart . . ." Al is panicking when Justin returns. His hands are scraping at his chest, and he's gasping for air, stretching his head upward and taking in gulps like a goldfish reaching to the surface of the fish bowl for food.

"Are you having a heart attack?" Doris shrieks.

Justin sighs, "He's not having a—"

"Stop it, Al!" Justin is interrupted by a screeching Doris. "Don't you dare have a heart attack, do you hear me?" She picks up a newspaper from the ground and starts hitting Al with it with each word. "Don't. You. Dare. Even. Think. Of. Dying. Before. Me. Al. Hitchcock."

"Ow." He rubs his arm. "That hurts."

"Hey, hey, hey!" Justin breaks it up. "Give me that paper, Doris."

"No!"

"Where did you get it?" He tries to grab it out of her hands.

"It was just there, beside Al," she shrugs. "Paperboy delivered it."

"They don't have paperboys around here," he explains.

"Then I guess it's Al's."

"There's a coffee-to-go too," Al manages to say, finally getting his breath back.

"A coffee-to-*what?*" Doris screeches so loudly, a window from the neighbor's flat upstairs is banged closed loudly. This does not deter her. "You bought a coffee?" She begins spanking him again with the newspaper. "No wonder you're dying!"

"Hey"—he crosses his arms over his body protectively—"it's not mine. It was outside the door with the newspaper when I got here."

"It's mine." Justin finally succeeds in snatching the paper from Doris's hands and the coffee cup that is on the ground beside Al.

"There's no note attached." Doris narrows her eyes and looks from one brother to the other. "Trying to defend your brother is only going to kill him in the long run, you know."

"I might do it more often, then," Justin grumbles, shaking the newspaper and hoping for a note to fall out. He checks the coffee cup for a message. Nothing. Yet he's sure it's for him, and whoever left it there can't be long gone. He focuses then on the front page. Above the headline, in the corner of the page, he notices the instruction "Go to p. 42."

He can't open the paper quickly enough and battles with the oversize pages to get to the correct spot. Finally he gets to the classified pages. He scans the advertisements and birthday greetings and is about to close the paper altogether and join Doris in chastising Al for his caffeine habit when he spots it.

Eternally grateful recipient wishes to thank Justin Hitchcock, donor and hero, for saving life. Thank you.

He holds his head back and howls with laughter. Doris and Al look at him with surprise.

"Al"—Justin lowers himself to his knees before his brother—"I need you to help me now." His voice is urgent, the pitch going up and down with excitement. "Did you see anybody when you were jogging back to the house?"

"No." Al's head rolls tiredly from one side to the other. "I can't think."

"Think." Doris slaps his face lightly.

"That's not entirely necessary, Doris."

"They do it in the movies when they're looking for information. Go on, tell him, baby." She nudges him a little more lightly.

"I don't know," Al whines. "By the time I got to the house, I couldn't breathe, let alone see. I don't remember anyone. Sorry, bro. Man, I was so scared. All of these black dots were in front of my eyes, I was getting so dizzy and—"

"Okay," Justin leaps to his feet and runs up the stairs to the front yard. He runs to the driveway and looks up and down the street. It's busier now; at seven thirty there is more life and traffic noise as people leave to head to work.

"*Thank you!*" Justin shouts at the top of his lungs. A few people turn around to look at him, but most keep their heads down. A light drizzle of October London rain begins to fall while another man loses his mind on a Monday morning.

"*I can't wait to read this!*" He waves the newspaper around in the air, shouting up and down the road so that he can be heard from all angles.

What do you say to someone whose life you saved? Something deep. Something funny. Something philosophical.

"*I'm glad you're alive!*" he shouts.

"Eh, thanks." A woman scurries past him with her head down.

"*Um, I won't be here tomorrow!*" Pause. "*In case you're planning on doing this again.*" He lifts the coffee into the air and waves it around, sending droplets jumping from the small drinking hole, burning his hand. Still hot. Whoever it was, they weren't here that long ago.

"*Um. Getting the first flight to Dublin tomorrow morning. Are you from there?*" he shouts to the wind. The breeze sends more crispy autumn leaves parachuting from their branches to the ground, where they land running, make a tapping sound, and scrape along the ground until it's safe to stop.

"Anyway, thanks again." He waves the paper in the air one more time and turns to face the house.

Doris and Al are standing at the top of the stairs with their arms folded, their faces a picture of concern. Al has caught his breath and composed himself but is still leaning against the iron railings for support.

Justin tucks the newspaper under his arm, straightens himself up, and tries to appear as respectable as possible. He puts his hand in his pocket and strolls back toward the house. Feeling a piece of paper in the pocket, he retrieves it and reads it quickly before crumpling it and tossing it into the trash. He has saved a person's life, just as he thought; he must focus on the most important matter at hand.

From the bottom of the trash bin, beneath rolls of tired old smelly carpets, crushed tiles, paint tubs, and drywall, I lie in a discarded bathtub and listen as the voices recede until the front door finally closes.

A crumpled ball of paper has landed nearby, and as I reach for it, my shoulder knocks over a two-legged stool, which toppled onto me in my rush to leap into the bin. I locate the paper and open it up, smoothing out the edges. My heart starts its rumba beat again as I see my first name, Dad's address, and his phone number scrawled upon it.

Chapter 32

◇◇◇◇◇

W HERE ON EARTH HAVE YOU been? What happened to you, Gracie?"

"Joyce" is my response as I burst into the hotel room, breathless and covered in paint and dust. "Don't have time to explain." I rush around the room, throwing my clothes into my bag, taking a change of clothes, and hurrying by Dad, who's sitting on the bed, in order to get to the bathroom.

"I tried calling you on your hand phone," Dad calls to me.

"Yeah? I didn't hear it ring." I struggle to squeeze into my jeans, hopping around on one foot while I pull them up and try to brush my teeth at the same time.

I hear his voice saying something. Mumbles but no words.

"Can't hear you, brushing my teeth!"

Silence while I finish, and when I head back to the room fifty minutes later, he continues where he left off.

"That's because when I called it, I heard it ringing here in the bedroom. It was on top of your pillow. Just like one of those chocolates the nice ladies here leave behind."

"Oh. Okay." I jump over his legs to get to the dressing table and reapply my makeup.

"I was worried about you," he says quietly.

"You needn't have been." I realize I have one shoe on, and start searching everywhere for the other.

"So I called downstairs to reception to see if they knew where you were."

"Yeah?" I give up looking for my shoe and concentrate on inserting my earrings. My fingers, trembling with the adrenaline of the Justin situation, have become too big for the task at hand. The back of one earring falls to the floor. I get down on my hands and knees to find it.

"So then I walked up and down the street, checking all of the shops that I know you like, asking all the people in them if they'd seen you."

"You did?" I say, distracted, feeling carpet burns through my jeans as I shuffle around the floor on my knees.

"Yes," he says quietly again.

"Aha! Got it!" I find the backing beside the bin below the dresser. "Now where the hell is my shoe?"

"And along the way," Dad continues, "I met a policeman, and I told him I was very worried, and he walked me back to the hotel and told me to wait here for you but to call this number if you didn't come back after twenty-four hours."

"Oh, that was nice of him." I open the wardrobe in the hunt for my shoe, and find it still full of Dad's clothes. "Dad!" I exclaim. "You forgot to pack your other suit. And your good sweater!"

I look at him—for the first time since I've entered the room, I realize—and only now notice how pale he looks. How old he seems in this soulless hotel room. Perched at the edge of his single bed, he's dressed in his three-piece suit, cap beside him on the bed, his case packed or half packed and sitting upright beside him. In one hand is the photograph of Mum, in the other is the card the policeman gave him. The fingers that hold them tremble; his eyes are red and sore-looking.

"Dad," I say as panic builds inside me, "are you okay?"

"I was worried," he repeats again in the tiny voice I'd been as good as ignoring. He swallows hard. "I didn't know where you were."

"I was visiting a friend," I say softly, joining him on the bed.

"Oh. Well, this friend here was worried." He gives a small smile. It's a weak smile, and I'm jolted by how fragile he appears, how much like an old man. His usual attitude, his jovial nature, is gone. His smile disappears quickly, and his trembling hands, usually steady as a rock, force the photo of Mum and the card from the policeman back into his coat pocket.

I look at his bag. "Did you pack that yourself?"

"Tried to. Thought I got everything." He looks away from the open wardrobe, embarrassed.

"Okay, well, let's take a look in it and see what we have." I hear my voice, and it startles me to hear myself speaking to him as though addressing a child.

"Aren't we running out of time?" he asks. His voice is so quiet, I feel I should lower mine so as not to break him.

"No"—my eyes fill with tears, and I speak more forcefully than I intend—"we have all the time in the world, Dad."

I look away and distract those tears from falling by lifting his case onto the bed and trying to compose myself. Day-to-day things, the mundane, are what keeps the motor running. How extraordinary the ordinary really is, a tool we all use to keep going, a template for sanity.

When I open the case, I feel my composure slip again, but I keep talking, sounding like a delusional 1950s suburban TV mother, repeating the hypnotic mantra that everything's just dandy and swell. I "oh, gosh" and "shucks" my way through his suitcase, which is a mess, though I shouldn't be surprised, as Dad has never had to pack a suitcase in his life. What upsets me is the possibility that at seventy-five years old, after ten years without his wife, he simply doesn't know how to. A simple thing like that, my big-as-an-oak-tree, steady-as-a-rock father cannot do. Instead he sits on the edge of the bed, twisting his cap around in his gnarled fingers.

Things have attempted to be folded, but instead are crumpled in small balls with no order at all, as though they have been packed by a child. I find my shoe inside some bathroom towels. I take it out and put it on my foot without saying anything, as though it's the most normal thing in the world. The towels go back where they belong. I start folding and packing all over again. His dirty underwear, socks, pajamas, vests, toiletry bag. Then I walk over to get the clothes from the wardrobe, and I take a deep breath.

"We have all the time in the world, Dad," I repeat. Though this time, it's for my own benefit.

On the tube on the way to the airport, Dad keeps checking his watch and fidgeting in his seat. Every time the train stops at a station, he pushes the seat in front of him impatiently as if to move it along himself.

"Do you have to be somewhere?" I smile.

"The Monday Club." He looks at me with worried eyes. He's never missed a week, not even when I was in the hospital.

"But today is Monday. We have time."

He fidgets. "I just don't want to miss this flight. We might get stuck over here."

"Oh, I think we'll make it." I do my best to hide my smile. "And there's more than one flight a day, you know."

"Good." He looks relieved. "I might even make evening mass. Oh, they won't believe everything I tell them tonight," he says with excitement. "Donal will drop dead when everybody listens to me and not to him for a change." He settles back into his seat and watches out the window as the underground speeds by. He stares into the black, no longer seeing his own reflection but seeing somewhere else and someone else a long way off, a long time ago. While he's in another world, I take out my cell phone and start planning my next move.

"Frankie, it's me. Justin Hitchcock is getting the first plane to Dublin tomorrow morning, and I need to know what he's doing, stat."

"And how am I supposed to do that, Dr. Conway?"

"I thought you had ways."

"You're right, I do. But I thought you were the psychic one."

"I'm certainly not psychic, but even still, I'm not getting anything about where he could be going."

"Are your powers fading?"

"I don't have powers."

"Whatever. Give me an hour, I'll get back to you."

Two hours later, while Dad and I wait at the gate, Frankie calls back.

"He's going to be in the National Gallery tomorrow morning at ten thirty. He's giving a talk on a painting called *Woman Writing a Letter*. Sounds fascinating."

"Oh, it is, it's one of Terborch's finest. In my opinion."

Silence.

"You were being sarcastic, weren't you?" I realize. "Okay, well, does your uncle Thomas still run that company?" I smile mischievously, and Dad looks at me curiously.

"What are you planning?" Dad asks suspiciously once I've ended the call.

"I'm having a little bit of fun."

"Shouldn't you get back to work? It's been weeks now. Conor called your hand phone while you were gone this morning, it slipped my mind to tell you. He's in Japan, but I could hear him very clearly," he says, impressed with either Conor or the phone company, I'm not sure which. "He wanted to know why the house doesn't have a For Sale sign yet. He said you were supposed to do that." He looks worried.

"Oh, I haven't forgotten." I'm agitated by the news of Conor's call, but I try not to let it show. "I'm selling it myself. I have my first viewing tomorrow."

Dad looks unsure, and he's right to, because I'm lying through my teeth.

"Your company knows this?" His eyes narrow.

"Yes." I smile tightly. "They can take the photos and put the sign up in a matter of hours. I know a few people in the real estate world."

He rolls his eyes.

We both look away in a huff, and just so I don't feel that I'm fully lying, while we shuffle along the line to board the plane, I text a few clients to see if they're interested in a viewing. Then I ask my trusty photographer to take the shots of the house. By the time we're fastening our seat belts, I have already arranged for the For Sale sign for later today and a viewing appointment tomorrow, for a couple I've been working with. Both teachers at the local school, they will come by the house during their lunch break. At the bottom of their text is the mandatory "Was so sorry to hear about what happened. Have been thinking of you. See you tomorrow, Linda xx."

I delete it right away.

Dad looks at my thumb working over the buttons on my phone with speed. "You writing a book?"

I ignore him.

"You'll get arthritis in your thumb, and it's not much fun, I can tell you that."

I press send and switch the phone off.

"You really selling the house yourself?" he asks.

"Yes," I say, confidently now.

"Well, I didn't know that, did I? I didn't know what to tell him."

Score one to me.

"That's okay, Dad, you don't have to feel you're in the middle of all this."

"Well, I am."

Score one to him.

"Well, you wouldn't have been if you hadn't answered my phone."

Two–one.

"You were missing all morning—what was I supposed to do, ignore it?"

Two–all.

"He was concerned about you, you know. He thought you should see someone. A professional person."

Off the charts.

"Did he, now?" I fold my arms, wanting to call him and rant about all the things I hate about him and that have always annoyed me. The cutting of his toenails in bed, the nose-blowing that rattled the house every morning, his inability to let people finish their sentences, his stupid party coin trick that I fake-laughed at from the first time he did it, his inability to sit down and have an adult conversation about our problems, his constant walking away during our fights . . . Dad interrupts my silent torture of Conor.

"He said you called him in the middle of the night, spurting Latin."

"Really?" I feel anger surge. "And what did you say?"

He looks out the window as we pick up speed down the runway.

"I told him you made a fine fluent Italian-speaking Viking too." I see his cheeks lift, and I throw my head back and laugh.

All even.

He suddenly grabs my hand. "Thanks for all this, love. I had a great time." He gives my hand a squeeze and goes back to looking out the window as the green of the fields surrounding the runway goes racing by.

He doesn't let go of my hand, so I rest my head on his shoulder and close my eyes.

Chapter 33

◇◇◇◇

J USTIN WALKS THROUGH ARRIVALS AT Dublin Airport on Tuesday morning with his cell phone glued to his ear, listening once again to the sound of Bea's outgoing message. He sighs when he hears the beep, beyond bored now with her childish behavior.

"Hi, honey, it's me. Dad. Again. Listen, I know you're angry with me, and at your age everything is oh-so-very-dramatic, but if you'd just listen to what I have to say, the odds are you'll agree with me and thank me for it when you're old and gray. I only want the best for you, and I will not hang up this phone until I have convinced you—" He immediately hangs up.

Behind the barricade at arrivals is a man in a dark suit holding a large white placard with Justin's surname written in large capital letters. Underneath are those two magical words: THANK YOU.

Those words have been capturing his attention on billboards, in the newspaper, on the radio, and on television all day and every day, ever since the first note arrived. Whenever the words drift from the lips of a passerby, he does a double take, following them as though hypnotized, as though they contain a special encrypted code just for him. Those words float in the air like the scent of freshly cut grass on a summer's day; more than a smell, they carry with them a feeling, a place, a time, a happiness. They transport him just like a special song from youth, when nostalgia, like the ocean's tide, sweeps in and catches you on the sand, pulling you in and under when you least expect it, and often when you least want it.

Those words are now constantly in his head. Thank you, thank you, thank you. The more he hears them and rereads the short notes, the more alien they become, as though he is seeing the sequence of those particular letters for the first time in his life— like how music notes, so familiar, so simple, arranged in a different way become pure masterpieces.

This transformation of everyday common things into some- thing magical, this growing understanding that what he once per- ceived to be was not at all, reminds him of the times he spent as a child staring at his face in the mirror. As he stood on a footstool so that he could reach, the more intensely he stared, the more his face began to morph into one he was wholly unfamiliar with. In those moments he wondered if he was seeing the real him: eyes farther apart than he'd thought, one eyelid lower than the other, one nostril also ever so slightly lower, the corner of one side of his mouth turning downward, as though there was a line going through one side of his face and dragging everything south, like a knife through sticky chocolate cake. The surface, once smooth, drooped and hung down. A quick glimpse, and it was unnotice- able. Careful analysis, though, before brushing his teeth at night, revealed he wore the face of a stranger.

Now he takes a step back from those two words, circles them a few times, and views them from all angles. Just as with paintings in a gallery, the words themselves dictate the height at which they should be displayed, the position from which they should be best approached and contemplated. He has found the correct angle now. He can now see the weight they hold; they have a sense of purpose, the strength of beauty and ammunition. Rather than a polite utterance heard a thousand times a day, "Thank you" now has meaning.

Without another thought about Bea, he flips his phone closed and approaches the man holding the sign. "Hello."

"Mr. Hitchcock?" The six-foot man's eyebrows are so dark and thick Justin can barely see his eyes.

"Yes," he says suspiciously. "Is this car for a Justin Hitchcock?"

The man consults a piece of paper in his pocket. "Yes, it is, sir. Is that still you, or does that change things?"

"Ye-es," he says slowly. "That's me."

"You don't seem so sure," the driver says, lowering the sign. "Where are you going this morning?"

"Shouldn't you know that?"

"I do. But the last time I let somebody in my car as unsure as you, I delivered an animal rights activist directly into an IMFHA meeting."

Unfamiliar with the initials, Justin asks, "Is that bad?"

"The president of the Irish Masters of Fox Hounds Association thought so. He was stuck at the airport with no car while the lunatic I collected was splashing red paint around the conference room. Let's just say, in terms of a tip for me, it was what the hounds would call a 'blank day.' "

"Well, I don't think the hounds would call it anything, necessarily," Justin jokes, "other than 'Ooo-ooo.' " He lifts his chin and howls into the air, playfully.

The driver stares back blankly, and Justin's face flushes. "Well, I'm going to the National Gallery." Pause. "I'm pro-Gallery, by the way. I'm going to talk about painting, not turn people into canvases as a method of venting my frustration. Though if my ex-wife was in the audience, I'd run at her with a paintbrush." He laughs, and the driver responds with another stony expression.

"I wasn't expecting anybody to greet me," Justin yaps at the driver's heels as they walk out of the airport into the gray October day. "Nobody at the gallery informed me you'd be here," he tests him as they hurry across the pedestrian walkway through parachuting raindrops that plummet toward Justin's head and shoulders.

"I didn't know about the job until late last night, when I got the call. I was supposed to be going to my wife's aunt's funeral today." They reach the lot, and he roots around his pockets for the car parking ticket and slides it into the machine to validate it.

"Oh, I'm sorry to hear that." Justin stops wiping away the parachuting raindrop casualties that have landed with a *shplat* on the shoulders of his brown corduroy jacket and looks at the driver grimly, out of respect.

"So was I. I hate funerals."

"Well, you wouldn't be alone in thinking that."

The driver stops walking and turns to face Justin with a look of intensity on his face. "They always give me the giggles," he says. "Does that ever happen to you?"

Justin is unsure whether to take him seriously, but the driver doesn't crack even the slightest smile. Justin thinks back to his father's funeral, when he was nine years old. The two families huddled together at the graveyard, all dressed head to toe in black like dung beetles around the dirty open hole in the ground where the casket was placed. His dad's family had flown over from Ireland, bringing with them the rain, which was unconventional for Chicago's hot summer. They stood beneath umbrellas, he close to his aunt Emelda, who held their umbrella in one hand and the other tightly on his shoulder, Al and his mother beside him under another umbrella. Al had brought along his fire engine, which he played with while the priest talked about their father's life. This annoyed Justin. In fact, everybody and everything annoyed Justin that day.

He hated Aunt Emelda's hand being there, heavy and tight on his shoulder, though he knew she was trying to be helpful.

He'd greeted her that morning dressed in his best suit, as his mother had requested in her new quiet voice, which Justin had to lean in closely to hear. Aunt Emelda had pretended to be psychic, just as she always did when they saw each other after long stints apart.

"I know just what you want, little soldier," she'd said in her strong Cork accent, which Justin could barely understand and sometimes mistook for her breaking out into song. She'd rummaged in her oversize handbag and dug out a toy soldier with a plastic smile and a plastic salute, quickly peeling off the price tag and, with it, the sticker with the soldier's name, before handing it to him. Justin stared down at Colonel Blank, who saluted him with one hand and held a plastic gun in the other, and immediately mistrusted him. The plastic gun got lost in the heavy pile of black coats by the front door as soon as he'd pulled the package open. As usual, Aunt Emelda's psychic powers had been tuned into the desires of the wrong nine-year-old boy, for Justin had not wanted this plastic soldier on this day of all days, and he couldn't help but imagine a young boy across town waiting for a plastic soldier and instead being handed Justin's father by the tuft of his jet-black hair. But he accepted her gift with a smile as big and sincere as Colonel Blank's. Later that day, as he stood with her beside the hole in the ground, he thought maybe for once she could read his mind as her hand gripped him tighter, her nails digging into his bony shoulders as though holding him back. For Justin had thought about jumping into that damp, dark hole.

Justin realizes the driver is now staring at him intently. His head moves in close, as though he's awaiting the answer to a very personal question.

Justin clears his throat and adjusts his eyes to the world of thirty-five years later. Time travel of the mind; a powerful thing.

"That's us over there." The driver presses the button on his keys, and the lights of an S-class Mercedes light up.

Justin's mouth drops. "Do you know who organized this?"

"No idea." The driver holds one of the back doors open for him. "I just take the orders from my boss. Thought it was unusual having to write 'Thank You' on the sign. Does that make sense to you?"

"Yes, it does but . . . it's complicated. Could you find out from your boss who's paying for this?" Justin settles into the backseat of the car and places his briefcase on the floor beside him.

"I could try."

"That would be great." I'll have gotcha then! Justin relaxes into the leather chair, stretches his legs out fully, and closes his eyes, barely able to hold back his smile.

"I'm Thomas, by the way," the driver introduces himself. "I'm here for you all day, so wherever you want to go after this, just let me know."

"For the entire day?" Justin almost chokes while sipping from his free bottle of chilled water, which was waiting for him in the hand rest. He saved a rich person's life. Yes! He should have mentioned more to Bea than just muffins and daily newspapers. A villa in the south of France.

"Would your company not have organized this for you?" Thomas asks.

"No." Justin shakes his head. "Definitely not."

"Maybe you've a fairy godmother you don't know about," Thomas says, deadpan.

"Well, let's see what this pumpkin's made of." Justin laughs.

"Won't get to test it this morning," Thomas says, braking as they enter Dublin traffic, worsened by the rainy weather.

Justin presses a button on the door to heat his seat and feels his back and behind warming. He kicks off his shoes and relaxes in comfort as he watches the miserable faces in the fogged-up windows of the buses gliding past him.

"After the gallery, do you mind bringing me to D'Olier Street? I need to visit somebody at the blood donor clinic."

"No problem, boss."

The October gust huffs and puffs and attempts to blow the last of the leaves off the nearby trees. They hang on tight like the nannies in Mary Poppins, who cling to the lampposts of Cherry Tree Lane in a desperate attempt to prevent their airborne competition from blowing them away from the big Banks job interview. The leaves, like many people this autumn, are not yet ready to let go. They cling on tight to yesterday, putting up a fight before giving up the place that has been their home for two seasons. I watch as one leaf lets go and dances around in the air before falling to the ground. I pick it up and slowly twirl it around by its stalk in my fingers. I'm not fond of autumn. Not fond of watching things so sturdy wither as they lose against nature, the higher power they can't control.

"Here comes the car," I comment to Kate.

We're standing across the main road from the National Gallery, behind the parked cars shaded by the trees rising above and over the gates of Merrion Square.

"You paid for that?" Kate says. "You really are nuts."

"Tell me something I don't know. Actually, I paid half. That's Frankie's uncle driving—he runs the company. Pretend you don't know him if he looks over."

"But I don't know him."

"Good, that's convincing."

"Joyce, I have never seen that man in my life."

"Wow, that's really good."

"How long are you going to keep this up, Joyce? The London thing sounded fun while it lasted, but really, all we know is that the man donated blood."

"To me."

"We don't know that."

"I know that."

"But you can't know that."

"But I can. That's the funny thing."

She looks doubtful at me with such pity, it makes my blood boil.

"Kate, yesterday I had carpaccio and fennel for dinner, and I spent the evening singing along to practically all the words of Pavarotti's *Ultimate Collection*."

"I still don't understand how you think that it's this Justin Hitchcock who's responsible for all that. Remember that film *Phenomenon*? John Travolta just suddenly became a genius overnight."

"He had a brain tumor that somehow increased his ability to learn," I snap.

The Mercedes pulls up by the gates of the gallery. The driver gets out of the car to open the door for Justin and he emerges, brief-case in hand, beaming from ear to ear, and I'm happy to see that next month's mortgage payment has gone to good use. I shall worry about that, and everything else in my life, when the time comes.

He still has the aura I felt from the day I first laid eyes on him in the hair salon—a presence that makes my stomach walk a few flights of stairs and then climb the final ladder to the ten-meter diving platform at the Olympics final. He looks up at the gallery and around at the park, and with that strong jawline he smiles, a smile that causes my stomach to do one, two, three bounces, before attempting the toughest dive of all, a reverse one-point-five somersault and three and a half twists before entering the water with a belly flop.

The leaves around me rustle as another soft breeze blows, and I imagine that it carries to me the smell of his aftershave, the scent I remember from the salon. I have a brief flash of him picking up a parcel wrapped in emerald-green paper, which sparkles under Christmas-tree lights and surrounding candles. It's tied with a large red bow, and my hands are momentarily his as he unties it slowly, carefully peeling back the tape from the paper, taking care not to rip it. I am struck by his tenderness for the package, which has been lovingly wrapped, and I am in on his plans to pocket the paper and use it for the unwrapped presents he has sitting out in the car. Inside is a bottle of aftershave and a shaving set. A Christmas gift from Bea.

"He's handsome," Kate whispers. "I support your stalking campaign one hundred percent, Joyce."

"I'm not stalking," I hiss, "and I'd have done this even if he was ugly."

"Can I go in and listen to his talk?" Kate asks.

"No!"

"Why not? He's never seen me; he won't recognize me. Please, Joyce, my best friend believes she is connected to a complete stranger by blood. At least I can go and listen to him to see what he's like."

"What about Sam?"

"Do you want to watch him for a little while?"

I freeze.

"Oh, forget that," she says quickly. We still haven't talked about how I ran from the gymnasium the other day, leaving Frankie to try to stop Sam from crying. "I'll bring him in with me. I'll stay down the back and leave if he disturbs anyone."

"No, no, it's okay. I can do it." I swallow and paste a smile on my face.

"Are you sure?" She looks unconvinced. "I won't stay for the entire thing. I just want to see what he's like."

"I'll be fine. Go." I push her away gently. "Go in and enjoy yourself. We'll be fine here, won't we, Sammy?"

Sam puts his socked toe in his mouth in response.

"I promise I won't be long." Kate leans in to the stroller, gives her son a kiss, and dashes across the road and into the gallery.

"So . . ." I look around nervously. "It's just you and me, Sean."

He looks at me with his big blue eyes, and mine instantly fill.

I look around to make sure nobody has heard me. I meant to say Sam.

Justin takes his place at the podium in the lecture hall in the basement of the National Gallery. A packed room of faces stares back at him, and he feels he's back in his element. A late arrival, a young woman, enters the room and quickly takes a place among the crowd.

"Good morning, ladies and gentlemen, and thank you so much for joining me on this rainy morning. I am here to talk about this painting, *Woman Writing a Letter*, by Gerard Terborch, a Dutch Baroque artist from the seventeenth century who was largely responsible for the popularization of the letter theme. This painting—well, not this painting alone—this genre of letter-writing is a personal favorite of mine, particularly when in this current age it seems a personal letter has almost become extinct." He stops.

Almost but not quite, for there's somebody sending me notes.

He steps away from the podium and looks at the crowd, suspicion written upon his face. His eyes narrow as he studies his audience. He scans the rows, knowing that somebody here could be the mystery note-writer.

Somebody coughs, snapping him out of his trance, and he is back with them again. Mildly flustered, he continues where he left off.

"In an age when a personal letter has almost become extinct, this painting is a reminder of how the great masters of the Golden Age depicted the subtle range of human emotions affected by such a seemingly simple aspect of daily life. Terborch was not the only artist responsible for these images. I cannot go further on this subject without paying lip service to Vermeer, Gabriel Metsu, and Pieter de Hooch, who all produced paintings of people reading, writing, and receiving and dispatching letters, which I have written about in my book *The Golden Age of Dutch Painting.* Terborch's paintings use letter-writing as a pivot on which to turn complex psychological dramas, and his are among the first works to link lovers through the theme of a letter."

He studies the woman who arrived a little late, wondering if she is reading deeper into his words. He almost laughs aloud at his assumption, first, that the person whose life he saved would be in this room; second, that it would be a young woman; and third, that she'd be attractive. Which makes him ask himself, What exactly are you hoping will come out of this current drama?

As I push Sam's stroller into Merrion Square, we're instantly transported from the Georgian center of the city to another world shaded by mature trees and surrounded by color. The burnt oranges, reds, and yellows of the autumn foliage litter the ground and, with each gentle breeze, hop alongside us like inquisitive little birds. I choose a bench along the quiet walk and turn Sam's stroller around so that he faces me. I watch him for a while as he strains his neck to see the remaining leaves that refuse to surrender their branches far above him. He points a tiny finger up at the sky and gurgles some sounds.

"Tree," I tell him, which makes him smile, and his mother is instantly recognizable in his face.

The vision has the same effect as a boot hitting my stomach. I take a moment to catch my breath.

"Sam, while we're here we should really discuss something," I say.

His smile widens.

"I have to apologize for something." I clear my throat. "I haven't been paying much attention to you lately, have I? The thing is . . ." I wait until a man has passed us before continuing. "The thing is"—I lower my voice—"I couldn't bear to look at you . . ." I trail off again as his grin widens.

"Oh, here." I lean over, remove his blanket, and press the button to release his safety straps. It opens easily this time. "Come up here to me." I lift him out of the buggy and sit him on my lap. His body is warm, and I hug him close. I breathe in the top of his head, his wispy hairs silky as velvet, his body so chubby and soft in my arms, I want to squeeze him tighter. "The thing is," I say quietly to the top of his head, "it broke my heart to look at you, because each time I did, I remembered what I'd lost." He looks up at me and babbles in response. "Though how could I ever be afraid to look at you?" I kiss his nose. "I shouldn't have taken it out on you, but it was so hard." My eyes fill, and this time I let the tears fall. "I wanted to have a little boy or girl so people would say, 'Oh, look, you're the picture of your mummy.' Or maybe the baby would have my nose or my eyes, because that's what people say to me, that I look like my mum. And I love hearing that, Sam, I really do, because I miss her and I want to be reminded of her every single day. But looking at you was different. I didn't want to be reminded that I'd lost my baby."

"Ba-ba," he says.

I sniffle. "Ba-ba gone, Sam. Sean for a boy, Grace for a girl." I wipe my nose.

Sam, uninterested in my tears, looks away and studies a bird. He points a chubby finger again.

"Bird," I say.

"Ba-ba," he responds.

"But there's no Sean or Grace now." I hug him tighter and continue to let my tears fall, knowing that Sam won't be able to report my weeping to anybody.

The bird hops a few inches and then takes off, disappearing into the sky.

"Ba-ba gone," Sam says, holding his hands out, palms up.

I watch it fly into the distance, still visible like a speck of dust against the pale blue sky. My tears stop. "Ba-ba gone," I repeat.

"So what do we see in this painting?" Justin asks.

Silence as everyone views the projected image.

"Well, let us state the obvious first. A young woman sits at a table in a quiet interior. She is writing a letter. We see a quill moving across a sheet of paper. We do not know what she is writing, but her soft smile suggests she is writing to a loved one or perhaps a lover. Her head tilts forward, exposing the elegant curve of her neck . . ."

While Sam is back in his buggy, drawing circles on paper with his blue crayon, or more accurately, banging out dots on the paper, sending wax shrapnel all over his buggy, I produce my own pen and paper from my bag. I imagine I'm hearing Justin's words from across the road. I don't need to see the work of *Woman Writing a Letter* on canvas, for it has been painted in my mind after Justin's years of intensive study during college and again during research for his book. I begin to write.

As part of a mother/daughter bonding activity when I was seventeen years old, during my goth phase, when I had dyed black hair, a white face, and red lips that were victim to piercing, Mum enrolled us both in a calligraphy class at the local primary school. Every Wednesday at seven p.m.

Mum read in a rather New Age book that Dad didn't agree with that if you partook in activities with your children, they would more easily, and of their own accord, open up and share things about their lives, rather than being forced into a face-to-face interrogative-style sit-down, which Dad was more accustomed to.

The classes worked, and although I moaned and groaned when I first heard we'd be doing this, I eventually opened up and told her all. Well, almost all. The rest she had the intuition to guess. I came away with a deeper love, respect, and understanding of my mother as a person, a woman, and not just as a mum. I also came away with a skill in calligraphy.

I find that when I put pen to paper and get into the rhythm of quick upward flicks, just as we were taught, it takes me back to those classrooms where I sat with my mother. It was a perfect activity for her to choose for me at seventeen, better than she ever knew. Calligraphy had rhythm, with roots in Gothic style; it was written in the vigor of the moment and had attitude. A uniform style of writing, but one that was unique. A lesson to teach me that conformity may not quite mean what I once thought that it had meant, for there are many ways to express oneself in a world with boundaries, without overstepping them.

Suddenly I look up from my page. "Trompe l'oeil," I say aloud with a smile.

Sam looks up from his crayon banging and regards me with interest.

"What does that mean?" Kate raises her hand and asks.

"Trompe l'oeil is an art technique involving extremely realistic imagery in order to create the optical illusion that the depicted objects really exist, instead of being two-dimensional painting. It's derived from French, *trompe* meaning 'trick' and *l'oeil* meaning 'the eye,' " Justin tells the room. "Trick the eye," he repeats, looking around at all the faces in the crowd.

Where are you?

Chapter 34

◇◇◇◇◇

"S o how did it go?" Thomas the driver asks as Justin gets back into the car after his talk.

"I saw you standing at the back of the room. You tell me."

"Well, I don't know much about art, but you certainly knew how to talk about one girl writing a letter."

Justin smiles and reaches for another free bottle of water. He's not thirsty but it's there, and it's free.

"Were you looking for somebody?" Thomas asks.

"What do you mean?"

"In the crowd. I noticed you looking around pretty intently a few times. A woman, is it?" He grins.

Justin shakes his head. "I have no idea. You'd think I was crazy if I told you."

"So, what do you think?" I ask Kate as we walk around Merrion Square and she fills me in on Justin's lecture.

"What do I think?" she repeats, strolling slowly behind Sam's buggy. "I think that it doesn't matter if he ate carpaccio and fennel yesterday, because he seems like a lovely man. I think that no matter what your reasons are for feeling connected or even attracted to him, they're not important. You should stop all this running around and just introduce yourself."

I shake my head. "No can do."

"Why not? He seemed to be pretty interested when he was chasing your bus down the road and when he saw you at the ballet. What's changed now?"

"He doesn't want anything to do with me."

"How do you know that?"

"I know."

"How? And don't tell me it's because of some mumbo jumbo thing you saw in your tea leaves."

"I drink coffee now."

"You hate coffee."

"He obviously doesn't."

She does her best not to be negative but looks away.

"He's too busy looking for the woman whose life he saved; he's no longer interested in me. He had my contact details, Kate, and he never called. Not once. In fact, he went so far as to throw them in the trash, and don't ask me how I know that."

"Knowing you, you were probably lying in the bottom of it."

I keep tight-lipped.

Kate sighs. "How long are you going to keep this up?"

I shrug. "Not much longer."

"What about work? What about Conor?"

"Conor and I are done. There's nothing more to say. Four years of separation, and then we'll be divorced. Why does everyone want me to fall apart, Kate? Can't everyone just accept that I'm happy with what's happened? Or that I'm stronger than some people?"

"Nobody wants to see you fall apart, Joyce. I'm glad you're

happy about the separation, really I am. But you never talk about . . . you know."

"Losing my baby," I say firmly.

"I don't want you to feel that you have to talk about it."

"Yes, you do. Everybody does. But I'm not going to be the person that breaks down every time it's mentioned. I'm dealing with it in my own way."

"Okay."

"I'm moving on, Kate. And as for work, I've already told them I'm going back next week; my diary is already full with appointments. And as for the house—shit!" I pull up my sleeve to look at my watch. "I have to get back. I'm showing the house in an hour."

A quick kiss, and I run for the nearest bus home.

"Okay, this is it." Justin stares out the car window and up to the second floor of the building that houses the blood donor clinic.

"You're donating blood?" Thomas asks.

"No way. I'm just paying somebody a visit. I shouldn't be too long. If you see any police cars coming, start the engine." He smiles, but it is unconvincing.

He nervously asks for Sarah at reception and is told to wait in the waiting room. Around him men and women on their lunch breaks sit in their suits and read newspapers, waiting to be called for their blood donations.

He inches closer to the woman beside him, who's flicking through a magazine. He leans over her shoulder, and as he whispers, she jumps.

"Are you sure you want to do this?"

Everyone in the room lowers their papers and magazines to stare at him. He coughs and looks away, pretending somebody else said it. On all the walls around them are posters encouraging people to donate, as well as ones of young children, survivors of leukemia and other illnesses. He has already waited half an hour and checks his watch every minute now, conscious he has a plane to catch. When the last person leaves him alone in the room, Sarah appears at the door.

"Justin." She isn't icy, she isn't tough or angry. Just quiet. Hurt. That's worse. He'd rather she was angry.

"Sarah." He stands and greets her in an awkward half embrace and with a kiss on one cheek, which turns into two. A questionable third is aborted and almost becomes a kiss on the lips. She pulls away, ending the farcical greeting.

"I can't stay long, I have to get to the airport for a flight, but I wanted to come by and see you face-to-face. Can we talk for a few minutes?"

"Yes, sure." She walks into the reception room and sits down, arms still folded.

"Oh." He looks around. "Don't you have an office or something?"

"This is nice and quiet."

"Where is your office?"

Her eyes narrow with suspicion, and he gives up that particular line of questioning and quickly takes a seat beside her.

"I'm here, really, to apologize for my behavior the last time we met. Well, every time we met and every moment after that. I really am sorry."

She nods, waiting for more.

Damn it, that's all I had! Think, think. You're sorry and . . .

"I didn't mean to hurt you. I got very distracted that day with those crazy Vikings. In fact, you could say I've been distracted by crazy Vikings almost every day for the last month or two, and uh . . ." Think! "Could I go to the men's room? If you wouldn't mind, I mean."

She looks a little taken aback but directs him to it. "Sure, it's straight down the hall at the end."

Standing outside, where a newly hammered For Sale sign is attached to the front wall, Linda and her husband, Joe, are pressing their faces up against the window and gawking into the living room. A protective feeling comes over me. Then as soon as it comes, it vanishes. Home is not a place—not this place, anyway.

"Joyce? Is that you?" Linda slowly lowers her sunglasses.

I give them a big wobbly smile while reaching into my pocket for the bunch of keys, which is already minus my car keys and the furry ladybird key chain that used to be on Mum's set. Even the keys have lost their heart, their playfulness; all they have now is their function.

"Your hair—you look so different."

"Hi, Linda. Hi, Joe." I hold out my hand to greet them. But Linda has other plans and reaches out to offer me a huge, tight hug.

"Oh, I'm so sorry for you," she mutters as she squeezes me. "Poor you."

A nice gesture, if perhaps I'd known her a bit better and longer than merely having shown her three houses over a month ago.

She lowers her voice to a whisper. "Did they do that at the hospital?" She eyes my hair.

"Uh, no, they did that at the hair salon," I chirp, my usual Lady of Trauma coming back to save the day. I turn the key in the door and allow them to enter first.

"Oh," she breathes excitedly, and her husband smiles and takes her hand. I have a flashback of Conor and me coming to view the house ten years ago; it had just been deserted by an old lady who had lived alone for the previous twenty years. I follow my younger self into the house, and suddenly she is real and I am the ghost, remembering what we saw and replaying the moment again.

The home had reeked inside, with its old carpets, creaking floors, rotting windows, and out-of-fashion wallpaper. It was disgusting and a money pit, and we loved it as soon as we stood where Linda and her husband stand right now.

We had everything in front of us back then, when Conor was the Conor I loved and I was the old me; a perfect match. Then Conor became who he is now, and I became the Joyce he no longer loved. As the house became more beautiful, our relationship became uglier. We could have lain on a cat-hair-infested rug on our first night and still been happy, but every minute detail of what was wrong in our marriage going forward we attempted to fix by getting a new couch, repairing doors, replacing drafty windows. If only we'd put that much time and concentration into ourselves; self-improvement rather than home improvement. Neither of us thought to fix the draft in our marriage. It whistled through the growing cracks until we both woke up one morning with cold feet.

"I'll show you around downstairs, but, um—" I look up at the nursery door, no longer vibrating as it had when I first returned home from the hospital. It is just a door now, quiet and still. Doing what a door does. Nothing. "I'll let you wander around upstairs by yourselves."

"Are the owners still living here?" Linda asks.

I look around. "No. No, they're long gone."

As Justin makes his way down the hall to the toilet, he examines each of the names on the doors, looking for Sarah's office. He has no idea where to start, but maybe if he can find the folder that deals with blood recently taken from Trinity College . . .

He finally sees her name on one door and raps on it gently.

When he hears no response, he enters and closes it quietly behind him. He looks around quickly, sees piles of folders on the shelves. He runs immediately to the filing cabinets and starts rifling through them. Moments later the doorknob turns. He drops a file back into the cabinet, spins toward the door, and freezes. Sarah stands there looking at him, shocked.

"Justin?"

"Sarah?"

"What are you doing in my office?"

You're an educated man, think of something smart.

"I took a wrong turn."

She folds her arms. "Why don't you tell me the truth now?"

"I was on my way back and saw your name on the door and thought I'd come in and have a look around, see what your office is like. I have this thing, you see, where I believe that an office really represents what a person is like, and if we're to have a future tog—"

"We're not going to have a future."

"Oh. I see. But if we were to—"

"No."

His eyes scan her desk and fall upon a photograph of Sarah with her arms around a young blond girl and a man. They pose happily together on a beach.

Sarah follows his gaze.

"That's my daughter, Molly." She tightens her lips then, angry at herself for saying anything.

"You have a daughter?" He reaches for the frame and pauses before touching it, looking to her for permission first.

She nods, lips loosening, and he takes the photo in his hands.

"She's beautiful."

"She is."

"How old is she?"

"Six."

"I didn't know you had a daughter."

"You don't know a lot of things about me. You never stuck around long enough on our dates to talk about anything that wasn't about you."

Justin cringes. "Sarah, I'm so sorry."

"So you said, so sincerely, right before you came into my office and started rooting around."

"I wasn't rooting—"

Her look is enough to stop him from telling another lie. She takes the photo frame gently from his hands. Nothing about her is rough or aggressive. She is clearly filled with disappointment; this is not the first time an idiot like Justin has let her down.

"The man in the photo?"

She looks sad as she studies it before placing it back on the table.

"I would have been happy to tell you about him before," she says softly. "In fact, I remember trying to on at least two occasions."

"I'm sorry," he repeats, feeling so small he almost can't see over her desk. "I'm listening now."

"And I'm sure I remember you telling me you had a flight to catch," she says.

"Right." He nods and makes his way to the door. "I am so truly and very, very sorry. I am hugely embarrassed and disappointed in myself." And he realizes he actually means this from the bottom of his heart. "I am going through some strange things at the moment."

"Find me someone who isn't. We all have crap to deal with, Justin. Just please do not drag me into yours."

"Okay." He nods again and offers another apologetic, embarrassed smile before exiting her office, rushing down the stairs and jumping into the car, feeling two feet tall.

Chapter 35

◇◇◇◇◇

"WHAT'S THAT?"

"I don't know."

"Just give it a wipe."

"No, you."

"Have you seen something like that before?"

"Yeah, maybe."

"What do you mean, maybe? You either have or you haven't."

"Don't get smart with me."

"I'm not, I'm just trying to figure it out. Do you think it will come off?"

"I've no idea. Let's ask Joyce."

I hear Linda and Joe mumbling together in the hallway. I've left them to their own devices and have been standing in the galley kitchen, drinking a black coffee and staring out at my mother's rosebush at the back of the garden. I see the ghosts of Joyce and Conor sunbathing on the grass during a hot summer with the radio blaring.

"Joyce, could we show you something for a moment?"

"Sure."

I put the coffee cup down, passing the ghost of Conor making his lasagna specialty in the kitchen, passing the ghost of Joyce sitting in her favorite armchair in her pajamas, and make my way to the hall. Linda and Joe are on their hands and knees, examining the stain by the stairs. My stain.

"I think it might be wine," Joe says, looking up at me. "Did the owners say anything about the stain?"

"Uh . . ." My legs wobble slightly, and for a moment I think my knees are going to go. I hold on to the banister and pretend to lean down to look at it more closely. I close my eyes. "It's been cleaned a few times already, as far as I know. Would you be interested in keeping the carpet?"

Linda makes a face while she thinks, looks up and down the stairs, through the house, examining my choice of decor with a ruffled nose. "No, I suppose not. I think wooden floors would be lovely. Don't you?" she asks Joe.

"Yeah," he nods. "A nice pale oak."

"So, no," she says. "I don't think we'd keep this carpet."

I haven't intended to keep the owners' details from them deliberately—there's no point, as they'll see them on the contract anyway. I had assumed they knew that the property was mine, but as they poked holes in the decor and in the choice of room layout, I didn't think it would be necessary to make them uncomfortable by pointing it out now.

"You seem keen." I smile, watching their faces aglow with warmth and excitement at finally finding the right home for themselves.

"We are." She grins. "We have been so fussy, as you well know. But now the situation has changed, and we need to get out of that flat and find something bigger as soon as we can, seeing as we're expanding—or at least I am," she jokes nervously, and it's only then that I notice the small bump beneath her shirt, her belly button hard and protruding against the fabric.

"Oh, wow . . ." Lump to throat, wobble of knees again, please let this moment be over quickly, please make them look away from me. They have tact, and so they do. "That's fantastic, congratulations," my voice says cheerily, and even I can hear how hollow it is, so devoid of sincerity, the empty words almost echoing within themselves.

"So that room upstairs would be perfect." Joe nods to the nursery.

"Oh, of course, that's just wonderful." The 1950s surbuban housewife is back as I gosh, gee-whiz, and shucks my way through the rest of the conversation.

"I can't believe they don't want any of the furniture," Linda says, looking around.

"Well, they're both moving to smaller properties, where their belongings just won't fit."

"But they're not taking anything?"

"No," I say, looking around. "Nothing but the rosebush in the back garden."

And a suitcase of memories.

Justin falls into the car with a giant sigh.

"What happened to you?"

"Nothing. Could you just drive directly to the airport now, please? I'm a little behind schedule." Justin places his elbow on the window ledge and covers his face with his hand, hating himself, hating the selfish, miserable man he has become. He and Sarah weren't right for each other, but what right had he to use her like that, to bring her down into his pit of desperation and selfishness?

"I've got something that will cheer you up," Thomas says, reaching for the glove compartment.

"No, I'm really not in the—" Justin stops, seeing Thomas retrieve a familiar envelope from the compartment. Thomas hands it over to him.

"Where did you get this?"

"My boss called me, told me to give it to you before you got to the airport."

"Your boss." Justin narrows his eyes. "What's his name?"

Thomas is silent for a while. "John," he finally replies.

"John Smith?" Justin says, his voice thick with sarcasm.

"The very man."

Knowing he'll squeeze no information from Thomas, he turns his attention back to the envelope. He circles it slowly in his hand, trying to decide whether to open it or not. He could leave it unopened and end all of this now, get his life back in order, stop using people, taking advantage. Meet a nice woman, treat her well.

"Well? Aren't you going to open it?" Thomas asks.

Justin continues to circle it in his hand.

"Maybe."

Dad opens the door to me, earphones in his ears, iPod in his hand. He looks my outfit up and down.

"Ooh, you looking very nice today, Gracie," he shouts at the top of his voice, and a man walking his dog across the road turns to stare. *"Were you out somewhere special?"*

I smile. Relief at last. I put my finger on my lips and take the earphones out of his ears.

"I was showing the house to some clients of mine."

"Did they like it?"

"They're going to come back in a few days to measure. So that's a good sign. But being back over there, I realized there are so many things that I have to go through."

"Haven't you been through enough? You don't need to sob for weeks just to make yourself feel okay about all this."

I smile. "I mean that I have to go through possessions. Things

I've left behind. I don't think they want a lot of the furniture. Would it be okay if I stored it in your garage?"

"My woodwork studio?"

"That you haven't been in for ten years."

"I've been in there," he says defensively. "All right, then, you can use it. Will I ever be rid of you?" he says with a slight smile.

I sit at the kitchen table, and Dad immediately busies himself, filling the kettle as he does for everyone who enters his domain.

"So how did the Monday Club go last night? I bet Donal McCarthy couldn't believe your story. What was his face like?" I lean in, excited to hear and to change the topic.

"He wasn't there," Dad says, turning his back to me as he takes out a cup and saucer for himself and a mug for me.

"What? Why not? And you with your big story to tell him! The cheek of him. Well, you'll have next week, won't you?"

He turns around slowly. "He died over the weekend. His funeral's tomorrow. Instead we spent the night talking about him and all the old stories that he told a hundred times."

"Oh, Dad, I'm so sorry."

"Ah, well. If he hadn't have gone over the weekend, he would have dropped dead when he'd heard I met Michael Aspel. Maybe it was just as well." He smiles sadly. "Ah, he wasn't such a bad man. We had a good laugh even if we did enjoy getting a rise out of each other."

I feel for Dad. It is such a trivial thing compared to the loss of a friend, but he had been so excited to share his stories with his great rival.

We both sit in silence.

"You'll keep the rosebush, won't you?" Dad asks finally.

I know immediately what he's talking about. "Of course I will. I thought that it'd look good in your garden."

He looks out the window and studies his garden, most likely deciding where he'll plant it.

"You have to be careful moving it, Gracie. Too much shock causes a serious, possibly a grave, decline."

I smile sadly. "That's a bit dramatic, but I'll be fine, Dad. Thanks for caring."

He turns his back again. "I was talking about the roses."

My phone rings at that moment, vibrates along the table and almost hops off the edge.

"Hello?"

"Joyce, it's Thomas. I just saw your young man off at the airport."

"Oh, thank you so much. Did he get the envelope?"

"Uh, yeah. About that: I gave it to him all right, but I've just looked in the backseat of the car, and it's still there."

"What?" I jump up from the kitchen chair. "Go back, go back! Turn the car around! You have to give it to him. He's forgotten it!"

"Thing is, he wasn't too sure on whether he wanted to open it or not."

"What? Why?"

"I don't know, love! I gave it to him when he got back into the car and before we got to the airport, just like you asked. He seemed very down, and so I thought it'd cheer him up a bit."

"Down? Why? What was wrong with him?"

"Joyce, love, I don't know. All I know is he got into the car a bit upset, so I gave him the envelope and he sat there looking at it and I asked him if he was going to open it and he said maybe."

"Maybe," I repeat. Had I done something to upset him? Had Kate said something? "He was upset when he came out of the gallery?"

"No, not the gallery. We stopped off at the blood donor clinic on D'Olier Street before heading to the airport."

"He was donating blood?"

"No, he said he had to meet somebody."

Oh, my God, maybe he'd discovered it was me who'd received his blood and he wasn't interested.

"Thomas, do you know if he opened it?"

"Did you seal it?"

"No."

"Then there's no way of my knowing. I didn't see him open it. I'm sorry. Do you want me to drop it at your house on the way back from the airport?"

"Please."

An hour later I meet Thomas at the door, and he gives me the envelope. I can feel the contents still inside, and my heart falls. Why didn't Justin open it and take it with him?

"Here, Dad." I slide the envelope across the kitchen table. "A present for you."

"What's in it?"

"Front-row seats to the opera for next weekend," I say sadly, leaning my chin on my hand. "It was a gift for somebody else, but he clearly doesn't want to go."

"The opera." Dad makes a funny face. "It's far from operas I was raised." He opens the envelope anyway as I get up to make some more coffee.

"Oh, I think I'll pass on this opera thing, love, but thanks anyway."

I spin round. "Oh, Dad, why? You liked the ballet, and you didn't think that you would."

"Yes, but I went to that with you. I wouldn't go to this on my own."

"You don't have to. There are two tickets."

"No, there aren't."

"Yes, there definitely are. Look again."

He turns the envelope upside down and shakes it. A loose piece of paper falls out and flutters to the table.

My heart skips a beat.

Dad props his glasses on the tip of his nose and peers down at the note. " 'Accompany me,' " he says slowly. "Ah, love, that's awful nice of you—"

"Show me that." I grab it from his hands disbelievingly and read it for myself. Then I read it again. And again and again.

Accompany me? Justin.

Chapter 36

◇◇◇◇◇

H E WANTS TO MEET ME," I tell Kate nervously as I twirl a string from my shirt around my finger.

"You're going to cut off your circulation, be careful," Kate responds in a motherly fashion.

"Kate! Did you not hear me? I said he wants to meet me!"

"And so he should. Did you not think that this would eventually happen? Really, Joyce, you've been taunting the man for weeks. And if he did save your life, as you're insisting he did, wouldn't he want to meet the person whose life he saved? Boost his male ego? Come on, it's the equivalent to a white horse and a shiny suit of armor."

"No, it's not."

"It is in his male eyes. His male wandering eyes," she spits out aggressively.

My eyes narrow as I study her closely. "Is everything okay? You're beginning to sound like Frankie."

"Stop biting your lip, it's starting to bleed. Yes, everything's great. Just hunky-dory."

"Okay, here I am." Frankie breezes through the door and joins us on the bleachers.

We are seated on a split-level viewing balcony at Kate's local swimming pool. Below us Eric and Jayda splash noisily in their swimming class. Sam sits beside us in his stroller, looking around.

"Does this one do anything?" Frankie watches him suspiciously.

Kate ignores her.

"Issue number one for discussion today: Why do we have to constantly meet in these places with all these *things* crawling around?" She looks around at all the toddlers. "What happened to cool bars, new restaurants, and shop openings? Remember how we used to go out and have fun?"

"I have plenty of fucking fun," Kate says a little too defensively. "I'm just one great big ball of fucking fun," she repeats and looks away.

Frankie doesn't hear the unusual tone in Kate's voice, or hears it and decides to push anyway. "Yes, at dinner parties for other couples who also haven't been out for months. That's not so fun."

"You'll understand when you have kids."

"I don't plan to have any." She pauses. "Is everything okay?"

"Yes, she's 'hunky-dory,' " I say to Frankie, using my fingers as quotation marks.

"Oh, I see," Frankie says slowly and mouths "Christian" at me. I shrug.

"Is there anything you want to get off your chest, Kate?" Frankie asks.

"Actually, yes." Kate turns to her with fire in her eyes. "I'm tired of your little comments about my life. If you're not happy here or in my company, then piss off somewhere else, but just know that it'll be without me." She turns away then, her cheeks flushed with anger.

Frankie is silent for a moment as she observes her friend. "Okay," she says perkily and turns to me. "My car is parked outside; we can check out the new bar down the road."

"We're not going anywhere," I protest.

"Ever since you left your husband and your life has fallen apart, you've been no fun," she says to me sulkily. "And as for you, Kate, ever since you got that new Swedish nanny and your husband's been eyeing her up, you've been absolutely miserable. As for me, I'm tired of hopping from one night of meaningless sex with handsome strangers to another, and having to eat microwave dinners alone every evening. There, I've said it."

My mouth falls open. So does Kate's. I can tell we are both trying our best to be angry with Frankie, but her comments are so spot-on, it's actually quite humorous. She nudges me with her elbow and chuckles mischievously in my ear. The corners of Kate's lips begin to twitch too.

"I should have got a manny," Kate finally says.

"Nah, I still wouldn't trust Christian," Frankie responds. "You're being paranoid, Kate," she assures her seriously. "I've been around you guys, I've seen him. He adores you, and she is not attractive at all."

"You think?"

"Uh-huh." She nods, but when Kate looks away, she mouths "Gorgeous" to me.

"Did you mean all that stuff you said about your life?" Kate says, brightening up now.

"No." Frankie throws her head back and laughs. "I love meaningless sex. I need to do something about the microwave dinners, though. My doctor says I need more iron. Okay"—she claps her hands, causing Sam to jump with fright—"what's on the agenda for this meeting?"

"Justin wants to meet Joyce," Kate explains, then snaps at me, "Stop biting your lip."

I stop.

"Ooh, great," Frankie says excitedly. "So what's the problem?" She sees my look of terror.

"He's going to realize that I'm me."

"As opposed to you being . . . ?"

"Someone else." I bite my lip again.

"This is really reminding me of the old days. You are thirty-three years old, Joyce, why are you acting like a teenager?"

"Because she's in love," Kate says, bored, turning to face the swimming pool and clapping for her coughing daughter, Jayda, whose face is half underwater.

"She can't be in love." Frankie rolls her nose up in disgust.

"Is that normal, what's she doing out there, you think?" Kate, beginning to get worried about Jayda, tries to get our attention.

"Of course it's not normal," Frankie responds. "She hardly knows the guy."

"Girls, um, stop for a minute," Kate tries to butt in.

"I know more about him than any other person will ever know," I defend myself. "Apart from himself."

"Uh, lifeguard." Kate gives up on us and calls to the woman sitting below us. "Is my daughter okay?"

"*Are* you in love?" Frankie looks at me seriously.

I turn to hide my smile, just as the lifeguard crashes into the water to save Jayda.

"You'll have to take us over to Ireland with you," Doris says with excitement, placing a vase on the kitchen windowsill. The place is almost done now, and she's arranging the finishing touches. "We need to be nearby just in case something happens. They could be a murderer or a serial stalker who dates people and then kills them. I saw something like that on *Oprah*."

Al begins hammering nails into the wall, and Justin joins in with the rhythm, gently and repeatedly bashing his head against the kitchen table in response.

"I am not taking you both to the opera with me," Justin says.

"You took me along on a date when you and Delilah Jackson went out." Al stops hammering and turns to him. "Why should this be any different?"

"Al, I was twelve years old."

"Still—" He shrugs, returning to his hammering.

"What if she's a celebrity?" Doris says excitedly. "Oh, my God, she could be! I think she is! Jennifer Aniston could be sitting in the front row of the opera, and there could be a place free beside her. Oh, my God, what if it is?" She turns to Al with wide eyes. "Justin, you have to tell her I'm her biggest fan."

"Whoa, whoa, whoa, hold on a minute, you're starting to hyperventilate. How on earth have you come to that conclusion? We don't even know if it's a woman." Justin sighs.

"Yeah, Doris," Al joins in. "It's probably just a normal person."

"Yeah"—Justin imitates his brother's tone—"because celebrities aren't normal people, they're really underworld beasts that grow horns and have three legs."

"We're going to Dublin tomorrow," Doris says with an air of finality. "It's your brother's birthday, and a weekend in Dublin—in a very nice hotel like the Shelbourne Hotel—would be a perfect birthday present for him, from you."

"I can't afford the Shelbourne Hotel, Doris."

"Well, we'll need a place that's close to a hospital in case he has a heart attack. In any case, we're all going!" She claps her hands excitedly.

Chapter 37

◇◇◇◇◇

I'M ON MY WAY INTO the city to meet Kate and Frankie for help on what to wear to tonight's opera when my phone rings.

"Hello?"

"Joyce, it's Steven."

My boss.

"I just received another phone call."

"That's really great, but you don't have to call me every time that happens."

"It's another complaint, Joyce."

"From who and about what?"

"That couple you showed the new cottage to yesterday?"

"Yes?"

"They've pulled out."

"Oh, that's a shame," I say, lacking all sincerity. "Did they say why?"

"Yes, in fact they did. It seems a certain person in our company advised them that to properly re-create the look of the period cottage, they should demand that the builders carry out excess work. Guess what? The builders weren't entirely interested in their list, which included"—I hear paper rustling—" 'Exposed beams, exposed brickwork, a log-burning stove, open fires . . .' The list goes on. So now they've backed out."

"It sounds reasonable enough to me. The builders were re-creating period cottages without any period features. Does that make sense to you?"

"Who cares? Joyce, you were only supposed to let them in to measure for their couch. Douglas had sold this place to them already when you were . . . out."

"Evidently, he hadn't."

"Joyce, I need you to stop turning our clients away. Do you need to be reminded that your job is to sell, and if you're not doing that, then . . ."

"Then what?" I say haughtily, my head getting hot.

"Then nothing." He softens. "I know you've had a difficult time . . . ," he begins awkwardly.

"That time is over and has nothing to do with my ability to sell a house," I snap.

"Then sell one," he finishes.

"Fine." I snap my phone shut and glare out the bus window at the city. A week back at work, and already I need a break.

"Doris, is this really necessary?" Justin moans from the bathroom.

"Yes!" she calls. "This is what we're here for. We have to make sure you're going to look right tonight. Hurry up, you take longer than a woman to get ready."

Doris and Al are sitting on their bed in a Dublin hotel—not the Shelbourne, much to Doris's dismay. It is more of a Holiday Inn, but it's central to the city and to the stores, and that's good enough for her. As soon as they'd landed earlier that morning, Justin had been set to show them around all the sites, the museums, churches, and castles, but Doris and Al had other things on their minds. Shopping.

The Viking tour was as cultured as they got, and Doris howled when water sprayed her in the face as they entered the river Liffey. They'd ended up rushing to the nearest restroom as soon as they could so that Al could wash the mascara out of her eye.

There were only hours to go until the opera, until Justin would finally discover the identity of this mystery person. He was filled with anxiety, excitement, and nerves at the thought of it. It would be a pleasant evening or one of sheer torture, depending on his luck. He had to figure out an escape plan if his worst-case scenario was to play out.

"Oh, hurry up, Justin," Doris howls again just as he fixes his tie and exits the bathroom.

"Work it, work it, work it!" Doris whoops as he strolls up and down the room in his best suit. He pauses in front of them and fidgets awkwardly, feeling like a little boy in his communion suit.

He is greeted by silence. Al, who has been shoveling popcorn into his mouth at a serious speed, also stops.

"What?" Justin says nervously. "Something wrong? Something on my face? Is there a stain?" He looks down, studying himself.

Doris shakes her head. "Ha-ha, very funny. Now seriously, stop wasting time and show us the real suit."

"Doris!" Justin exclaims. "This *is* the real suit!"

"Your best one?" she drawls, looking him up and down.

"I think I recognize that from our wedding." Al's eyes narrow.

Doris stands up and picks up her handbag. "Take it off," she says calmly.

"What? Why?"

She takes a deep breath. "Just take it off. Now."

"These are too formal, Kate." I turn my nose up at the dresses she has chosen at the store. "It's not a ball, I just need something . . ."

"Sexy," Frankie says, waving a little dress in front of me.

"It's an opera, not a nightclub." Kate whips it away from her. "Okay, wow, look at this one. Not formal, not slutty."

"Yes, you could be a nun," Frankie says sarcastically.

They both turn away and continue to root through the hangers.

"Aha! I got it," Frankie announces.

"No, I've found the perfect one."

They both spin round with the same dresses in their hands, Kate holding one in red, Frankie holding another in black. I chew on my lip.

"Stop it!" they say in unison.

"Oh, my God," Justin whispers.

"What? You've never seen a pink pinstripe before? It's divine. Worn with this pink shirt and this pink tie—perfection. Oh, Al, I wish you'd wear suits like this."

"I prefer the blue," Al disagrees. "The pink is a bit gay. Or maybe that's a good idea in case she turns out to be a disaster. You can tell her your boyfriend's waiting for you. I can back you up on that," he offers.

Doris ignores her husband. "See, isn't this so much better than that other thing you were wearing? Justin? Earth to Justin? What are you looking at? Oh, she's pretty."

"That's Joyce," he whispers, staring at the other side of the store. He once read that a blue-throated hummingbird has a heart rate of one thousand two hundred and sixty beats per minute, and he wondered how anything could survive that. He understands now. With each beat, his heart pushes out blood and sends it flowing around his body. He feels his entire body throb and pulsate in his neck, wrists, heart, stomach.

"That's Joyce?" Doris asks, shocked. "The phone woman? Well, she looks . . . normal. What do you think, Al?"

Al looks to where they've been staring and nudges his brother. "Yeah, she looks real normal. You should ask her out once and for all."

"Why are you both so surprised she looks normal?" *Thump-thump. Thump-thump.*

"Well, sweetie, the very fact that she exists is a surprise." Doris snorts. "The fact that she's pretty is damn near a miracle. Go on, ask her out for dinner tonight."

"I can't tonight."

"Why not?"

"I've got the opera!"

"Opera shopera. Who cares about that?"

"You have been talking about it nonstop for over a week. And now it's opera shopera?" *Thump-thump. Thump-thump.*

"Well, I didn't want to alarm you before, but I was thinking about it on the plane ride over, and"—she takes a deep breath and touches his arm gently—"it can't be Jennifer Aniston. It's just going to be some old lady sitting in the front row waiting for you with a bouquet of flowers that you don't even want, or some overweight guy with bad breath. Sorry, Al, I don't mean you."

Justin's heart beats the speed of a hummingbird's heart, his mind now at the speed of its wings. He can barely think; everything is happening too fast. Joyce, far more beautiful up close than he remembers, her newly short hair soft around her face. She is beginning to move away now. He has to do something quick. Think, think, think!

"Ask her out for tomorrow night," Al suggests.

"I can't! My exhibition is tomorrow."

"Skip it. Call in sick."

"I can't, Al! I've been working on it for months. I'm the damn curator, I have to be there." *Thump-thump, thump-thump.*

"If you don't ask her out, I will." Doris pushes him.

"She's busy with her friends."

Joyce starts to leave.

Do something!

"Joyce!" Doris calls out.

"Jesus Christ." Justin tries to turn round and run in the other direction, but both Al and Doris block him.

"Justin Hitchcock," a voice says loudly, and he stops trying to break through their barrier and slowly turns round. One of the women standing beside Joyce looks familiar. She has a baby in a stroller beside her.

"Justin Hitchcock," the woman says again and reaches out her hand. "Kate McDonald." She shakes his hand firmly. "I was at your talk last week at the National Gallery. It was incredibly interesting. I didn't know you knew Joyce." She smiles brightly and elbows Joyce. "Joyce, you never said! I was at Justin Hitchcock's talk just last week! Remember I told you? The painting about the woman and the letter? And the fact that she was writing it?"

Joyce's eyes are wide and startled. She looks from her friend to Justin and back again.

"She doesn't know me, exactly," Justin finally speaks up, and feels a slight tremble in his voice. So much adrenaline is surging through him, he feels he's about to take off like a rocket through the department store's roof. "We've passed each other on many occasions but never had the opportunity to meet properly." He holds out his hand. "Joyce, I'm Justin."

She reaches out to take his hand, and static electricity rushes through as they get a quick shock from each other.

They both let go quickly. "Whoa!" She pulls back and cradles her hand in the other, as though burned.

"Oooh," Doris sings.

"It's static electricity, Doris. Caused when the air and materials are dry. They should use a humidifier in here," Justin says like a robot, not moving his eyes from Joyce's face.

Frankie cocks her head and tries not to laugh. "Charming."

"I tell him that all the time," Doris says.

After a moment, Joyce extends her hand again to finish the handshake properly. "Sorry, I just got a—"

"That's okay, I got it too." He smiles.

"Nice to meet you, finally," she says.

They remain holding hands, just staring at each other.

Doris clears her throat noisily. "I'm Doris, his sister-in-law."

She reaches diagonally over Justin and Joyce's handshake to greet Frankie.

"I'm Frankie."

They shake hands. While doing so, Al reaches over diagonally to shake hands with Kate. It becomes a hand-shaking marathon as they all greet at once, Justin and Joyce finally releasing their grip.

"Would you like to go for dinner tonight with Justin?" Doris blurts out.

"Tonight?" Joyce's mouth drops.

"She would love to," Frankie answers for her.

"Tonight, though?" Justin turns to face Doris with wide eyes.

"Oh, it's no problem, Al and I want to eat alone anyway." She nudges him. "No point being the gooseberry." She smiles.

"Are you sure you wouldn't rather stick to your other plans tonight?" Joyce says, slightly confused.

"Oh, no." Justin shakes his head. "I'd love to have dinner with you. Unless of course you have plans?"

Joyce turns to Frankie. "Tonight? I have that thing, Frankie . . ."

"Oh, no, don't be silly. It doesn't really make a difference, now, does it?" Frankie waves her hand dismissively. "We can have drinks any other time." She smiles sweetly at Justin. "So where are you taking her?"

"The Shelbourne Hotel?" Doris says. "At eight?"

"Oh, I've always wanted to eat there." Kate sighs. "Eight suits her fine," she responds.

Justin looks at Joyce. "Does it?"

Joyce seems to consider this, her mind ticking at the same rate as his heart.

"You're absolutely sure you're happy to cancel your other plans for tonight?" Frown lines appear on her forehead. Her eyes bore into his, and guilt overcomes him as he thinks of whoever it is he'll be standing up. He gives a single nod and is unsure of how convincing he seems.

Sensing this, Doris begins to pull him away. "Well, it was wonderful to meet you all, but we really better get back to shopping. Nice to meet you, Kate, Frankie, Joyce sweetie." She gives her a quick hug. "Enjoy dinner. At eight. Shelbourne Hotel. Don't forget, now."

"Red or black?" Joyce holds up the two dresses to Justin, just before he turns.

He considers this carefully. "Red."

"Black it is, then." She smiles, mirroring their first and only conversation from the hair salon, the first day they met.

He laughs and allows Doris to drag him away.

Chapter 38

◇◇◇◇◇

W HAT THE HELL DID YOU do that for, Doris?" Justin asks
as they walk back toward their hotel.

"You've gone on and on about this woman for weeks, and now
you've finally got a date with her. What's so wrong with that?"

"I have plans tonight! I can't just stand this other person up."

"You don't even know who it is!"

"It doesn't matter, it's still rude."

"Justin, seriously, listen to me. This whole thank-you message
thing could honestly be somebody playing a cruel joke."

He narrows his eyes with suspicion. "You think?"

"I honestly don't know."

Doris and Justin slow down, noticing that Al has begun to
pant.

"Would you rather risk going to something where you have
no idea what or who to expect? Or go to dinner with a pretty lady,
one you have been thinking about for weeks?"

"Come on," Al joins in, "when was the last time you were this
interested in anyone?"

Justin smiles.

"So, bro, what's it gonna be?"

"You should really take something for that heartburn, Mr. Conway," I can hear Frankie telling Dad in the kitchen.

"Like what?" Dad asks, enjoying the company of two young ladies. "Poteen?"

They all laugh, and I hear Sam's babbling echo around the kitchen.

"By the way, Mr. Conway, there's something about that night in question that I wanted to tell you about."

"Is there now?" Dad responds.

"All this time you thought it was me who made Joyce drink the poteen, but in truth, it was Frankie! Ha!" Kate says, clapping her hands.

"Frankie told me you'd blame her," Dad says.

"What?" Kate screeches, and I hear Frankie's laughter.

"It's a long time ago now since it all happened, so how's about you just own up to it and be thankful you didn't do Joyce too much damage," Dad adds, sounding like the father who dominated my teenage years.

"Okay, I'm coming!" I call down the stairs, interrupting what could become an explosive argument.

"Yahooo!" Frankie hollers.

"I've got the camera ready!" Kate calls back.

Dad starts making trumpet noises as I walk down the stairs. I look at Mum's photo on the hall table, maintaining eye contact with her all the way as she stares up at me. I wink at her as I pass.

As soon as I step into the hall and turn to the three of them in the kitchen, they all go quiet.

My smile fades. "What's wrong?"

"Oh, Joyce," Frankie whispers, "you look beautiful."

I sigh with relief and join them in the kitchen.

"Do a twirl." Kate films me with the video camera.

I spin in my new red dress while Sam claps his chubby hands.

"Mr. Conway, you haven't said anything!" Frankie nudges him. "Isn't she beautiful?"

We all turn to face Dad, who has gone silent, his eyes filled with tears. He nods up and down quickly, but no words come out.

"Oh, Dad"—I reach out and wrap my arms around him—"it's only a dress."

"You look beautiful, love," he manages to say. "Go get him, kiddo." He gives me a kiss on the cheek and hurries into the living room, embarrassed by his emotion.

"So," Frankie says, "have you decided whether it's going to be dinner or the opera tonight?"

"I still don't know."

"He asked you out to dinner," Kate says. "Why do you think he'd rather go to the opera?"

"Because firstly, he didn't ask me out for dinner. His sister-in-law did. And I didn't say yes. You did." I glare at Kate. "I think it's killing him not knowing whose life he saved. He didn't seem so convinced about our date before he left the shop, did he?"

"Stop reading so much into it," Frankie says. "He asked you out, so go out."

"Yeah," Kate agrees. "He seemed to really want you at that dinner. And anyway, why can't you just come clean and tell him that it's you?"

"My way of coming clean was supposed to be him seeing me at the opera. This was going to be it, the night he found out."

"So go to dinner and tell him that it was you all along."

"But what if he goes to the opera?"

We talk in circles for a while longer, and when they leave, I discuss the pros and cons of both situations with myself until my head is spinning so much I can't think anymore. When the taxi arrives, Dad walks me to the door.

"I don't know what you girls were in such deep conversation about, but I know you've to make a decision about something. Have you made it?" Dad asks softly.

"I don't know, Dad." I swallow hard. "I still don't know what the right decision is."

"Of course you do. You always take your own route, love. You always have."

"What do you mean?"

He looks out to the garden. "See that trail there?"

"The garden path?"

He shakes his head and points to a track in the lawn where the grass has been trampled on and the soil is slightly visible beneath. "You made that path."

"What?" I'm confused now.

"As a little girl." He smiles. "We call them 'desire lines' in the gardening world. They're the tracks and trails that people make for themselves. You've always avoided the paths laid down by other people, love. You've always gone your own way, found your own way, even if you do eventually get to the same point as everybody else. You've never taken the official route." He chuckles. "No, indeed you haven't. You're certainly your mother's daughter, cutting corners, creating spontaneous paths, while I stick to the routes and make my way the long way round."

We both study the small well-worn ribbon of grass.

"Desire lines," I repeat, seeing myself as a little girl, as a teenager, a grown woman, cutting across that patch each time. "I suppose desire isn't linear. There is no straightforward way of going where you want."

"Do you know what you're going to do now?" he asks as the taxi arrives.

I kiss him on his forehead. "I do."

Chapter 39

◇◇◇◇◇

I STEP OUT OF THE taxi at Stephen's Green and immediately see the crowds flowing toward the Gaiety Theatre, all dressed in their finest for the National Irish Opera's production. I have never been to an opera before, have only ever seen one on television, and my heart, tired of a body that can't keep up with it, is pounding to run into the building itself. I'm filled with nerves, with anticipation, and with the greatest hope I have ever felt in my life that the final part of my plan will come together. I'm terrified that Justin will be angry that it's me, though why he would be? I've run a hundred different scenarios in my head, and I can't seem to come to any rational conclusion.

I stand halfway between the Shelbourne Hotel and the Gaiety Theatre, no less than three hundred yards between them. I look from one to the other and then close my eyes, not caring how stupid I look in the middle of the road as people pass by me. I wait to feel the pull. Which way to go. Right to the Shelbourne. Left to the Gaiety. My heart drums in my chest.

I turn to the left and stride confidently toward the theater.

He has been stood up.

By the one woman he's had any sort of interest in since his divorce. Not counting poor Sarah. He had never counted poor Sarah.

I am a horrible person.

"I'm sorry to disturb you, sir," the maître d' says politely, "but we have received a phone call from your brother, Al?"

Justin nods.

"He wanted to pass on the message that he is still alive and that he hopes you are, um, well, that you're enjoying your night."

"Alive?"

"Yes, sir, he said you would understand, as it's twelve o'clock. His birthday?"

"Twelve?"

"Yes, sir. I'm also sorry to tell you that we are closing for the evening. Would you like to settle your bill?"

Justin looks up at him, bleary-eyed, and tries to nod again but feels his head loll to one side.

"I've been stood up."

"I'm sorry, sir."

"Oh, don't be. I deserve it. I stood up another person I don't even know."

"Oh. I see."

"But this stranger has been so kind to me. So, so kind. I've been given muffins and coffee, a car and a driver, and I've been so horrible in return." He stops suddenly.

The opera house might be still open!

"Here." He thrusts his credit card out. "I might still have time."

I stroll around the quiet streets of the neighborhood, wrapping my cardigan tighter around me. I told the taxi driver to let me out round the corner so that I could get some air and clear my head before I return home. I also want to be rid of my tears by the time Dad sees me; I'm sure he is currently sitting up in his armchair as he used to do when I was younger, eager to find out what had happened on my date, though he would pretend to be asleep as soon as he heard my key in the door.

I walk by my old house, which I successfully managed to sell only days ago, not to the eager Linda and Joe, who found out it was my home and were afraid my bad luck was an omen for them and their unborn child. Or more, that the stairs that caused my fall would perhaps be too dangerous for Linda during her pregnancy. Nobody takes responsibility for their own actions anymore, I notice. It wasn't the stairs, it was me. I was rushing. It was my fault. Simple as that. Something I'm going to have to dig deep to forgive myself for.

Perhaps I've been rushing my whole entire life, jumping into things headfirst without thinking them through. Running through the days without noticing the minutes. Not that the times when I slowed down and planned ever gave me more positive results. Mum and Dad had planned everything for their entire lives: summer holidays, a child, their savings, even nights out. Everything was done by the book. Her premature departure from life was the one thing they had never bargained on. A blip that knocked everything off course.

Conor and I had teed off straight for the trees and had bogeyed, big-time.

I stop outside our old home and stare up at the red bricks, at the door we argued about what color to paint, about the flowers we planted ourselves. I will have to start hunting for something smaller, something cheaper. I have no idea what he will do—an odd realization. This house isn't mine anymore, but the memories are; the memories can't be sold. The building that housed my once-upon-a-time dreams stands for someone else now, as it did for the people before us, and I feel happy to let it go. Happy that I can begin again, anew, though bearing the scars of before. They represent wounds that have healed.

It's midnight when I return to Dad's house, and behind the windows is blackness. There isn't a single light on, which is unusual, as he usually leaves the porch light on, especially if I'm out.

I open my bag to get my keys, and my hand bumps against my cell phone. It lights up to show I have missed ten calls, eight of which are from the house. I had it on silent at the opera and, knowing that Justin didn't have my number, didn't even think to look at it. I scramble for my keys, my hands trembling as I try to fit the right one into the lock. They fall to the ground, the noise echoing in the silent dark street. I lower myself to my knees, not caring about my new dress, and shuffle around the concrete, feeling for the metal in the darkness. Finally my fingers touch upon them, and I'm through the door like a rocket, turning on all the lights.

"Dad?" I call down the hallway. Mum's photograph is on the floor, underneath the table. I pick it up and place it back where it belongs, trying to stay calm, but my heart is having its own idea.

No answer.

I walk to the kitchen and flick the switch. A full cup of tea sits on the kitchen table. A slice of toast with jam, with one bite taken from it.

"Dad?" I say more loudly now, walking into the living room and turning on the light.

His pills are spilled all over the floor, their containers opened and emptied, all the colors mixed.

I panic now, going back through the kitchen and through the hall, and running upstairs, turning on all the lights as I yell at the top of my lungs.

"*Dad! Dad! Where are you? Dad, it's me, Joyce! Dad!*" Tears are flowing now; I can barely speak. He is not in his bedroom or in the bathroom, not in my room or anywhere else. I pause on the landing, trying to listen in the silence to hear if he's calling. All I can hear is the drumbeat of my heart in my ears, in my throat.

"*Dad!*" I yell, my chest heaving, the lump in my throat threatening to seize my breath. I've nowhere else to look. I start pulling open wardrobes, searching under his bed. I grab a pillow from his bed and breathe in, holding it close to me and instantly soaking it with tears. I look out the back window and into the garden: no sign of him.

My knees now too weak to stand, my head too clouded to think, I sink onto the top stair on the landing and try to figure out where he could be.

Then I think of the spilled pills on the floor, and I yell the loudest I have ever shouted in my life. "*Daaaaaad!*"

Silence greets me, and I have never felt so alone. More alone than at the opera, more alone than in an unhappy marriage, more alone than when Mum died. Completely and utterly alone, the last person I have in my life taken away from me.

Then, "Joyce?" A voice calls from the front door, which I've left open. "Joyce, it's me, Fran." She stands there in her dressing gown and slippers, her eldest son standing behind her with a flashlight in his hand.

"Dad is gone." My voice trembles.

"He's in the hospital, I was trying to call y—"

"What? Why?" I stand up and rush down the stairs.

"He thought he was having another heart—"

"I have to go. I have to go to him." I rush around, searching for my car keys. "Which hospital?"

"Joyce, relax, love, relax." Fran's arms are around me. "I'll drive you."

Chapter 40

◇◇◇◇◇

I RUN DOWN THE HOSPITAL corridors, examining each door, trying to find the correct room. I panic, my tears blinding my vision. A nurse stops me and tries to help me. Knows instantly who I'm talking about. I shouldn't be allowed in at this time, but she can tell I'm distraught, wants to calm me by showing me he's all right.

I follow her down a series of corridors before she finally leads me into his room. I see Dad lying in a small bed, tubes attached to his wrists and nose, his skin deathly pale, his body so small under the blankets.

"Was that you making all that fuss out there?" he asks, his voice sounding weak.

"Dad." My voice comes out muffled.

"It's okay, love. I just got a shock, is all. Thought my heart was acting up again, went to take my pills, but then I got dizzy and they all fell out. Something to do with sugar, they tell me."

"Diabetes, Henry." The nurse smiles. "The doctor will be around to explain it all to you in the morning."

I sniffle, trying to remain calm.

"Ah, come here, you silly sod." He lifts his arms toward me.

I rush to him and hug him tight, his body feeling frail but protective.

"I'm not going anywhere, you. Hush, now." He runs his hands through my hair and pats my back comfortingly. "I hope I didn't ruin your night. I told Fran not to bother you."

"Of course you should have called me," I say into his shoulder. "I got such a fright when you weren't home."

"Well, I'm fine. You'll have to help me, though, with all this stuff," he whispers. "I told the doctor I understand, but I don't really. He's a real snooty type." He wrinkles up his nose.

"Of course I will." I wipe my eyes and try to compose myself.

"So, how did it go?" he asks, perking up. "Tell me all the good news."

"He, um"—I purse my lips—"he didn't show up." My tears start again.

Dad is quiet; sad, then angry, then sad again. He hugs me again, tighter this time.

"Ah, love," he says gently. "He's a bloody fool."

Chapter 41

◇◇◇◇◇

JUSTIN FINISHES EXPLAINING THE STORY of his disastrous weekend to Bea, who is sitting on the couch, her mouth open in shock.

"I can't believe I missed all this. I'm so bummed!"

"Well, you wouldn't have missed it if you'd been talking to me," Justin teases.

"Thank you for apologizing to Peter, Dad. I appreciate it. He appreciates it."

"I was acting like an idiot; I just didn't want to admit my little girl was all grown up."

"You better believe it." She smiles. "God"—she thinks back to his story—"I still can't imagine somebody sending you all that stuff. Who could it be? The poor person must have waited and waited for you at the opera."

Justin covers his face and winces. "Please, I know, it's killing me."

"But you chose Joyce, anyway."

He nods and smiles sadly.

"You must have really liked her."

"She must have really not liked me, because she didn't show up. No, Bea, I'm over it now. It's time to move on. I hurt too many people in the process of trying to find out about this person. If you can't remember anyone else you told about my wish list, then we'll never know."

Bea thinks hard. "I only told Peter, the costume supervisor, and her father. But what makes you think it wasn't either of them?"

"I met the costume supervisor that night. She didn't act like she knew me, and she's English—why would she have gone to Ireland for a blood transfusion? I even called her to ask her about her father. Don't ask what happened." He sets off Bea's glare. "Anyway, turns out her father's Polish."

"Hold on, where are you getting that from? She wasn't English, she was Irish." Bea frowns. "They both were."

Thump-thump. Thump-thump.

"Justin—" Laurence enters the room with cups of coffee for him and Bea. "I was wondering, when you have a minute, if we could have a word."

"Not now, Laurence," Justin says, moving to the edge of his seat. "Bea, where's your ballet program?"

"Honestly, Justin." Jennifer arrives at the door with her arms folded. "Could you please just be respectful for one moment? Laurence has something he wants to say, and you owe it to him to listen."

Bea runs to her room, pushing through the battling adults, and returns, waving the program in her hand.

Justin grabs it from her and flips through it quickly. "There!" he stabs his finger on the page.

"Guys"—Jennifer steps in between them—"we really have to settle this now."

"Not now, Mum. Please!" Bea yells. "This is important!"

"And this is not?"

"That's not her." Bea looks at the photo and shakes her head furiously. "That's not the woman I spoke to."

"Well, what did she look like?" Justin is up on his feet now. *Thump-thump. Thump-thump.*

"Let me think, let me think." Bea panics. "I know! Mum!"

"What?" Jennifer looks from Justin to Bea in confusion.

"Where are the photographs we took at the bar on opening night?"

"Oh, um—"

"Quick."

"They're in the corner kitchen cupboard," Laurence says, frowning.

"Yes, Laurence!" Justin punches the air. "They're in the corner kitchen cupboard! Go get them, quick!"

Alarmed, Laurence runs into the kitchen while Jennifer watches everyone in shock. Justin paces the floor at top speed until Laurence returns with the photos.

"Here they are." He holds them out, and Bea snaps them out of his hand.

Jennifer tries to interject, but Bea and Justin are too fast for her.

Bea shuffles through the photos at top speed. "You weren't in the room at the time, Dad. You had disappeared somewhere, but we all got a group photo, and here it is!" She leans in to her father to show him. "That's them. The woman and her father, there at the end." She points.

Silence.

"Dad?"

Silence.

"Dad, are you okay?"

"Justin?" Jennifer moves in closer. "He's gone very pale. Go get him a glass of water, Laurence, quick."

Laurence rushes back to the kitchen.

"Dad." Bea clicks her fingers in front of his eyes. "Dad, are you with us?"

"It's her," he whispers.

"Her who?" Jennifer asks.

"The woman whose life he saved." Bea jumps up and down excitedly.

"You saved a woman's life?" Jennifer asks, shocked. "You?"

"It's Joyce," he whispers.

Bea gasps. "The woman who phoned me?"

He nods.

Bea gasps again. "The woman you stood up?"

Justin closes his eyes and silently curses himself.

"You saved a woman's life and then stood her up?" Jennifer laughs.

"Bea, where's your phone?"

"Why?"

"She called you, right? Her number must be in your phone."

"Oh, Dad, my phone log only holds ten recent numbers. That was weeks ago!"

"Dammit!"

"I gave the number to Doris, remember? She wrote it down. You called the number from your house!"

Then threw it in the trash, you jerk! But wait—the bin! It's still there!

"Here." Laurence runs in with the glass of water, panting.

"Laurence." Justin reaches out, takes him by the cheeks, and kisses his forehead. "I give you my blessing. Jennifer"—he does the same and kisses her directly on the lips—"good luck."

With that, he runs out of the apartment as Bea cheers him on, Jennifer wiping her lips in disgust and Laurence wiping the spilled water from his clothes.

As Justin sprints from the tube station to his house, rain pours from the clouds like a cloth being squeezed. He doesn't care—he just looks up at the sky and laughs, loving how it feels on his face, unable to believe that Joyce was the woman all along. He should have known. It all makes sense now, her reluctance to make dinner plans, her friend being at his talk, all of it!

He turns the corner and sees the bin, now filled to the brim with items. He jumps in and begins sorting through it.

From the window, Doris and Al stop packing their suitcases and watch him with concern.

"Dammit, I really thought he was getting back to normal," Al says. "Should we stay?"

"I don't know," she replies worriedly. "What on earth is he doing? It's ten o'clock at night—surely the neighbors will call the cops."

They watch him whooping and hollering as he throws the contents of the bin onto the ground beside it, seemingly unaware that he's soaked to the bone.

Chapter 42

◇◇◇◇◇

I LIE IN BED STARING at the ceiling. Dad is still in the hospital undergoing tests, and will be home tomorrow. With nobody around, I've been able to process my life. I've worked my way through despair, guilt, sadness, anger, loneliness, depression, and cynicism, and have finally found my way to hope. Like an addict going cold turkey, I have paced the floors of these rooms with every emotion bursting from my skin. I have spoken aloud to myself, screamed, shouted, wept, and mourned.

It's eleven p.m.—dark, windy, and cold outside as the winter months are fighting their way through—when the phone rings. Thinking it's Dad, I hurry downstairs, grab the phone, and sit on the bottom stair.

"Hello?"

"It was you all along."

I freeze. My heart thuds. I take a deep breath.

"Justin?"

"It was you all along, wasn't it?"

I'm silent.

"I saw the photograph of you and your father with Bea. That's the night she told you about my donation. About wanting all those thank-yous." He sneezes.

"Bless you."

"Why didn't you say anything to me? All those times I saw you? Did you follow me or . . . or what's going on, Joyce?"

"Are you angry with me?"

"No! I mean, I don't know. I don't understand. I'm so confused."

"Let me explain." I take another deep breath and try to steady my voice. "I didn't follow you to any of the places we met, so please don't be concerned. I'm not a stalker. Something happened, Justin. Something happened when I received my transfusion, and whatever that was, when your blood was transfused into mine, I suddenly felt connected to you. I kept turning up at places where you were, like the hair salon, the ballet. It was all a coincidence." I'm speaking too fast now, but I can't slow down. "And then Bea told me you'd donated blood around the same time that I'd received it, and . . ."

"You mean, you know for sure it's my blood that you received? Because I couldn't find out, nobody would tell me. Did somebody tell you?"

"No. Nobody told me. They didn't need to. I—"

"Joyce." He stops me, and I'm immediately worried by his tone.

"I'm not some weird person, Justin. Trust me. I have never experienced this before." I tell him the story. Of experiencing his skills, his knowledge, his tastes.

He is quiet.

"Say something, Justin."

"I don't know what to say. It sounds . . . odd."

"It *is* odd, but it's the truth. This will sound even odder, but I feel like I've gained some of your memories too."

"Really?" His voice is cold, far away. I'm losing him.

"Memories of the park in Chicago, Bea dancing in her tutu on the red-checked cloth, the picnic basket, the bottle of red wine. The cathedral bells, the ice-cream parlor, the seesaw with Al, the sprinklers, the—"

"Whoa, whoa, whoa. Stop now. Who are you? Who's told you these things?"

"Nobody. I just know them!" I rub my eyes tiredly. "I know it sounds bizarre, Justin, I really do. I am a normal decent human being who is as cynical as they come, but this is my life, and these are the things that are happening to me. If you don't believe me, then I'll hang up and go back to my life, but please know that this is not a joke or a hoax or any kind of setup."

He is quiet for a while. And then, "I want to believe you."

"You feel something between us?"

"I do." He speaks very slowly, as though pondering every letter of every word. "The memories, tastes, and hobbies and whatever else of mine that you mentioned are things that you could have seen me do or heard me say. I'm not saying you're doing this on purpose—maybe you don't even know it, maybe you've read my books; I mention many personal things in my books. You saw the photo in Bea's locket, you've been to my talks, you've read my articles. I may have revealed things about myself in them, in fact I know I have." He pauses. "How can I know that you knowing these things is through a transfusion? How do I know that—no offense—but that you're not some lunatic young woman who's convinced herself of some crazy story she read in a book or saw in a movie? How am I supposed to know?"

My heart sinks. I have no way of convincing him. "Justin, I don't believe in anything right now, but I believe in this."

"I'm sorry, Joyce," he says, sounding as if he's ending the conversation.

"No, wait," I stop him. "Is this it?"

Silence.

"Aren't you going to even try to believe me?"

He sighs deeply. "I thought you were somebody else, Joyce. I don't know why, because I'd never even met you, but I thought you were a different kind of person. This . . . this I don't understand. This, I find . . . it's just not right, Joyce."

Each sentence is a stab through my heart and a punch to my stomach. I could stand hearing this from anyone else in the world, but not him. Anyone but him.

"You've been through a lot, by the sound of it. Perhaps you should talk to someone. In any case, good-bye, Joyce. I hope everything works out for you, really I do."

"Hold on! Wait! There is one thing. One thing that only you could know."

He pauses. "What?"

I squeeze my eyes shut and take a deep breath. Do it or don't do it. Do it or don't. I open my eyes and blurt it out, "Your father."

There's silence.

"Justin?"

"What about him?" His voice is ice cold.

"I know what you saw," I say softly. "How you could never tell anyone."

"What the hell are you talking about?"

"I know about you being on the stairs, seeing him through the banisters. I see him too. I see him with the bottle and the pills, closing the door. I see the green feet on the floor—"

"*Stop!*" he yells, and I'm shocked to silence. But I must keep trying, or I'll never have the opportunity to say these words again.

"I know how hard it must have been for you as a child. How hard it was to keep it to yourself—"

"You know nothing," he says coldly. "Absolutely nothing.

Please stay away from me. I don't ever wish to hear from you again."

"Okay." My voice is a whisper, but he has already hung up.

I sit on the steps of the dark empty house and listen as the cold October wind rattles through.

So that's that.

PART THREE

One Month Later

Chapter 43

◇◇◇◇◇

"N ext time we should take the car, Gracie," Dad says as we make our way down the road back from our walk in the Botanics. I link his arm, and I'm lifted up and down with him as he sways. Up and down, down and up. The motion is soothing.

"No, you need the exercise, Dad."

"Speak for yourself," he mutters. "Howya, Sean? Miserable day, isn't it?" he calls across the street to an old man on a walker.

"Terrible," Sean shouts back.

"So what did you think of the apartment, Dad?" I broach the subject for the third time in the last few minutes. "You can't dodge this conversation."

"I'm dodging nothing, love. Howya, Patsy? Howya, Suki?" He stops and bends down to pat a sausage dog walking by with its owner. "Aren't you a cute little thing," he says, and we continue on. "I hate that little runt. Barks all bloody night when she's away," he mutters, pushing his cap down farther over his eyes as a great big gust blows. "Christ Almighty, are we gettin' anywhere at all? I feel like we're on one of those milltreads with this wind."

"Treadmills." I laugh. "So come on, do you like the apartment or not?"

"I'm not sure. It seemed awful small, and there was a funny man that went into the flat next door. Don't think I liked the look of him."

"He seemed very friendly to me."

"Ah, he would to you." He shakes his head. "Any man would do for you now, I'd say."

"Dad!" I laugh.

"Good afternoon, Graham. Miserable day, isn't it?" he says to another neighbor passing.

"Awful day, Henry," Graham responds, shoving his hands in his pockets.

"Anyway, I don't think you should take that apartment, Gracie. Hang on with me a little longer until something more appropriate pops up. There's no point in taking the first thing you see."

"Dad, we've seen ten apartments, and you don't like any of them."

"Is it for me to live in or for you?" he asks. Up and down. Down and up.

"For me."

"Well, then, what do you care?"

"I value your opinion."

"You do in your— Hello there, Kathleen!"

"You can't keep me at home forever, you know."

"Forever's been and gone, my love. There's no budging you. You're the Stonehenge of grown-up children living at home."

"Can I go to the Monday Club tonight?"

"Again?"

"I have to finish off my chess game with Larry."

"Larry just keeps positioning his pawns so that you'll lean over and he can see down your top. That game will never end," Dad jokes.

"Dad!"

"What? Anyway, you need to get more of a social life than hanging around with the likes of Larry and me."

"I like hanging around with you."

He smiles to himself, pleased to hear that.

We turn into Dad's house and sway up the small garden path to the front door.

The sight of what's on the doorstep stops me in my tracks.

A small basket of muffins covered in plastic wrap and tied with a pink bow. I look at Dad, who steps right over them and unlocks the front door. His obliviousness makes me question my eyesight. Have I imagined them?

"Dad! What are you doing?" Shocked, I look behind me, but nobody's there.

Dad turns and winks at me, looks sad for a moment, then gives me a great big smile before closing the door in my face.

I reach for the envelope that is taped to the plastic and with trembling fingers slide the card out.

Thank you . . .

"I'm sorry, Joyce." I hear a voice behind me that almost stops my heart, and I twirl round.

There he is, standing at the gate, a bouquet of flowers in his gloved hands, the sorriest look on his face. He is wrapped up in a scarf and a winter coat, the tip of his nose and cheeks red from the cold, his green eyes twinkling in the gray day. He is a vision; he takes my breath away with one look, his proximity to me almost too much to bear.

"Justin . . ." Then I'm utterly speechless.

"Do you think"—he takes a couple steps forward—"you could find it in your heart to forgive a fool like me?" He stands at the end of the garden now.

I'm unsure what to say. It's been a month. Why now?

"On the phone, you hit a sore point," he says, clearing his throat. "Nobody knows that part about my dad. Or knew that. I don't know how you do."

"I told you how."

"I don't understand it."

"Neither do I."

"But then I don't understand most ordinary things that happen every day. I don't understand what my daughter sees in her boyfriend. I don't understand how my brother has defied the laws of science by not turning into an actual potato chip. I don't know how Doris can open the milk carton with such long nails. I don't understand why I didn't beat down your door a month ago and tell you how I felt . . . I don't understand so many simple things, so I don't know why this should be any different."

I take in the sight of his face, his small nervous smile, his curly hair covered by a woolly hat. He studies me too, and I shiver, but not from the cold. I don't feel it now.

Frown lines suddenly appear on his forehead as he looks at me.

"What?"

"Nothing. You just remind me so much of somebody right now. It's not important." He clears his throat and smiles, trying to pick up where he left off.

"Eloise Parker," I guess, and his grin fades.

"How the hell do you know that?"

"She was your next-door neighbor who you had a crush on for years. When you were five years old, you decided to do something about it, and so you picked flowers from your front yard and brought them to her house. She opened the door before you got up the path and stepped outside wearing a blue coat and a black scarf," I say, pulling my blue coat around me tighter.

"Then what?" he asks, shocked.

"Then nothing." I shrug. "You dropped them on the ground and chickened out."

He shakes his head softly. "How on earth . . . ?"

I shrug.

"What else do you know about Eloise Parker?" He narrows his eyes.

I giggle and look away. "You lost your virginity to her when you were sixteen, in her bedroom when her mom and dad were away on a cruise."

He lowers the bouquet so that it faces the ground. "Now, you see, that is not fair. You are not allowed to know stuff like that about me."

I laugh.

"You were christened Joyce Bridget Conway, but you tell everyone your middle name is Angeline," he retaliates.

My mouth falls open.

"You had a dog called Bunny when you were a kid." He lifts an eyebrow cockily. "You got drunk on poteen when you were"—he closes his eyes and thinks hard—"fifteen. With your friends Kate and Frankie."

He takes a step closer with each piece of knowledge.

"Your first French kiss was with Jason Hardy when you were ten, who everyone used to call Jason Hard-On."

I laugh.

"You're not the only one who's allowed to know stuff." He takes a final step closer and can't move any nearer now. His shoes, the fabric of his thick coat, every part of him, is on the verge of touching me.

My heart takes out a trampoline and enrolls in a marathon session of leaping. I hope Justin doesn't hear it whooping with joy.

"Who told you all of that?" My words touch his face in a breath of cold smoke.

"Getting me here was a big operation." He smiles. "Big. Your friends had me run through a series of tests to prove I was sorry enough to be deemed worthy of coming here."

I laugh, shocked that Frankie and Kate could finally agree on something, never mind keeping anything of this magnitude a secret.

Silence now. We are so close, if I look up at him my nose will touch his chin. I keep looking down.

"You're still afraid to sleep in the dark," he whispers, taking my chin in his hand and lifting it so that I can look nowhere else but at him. "Unless somebody's with you," he adds with a small smile.

"You cheated on your first college paper," I whisper.

"You used to hate art." He kisses my forehead.

"You lie when you say you're a fan of the *Mona Lisa*." I close my eyes.

"You had an invisible friend named Horatio until you were five." He kisses my nose, and I'm about to retaliate, but his lips touch mine so softly the words give up, sliding back to the memory bank where they came from.

I am faintly aware of Fran exiting her house next door and saying hello, of a car driving by with a beep, but everything is blurred in the distance as I get lost in this moment with Justin, in this new memory for him and me.

"Forgive me?" he says as he pulls away.

"I have no choice but to. It's in my blood." We laugh. I look down at the flowers in his hands, which have been crushed between us. "Are you going to drop these on the ground too and chicken out?"

"Actually, they're not for you." His cheeks redden even more. "They're for somebody at the blood clinic who I really need to apologize to. I was hoping you would come with me, help explain the reason for my crazy behavior, and maybe she could explain a few things to us in turn."

I look back to the house and see Dad spying at us from behind the curtain. He gives me the thumbs-up, and my eyes fill.

"Was he in on this too?"

"He called me a worthless silly sod and an up-to-no-good fool." Justin makes a face. "So, yes."

I blow Dad a kiss. I feel him watching me, and feel Mum's eyes on me too, as I walk down the garden path, cut across the grass, and follow the desire line I had created as a little girl, out onto the pavement that leads away from the house I grew up in.

Though this time, I'm not alone.

Acknowledgments

◇◇◇◇◇

THANKS TO MY PRECIOUS PEOPLE for their love, guidance, and support; David, Mimmie, Dad, Georgina, Nicky, Rocco, Jay, Breda, and Neil. To Marianne for her Midas touch and for her "clatter" of vision. Thanks to Lynne Drew, Amanda Ridout, Claire Bord, Moira Reilly, Tony Purdue, Fiona McIntosh, and the whole team at HarperCollins. Huge thanks as always to Vicki Satlow with the incredible HV, and Pat Lynch. I'd like to thank all my friends for supporting and sharing the adventure with me. Special thanks to Sarah for being the godliest of all godlies. Thanks to Mark Monahan at Trinity College, Karen Breen at the Irish Blood Transfusion Service, and Bernice at Viking Splash Tours.

Sources

◇◇◇◇◇

www.tcd.ie
www.ibts.ie
www.rotunda.ie

About the Author

◇◇◇◇◇

BEFORE EMBARKING ON HER WRITING career, **CECELIA AHERN** completed a degree in journalism and media communications. At twenty-one she wrote her first novel, *P.S. I Love You*, which became an international bestseller and was adapted into a major motion picture starring Hilary Swank. Her successive novels *Love, Rosie*; *If You Could See Me Now*; and *There's No Place Like Here* were also international bestsellers. Her books are published in forty-six countries and have collectively sold more than nine million copies. She is also the cocreator of the hit ABC comedy series *Samantha Who?* starring Christina Applegate. The daughter of Ireland's former prime minister, Ahern lives in Dublin, Ireland.